The Many Sins of Lord Cameron

JENNIFER ASHLEY

BERKLEY SENSATION, NEW YORK

THE BERKLEY PUBLISHING GROUP
Published by the Penguin Group
Penguin Group (USA) Inc.
375 Hudson Street, New York, New York 10014, USA
Penguin Group (Canada), 90 Eglinton Avenue East, Suite 700, Toronto, Ontario M4P 2Y3, Canada
(a division of Pearson Penguin Canada Inc.)
Penguin Books Ltd., 80 Strand, London WC2R 0RL, England
Penguin Group Ireland, 25 St. Stephen's Green, Dublin 2, Ireland (a division of Penguin Books Ltd.)
Penguin Group (Australia), 250 Camberwell Road, Camberwell, Victoria 3124, Australia
(a division of Pearson Australia Group Pty. Ltd.)
Penguin Books India Pvt. Ltd., 11 Community Centre, Panchsheel Park, New Delhi—110 017, India
Penguin Group (NZ), 67 Apollo Drive, Rosedale, Auckland 0632, New Zealand
(a division of Pearson New Zealand Ltd.)
Penguin Books (South Africa) (Pty.) Ltd., 24 Sturdee Avenue, Rosebank, Johannesburg 2196,
South Africa

Penguin Books Ltd., Registered Offices: 80 Strand, London WC2R 0RL, England

THE MANY SINS OF LORD CAMERON

A Berkley Sensation Book / published by arrangement with the author

PRINTING HISTORY
Berkley Sensation mass-market edition / August 2011

Cover art by Gregg Gulbronson.
Cover design by George Long.
Cover hand lettering by Ron Zinn.
Interior text design by Laura K. Corless.

For information, address: The Berkley Publishing Group,
a division of Penguin Group (USA) Inc.,
375 Hudson Street, New York, New York 10014.

ISBN: 978-0-425-24049-6

BERKLEY® SENSATION
Berkley Sensation Books are published by The Berkley Publishing Group,
a division of Penguin Group (USA) Inc.,
375 Hudson Street, New York, New York 10014.
BERKLEY® SENSATION and the "B" design are trademarks of Penguin Group (USA) Inc.

PRINTED IN THE UNITED STATES OF AMERICA

10 9 8 7 6 5 4 3 2 1

"Jennifer Ashley just gets better and better! With a smart, intriguing heroine and a sinfully sexy hero, *The Many Sins of Lord Cameron* is impossible to put down. I loved it!"

—Elizabeth Hoyt, *New York Times* bestselling author

Praise for

Lady Isabella's Scandalous Marriage

"I adore this novel: It's heartrending, funny, honest, and true. I want to know the hero—no, I want to *marry* the hero!"

—Eloisa James, *New York Times* bestselling author

"Skillfully nuanced characterization and an abundance of steamy sensuality give Ashley's latest impeccably crafted historical its irresistible literary flavor." —*Chicago Tribune*

"Readers rejoice! The Mackenzie brothers return as Ashley works her magic to create a unique love story brimming over with depth of emotion, unforgettable characters, sizzling passion, mystery, and a story that reaches out and grabs your heart. Brava!" —*RT Book Reviews* (Top Pick)

"A heartfelt, emotional historical romance with danger and intrigue around every corner . . . A great read!"

—*Fresh Fiction*

"A wonderful novel filled with sweet, tender love that has long been denied, fiery passion, and a good dash of witty humor . . . For a rollicking good time, sexy Highland heroes, and touching romances, you just can't beat Jennifer Ashley's novels!" —*Night Owl Romance*

"You can't help but fall in love with the Mackenzie brothers."

—*Loves Romances and More*

"I really think this series is a must read for all historical romance fans." —*Smexy Books*

continued . . .

"I'm a big fan of Jennifer Ashley's, whose characters are always fantastic and well written . . . The cat and mouse game between Mac and Isabella is deliciously fun."

—*All About Romance*

"Since this is the first book I'd ever read by Ashley, I wasn't sure what to expect. The buzz about *The Madness of Lord Ian Mackenzie* made me think I wouldn't be disappointed, however, and I was right." —*Book Binge*

"Ms. Ashley is a superb author who can bring sensuality and passion to life with her characters and pour the emotion off the pages." —*Fiction Vixen Book Reviews*

"Isabella is a heroine strong enough to make tough choices even with a broken heart. Mac is a hero willing to admit his mistakes, who determines to become worthy of his heroine's love once more. While he is at it, he may melt some readers' hearts as well." —*A Romance Review*

"Ms. Ashley did not let me down amid her story of a second chance at love." —*The Good, The Bad and The Unread*

"I've always loved a marriage-in-trouble story and this is a slightly different take on a favorite trope." —*Dear Author*

THE MADNESS OF LORD IAN MACKENZIE

"Ever-versatile Ashley begins her new Victorian Highland Pleasures series with a deliciously dark and delectably sexy story of love and romantic redemption that will captivate readers with its complex characters and suspenseful plot."

—*Booklist*

"Ashley's enthralling and poignant romance . . . touches readers on many levels. Brava!" —*RT Book Reviews*

"Mysterious, heartfelt, sensitive, and sensual . . . Two big thumbs up." —*Publishers Weekly,* "Beyond Her Book"

"A story of mystery and intrigue with two wonderful, bright characters you'll love . . . I look forward to more from Jennifer Ashley, an extremely gifted author."

—*Fresh Fiction*

"Brimming with mystery, suspense, an intriguing plot, villains, romance, a tormented hero, and a feisty heroine, this book is a winner. I recommend *The Madness of Lord Ian Mackenzie* to anyone looking for a great read."

—*Romance Junkies*

"Wow! All I can say is *The Madness of Lord Ian Mackenzie* is one of the best books I have ever read. [It] gets the highest recommendation that I can give. It is a truly wonderful book." —*Once Upon A Romance*

"When you're reading a book that is a step or two—or six or seven—above the norm, you know it almost immediately. Such is the case with *The Madness of Lord Ian Mackenzie*. The characters here are so complex and so real that I was fascinated by their journey . . . [and] this story is as flat-out romantic as any I've read in a while . . . This is a series I am certainly looking forward to following."

—*All About Romance*

"A unique twist on the troubled hero . . . Fresh and interesting." —*Night Owl Romance*

"A welcome addition to the genre." —*Dear Author*

"Intriguing . . . Unique . . . Terrific."

—*Midwest Book Review*

Berkley Sensation Titles by Jennifer Ashley

THE MADNESS OF LORD IAN MACKENZIE
LADY ISABELLA'S SCANDALOUS MARRIAGE
THE MANY SINS OF LORD CAMERON

PRIDE MATES
PRIMAL BONDS

Thanks go to my editor, Kate Seaver, for her ongoing support for this series. Also, thanks to the many readers who have told me how much they adore the Mackenzie brothers! Thank you! For more information on the brothers and the series, please see the Mackenzies' page at my website:

www.jennifersromances.com

Chapter 1

Scotland, September 1882

I saw Mrs. Chase slide that letter into Lord Cameron's pocket. She did it almost under my nose. Bloody woman.

Ainsley Douglas sank to her knees in her ball dress and thrust her arms deep into Lord Cameron Mackenzie's armoire.

Why did it have to be Cameron Mackenzie, of all people? Did Mrs. Chase know? Ainsley's heart thrummed before she calmed it down. No, Phyllida Chase could not know. No one did. Cameron must not have told her, because the tale would have come 'round to Ainsley again with breathtaking speed, society gossip being what it was. Therefore, it stood to reason that Cameron had kept the story to himself.

Ainsley felt only marginally better. The queen's letter hadn't been in the pockets of any of the coats in the dressing room. In the armoire, Ainsley found shirts neatly folded, collars stacked in collar boxes, cravats carefully separated with tissue paper. Rich cambric and silk and softest lawn, costly fabrics for a rich man.

She pawed hastily through the garments, but nowhere did she find the letter tucked carelessly into a pocket or fallen between the shirts on the shelf. The valet had likely gone through his master's pockets and taken away any stray paper to return it to Lord Cameron or put it somewhere for safekeeping. Or Cameron had already found it, thought it female silliness, and burned it. Ainsley prayed fast and hard that he'd simply burned it.

Not that such a thing would completely solve Ainsley's dilemma. Phyllida, blast the woman, had more of the queen's letters stashed away somewhere. Ainsley's assignment: Retrieve them at all costs.

The immediate cost was to Ainsley's dove gray ball dress, the first new gown she'd had in years that wasn't mourning black. Not to mention the cost to her knees, her back, and her sanity.

Sanity was further disturbed by the sound of the door opening behind her.

Ainsley backed swiftly out of the wardrobe and turned around, fully expecting Cameron's rather frightening Romany valet to be glaring down at her. Instead, the door blocked whoever had pushed it open, giving Ainsley a few more seconds to panic.

Hide. Where? The door to the dressing room lay across the length of the chamber, the armoire behind her too full for a young woman in a ball dress. Under the bed? No, she'd never dash across the carpet and wriggle beneath it in time.

The window with its full seat was two steps away. Ainsley dove for it, stuffed her skirts beneath her and jerked the curtains closed.

Just in time. Through the crack in the drapes, she saw Lord Cameron himself back into the room with Phyllida Chase, former maid of honor to the queen, hanging around his neck.

The sudden burn in Ainsley's heart took her by surprise.

She'd known for weeks that Phyllida had stuck her claws into Cameron Mackenzie. Why should Ainsley mind? Phyllida was the sort of woman Lord Cameron preferred: lovely, experienced, uninterested in her husband. Likewise Cameron was the sort Phyllida liked: rich, handsome, not looking for a deep attachment. They suited each other well. What business was it of Ainsley's?

Even so, a lump formed in her throat as Lord Cameron shut the door with one hand and slid the other to the small of Phyllida's back. She wound her arms around him, while Cameron leaned down and pressed leisurely kisses to her neck.

There was desire in that embrace, unashamed, unmistakable desire. Once, long ago, Ainsley had felt Cameron Mackenzie's desire. She remembered rippling heat softening her body, the point of fire of his kiss. Years had passed, but she still remembered the imprint of his mouth on her lips, on her skin—his hands so skilled.

Phyllida melted to Cameron with a hungry noise, and Ainsley rolled her eyes. She knew full well that *Mr.* Chase was still in the gardens, following the house party on a ramble, the paths lit by paper lanterns under the midnight sky. Ainsley knew this because she'd slipped away from the party as they moved from ballroom to gardens, so that she could search Lord Cameron's chamber.

They couldn't have let her search in peace, could they? No, the bothersome Phyllida could not stay away from her Mackenzie male and had dragged him up here for a liaison. Selfish cow.

Cameron's coat slid to the floor. The waistcoat and shirt beneath outlined muscles hardened by years of riding and training horses. Lord Cameron moved with ease for such a big man, comfortable with his height and strength. He rode with the same grace, the horses under him responding to his slightest touch. Ladies responded to the same touch, she had reason to know.

The deep scar on his cheekbone made some say that his

handsomeness was ruined, but Ainsley disagreed. The scar had never unnerved her, but his tallness had taken Ainsley's breath away when Isabella had introduced her to him six years ago, as had the way his gloved hand swallowed her smaller one. Cameron hadn't looked much interested in an old school friend of his sister-in-law's, but later . . . *Oh, that later.*

At *this* moment, Cameron's gaze was reserved for the slim, dark-haired beauty of Phyllida Chase. Ainsley happened to know that Phyllida kept her hair black with the help of a little dye, but Ainsley would never say so. She wouldn't be that petty. If she and Isabella had a good giggle over it, what harm was there in that?

Cameron's waistcoat came off, then his cravat and collar, giving Ainsley a fine view of his bare, damp throat.

She looked away, an ache in her chest. She wondered how long she would have to wait before attempting to slip away—surely once the couple was on the bed they'd be too engrossed in each other to notice her crawling for the door. Ainsley drew a long breath, becoming more unhappy by the minute.

When she summoned the nerve to peek back through the drape, Phyllida's bodice was open, revealing a pretty corset over plump curves. Lord Cameron bent to kiss the bosom that welled over the corset cover, and Phyllida groaned in pleasure.

The vision came to Ainsley of Lord Cameron pressing his lips to *her* bosom. She remembered his breath burning her skin, his hands on her back. And his kiss. A deep, warm kiss that had awakened every single desire Ainsley had ever had. She remembered the exact pressure of the kiss, the shape and taste of his mouth, the rough of his fingertips on her skin.

She also remembered the icicle in her heart when he'd looked at her and through her the next day. Her own fault. Ainsley had been young and allowed herself to be duped, and she'd compounded the problem by insulting him.

Phyllida's hand was under Cameron's kilt now. He moved to let her play, and the plaid inched upward. Cameron's strong thighs came into view, and Ainsley saw with shock that scars marked him from the back of his knees to the curve of his buttocks.

They were deep, knotted gashes, old wounds that had long since closed. Good heavens, Ainsley hadn't seen *that.* She couldn't stop the gasp that escaped her lips.

Phyllida raised her head. "Darling, did you hear something?"

"No." Cameron had a deep voice, the one word gravelly.

"I'm certain I heard a noise. Would you be a love and check that window?"

Ainsley froze.

"Damn the window. It's probably one of the dogs."

"Darling, *please*." Her pouting tone was done to perfection. Cameron growled something, and then Ainsley heard his heavy tread.

Her heart pounded. There were two windows in the bedchamber, one on either side of his bed. The odds were two-to-one that Lord Cameron would go to the other window. Even bet, Ainsley's youngest brother, Steven, would say. Either Cameron would jerk back the curtain and reveal Ainsley sitting there, or he would not.

Steven didn't like even bets. Not enough variables to be interesting, he insisted. That was because Steven wasn't the one huddled on a window seat waiting to be revealed to Lord Cameron and the woman who was blackmailing the Queen of England.

Lord Cameron's broad brown hands grasped the edges of the drapes in front of Ainsley and parted them a few inches.

Ainsley gazed up at Cameron, meeting his topaz gaze for the first time in six years. He looked at her fully, like a lion on a veldt eyeing a gazelle, and the gazelle in her wanted to run, run, run. The defiant tomboy from Miss Pringle's Academy, however, now a lofty lady-in-waiting, stared boldly back at him.

Silence stretched. Cameron's large body blocked her from the room behind him, but he could so easily turn and reveal her. Cameron owed her nothing. He must know good and well that she was hiding in his bedchamber because of another intrigue. He could betray Ainsley, hand her to Phyllida, and think it served her right.

Behind Cameron, Phyllida said, "What is it, darling? I saw you jump."

"Nothing," Cameron said. "A mouse."

"I can't bear mice. Do kill it, Cam."

Cameron let his gaze tangle with Ainsley's while she struggled to breathe in her too-tight lacings.

"I'll let it live," he said. "For now." Cameron jerked the curtains closed, shutting Ainsley back into her glass and velvet tent. "We should go down."

"Why? We've just arrived."

"I saw too many people coming back into the house, including your husband. We'll go down separately. I don't want to embarrass Beth and Isabella."

"Oh, very well."

Phyllida didn't seem much put out, but then, she likely assumed she could hole up with her Mackenzie lord anytime she pleased to enjoy his touch.

For one moment, Ainsley experienced deep, bone-wrenching envy.

The two fell silent, no doubt restoring clothing, and then Phyllida said, "I'll speak with you later, darling."

Ainsley heard the door open, more muffled conversation, and then the door closed, and all was silent. She waited a few more heart-pounding minutes to make certain they'd gone, before she flung back the draperies and scrambled down from the window seat.

She was across the room and reaching for the door handle when she heard a throat clear behind her.

Slowly, Ainsley turned around. Lord Cameron Mackenzie stood in the middle of the room in shirtsleeves and kilt, his golden gaze once more pinning her in place. He held up a key in his broad fingers.

"So tell me, Mrs. Douglas," he said, his gravelly voice flowing over her. "What the devil are you doing in my bedchamber—this time?"

Chapter 2

Six years ago

Well, this is damned pleasant.

Six years ago, almost to the day, Cameron Mackenzie had stood in the doorway of this very bedchamber and spied a beautiful stranger in the act of closing the drawer of his bedside table.

The lady had worn blue—a shimmering, deep blue gown that bared her shoulders, cupped her waist, and flared back over a modest bustle. Pink roses drooped through her hair and down the gown's train. She'd removed her slippers—the better for stealth—revealing slender feet in white silk stockings.

She hadn't heard him. Cameron leaned on the door frame, enjoying watching her so blithely going through his bedside table.

Drunk and bored, Cameron had left Hart's interminable house party downstairs, unable to take another minute of it.

Now warmth stirred through his ennui. He couldn't remember who the young woman was—he knew he'd been introduced to her, but Hart's guests had long since blurred into one dull mass of humanity.

This lady now separated from that mass, becoming more real to him by the second.

Cameron softly crossed the room, the numbness in which he existed when not with his horses or Daniel lifting away. He stepped behind the blue-clad lady and clasped her satiny waist.

It was like catching a kitten in his hands—a startled cry, a rapid heartbeat, breath coming fast. She looked back and up at him and tangled his heart in a pair of wide gray eyes.

"My lord. I was . . . um . . . I was just . . ."

"Looking for something," he supplied. The roses in her hair were real, the scent of them deepened by her own warmth. A plain silver chain and locket adorned her neck.

"Pencil and paper," she finished.

She was a bad liar. But she was soft and smelled good, and Cameron was drunk enough not to care that she lied. "So you could write me a letter?"

"Yes. Of course."

"Tell me what this letter would say."

"I'm not certain."

Her stammer was endearing. That she wanted a liaison was perfectly obvious. Cameron tightened his hand on her waist and pulled her back ever so gently against him. Her small bustle pressed his groin, the cage keeping him from what he wanted to feel.

When she looked up at him again, something snapped inside him. The scent of her mingling with roses, the feel of her in the curve of his arm, the tickle of her fair hair against his chin awoke emotions he'd thought long dead.

He needed this woman, wanted her. He could drown in her, make her sigh in pleasure, enjoy oblivion with her for a little while.

Cameron touched an openmouthed kiss to her shoulder, tasting her skin. Salt, sweet, a little bit of spice. Not enough—he wanted more.

Cameron didn't often kiss women on the lips. Kissing led to expectations, to hopes for romance, and Cameron did not want romance with his ladies.

But he wanted to know what she tasted like, this young woman who pretended such innocence. A name swam to him—Mrs. . . . Douglas? Cameron vaguely remembered a husband standing next to her downstairs, a man clearly too old for her. She must have married him for convenience. The man probably hadn't touched her in years.

Cameron would touch her and taste her and then send her back to her ineffectual husband sated and happy. At least one night of this be-damned house party wouldn't be so tedious.

He tilted her head back and brushed his lips gently to her mouth. Mrs. Douglas started in surprise but didn't push away. Cameron coaxed her lips open, deepening the kiss.

Pleasant fire spun through him when Mrs. Douglas dipped her tongue into *his* mouth, hesitant, but beautifully curious. His lady was unpracticed, as though she'd not kissed like this in a long time, but Cameron could tell she'd done it at least once. He cupped her head in his hand and let her explore.

Cameron broke the kiss to lick across her lips, finding the moisture between them honey sweet. He transferred his mouth to her throat while he undid the hooks on the back of her bodice. The silk easily parted, his hands pushing down the fabric so he could lean in and kiss her bosom. Mrs. Douglas's soft sound of pleasure made his arousal jump, the need to hurry beating through his brain. But Cameron didn't want to hurry. He wanted to go slowly, to savor every moment.

He let the bodice crumple to her waist, and with the ease of practice, slid his hand to the laces of her corset.

Ainsley thought she'd burn up and die. This was not what she'd meant to happen—she meant to be far from this chamber before Lord Cameron returned for the night. But now Lord Cameron coaxed to life sensations she thought she'd never feel again.

The necklace she'd taken from Cameron's dressing table was safely buttoned into the pocket of her petticoat. She'd nearly tucked it into her bosom, but the emeralds were bulky, and she'd feared the outline would show against her bodice. Luckily for her she had changed her mind, or Cameron's roving fingers would have already found it.

The necklace belonged to one Mrs. Jennings, a widowed friend of Ainsley's brother. Mrs. Jennings had tearfully confided in Ainsley that she'd left her necklace in Cameron's chamber, and now the very bad man would not let her have it back. He was blackmailing her over it, she claimed. Mrs. Jennings feared exposure, scandal. Ainsley, outraged at Cameron's behavior, had offered to fetch it for her.

She understood now why Mrs. Jennings had fallen for Lord Cameron's seduction. Cameron's tall body dwarfed hers, his hands so large that Ainsley's were lost in them. But instead of being frightened, Ainsley felt *right* in the curve of his arms, as though she'd been made to fit him.

Dangerous, dangerous thoughts.

Cameron pressed kisses to Ainsley's neck. She touched his hair, marveling at the rough silk of it. His breath was furnace-hot, his mouth a place of fire, and Ainsley burned.

The corset's laces parted, and Cameron glided his hand inside her chemise and down her back.

Reality hit Ainsley with a slap. The notorious Cameron Mackenzie was parting her clothes with skilled, seductive hands, preparing to take her to bed. But Ainsley Douglas was not a courtesan or a wild-living lady free to make her own choices. She'd married respectably, thanks to her brother's quick thinking, and her elderly husband waited for her in their chamber.

John would be sitting with his slippered feet stretched to the fire, had probably already dozed off over his newspapers.

His tousled gray head would be slumped in sleep, his spectacles askew on his nose. So kind, so patient, was John Douglas, knowing that his young wife had more interesting things to do than be with him. Ainsley's heart broke.

"I can't." The words dragged from her, everything she thought right forcing them out. "I can't. My lord, I'm so sorry."

Cameron stilled, mouth on her neck, hand on her bare back.

"My husband is a good man," she whispered. "A very good man. He doesn't deserve this."

Damn it, something inside Cameron cried out. *Damn it all to hell.*

His entire body fought him as he lifted his hands away. Cameron knew women, knew when their bodies craved a man's touch. Mrs. Douglas wanted what Cameron offered, that was apparent, despite the anguish swimming in her gray eyes. Cam smelled her readiness faintly behind the roses and knew that if he took her, he'd find her slick and open for him.

Her husband obviously hadn't been satisfying her needs. Whether he wouldn't or couldn't didn't matter; he wasn't, or this lady would not be so ready to seek Cameron.

And yet, Mrs. Douglas was saying no for this husband's sake. It took a rare courage to make such a decision, strength that most of Cam's women didn't have. Those women wanted satiation and weren't much bothered by who they hurt to get it.

Cameron tugged Mrs. Douglas's corset back together and laced it closed and then fastened her bodice. He turned her to face him again and traced her cheek with the backs of his fingers.

"Go tell your good man how lucky he is, Mrs. Douglas."

"I am truly sorry, my lord."

Good lord, Cameron had tried to seduce her, and she was apologizing to *him.* Cameron had wanted pleasure, pure and simple, the mind-blanking fire of coupling. Nothing more. He'd assumed she sought that as well. Now she looked worried that she'd caused him inconvenience.

Cameron leaned and pressed another kiss to her parted lips, lingering until the last possible moment. "Go on, now."

Mrs. Douglas nodded, smiling her gratitude. Gratitude, God help him.

Cameron walked her to the door and opened it, kissed her damp lips once more, and guided her out. When Mrs. Douglas turned around to say something, he shook his head and shut the door, turning the key in the lock.

He pressed his forehead to the door's cool panels, listening to her patter away down the empty hall. "Good night, lass," he whispered.

Cameron spent the rest of the night on his bed, fully dressed, downing glass after glass of whiskey. He wasted much time trying not to fantasize about pretty young Mrs. Douglas and where the seduction would have gone. He failed utterly.

The fantasies wrapped him in a glow of warmth well into the next day as Cameron watched Mrs. Douglas. Her husband was tall and bony, awkward with her, though he lingered near her as though he needed to be reassured by her constant presence. Mrs. Douglas was kind to him, Cameron noticed. She didn't treat him with disdain. He also noticed the Mrs. Douglas studiously avoided any eye contact with Cameron.

What a wild affair Cameron could have with her—every night something new. He'd buy jewels to drape her naked body and scented oils to slide onto her skin. He'd be discreet, something Cameron rarely bothered with. He'd convince Mrs. Douglas that her husband would never be hurt by anything they did. They'd meet in secret, perhaps alone in Cameron's carriage, while they explored and tasted and thoroughly learned each other. Their liaison would be glorious, stuff to think on for years to come.

The pleasant fantasy came crashing down the next night when Cameron stood on the terrace outside the ballroom, drinking whiskey with his brother Mac. One of Cameron's former paramours, Felicia Hardcastle, of lovely body but foul temper, stormed out to the terrace and halted in front of Cameron. "You gave her my necklace!"

Necklace? What necklace? People inside the ballroom stared, and Mac watched in mixed astonishment and amusement.

"What the devil are you talking about?" Cameron demanded.

Felicia pointed a stiff finger through the terrace door to Mrs. Jennings, another former mistress. The lady in question stood in the middle of the ballroom in a low-necked evening dress that showed off the emeralds encircling her neck. Emeralds Cameron had purchased for Felicia, which Felicia had carelessly left in his chamber at the beginning of the week. Cameron had locked them into the drawer of his bedside table, planning to have his valet, Angelo, retrieve them and return them to Felicia's maid.

Now the emeralds hung around the neck of Mrs. Jennings, who turned to greet Ainsley Douglas and take her hand with a fond squeeze. Mrs. Douglas, the lady Cameron had found hovering near his bedside table last night.

Bloody hell.

Felicia swept back inside to screech accusations at Mrs. Jennings and Ainsley. Cameron watched Ainsley's pretty mouth drop open and her gaze move across the room to lock on Cameron's.

Her expression spoke of confusion, shock, betrayal. Genuine? Or more trickery?

It didn't matter. Mrs. Douglas had lied to him, used him, duped him with her tearful reluctance to betray her husband—all to steal a stupid necklace for some ridiculous feminine intrigue. And Cameron, fool that he was, had fallen for the little deception.

He entered the ballroom and moved through the crowd, striving to ignore Felicia, Mrs. Jennings, and the gawping crowd. Ainsley Douglas thrust herself into Cameron's path, and he nearly ran over her.

Her gray eyes pleaded with him to understand, forgive. The smell of the roses on her bosom came to him, and the sweet scent of herself, and Cameron realized he still wanted her.

He made himself look down at her in stony indifference, hardening his heart to the tears beading on her lashes. He turned away and continued through the crowd until he reached the ballroom door, then left the house and made his way to the stables.

The warm, horsy odors had comforted him a little, but Cameron told Angelo that he was leaving, mounted a horse, and departed. He boarded a train for London that night and left for the Continent the next morning.

Six years between that day and this rushed past Cameron. He'd returned tonight to his chamber in the midst of another boring house party, again drunk, to find pretty Ainsley Douglas here once more.

Something sharp and raw burned away his half inebriation. Cameron tossed up the key and caught it, the little ringing sound loud in the silence.

"Well?" he asked. "Have ye thought of an explanation yet?"

Chapter 3

Ainsley Douglas wet her lips, making them moist and red and enticing. "Oh yes," she said. "Dozens of them. I'm trying to decide which one you will believe."

She stood against the door in a gray evening frock that bared half her chest, the same silver necklace she'd worn six years ago glittering on her bosom. Her ballroom coiffure was a mess, the back of her gown crushed. So innocent she looked, watching him with wide eyes, but Cameron knew better than to believe in Ainsley Douglas's innocence.

"I'll make a bargain with you, lass," he said. "You tell me the truth, and I'll unlock the door and let you out."

Ainsley stared at him with those heart-wrenching gray eyes a moment longer, then she turned back to the door, yanked a hairpin from her hair, and dropped to her knees to examine the lock.

Cameron's heart pounded and his blood felt thick. He hadn't refastened his shirt or waistcoat, and they hung open to his waist, but the air didn't cool him. His skin was hot, and his mouth was dry as a tomb. He needed another drink. A large one.

Ainsley's position pushed her backside at him, showing Cameron a bustle and train covered with gray ruffles and small black bows. One of her curls straggled down her bare back. Her hair was a little darker than Cameron remembered, woven with golden streaks. Blond hair could darken as a person got older—she'd be all of, say, twenty-seven now.

Her elderly husband was dead, and Ainsley Douglas, according to Isabella, shuttled between being a paid lady-in-waiting to Her Dour Majesty and living with her older brother and his very respectable wife. No longer the ingénue, Mrs. Douglas was a lady whose lot in life had become waiting on others for her living.

Poor little dove.

Cameron swung himself onto the bed, putting his back against the headboard, and reached to his bedside table for a cigar. "That lock is ancient," he said to the bare oval of her back. "Good luck with it."

"Not to worry," she said, scratching away at it. "I've not yet met a lock I couldn't open."

Cameron lit the cheroot, the smell of the sulfur match and cigar smoke curling inside his nostrils. "Aye, you're quite the criminal, aren't you? Last time you broke in here to steal a necklace. What are you here for this time? Blackmail?"

Ainsley glanced swiftly back at him, face pink. "Blackmail?"

"I wouldn't advise you to blackmail Phyllida Chase, dove. She'd eat you for breakfast."

Ainsley gave him a quick, scornful look and returned to the door. "Me, blackmail *Mrs. Chase*? Hardly. And I explained to Isabella about that necklace. I truly thought it belonged to Mrs. Jennings."

Cameron threw the spent match into a bowl. "I'm past caring about the damned necklace. It was a long time ago, and bloody intrigues of bloody-minded women hold no interest for me."

"I'm very pleased to hear it, Lord Cameron," Ainsley said, concentrating on the lock.

Why did her saying his name make it music? Cameron leaned back and took a pull of his cigar. He should taste the fine, pressed leaves seasoned with brandy, but it could have been a charred stick for all he noticed.

If he weren't so drunk he would simply unlock the door, let her out, and forget about her. But flashes of the night six years ago kept coming to him—the fierce heat of her skin, her hesitant but needy touch, her swiftly drawn breath as he kissed across her bosom.

She was six years older now and the gray dress was all wrong for her, but time had only deepened her beauty. Lush breasts swelled over the top of her bodice, and her hips had widened to be enticing under the tightly drawn skirt. Her face reflected more experience of the world, her gray eyes held a bit more skepticism, her self-control was firmer.

If Cameron could convince her to stay tonight, he'd finally be able to savor the hot, sensual taste of Ainsley Douglas, which had bewitched him all these years. Warm, cinnamony, smooth. He'd press her against the door, lick her skin that was damp with sweat, tell her what he really wanted in return for letting her out. All she had to do was finish what they'd started six years ago, and he'd unlock the door and release her.

Cameron forced himself to look away from her and take another pull of the cheroot. His wandering gaze fell on the coat that lay sprawled across the bed and the corner of paper that stuck out of his pocket.

He'd forgotten about the letter, or whatever it was, that Phyllida had thrust at him earlier that day. She'd told him to keep it safe for her, and Cameron had tucked the paper away, uninterested. His valet, Angelo, must have found it and thought it important enough to slide into the coat of Cameron's formal suit.

Cameron fished out the paper and unfolded it. It was part of a letter, missing the greeting, and unsigned. His brows rose as he started reading. It was a sickening sweet panegyric to an apparently virile man, the prose drowning in exclamation marks and underlining. The style was sentimental and emphatic and all wrong for Ainsley Douglas.

He held up the page. "Is this what you were looking for, Mrs. Douglas?"

Ainsley looked around at him and slowly rose to her feet. The shock and dismay on her face told Cameron all he needed to know.

"That isn't yours," she said.

"God, I hope not. 'Your honest brow is crowned with honeyed dew, your muscles like Vulcan's at his forge.' How long did it take ye to think up this drivel?"

Ainsley marched across the carpet and halted beside the bed, arm outstretched. "Give it to me."

Cameron looked at her gloved palm so stiffly held out to him and wanted to laugh. She expected him to meekly return the letter, perhaps escort her to the door, apologize for inconveniencing her?

"Who did ye write it to?" Whoever it was didn't deserve this beautiful woman writing him at all, even a bloody awful letter like this one.

She reddened. "It's not mine. It's . . . a friend's. May I have it back, please?"

Cameron folded the letter in half. "No."

She blinked. "Why not?"

"Because ye want it so much."

Ainsley's chest hurt. Lord Cameron lounged back on his bed and laughed at her, eyes glints of gold as he dangled the letter between his strong fingers. His waistcoat and shirt hung open, showing her a V of chest dusted with dark hair. A man in dishabille who'd undressed for his mistress. His kilt rumpled across his knees, the hem caught on a scar she'd seen when Mrs. Chase had lifted it.

He was rude, ungentlemanly, brutish, and dangerous. Lord Cameron collected erotica, people told her, books and art. She saw no sign of that lying about, although the painting that hung over his bedside table—a woman sitting on her bed pulling on her stockings—held unashamed sensuality.

But though a lady ought to regard Lord Cameron in disapproval, even apprehension, he made Ainsley's blood tingle. He again was awakening things in her that had lain dead for too many years.

"Please give me the letter, Lord Cameron. It is very important."

Cameron took a puff from his cheroot, sending smoke into Ainsley's face. Ainsley coughed and waved it away.

"You're tipsy," she said.

"No, I'm bloody drunk and plan to get drunker. Would you like to join me in a single malt, madam? From Hart's finest stock."

The Mackenzies owned a small distillery that shipped Scots whiskey all over Scotland and to select clients in England. Everyone knew that. The distillery had done only modestly until Hart had inherited it—according to Isabella, Hart and Ian between them had turned it into a vastly profitable venture.

Ainsley imagined Cameron taking a slow sip of whiskey, licking away a drop from his lips. She swallowed. "If I show you that I'm not afraid of whiskey, will you give me the letter and let me out?"

"No."

Ainsley let out an exasperated breath. "Devil take you, Lord Cameron, you are the most maddening, wretched—"

She made a sudden grab for the letter, but Cameron lifted it out of reach. "No, you don't, Mrs. Douglas."

Ainsley narrowed her eyes and swatted, not at the letter, but the cheroot. The lit cigar flew from Cameron's fingers and bounced to the bedcovers. He dove after it, growling.

"Damn you, woman."

Ainsley had one knee on the bed, her fingers around the letter he'd dropped to snatch at the cheroot. The next instant, she found herself flat on the mattress with Lord Cameron on top of her, her wrists captured above her head by his massive hand. Lord Cameron might be drunk, but he was strong.

"Clever, clever Mrs. Douglas. But not fast enough."

Still holding Ainsley's wrists, Cameron tossed the cheroot onto the bedside table, then wrested the letter from Ainsley's fingers. She struggled but couldn't budge him; his big hand held her firmly in place.

Cameron stuffed the letter into his waistcoat pocket and leaned closer, his breath burning her skin. He was going to kiss her. She'd dreamed of his kiss in the lonely years between her first encounter with him and this one, reliving the warm pressure of his mouth, the heat of his tongue. And now, she would let him kiss her again. Gladly.

Closer. Closer. Cameron nuzzled the line of her hair, his lips just brushing it. "Who is the letter to?" he whispered.

Ainsley could barely speak. "None of your affair."

His smile held sin. "You look too innocent to have paramours. But I know you're a good little liar."

"I'm not lying, and I don't have a paramour. The letter belongs to a friend, I told you."

"She must be a very dear friend, for you to go to all this trouble." He fished the key from his pocket and touched it to her lips. "Ye want this, do you?"

"I would enjoy leaving the room, yes."

Cameron's eyes warmed. "Are ye certain?"

"Very certain." *I think.*

Cameron traced her lips with the key, the metal cool and hard. "What would you do for this key, pretty Mrs. Douglas?"

"I don't know." That was the plain truth. Whatever Cameron asked her for, Ainsley was afraid she'd do without protest.

"Would you kiss me for it?"

Ainsley's gaze went to his lips, and she wet her own. "Yes. Yes, I believe I would."

"Bold, wicked lady."

"I must be, mustn't I? I haven't screamed or slapped you or smacked my knee between your legs."

Cameron looked startled, then burst out laughing. It was a genuine laugh, his gravelly voice warm. The bed shook with it. Still laughing, Cameron tilted his head back and dropped the key into his mouth.

"What are you—" Ainsley's words cut off as Cameron brought his mouth down on hers, sweeping his tongue—and the cool key—inside. His lips were strong, mastering, his tongue forceful.

Cameron lifted his head again, still smiling.

Finding her hands released, Ainsley plucked the key from her mouth. "I could have choked on this, my lord."

"I wouldn't have let you." His tone was suddenly gentle, the one of the man who coaxed the most reluctant horses to come to his hand. In that instant, Ainsley saw loneliness in his eyes, a vast well of it, filling every space of him.

Ainsley knew about loneliness—she was often alone despite living among so many people—but she also knew that she had family and friends who would be at her side the moment she truly needed them. Lord Cameron had family, the notorious Mackenzies, four men who couldn't stay out of the scandal sheets, and a son, Daniel, who spent most of his time away at school. His two younger brothers had wives and new families to keep them busy, his older brother Hart had the dukedom. What did Cameron have?

Compassion squeezed her heart, and Ainsley reached up to touch his face.

Instantly, Cameron rolled off her, removing his heady warmth, at the same time pulling her upright. She found herself sitting on the edge of the bed, clutching the key, before his hand under her backside pushed her to her feet.

"Go," he said. "You have your way out, and I want to sleep."

Ainsley held out her hand. "With the letter?"

"Bugger the letter. Now get out, woman, and leave me in peace."

The shutters between himself and her had risen again. Hard and unpredictable was Lord Cameron. A new mistress every few months, ruthless when it came to winning races, and fiercely protective of his horses and his son.

Horses and women, she'd heard someone say about him. *That's all he cares about, in that order.*

And yet she'd seen that flash of longing in his eyes.

Cameron still had the page of the letter. Ainsley had lost this round, but there would be another. There would have to be.

"Good night then, Lord Cameron."

Hand under her arm, playful no longer, Cameron took her to the door, waited while she put the key in the lock, and more or less shoved her out of the room. Without looking at her, Cameron closed the door behind her, and she heard the decided click of the lock.

Well.

Ainsley blew out her breath and leaned against the nearest wall. She shook in every limb, her chest tight, her corset far too binding. She could still feel the weight of Cameron's long body on hers, the strength of his hand on her wrists, the imprint of his mouth on hers.

She hadn't forgotten his touch, the heat of his kiss, the strength of him, in six years. What a man he was, a forbidden, out-of-reach man who cared nothing for Ainsley Douglas and her troubles. Cameron still had the letter, and she had to get it back from him before he gave it to Phyllida, or worse, his brother Hart. If Hart Mackenzie knew what a treasure Cameron carried carelessly in his pocket, the ruthless duke wouldn't hesitate to use it, she was certain.

But at the moment, Ainsley could only think of the long length of Cameron pressing her into the mattress, the heat of his breath on her mouth. What would it be like to be his lover?

Wonderful, wicked, far too powerful for the likes of Ainsley Douglas. He'd called her a mouse, she remembered, when he'd found her tucked into his window seat to hide.

She also remembered, as she finally pried herself from the wall and headed for the back stairs, something she'd seen very clearly when Cameron had pinned Ainsley's hands above her head.

His loosened sleeve had slipped, revealing scars along the inside of his forearm. The scars had faded with time, but each was perfectly round, each about three quarters of an inch in diameter. Ainsley recognized the shape of them from an accident that had happened to one of her brothers, but Sinclair had suffered only one burn.

Someone, once upon a time, had amused themselves by touching a lighted cigar end repeatedly to Lord Cameron's flesh.

The morning was fine enough to put Angelo on Night-Blooming Jasmine and let her gallop in the one field that wasn't too boggy for the horses. Cameron rode behind them on a retired racer as Angelo let Jasmine run full out.

Cameron felt the power of the horse he rode, the air in his face, the rush of speed—all working to pull him out of his groggy, hungover state. He only ever came alive while astride a horse or watching their grace and strength as they ran. Sometimes when he hit the moment of passion with a woman, he'd feel the same surge of life, but at all other times, Cameron Mackenzie was half dead, walking through life and barely feeling it.

The exception: The two times he'd found Ainsley Douglas in his bedroom. Both times he'd come upon her there, he'd felt that rush and roar of excitement, the exhilaration pouring into his body.

Cameron hadn't slept after Ainsley had left the night before. He'd tried to soothe his lust and his anger with whiskey and cheroots, but nothing had worked. Now here he was too damn early in the morning, his head pounding, his mouth parched, while he tried to train the most challenging horse of his career.

Night-Blooming Jasmine, a three-year-old with incredible speed, had been nearly ruined by being pushed to win the big races before she was ready. Her owner, a fool of an English viscount called Lord Pierson, had already run through a string of trainers, finding fault with each and transferring Jasmine from one to the next in rapid succession. Pierson openly despised Cameron, because Cameron trained his own horses and sometimes horses for other owners. A gentleman hired others to do menial jobs for him, Pierson told him.

Cameron saw no reason to own horses if he couldn't be among them. He'd learned at a young age that he had a gift with the beasts. Not only could he bring out the best in each, but the horses followed him about the paddocks like dogs and came eagerly alert whenever he walked into a stable yard.

Jasmine was a dark brown filly with a coffee brown mane and tail, long of leg and sound of heart. She had the spirit and the speed, but Pierson had nearly destroyed her. He'd wanted to run her, as a three-year-old, in the most important flat races of the year: Epsom, Newmarket, Doncaster. Jasmine had fallen at Newmarket, but mercifully unhurt, had finished respectably, which was more to do with her jockey's skill than her trainer's care.

At Epsom, under a new trainer and new jockey, she'd flagged in the middle of the pack. Pierson, disgusted, had sacked that trainer and jockey and brought Jasmine to Cameron, saying that Cameron was his last hope. Pierson was damned sorry that his last hope was one of the bloody Scottish Mackenzies, but he had no other choice. Jasmine needed to win the St. Leger at Doncaster, and that was all there was to that.

Cameron would have told Pierson to fornicate himself, but one look at Jasmine's sleek body and mischievous eye, and Cameron couldn't turn her away. He knew there was something in the horse that he could bring out. He needed to rescue her from Pierson. So he agreed.

But Cam doubted she'd win Doncaster and told Pierson so, frankly. She was wrung out, tired, annoyed, and needed much care if she'd finish at all. Pierson didn't like that, but too damn bad.

Jasmine at least ran well today, showing her potential, neck arching proudly when Angelo reached down to pat her. Some of Hart's guests lined up beyond the field—keeping a safe distance as Cameron had instructed them all week.

Nowhere did he see a lady with a fine head of golden hair craning to watch, as much as Cameron looked for her while pretending to himself that he didn't. Ainsley Douglas was likely helping Isabella and Beth organize something. Isabella had spent much time this week singing the praises of Mrs. Douglas's gift for managing things.

Of course she had a gift. Criminals had to be organized, or they'd be caught. The crackling paper in Cameron's pocket was a reminder of that.

Cameron's son, Daniel, rode another racer, a more experienced horse to keep Jasmine paced. Cameron pulled his horse back to watch, noting with a tug of pride, as Daniel cantered side by side with Jasmine and Angelo, that his son had the touch with the horses. Danny would be a damned fine trainer if he chose to take up the sport.

Daniel's lanky form had not only shot up to reach Cameron's height over the summer, but his voice had deepened and his shoulders widened. He'd become a man when Cameron wasn't looking, and Cameron wasn't certain what to do about it. Daniel was turning out remarkably well, in spite of it all, which Cameron put down to his brothers' help and his sisters-in-law's influence.

Angelo and Daniel rode the horses around to where Cameron waited, the Romany Angelo smiling with pleasure. "She's in fine form this morning," Angelo said.

"Aye," Daniel reached over and patted Jasmine's neck with proprietary pride. "In spite of the trouble she causes us. Wish I could be a jockey and ride her to victory, but I'm already too big."

"Jockeys have a hell of a life, son," Cam said. He understood Daniel's longing, but he wanted his son's neck in one piece.

"Aye, all those horses and money and women must be a right trial," Daniel said.

Angelo laughed, and Jasmine stretched her neck to Cameron. Cameron rubbed her nose. "You're doing fine, lass. You've got heart, I know that."

"She won't win," Angelo said. "Doncaster is in three weeks."

"I know."

"What about Pierson?"

"I'll deal with Pierson. You stay away from him."

Angelo laughed. "No fear there."

Hart's guests might be shocked to hear Angelo speaking so familiarly to Cameron, but the two men were more friends than servant and master. Cameron found Angelo refreshingly frank, and Angelo had decided that Cameron had good sense, for an Anglo. Besides, Cameron knew horses, and the two men had become fast friends over that.

Across the field, the guests were moving off, being herded by the redheaded Isabella up to the lawn.

"Now, what are they doing?" Cameron growled.

"Croquet match," Angelo said. "To the death, I think."

"Croquet is bloody boring," Daniel said.

Cameron wasn't listening. Another woman had come to join Isabella, one in a dull gray frock with hair the color of sunshine.

"Jasmine's had enough this morning," Cameron said. "Cool her down and take her in, Angelo."

Angelo flashed another smile and turned Jasmine away. Daniel followed Angelo without a word. Cameron rode to the edge of the paddock to dismount his own horse, tossed his reins to a groom, and climbed the slope toward the house.

"Get me into this game, Izzy," Cameron said when he reached Isabella at the edge of Hart's well-groomed lawn. Pairs of ladies and gentlemen waited beyond, a few gentlemen swinging mallets and rolling shoulders to show off for the ladies.

Isabella turned to Cameron in surprise. "We're playing croquet."

"Yes, I know what the devil it is. Give me a damned mallet."

"But you hate croquet." Isabella continued to blink green eyes at him.

"I don't hate it today. I want you to pair me with Mrs. Douglas."

"Ah." Isabella's surprised look turned to one of interest. "Mrs. Douglas, is it?"

They both turned to where Ainsley stood under a tree across the lawn, the Italian count at her side trying to catch her attention. Ainsley's dress, trimmed with darker gray piping, was long-sleeved and high-collared, buttoned up to her neck. Cameron didn't like her like that—the effect was one of a brightly plumed bird wrapped in a confining sheet.

"You should have told me beforehand," Isabella was saying. "I've already put her with a partner."

"So change him."

"Change him? My dear Cameron, assigning Hart's guests to partners is an extremely delicate task. The entire game of croquet is a like a balance of European power. If I change one team, I have to change them all. I bless Ainsley for being able to take on the count."

Mac came up behind Isabella, slid his arm around her waist, and nuzzled her cheek. "Hart and his political games of croquet. I can think of so many better things to do this morning besides whacking a ball around a green."

Isabella blushed but didn't push her husband's hand away

as it moved to her abdomen, where their second child had started to grow. "I promised Hart I'd help him," Isabella said. "He looked so desperate when he asked."

"He would." Mac continued to nuzzle. "Where is Hart, anyway?"

"Wooing diplomats with brandy and cigars behind closed doors," Isabella said.

"Leaving us with the dull work," Mac rumbled.

Their youngest brother, Ian, was absent as well, but none of them needed to ask why. Cameron had spoken to Ian earlier that morning, but Ian didn't like crowds, nor did he like games in which he could calculate the winning trajectories in two minutes. He'd be bored and uncomfortable and dart away to be alone, giving Hart's guests something to talk about.

In the past, Cameron, worrying about Ian, would go make sure that he wasn't sitting alone in a huddle, or staring for hours at a Ming bowl, or pouring over some endless mathematical exercise. These days, Cameron knew that Ian used the excuse of not liking crowds to spend more time alone with his wife—in bed. Crafty sod.

"If you truly want in the game, Cameron, I'll have you look after Mrs. Yardley," Isabella said. "She volunteered to sit out as we have an odd number, but I know she'd love to play."

Cameron's gaze strayed to the green where the count had taken Ainsley's arm to lead her to the first wicket. "Fine," Cameron said. "Mrs. Yardley it is."

"Excellent. She'll be pleased." Isabella smiled. She held out a mallet to him. "Think of it as a very slow game of polo. Enjoy yourself, Cam."

"Oh, I intend to." Cameron took the mallet and marched determinedly to the lawn. Ainsley Douglas, ensconced with her count, never once looked his way.

Chapter 4

Mrs. Yardley, a very plump, gray-haired woman who could barely move her legs to walk, proved to be intelligent and pleasant. Cameron flirted with her mildly as he carried her mallet and folding chair and settled her in at each wicket. She stated that she appreciated Isabella pairing her with the black sheep of the Mackenzie family—a lady of her years and girth had only so much excitement in life.

Cameron leaned on his mallet, trying to stave off his headache as the tedious game commenced tediously. He'd drunk far too much last night, and while he'd felt better riding this morning, his head was still thick with his hangover.

Ainsley, on the other hand, looked fresh and bright, every gleaming hair in place. Cameron had liked her much better mussed. On his bed last night he'd wanted to spread her golden hair in his hands, drag it over her bare breasts, kiss the lips that talked back to him so saucily. He let his senses drift to the scent of her, the feel of her beneath him, the taste of her mouth when he'd pushed the key into it.

"Ah," Mrs. Yardley said. "I see a spring lassie catching a laddie's eyes."

Cameron opened his eyes and frowned as the count tried to guide Ainsley's hands on her mallet. There was no need for the count to instruct her—Ainsley had already racked up a number of points with her competent strokes.

"It's autumn," Cameron said. The trees at the bottom of the park blazed scarlet and gold, mixed with the deeper black green of the pines.

"But a beautiful lady always means spring in the heart."

"I mean that it's autumn for me." Cameron watched Ainsley as she bent to tap her ball with precision. The sight of Ainsley's hands firmly gripping her mallet made him dizzy.

"Nonsense. You've lived only half as long as I have, and it's a long time through the next half of your life. Such a strange marriage Mrs. Douglas made. John Douglas was in his fifties, she barely eighteen. I imagine it was a family arrangement, but I can't imagine what sort of arrangement. Douglas never had much money, and he left Ainsley almost destitute, poor thing. I tell you all this for a reason, Lord Cameron."

Because she'd noted Cameron's obsessive interest with Ainsley Douglas. Hell, the whole house party would see it if they weren't busy trying to be noticed themselves.

"She's young," Cameron said. "She can remarry."

"True, she is young and still quite lovely, but she's shut away from company much of the time. Her Majesty keeps Mrs. Douglas tucked by her side—she's become quite the favorite, and Mrs. Douglas needs the money the post with the queen brings. Ainsley's oldest brother helps her, but he has a family of his own, and Ainsley rather feels the pinch of living in his back spare room. Ainsley's mother had been one of the queen's favorites before she lost that pleasure by marrying beneath her. Mr. McBride was *not* who the queen had in mind for poor, dear Jeanette. But all that was forgotten when the queen met Ainsley. She was enchanted with Ainsley and insisted on bringing her into the household. The post was a godsend. Ainsley's brother is kind, but she was utterly dependent on him. Of course she took it."

All of which explained Ainsley's obsessive determination to retrieve the disgraceful letter from the clutches of the evil Lord Cameron before he showed it to anyone. Ainsley couldn't afford to lose her position with the queen.

"But the poor girl is never seen out and about during the Season," Mrs. Yardley went on. "Or any other time for that matter. The queen likes to keep her close. By the time Ainsley is allowed a holiday, she's too exhausted for much of a social life. She stays with her brother during her meager days off—kind people, as I said, but stuffy. Family suppers and reading aloud. Playing the piano if they're feeling *truly* frivolous. Patrick and his wife are a bit overprotective, have always been, but then Patrick and Rona raised Ainsley and her three other brothers when their parents died. I'm happy that Isabella plucks Ainsley out once in a while, even if only for a week." Cameron felt Mrs. Yardley's keen eyes on him. "Are you listening, my lord? I'm not babbling to fill the time, you know."

Cameron couldn't look away from Ainsley, her head bent to the count's as they discussed their next play. "Yes, I'm listening."

"I wasn't born old, my lord. I recognize when a man wants a woman. And you're not a monster, despite the reputation you try to maintain. Ainsley needs a bit of excitement in her life, poor lamb. She was a very lively young woman and then suddenly had to become a drudge."

She didn't seem drudging now. Ainsley was laughing, her laughter sparkling across the green. Her smile was all for the count, and something dangerous stirred inside Cameron.

"Forgive me, my lord," Mrs. Yardley said. "I don't have

much to do these days but observe my fellow men—and women—and I do have great experience in who fits with whom. Why not make a match of it? What on earth else do you intend to do with the rest of your life?"

"Much as I do now, I imagine." Cameron rubbed his upper lip as Ainsley patted the count's arm in praise. "Horses take much attention, and the racing calendar fills the year."

"So I hear. But happiness is a different thing. It's worth a little effort."

"I made that effort once." *Too damn bloody much effort.*

"Yes, dear, I knew your wife."

A glance at Mrs. Yardley told Cameron she'd known some of the truth about Lady Elizabeth. The memory of Elizabeth's beautiful face, her mad eyes as she came at him, ready to strike, made his body tighten. Old pain, old darkness dimmed the bright morning.

Cameron heard Ainsley's laughter again, and he opened his eyes, the visions dissolving.

"If you knew my wife, then you'll understand why I view marriage as a miserable existence," Cameron said, still watching Ainsley. "I won't enter it again."

"It *can* be a miserable existence, I don't deny that. But with the right person, it can be the best existence in the world. Trust me, I know."

"It's our turn," Cameron said curtly. "Are you up for a go?"

Mrs. Yardley smiled. "I'm rather tired, my lord. You take my turn for me."

Cameron felt the paper of the stolen letter crackle in his pocket and watched Ainsley smile at the count.

"You're a wise woman, Mrs. Yardley." He lowered the mallet he'd rested on his shoulder and approached their waiting ball.

"I know that, dear," Mrs. Yardley said behind him.

Ainsley knew the precise moment Cameron stepped from the shade to take his shot, while the slow-moving Mrs. Yardley kept her seat. Ainsley had been aware of every movement Cameron made since he'd appeared even though she'd avoided looking directly at him.

She hadn't missed how Cameron carried Mrs. Yardley's chair and mallet for her, slowing his long stride for hers as they moved about the pitch. He was being patient, kind even, conversing with the elderly lady, who smiled back at him in appreciation.

Cameron was this patient and gentle with his horses, guiding them with care that he rarely used on people, unless they were like Mrs. Yardley. It was a side of himself no one acknowledged, and Ainsley wondered if anyone but she even noticed it.

She saw no sign of that patience, however, when Cameron looked up from his ball at Ainsley. His eyes glinted with determination, like a billiards shark ready to win the pool.

It did not help that Lord Cameron was devastating in his riding clothes: buff breeches smooth over his thighs, boots muddy, casual coat hanging open over a plain shirt. Cameron's large masculinity rendered the slender Englishmen pale and ineffectual, as though a bear had wandered into a gathering of docile deer. He wielded his mallet with precision, which was why he and Mrs. Yardley had already racked up a number of points, and therefore guineas, because no one who came to visit the Duke of Kilmorgan didn't gamble outrageously.

Cameron drew back his mallet and struck his ball with force. The ball leapt with a straight trajectory up the little rise and smacked into Ainsley's with a decided *click.*

Her heart jumped. "Botheration," she muttered.

Her partner, the rather feeble-brained count, called out, "Excellent roquet, my lord."

Cameron strode to them, mallet on his shoulder. He said nothing to Ainsley as he placed his large booted foot over his ball, Ainsley's still touching it, and drew back the mallet. His riding coat stretched across his shoulders as Cameron smacked the ball under his foot, the impact sending Ainsley's galloping across the green. She watched in dismay as the bright yellow and white striped sphere rolled merrily to the edge of the lawn and plunged into the undergrowth of the woods.

"I believe you're out of bounds, Mrs. Douglas," Cameron said.

Ainsley ground her teeth. "I see that, my lord."

The count said in careful English, "That was perhaps not, as you English say, very sporting."

"Games are played to win," Cameron said. "And we're Scottish."

The count looked into the undergrowth and then down at his well-polished shoes. "I will fetch the ball for you, signora," he said without much enthusiasm.

Which would leave Ainsley alone with Cameron. "No, indeed, I'll find it myself. Won't be a tick."

Ainsley turned and ran for the undergrowth before the count could do more than make a token protest. She hadn't missed the relief on the count's face that he wouldn't have to take his pristine suit into the bushes, nor had she missed the slow smile on Cameron's.

It was cool under the trees, the mud sticky. Ainsley walked about ten yards into the woods before she spied the painted stripe on the ball under the thickest bush. She stuck her mallet into the brush and thrashed around for it.

"Allow me." Cameron was beside her, no apology, no explanation. His longer arm allowed his mallet to reach under the brush, and in a few seconds, he scraped Ainsley's ball back to bare mud.

"Thank you." She started to tap the ball back, not wanting to pick up the mud-caked thing, but Lord Cameron's body was in her way. A screen of trees blocked them from view of the green, making them effectively alone.

"Why are you all buttoned up like that?" Cameron ran his gaze down the blackberry-shaped buttons of her bodice. A smart frock, Ainsley had thought when Isabella had coerced her into buying it. Gray with darker gray piping along the little peplum jacket and skirt, the chin-hugging collar trimmed with a bit of black lace.

"You were happy to bare all last night," Cameron said. He let his mallet handle hover an inch from her chest. "Your bodice was down to here."

Ainsley cleared her throat. "Low neckline for evening, high for morning." She'd tried to tell Isabella that the ball gown was too revealing, but Isabella had said: "It has to be, darling. I'll not have my dearest friend look like a frumpy matron."

"This doesn't suit you," Cameron said.

"I can't help the fashion, Lord Cameron."

Cameron poked the top button with his gloved finger. "Undo this."

Ainsley jumped. "What?"

"Unbutton your damned frock."

She nearly choked. "Why?"

"Because I want you to." Cameron's smile spread across his face, slow and sinful, and his voice went low. Dangerous. "Tell me, Mrs. Douglas. How many buttons will you undo for me?"

Chapter 5

This could not be happening to her. Lord Cameron Mackenzie could not be standing in front of Ainsley, asking her to unfasten her bodice for him. Here in the woods, steps away from the crème de la crème of Europe playing croquet on the Duke of Kilmorgan's front lawn.

"How many?" Cameron repeated.

All of them. Ainsley wanted to tear open the placket and sink down into the mud and let the brand-new dress be ruined.

"Three," she croaked.

Something wicked gleamed in his eyes. "Fifteen."

"*Fifteen?*" The blackberry buttons were close together, but fifteen would bare her to the middle of her corset. "Four."

"Twelve."

"Five," Ainsley countered. "That is as much as you can expect, and I'll have to do them up again before we return to the game."

"I don't give a tinker's damn what you do before you return to the game. Ten."

"Six. No more."

"Ten."

"Lord Cameron."

"Ten, bloody stubborn female." He leaned closer, breath touching her skin. "I'll ask politely until I get tired of asking, and then I'll rip off those pretty buttons myself."

Her world sharpened. "You wouldn't."

"I would."

Ainsley wet her lips. Her pleas of propriety were false, and he knew it. "Ten then."

"Done."

She had to be mad. She could not stand here and let Lord Cameron unbutton her frock. Once upon a time, she'd let him half undress her, and she'd barely gotten away with her sanity intact.

Untrue. She'd lost her sanity that night and never regained it.

Ainsley watched, one heartbeat at a time, as Cameron tugged off his gloves and reached for her top button.

His smile held triumph as the button slid through the hole. The fabric sprang back, as brazen as Ainsley felt. Cameron brushed the tiny bit of flesh he'd bared, licking heat all the way down her body. She would die before he reached ten.

Buttons two and three. Cameron touched her after he opened each one, as though learning her as she came undone for him.

Ainsley closed her eyes as he unfastened buttons four and five. He brushed the hollow of her throat, his touch like fire, before moving down to button six.

A skilled seducer, she told herself at buttons seven and eight. He was a man who knew how to make women yearn to give him what he wanted. Ainsley, for all her seeming recklessness, had learned to be cautious—everything done for a reason, every risk calculated against its reward. But with Cameron, the old reckless Ainsley reared up, wanting him to undo her bodice down to her waist and take what he pleased.

She almost begged him to at button nine.

At button ten, Ainsley opened her eyes.

"Done," Cameron said softly, and he pulled open the placket.

Ainsley's breasts swelled over the top of her corset. Ladies were supposed to be slender, hence the cage of the corset, but Ainsley always seemed to overfill her stays.

Cameron pushed the placket out of the way, his hand going almost reverently to her skin.

"Ainsley," he said in his raw voice. "Do you know how beautiful you are?"

When he touched her, when his voice flowed over her, she felt beautiful. "You are kind to say so."

"It doesn't have anything to do with kindness." He sounded irritated. Cameron slid his thumb over her breast then leaned and kissed her there.

Even him lying fully on top of her hadn't burned her as his lips did now. Ainsley's feminine places grew hot as he kissed her flesh, slow kisses, taking his time. His lips were warm, practiced, the rough warmth of his hair brushing her chin. She wanted to pull him to her, to cradle him against her as he laid her down in the sticky mud, even with the tap of croquet balls not far away.

Cameron kissed the top of her cleavage, his unshaved whiskers a pleasant burn. Then he straightened up, stepped away, and slid a folded paper down between her breasts.

Ainsley's eyes widened, and she clapped her hand over her corset. "What—"

"I believe that is yours, Mrs. Douglas."

Ainsley snatched out the letter, unfolded it, and saw the even strokes of the queen's handwriting, words to her horseman, John Brown.

"I decided I didn't have any interest in your letters," Cameron said. "Or your be-damned intrigues."

Ainsley stared, openmouthed, then she crumpled the page and thrust it into her jacket pocket. "Thank you," she said, heartfelt. "I can't explain, but thank you."

"You're still unbuttoned."

Ainsley looked down at her gaping placket, her breasts welling over the plain corset.

Cameron's wicked smile returned. "I don't mind. But if another ball comes rolling out here, you might be embarrassed."

Ainsley stripped off her gloves and started buttoning with shaking fingers. It took what seemed forever, while Cameron did nothing but watch, but at last Ainsley closed the top button. She snatched up the mallet she'd dropped, but when she turned to go, she found Cameron still barring her way.

"We have unfinished business, Mrs. Douglas."

"Do we? What business would that be?"

Cameron touched the handle of his mallet to her chin. "The business you began when you came to my room six years ago."

"I told you, that was a mistake. I thought you were withholding the emerald necklace from Mrs. Jennings."

"Forget about the damned necklace. I mean what you started with me that night. You half seduced me to keep me finding out what you were up to, then wriggled out of it with your pleas about your good husband." His eyes were hard, glints of angry gold.

"I'd not planned any of that. I expected to be finished and gone before you returned. Besides, you were perfectly willing to seduce *me*, even though you knew I was married."

"I'm used to women seeking me as refuge from their dull husbands."

"Like Phyllida Chase?" Ainsley heard the bitterness in her voice but couldn't mask it.

"Exactly like Phyllida Chase. Her husband ignores her and blatantly philanders, so she turns elsewhere for entertainment. Why not? Other women are much the same."

"You despise them," Ainsley said in surprise.

"What?"

"You despise these ladies who cuckold their husbands. And yet you seduce them. Why do you want to be with women you despise?"

Cameron's brows shot down, but the look he gave her struck her to the heart. "Men enjoy pleasure, Mrs. Douglas. We want it, we crave it; we think of little else. Even men who pretend to be prim and pious are driven by it. The beast lies very close to the surface. If a lady cuckolds her husband to provide me that pleasure, so be it, but I refuse to admire her for it."

"It sounds so lonely," Ainsley said softly.

"I'm rarely alone."

"I know," she said. "That makes it worse."

Cameron's gaze focused hard on her. Again the shutters between him and the world fell, and again Ainsley saw the lonely depths of him. For a split second only. Then the shutters were restored, his scowl back in place.

"You've misbuttoned yourself."

Ainsley looked down at her placket. "Blast."

Cameron leaned to her. "Unfinished business, Mrs. Douglas. Before you leave at the end of the week, we will finish it. Depend on that."

He jerked her up to him in a sudden movement and caught her lower lip between his teeth. Before Ainsley could gasp or pull away, he let her go, shouldered his mallet, and strode off, back through the curtain of trees.

He moved like a god in charge of his world, used to leaving panting females behind him. Ainsley's lip throbbed from Cameron's bite as she tried to grasp buttons with her shaking fingers, and she still felt his grip on the back of her neck. Lord Cameron was strong and dangerous, and she should be frightened of him. But the reckless Ainsley only mourned that he'd walked away too soon.

Something rustled in the brush, followed by a bleating voice. "Signora? Can you find not your ball?"

"Yes, yes, I have it!"

Ainsley jerked her placket together and swiftly buttoned it, then snatched up her muddy ball. She burst out of the brush to the waiting count and found that Cameron Mackenzie was no longer in sight.

"Dad!"

Under the fireworks in the dark gardens, Cameron's thoughts jerked from the memory of Ainsley's firm breasts under his lips when he'd unbuttoned her in the woods. Her pulse had been beating as fast as a rabbit's—would it beat as quickly in passion?

"*Dad!*"

Daniel Mackenzie planted himself in front of Cameron. The lad's kilt sagged from his hips, and his shirt was stained and jacket askew as though he'd been running through the woods. Probably he had been.

Daniel had inherited Elizabeth's eyes, a deep, rich brown, with only a hint of the Mackenzie gold. Likewise, his hair was very dark with mere highlights of red. Elizabeth had been a beautiful woman, and Daniel reflected this in the sturdy structure of his face, the straight, clear lines that age would never erase.

His eyes now held a mixture of rage and uncertainty. "Did ye forget?"

"Of course I didn't forget." Cameron dug through his brain trying desperately to remember what the devil he was supposed to remember. "Your aunt Isabella tethered me all morning."

"Yes, I know, the croquet. But I wanted to talk to you."

No one had explained to Cameron when he was twenty years old and proud as hell that he'd managed to get his wife with child, how difficult it would be to raise a son. Nannies and tutors and schools were supposed to do that, weren't they?

But sons needed so much more than food, clothing, and

tutoring. They expected fathers to know things, to teach them about life, to be there when needed. Cameron's own father had set no good example, so most of the time Cameron found himself floundering in deep waters, searching for his footing.

It had been damn hard going, and Cameron knew that he'd never, ever done enough. He thanked God for his brothers, as unruly as they were, for helping take Daniel under their collective wing. Between the four of them, and then Isabella and Beth, they'd somehow managed to bring Daniel up.

"I'm here now," Cameron said.

Daniel heaved an aggrieved sigh, tall enough to look his father directly in the eyes. "What I wanted to ask was—how old ye were when ye first took a mistress?"

Cameron felt the floundering start, but Daniel was perfectly serious. The lad's face was full of curiosity and something anxious as he waited for Cameron's answer.

"Why do you want to know?" Cameron had been fifteen, the lady in question, eighteen, knowing that a rich man's son eager for his first encounter would probably pay well. Cameron had had enthusiasm but no finesse, and he'd been under no illusion as to why a sophisticated courtesan had put up with him.

"Why'd ya think? I'm sixteen, and it's high time I had me own. You and Uncle Hart, not to mention Uncle Mac, had mistresses when you were still in school. Even Uncle Ian had one. The reputation of the Mackenzie family is no secret. I should know. I live with th' bloody lot of ye."

Bloody hell. Cameron's own father's advice on the matter of women had been: *Keep your cock happy with tarts, take a lady to breed heirs, and don't mix the two of them. Women should be sauce, not the meal, or they'll make your life hell.* Not what Cameron wanted to tell his son.

"A tart who takes up with a lad as young as you only wants your money," he said carefully. "It's no slight on you, Danny. It's the only way they know how to live."

"I don't mean a courtesan, Dad. I mean a real lady."

Cameron held on to his patience. "A real lady, as you call her, will expect marriage. If you want someone to bed, stick with tarts, but understand why they're with you. Then you'll both know where you stand."

"Oh, very wise, Father. *You* married before you were even out of Cambridge. And Mother was older than you too."

The scar on Cameron's left cheek tingled. He rubbed it. "And it was a bloody nightmare. Remember that."

"Aye, I know you hated me mum."

"I did not hate your mum . . ." Elizabeth had been crazy, violent, and insatiable, but had it been hatred that Cameron had felt? Or rage, sorrow, disgust?

"I have one all picked out," Daniel was saying. "And she's not a tart."

Cameron prayed for strength. "Who? A daughter of Hart's guests? Please, Danny, tell me you haven't already seduced her." Hart would be in a black fury over that and put the blame squarely on Cameron.

"*No,* Dad. It's Aunt Isabella's friend, Mrs. Douglas."

Cameron choked, coughed, searched desperately for breath. "What? No!"

"Why not?"

"Because she's too bloody old for ye, that's why not!" Guests turned, interest caught even through the fireworks. Cameron tried to lower his voice. "She's not for you, Daniel."

"Aunt Isabella says she is twenty-seven," Daniel said. "I hear her widow's portion was nothing, so I'd think she'd be grateful for a rich lad, don't you think?"

Cameron glanced to where Ainsley stood not far from them with Mrs. Yardley, Ainsley again in gray. At least she wasn't buttoned up to her chin this time. Now that the sun was down, the Scottish September night growing cold, she wore short sleeves and a bodice scooped halfway down her breasts. To fight off certain pneumonia, Ainsley had topped her ensemble with a thin, lacy shawl that was more holes than fabric.

Cameron's thoughts slid back, as they had done all day, to Ainsley in the woods, her skin flushing as he undid the tenth button of her bodice. He'd pulled open the placket, and hadn't the package inside been sweet?

Beautiful Ainsley spilling over her corset, breasts full and lush. He'd wanted to lick all the way down her cleavage, unlace the corset to bare her nipples, catch a velvet areola in his teeth. He'd been too damn hard to return to the game—he'd had to walk around in the mud a long time before making his way back to Mrs. Yardley to finish the match with her. It must have been the longest bloody game of croquet in the history of the world.

"She's not for you, lad," Cameron repeated with difficulty. "You leave her be."

"Why? Are ye interested in her yourself?"

Hell, yes. "She's not my sort of woman, Danny."

Daniel clenched large-boned hands he was still growing into. "I know that. That's why I like her. Because she's nothing like your women, nothing at all. So she'll be safe from the likes of you." He snarled the last word, turned, and loped off into the darkness.

"Daniel . . ."

Daniel didn't stop or turn back, disappearing at a run, off to who knew where.

Being a father was absolute hell. Cameron swung around again and found his view blocked by his youngest brother, Ian.

Cam was a little surprised to see that Ian had come outside—Ian hated crowds, was unnerved out of all proportion to them. However, it was dark, most of the guests avoided him anyway, and his wife, Beth, stood not many feet from him.

Ian was an inch or so shorter than Cameron, but just as broad of shoulder. His stance held a new strength, much of which was due to the young woman standing behind him chatting to one of the guests.

"Ian, what the devil was I supposed to remember to do with Daniel this afternoon?" Cameron asked him.

Ian glanced to where Daniel had gone. Ian would never give Cam placating phrases that others might—*He admires you, Cameron; he's just trying to please you.* Ian took things as they were and understood the truth. He knew that Daniel's frustration with Cameron was about equal to Cameron's frustration with Daniel.

"Ride the bounds with him," Ian said.

"Damn it." Daniel loved to ride the perimeter of Mackenzie lands, which led through deep woods to craggy gorges. Cameron was usually too busy with his horses, but he'd assured Daniel they'd do it today. "Take some advice, Ian. Don't look to me as a model for fatherhood. Watch what I do and then do the exact opposite."

Cameron realized he'd lost his literal-minded little brother. Ian had glanced away to watch Beth's face be lit by the bursting fireworks.

"Ian, do you remember what was in that letter I showed you this morning?" Cameron asked.

Without looking away from Beth, Ian started rattling off the sentences, repeating the flowery phrases in a rapid monotone.

Cameron raised his hand. "Fine. That's enough. Thank you."

Ian stopped as though a tap had been closed. Cameron knew that Ian had paid little attention to what the letter actually *said* but could repeat the words in their precise order. Would be able to for years.

"The question is, did Mrs. Douglas write it?" Cameron asked, half to himself.

"I don't know."

"I know you don't. I was pondering out loud."

Ian looked him up and down. "Mrs. Douglas writes letters to Isabella." Having delivered his declaration, Ian returned his gaze to Beth.

"Yes, they're old friends, but this has nothing to do

with—" Cameron broke off. "Ah, I see. Sorry, Ian, I didn't understand."

Ian didn't answer. Cameron squeezed Ian's shoulder, but briefly, knowing his youngest brother didn't like to be touched by anyone but Beth. Or Isabella. Only beautiful women for Ian Mackenzie, damn him.

"Ian, do you know why everyone thinks you mad?"

Ian glanced at Cameron, not really caring, but he'd learned to look at people when they spoke to him.

Cameron continued. "Because you give us the answer, but you leave out all the steps we lesser mortals need to reach it. You mean that I should ask Isabella to show me one of Mrs. Douglas's letters and compare the handwriting."

Still Ian didn't respond. As though he'd forgotten they'd been speaking at all, he turned away again, pulled back to Beth, the anchor of his world. Ian wasn't watching the fireworks, Cameron saw; Ian watched his wife watching them, understanding their beauty through the conduit of Beth.

Cameron let him go. Another firework exploded, the heat touching Cameron's face.

In the light of that firework, Cameron saw Ainsley Douglas slip away from Mrs. Yardley and walk steadily down a path toward the main garden, into darkness. As the guests applauded the display, Cameron turned and followed her into the night.

Chapter 6

"So he gave you the letter, did he?" Phyllida Chase faced Ainsley under the flare of distant fireworks. Ainsley had met her, as arranged, by the fountain in the center of the garden. The guests were still clumped on the west side to watch pyrotechnics that blasted over the meadow beyond.

"Lord Cameron returned it to me, yes," Ainsley said. "You so obviously passed it to him while you knew I was looking. Why?"

Phyllida's eyes glittered. "Because, I wanted you to know that I could hand the letters to anyone I pleased whenever I pleased if you took too long with the money. I never expected that you'd try to conduct your own bargain with him. You are to deal with *me*, my dear. No one else."

"You are the thief, Mrs. Chase," Ainsley said coolly. "I'll deal with whoever is necessary. I've brought you the money, now I take the letters, as agreed."

"You should not have tried to go behind my back, Mrs. Douglas. Because you did, the rest of the letters will cost you much more than the original price. One thousand guineas."

Ainsley stared. "One *thousand*? We agreed on five hundred. It was difficult enough to persuade her to give me that much."

"She shouldn't have written such letters then. One thousand by the end of the week, or I sell them to a newspaper."

Ainsley thumped her fists to her skirts. "I can't possibly come up with a thousand guineas. Not in four days."

"You'd better start sending telegrams then. *She* can afford it, for all her fussing, and it's her own fault she was so indiscreet. One week."

Ainsley wanted to scream. "Why on earth are you doing this? You were a lady of the bedchamber, someone she trusted. Why did you turn on her?"

"I turn on *her*?" Phyllida's eyes blazed, and for the first time, Ainsley saw an emotion in Phyllida Chase other than cold calculation. "Go and ask her why *she* turned on *me*. All I wanted was a little happiness. I *deserved* a little happiness. She snatched it all away from me, and for that I will never forgive her. Never."

The fury in Phyllida's voice was genuine, anger and despair that ate deeply. Phyllida had already been gone from the queen's service before Ainsley came into it three years ago, but she'd never learned why Phyllida had been dismissed. She'd heard whispers about Mrs. Chase—such as her notorious pursuit of younger men—but the queen had always been tight-lipped about Phyllida and forbidden gossip.

"I don't have a thousand guineas," Ainsley said. "I have five hundred. You would at least have that."

"The original price is a thing of the past. Consider the second five hundred the cost of me keeping quiet about how you seduced the paper from Lord Cameron."

Ainsley's face heated. "I didn't seduce it from him."

Phyllida gave her a hard smile. "My dear Mrs. Douglas, Lord Cameron is not only a man and a spoiled aristocrat, he's a *Mackenzie*. He'd not simply hand you back the letter without exacting a price for it. It scarcely matters if you haven't yet given that price to him. You will."

Ainsley blessed the darkness, because she knew she must be blushing all the way down to her toes. She remembered the heat of Cameron's mouth pressing the key into hers, the equal heat of his mouth on her breasts in the woods.

Before you leave at the end of the week, we will finish it, he'd told her. *Depend on that.*

"I haven't gone to his bed," Ainsley said. "Nor will I."

"Naïve darling, Lord Cameron doesn't take his women in a *bed*. Anywhere else in the room, yes—or in the carriage, the summerhouse, or on the front lawn. Never in a bed. Quite known for it, is our Lord Cameron."

Ainsley thoughts flashed to Cameron's hard body pressing her into his mattress, his large hand on her wrist. He'd been ready, she'd felt through his kilt, not seeming to mind at all that they were on a bed.

But he'd released her. He could have taken what he wanted right then, could have coerced Ainsley into giving in to him. But he hadn't.

"I won't," Ainsley said.

Phyllida gave her a pitying look. "The unworldly Mrs. Douglas. You are no match for Lord Cameron Mackenzie. He'll have what he wants from you very quickly, and you'll go to him. Cameron sees, he wants, he takes, and he is done."

We will finish it.

Ainsley's heart beat faster. "You seem very sanguine for the woman who is his lover."

"I went into my affair with Lord Cameron with my eyes wide open. He has the reputation for being a most pleasurable lover, and that is what I sought, to relieve my ennui at this dreadfully dull gathering. *Hart* Mackenzie used to hold exotic orgies that were all the rage, but now he invites stodgy people to do stodgy things for a stodgy week in the freezing Scottish countryside. Cameron is as bored as I am, but now that he's seen your pretty eyes, I'm certain he's finished with me. No matter, because I am finished with him."

Ainsley listened with growing warmth, realizing that she'd stumbled into a world she'd only glimpsed—husbands and wives seeking other partners for the novelty of it, lovers casually discarded for other lovers. In Ainsley's world, a young miss could be ruined in the blink of an eye; in Phyllida's, vows meant nothing, and pleasure was all.

Ainsley thought about Lord Cameron, with his fierce eyes and the passion that simmered below his surface. He tempered that passion into gentleness when he handled his horses or the frail Mrs. Yardley, protecting them at the same time he took care of them. That gentleness gave Ainsley the conviction that, even in his world of mistresses and secret lovers, Cameron Mackenzie deserved better than Phyllida Chase.

"I can give you the five hundred guineas," Ainsley said firmly.

Phyllida flicked her fingers. "I want a thousand. *She* can afford it."

Yes, but the small queen had very strong ideas on where money should be spent and how much at a time. She'd found it insulting that she'd have to pay at all.

But even the queen realized that the letters could seriously damage her reputation if it got out that she'd written such sentimentalities to Mr. Brown, never mind she'd never actually sent them to him. People were not happy with Victoria's reclusive life as it was, and there might be cries for her abdication if they thought she stayed home only to play with her Scottish equerry.

Phyllida had set out to punish the queen, and punish her she would. So the queen had sent Ainsley—the lady she ordered to do covert jobs that might involve something sordid such as picking locks and searching bedrooms—to deal with Phyllida. To retrieve the letters without parting with a penny if Ainsley could help it.

"You are optimistic if you think she'll give you a thousand," Ainsley said.

Firework after firework went off over the fields, filling the sky with light. Under their light, Phyllida smiled.

"One thousand is what I want," she said. "Raise it somehow by the end of the week, and you may have the letters back. If not . . ."

She made an empty gesture, then turned and strode down the gravel path without looking back.

"Bloody woman," Ainsley growled.

A cold nose thrust itself into her palm, and she looked down to see McNab, a Mackenzie dog, staring up at her with sympathetic eyes. Five dogs surrounded the Mackenzies at all times. Two of them—the hound Ruby and the terrier called Fergus—belonged to Ian and Beth and lived with them when they retreated to their own house not far from here. Ben and Achilles remained at the main house, but McNab, a springer spaniel, was more or less Daniel and Cameron's.

Ainsley sighed as she leaned to pet McNab. "How peaceful it must be to be a dog. *You* don't have to worry about intrigue or letters or blackmail."

McNab's tail smacked her legs with happy blows. The tail drove harder as McNab turned to greet the large man who'd followed him out of the darkness.

"So, Phyllida is blackmailing you," Cameron said.

Ainsley rapidly went through the conversation in her head, relaxing slightly when she realized that neither she nor Mrs. Chase had ever mentioned the queen by name.

"I'm afraid so."

Cameron patted McNab's head when the dog thrust it under Cameron's hand. "Phyllida can be the devil. Do you want me to shake your letters out of her?"

Ainsley's eyes widened in alarm. "Please don't. If you frighten her, she might run to a newspaper as she threatened."

McNab circled close behind Ainsley, which made her step

forward into Cameron's heat. Cameron didn't move. McNab sat down against Ainsley, happy they were all together in a small circle of space.

"I can solve your problem," Cameron said. "You know I'll give you the thousand for the asking."

He'd not simply hand you back the letter without exacting a price for it.

"I can raise the money," Ainsley said. "It will be difficult, but I can do it."

Across the garden, under the light of the Chinese lanterns, Phyllida stepped next to her husband and tucked her hand under his arm.

"She's is a hard woman," Cameron said.

"She's a bloody thorn in my side."

Cameron's chuckle grated like broken gravel. "If you think a thousand guineas will make Phyllida go away, it won't. She'll hold something back or find some other way to come at you again. Blackmailers are never satisfied." His laughter faded into bitterness.

"Aren't they? How do you know?"

His words were empty, hollow. "When you're the brother of a duke and your wife died in mysterious circumstances, sharks come out of the woodwork."

"That's a mixed metaphor."

"Bugger metaphors. They're human sharks and they come out of the shadows when you least expect them."

"I'm sorry," Ainsley said.

She sounded sorry. Damn her, why did she have to look at him like that?

Gray eyes shining in the darkness, the frank stare, the lacy shawl sliding from her shoulders as she reached down to pet his dog. Once again, Ainsley was making Cameron's world come alive, filling it with color instead of the deadly gray of his usual existence.

"All the world speculates on whether I killed my wife," he said. "Including you."

The flash of guilt in her eyes told him he was right. But why wouldn't Ainsley speculate on it? No one knew for certain what had happened in that room, only Cameron. Daniel had been a baby, and except for him, Cameron and Elizabeth had been alone.

Cameron thought of the inquest, everyone watching him as he gave evidence in a dead voice, everyone believing he'd killed Elizabeth. The eyes of the villagers, the journalists, Elizabeth's family, her lovers, his own father, the jury, the coroner—hard and cold, waiting for him to confess.

Only Hart had believed him, and Hart had perjured himself, telling the coroner that he'd seen Elizabeth drive the knife into her own throat as he'd broken open the door. Cameron had been across the room, holding Daniel, trying to still the lad's terrified screams. Hart had related the story, using the right mix of Mackenzie charm and horrified sympathy for his brother.

What Hart said had been true, but he hadn't seen it. Elizabeth had already been dead before Hart made it into the room. Hart had lied to save Cameron, and Cameron would be forever grateful. Hence, Cameron endured Hart's house parties and entertained Hart's guests by letting them watch him train his racers.

Ainsley's fingers landed on his arm, pulling him back from darkness. Her cool voice flowed over him, along with her scent—vanilla and cinnamon, that was Ainsley.

"People do speak of it, I can't deny that," she was saying. "But I don't think it's true."

"How the devil can you know?" Cameron heard the growl in his voice but couldn't stop it.

"I'm good at reading people, is all."

"That only means you're too damn trusting."

"It means it's my opinion, whether you like it or not. So cease trying to insult me, or bully me, or whatever it is you're doing."

She was waking him from his half-numb state again,

sharpening the world around him. "But you're a liar and a thief, Mrs. Douglas," he said, lightening his tone. "A confidence trickster. How can I take you at your word?"

Her hand remained on his arm, and Cameron liked that she didn't pull away. "You've met me under unfortunate circumstances. I am usually most reliable."

Cameron wanted to laugh. "You pick locks like a professional thief, search rooms, deal with blackmailers, and then ask me to believe in you."

Ainsley shot him an exasperated look. "I will remind you that I haven't seen *you* in the best of circumstances either, my lord. The last time we spoke, you unbuttoned my frock."

Yes, he remembered. Each button revealing more of her, the warmth of her skin, the brush of breath on his fingers. Cameron reached for her again, seeking that heat once more.

He touched her collarbone, cold even through the leather of his gloves. "Balls, woman, you're freezing."

Cameron slid off his coat and pulled it around her shoulders before she could protest, and then he held the lapels, not wanting to let go. Sweet Mrs. Douglas, looking into his face and saying she believed in him. No one else did. Only because of Hart had the verdict of the inquest been suicide. Cameron exonerated. The case finished.

Officially. Public opinion said otherwise, but only in whispers, because Hart wouldn't tolerate slander. Women in the demimonde and wives and widows wanting excitement sought Cameron because of the danger he represented, while respectable young ladies were swept out of his way. Cameron didn't care. He'd never sought to marry again—once was enough of that—but he doubted that anyone would have him even if he asked.

Now Ainsley Douglas looked at him with her clear gray eyes and told him she believed his innocence. No proof needed.

He wanted to taste the mouth that said such things. He wanted to pull her to him, feel her body under his, peel back her clothes and kiss every inch of her. Ainsley wore her hair in a tight coil tonight—he imagined loosening it, letting her hair flow over his body like warm silk.

McNab's tail lashed Cameron's legs, and Ainsley laughed and bent to pet the dog's head. "Lord Cameron, I need to ask you a favor."

Didn't she know it was dangerous to ask him for favors? Just because Cameron was innocent of murder didn't mean he was kind.

"What?"

"I searched Mrs. Chase's rooms, but I never found the letters. I've taken the opportunity to look over the rest of the house as well, but I've not been able to find them."

Cameron imagined Ainsley happily picking her way past the locked doors of every room in Hart's mansion. Assisting Isabella with the party would have given her an excuse to go almost anywhere in the house. Hart Mackenzie, the most careful and controlling man ever born, was no match for Ainsley and her hairpin.

"Of course you searched," he said. "Are ye certain you were thorough?"

"I am always very thorough, my lord. But there is one place I haven't looked." She touched her tongue to her lower lip, to the tiny bruise Cameron had left there. His mark. He who didn't always like kissing his women couldn't stop thinking about kissing Ainsley. "The one place she'd be able to stash the lot," Ainsley said, "where I'd likely not go, would be your chambers."

His heart missed a beat. "You did some searching in my chambers too, minx. Angelo told me someone had pawed through the wardrobe."

"But I wasn't able to finish."

No, Cam and Phyllida had come blundering in, Cameron seeking refuge from his ennui in mindless coupling.

Ainsley went on. "Would Mrs. Chase have had the chance to hide the rest somewhere in your rooms?"

Phyllida had latched on to Cameron the moment she'd arrived at the house party, and Cameron hadn't discouraged her. "Aye, she'd have had chance. But not, I'm thinking, the chance to retrieve them." He'd not invited Phyllida back to his chambers after last night, and she'd understood what his cool indifference meant.

"Excellent. Perhaps I could go in and look for them while you're training tomorrow? Would you be able to keep the servants away?"

The thought of her bustling around his rooms made him sweat. "Why wait for the morning? If you want to find the letters so much, go on up and have at it."

Ainsley's eyes widened. "What, *now*?"

"Why the hell not? The guests are riveted to Hart's pyrotechnics, and the house is empty. I'll show you the most likely places to look."

Ainsley pursed her lips, the soft pucker making him want to pull her close and finish what he'd started with her in the woods. He'd had to make himself walk away then or risk the count or Isabella or someone turning up looking for her, to find her in a most compromising position. No one at the croquet match seemed to have noticed her gone too long with the notorious Lord Cameron, though, probably thinking that Cameron wouldn't have anything to do with the nobody friend of his sister-in-law. Few of them noticed Ainsley at all, the blind fools. She kept to the shadows, certainly, but Cameron could see her there in all her blazing glory.

Ainsley finally let out a long sigh and nodded. "Very well, let us search. It's too blasted cold out here anyway." She turned without another word and headed for the house, his coat billowing behind her.

Chapter 7

Cameron followed Ainsley Douglas's swaying gray bustle up the steps to the dark end of the terrace. His coat half slid from her shoulders, her slippers were muddy, and one curl straggled down her back.

Why Cameron should come so alive watching a woman who had no intention whatsoever of sleeping with him, he didn't know. He only knew he was grateful for it. The only thing he could compare it to was waking on the opening day of an important race meet, knowing that the day would be filled with excitement, hurry, and elation. He'd spend the day with Daniel and his horses, and even the disappointments would be colored by the overall joy of the time.

Cameron held open a door on the end of the terrace, and Ainsley moved confidently inside and across the dark room without waiting for him.

"You know your way around," Cameron said when he caught up to her.

"I know Balmoral and Buckingham Palace like the

back of my hand," Ainsley said. She stepped from the room into the empty hall beyond. "This house is easy to navigate in comparison. We can get from here up to your wing unseen."

Ainsley opened another door, this one leading to a slanting back stair, which she started to ascend without hesitation.

"How do you know the servants won't see you?" Cameron asked as he followed. "Or did you tie them up and lock them in the kitchen?"

Ainsley answered breathlessly, skirts swishing as she climbed. "The only servant who uses these stairs is your man, and he's currently in the stables."

That was true enough. Angelo liked looking after Jasmine. "You'd make a bloody good jewel thief, knowing the back ways through other people's houses like this," Cameron said. "You could work house parties all over the country."

Ainsley looked back down at him over the banisters. "Don't be silly. I do have some morals, Lord Cameron."

Pity. Cameron followed her out through a narrow door to the landing to his floor. His rooms were two doors down, and he moved past her to unlock his bedchamber with his key.

"Saves you the time of picking it," he said.

Without comment Ainsley slid off Cameron's coat, handed it to him, and walked inside. She went straight to his wardrobe, opened it, and started to rummage. Cameron tossed the coat to a chair and watched the fine perspective of her backside moving as she lifted his shirts and collar boxes, peeked under lids and felt through fabric.

He stripped off his gloves and his too-binding formal waistcoat before moving to pour himself a cut crystal glass of whiskey. Taking up the whiskey, he leaned against a bedpost to continue watching her work.

Ainsley closed the wardrobe and turned to the glass-fronted bookcase. "You're an odd sort of man, Lord Cameron. You drink whiskey and smoke cheroots in front of a lady without asking leave, not to mention smacking away her ball in croquet instead of allowing her to win. In my world, that is simply not done. You'd be looked upon with horror."

"Lucky that I don't live in your world then. Besides, I know you're not a lady."

She shot him a startled look as she opened the bookcase. "What?"

Cameron gestured with his glass. "You pick locks and sneak into my bedroom, you know the back ways through my ancestral home, you're blatantly searching my bedchamber, and last night you wrestled with me on my bed." He took a deliberate sip of whiskey. "I'd say that makes you not a lady."

"Circumstances sometimes require odd behavior, my lord."

"Circumstances be damned. You haven't checked under the mattress."

"That is next." Ainsley plucked a book from the shelf and started leafing through it. She realized what kind of book it was and turned bright red.

Cameron suppressed his laughter as Ainsley stared at a page of blatantly naked Courbet figures, twined in an interesting position. He made a wager with himself whether she'd throw down the book in disgust and storm out, or whether his Mrs. Douglas would soldier on.

He won the bet when she drew a deep, determined breath and continued to fan through the pages.

Finding nothing, Ainsley placed the book back on the shelf and gingerly opened the next one, which was much the same. "You—*read*—this?"

"Of course I do. I collect it."

"It's in French."

"Don't you read books in French? Isabella told me you went with her to her fine ladies' academy."

"I learned it, yes, but I doubt any of these words were in our primer."

Cameron stopped trying to contain his laughter and let it burst out. It felt good.

"I would finish much more quickly if you helped me," she said.

Cameron leaned on the bedpost again. "But it's much more entertaining to watch you."

Ainsley made an exasperated noise, shoved the book back into the bookcase, and untied and opened a folio. She studied the first drawing. "I know I'm unworldly, Lord Cameron, but I'm not certain that what they're doing is quite possible."

Cameron leaned over her shoulder to look at the sensual sketch by Romano, drawn three centuries before. Admittedly the people depicted were in an awkward pose. "I buy it for the beauty of it, not for instruction."

"Well, that's a mercy, or you'd never have had a son."

Cam let out another laugh, the power of true mirth filling his body.

Could anything be more sensual than watching a lovely young woman leaf through page after page of his erotic pictures?

There was nothing of the prude about Ainsley, nor did she send him suggestive glances, using the drawings as seduction. She looked through each folio carefully, her cheeks sweetly pink, her breasts rising against her décolletage.

When she laid the last folio back on its shelf, Ainsley turned to him. "They're not here," she said, disappointed.

Cameron took another sip of whiskey. "There's my study next door."

"Is that a possibility?"

"Aye, it is."

He didn't miss Ainsley's flush as she speculated why Cameron might take a mistress to his private study. "Very well, let us search the study."

The room didn't connect to his bedroom. Cameron led her down the hall a few steps to the next door, which he unlocked. Normally he didn't lock his doors when he stayed at Kilmorgan—no need—but with all the comings and goings up here, he'd done it today.

Ainsley took on a look of dismay when she viewed the clutter of the study. This was Cameron's private room, his retreat from the overstated social life that he sometimes had to lead as Hart's brother and heir to the title.

Racing newspapers lay everywhere, as did books on all things equine. Cameron had contributed chapters or essays to a few of them, publishers begging for his opinion on the subject.

Cam's prized paintings hung here as well: pictures of the horses he'd grown up with, of his best racers, of the ones he simply loved. Mac had painted most of them, although Degas had done a sketch for him of a horse in motion, all rippling muscles and tossing mane.

Angelo was the only one allowed to touch this room, and the man knew better than to disturb anything. It all got a bit dusty, but the whiskey decanter and the humidor were always replenished, the ashtrays emptied and cleaned, and any stray pieces of clothing, boots, or riding equipment restored to their proper places.

Cameron took a clean glass from the tray holding the whiskey and held it up. "Drink? It will be thirsty work."

Ainsley eyed the glass in some trepidation. Cameron expected her to remind him that ladies didn't drink spirits, but she gave him a nod. "Yes, why not? I prefer it with soda. Do you have any?"

Cameron lifted the cut glass stopper from the decanter. "This is Mackenzie single malt. Hart would die of apoplexy if anyone cut it with soda. It's neat or nothing."

Ainsley began lifting papers from his desk. "Very well. My brothers taught me to enjoy it with soda, but then we never could afford Mackenzie blend. I can hear Steven's sighs of envy now."

By the time Cameron poured the glass and brought it to

her, Ainsley had seated herself on the floor, her skirts a swath of satin around her, a stack of papers and handwritten notes next to her. She accepted the whiskey, looking up at him with animated gray eyes.

Cameron clinked his glass against hers. "To a fruitful search."

She nodded, took a practiced sip, and continued sorting papers into neat stacks.

"Anything?" Cameron asked, leaning over her shoulder. From here he could look straight down the cleavage of her soft breasts, and he didn't mind that at all.

Ainsley wished to heaven he wouldn't stand next to her like that. Cameron's legs were firm and muscular under the socks he'd donned for the walk in the wet garden, the hem of his kilt on her eye level.

She glanced at his feet, large and muscular, pressing out the leather of his finely tailored shoes. Mud from the garden clung to one. Above the shoes were wide ankles behind thick gray wool, his legs those of a giant.

Ainsley couldn't stop her gaze from rising higher, to the shadow under his plaid kilt, where she glimpsed a brawny knee. He was warm, too, his legs radiating heat to her bare shoulder. She'd been so awfully cold in the garden, and standing against him had taken all the cold away.

She made herself continue sorting the papers. No erotica here, only horses, races and results, histories and bloodlines of stallions, notes on what horses were being bought and sold. She stacked them all into piles, wondering how on earth he found anything.

"Who is Night-Blooming Jasmine?" Ainsley asked. The name came up often.

"Filly I'm training. Horse with damned fine promise."

Ainsley looked up, unable to miss the glimpse of inner thigh in her view, the line of scar on it in shadow. She forced her gaze up, past the flat front of his kilt, to his shirt and the cravat he was in the act of loosening. His throat came into view, tanned and strong. Ainsley felt a flutter of pleasure. She liked him unbuttoned.

"Is she yours?" Ainsley asked, not missing the pride in his voice.

"Not yet." Cameron pulled the folds of cravat from his neck and tossed the cloth carelessly to the desk. "Bloody owner won't sell her to me."

"Why not?"

"Because he despises Mackenzies. He's only letting me train her because he's damned desperate. She's a fine bit of horseflesh, and she can run, by God, can she run." His voice warmed, a man talking about his heart's desire.

"Rather annoying of the man."

"Bloody stupid of him." Cameron's brows drew down as he drank. "I want her, and I'd do right by her, if I can only make Pierson see sense."

"Goodness, you sound almost like a man proposing marriage."

Cameron shuddered. "Dear God, never that. I even hate the sound of the word. I suppose landing a horse is similar, but horses aren't near as much bother as wives."

The pull of disgust in his voice was true. "I'm certain Isabella would be pleased to hear you say so," Ainsley said lightly.

"Isabella knows she's a bother. She delights in it. Just ask Mac."

Ainsley smiled at his quip, but he hadn't feigned his opinion of marriage. Ainsley looked away from him and quickly continued through the papers.

She found much evidence that Cameron was a womanizing, erotica-reading, whiskey-drinking, horse-mad gentleman but no letters from the queen. She set aside the last papers, shook out her skirts, and climbed to her feet. Cameron reached to help her, his firm hand under her elbow.

"I'm doubting now that Mrs. Chase hid them here," she said with a sigh. "I'll wager they've never left her house in Edinburgh, except the one paper she brought to show me. She knew I'd try to ferret them out."

"Ferret. A good name for you. I thought *mouse* when I saw you hiding in my window seat, but I can see the resemblance. Your eyes get bright when you're on the trail of what you want."

She liked his half smile, the teasing in his eyes. All loathing from his talk of marriage had gone. "How highly flattering you are, my lord. No wonder the ladies like you."

Cameron pulled out a drawer in the desk she'd already searched. The papers in it had been old, dates on them from fifteen, twenty years ago. Cameron dumped them on the floor—all over the newspapers she'd already straightened—and started prying inside the drawer.

"This one has a false bottom if I remember. Haven't touched it in a while."

He tugged fruitlessly at the wood. Ainsley pulled a hairpin from her coiled braid and handed it to him. "Try that."

"Ah, the tools of your trade." Cameron took it from her, inserted the end in a slightly gouged corner, and pulled.

The bottom of the drawer came away to reveal a single folded letter, creased from being pressed flat. Ainsley snatched it up and opened it but grunted in disappointment before she read a word. "Wrong handwriting. It's not hers."

She handed the paper back to Cameron and turned away.

Ainsley headed for the books on the mantelpiece, but a faint noise behind her made her turn around again. Cameron stood where she'd left him, still as stone, his gaze riveted to the unfolded letter in his hand.

"Lord Cameron?"

He didn't appear to hear. Cameron stared at the letter, his eyes unmoving, as though he'd taken in what it said and couldn't quite believe it.

Ainsley went to him. "What is it?"

When she touched his hand, he jerked and looked down at her, his eyes empty.

"It belonged to my wife."

Oh dear. Ainsley's own sadness about John Douglas could be triggered whenever she came unexpectedly across something that had belonged to him. Though Cameron had been widowed a long time now, his pain must have been intensified by Lady Elizabeth's violent death and people's morbid suspicions about it.

"I'm so sorry," Ainsley said, her heart in her words.

Cameron only looked at her. His amused tolerance and the camaraderie of the search had vanished.

Without a word, he strode to the hearth, where a fire burned against the cold September night, and tossed the letter onto the flames. Ainsley hurried to him as Cameron seized the poker and jabbed the paper deep into the coals.

"Why did you do that? Your wife's letter . . ."

Cameron dropped the poker. His hand was black with soot, and he drew out a handkerchief to wipe it. "My wife didn't write it." His voice was harsh. "It was a letter *to* her, from one of her lovers. Expressing his undying passion."

Ainsley stopped, stricken. "Cameron . . ."

"My wife had many lovers, both before and after our marriage." The statement was flat, devoid of emotion, but his eyes told Ainsley a different story. Lady Elizabeth had hurt him, and hurt him deeply.

From all Ainsley had heard about Lady Elizabeth Cavendish, she'd been high-strung, beautiful, and wild, a few years older than Cameron. Their marriage had been a scandal from beginning to end, finishing with her death six months after Daniel was born. Lady Elizabeth must have stood often in this very room, perhaps one day hiding the letter before Cameron or a servant came upon her.

Ainsley's anger surged. "Not very sporting of her."

"I carry on with married women. What is the difference?"

The difference was he didn't enjoy it, and he despised the women he carried on with. "I imagine you don't write those women letters expressing your undying passion."

"No."

Cameron rubbed his wrist, where his shirt had loosened. Ainsley saw the scars again, round and even.

"Who did that to you?" she asked.

Cameron slammed the cuff closed. "Leave it alone."

"Why?"

"Ainsley." The word was stark, holding rivers of pain.

"My lord?"

"Stop." Cameron cupped her head in his hands, his fingers spreading her hair. "Just . . . stop." He leaned to her and took her mouth in a kiss of harsh desperation.

Chapter 8

Cameron didn't simply kiss her. He opened her mouth with his strong one, took what he wanted, made Ainsley kiss him back. Made her like kissing him back, made her want more.

His hands kept her pinned in place, but Ainsley didn't want to go anywhere. His thighs flattened her skirts, the ridge of his hardness obvious and unashamed. Cameron knew how to make his mouth an instrument of sensuality, and he didn't bother to hide his wanting.

Ainsley curled her hands against his chest. Beneath the linen of his shirt was warm, living male, his heart beating as rapidly as hers.

Cameron slid his hand to the top of her bodice. "You have no buttons tonight, Mrs. Douglas."

"Clasps," she murmured as she kissed him. "In the back."

Cameron splayed his hand over the placket, fingers so strong that he could rip open every single clasp without thought. He kept his hand there, rock steady as he again swept his mouth across hers.

Ainsley couldn't breathe. Cameron tasted her to every corner, his mouth firm and bold, his a lover's kiss. No stolen moments in a corner, no cooing of lovebirds, just a man bent on bodily pleasure, damn what anyone thought. He licked across her mouth, hungry, feasting on Ainsley. She wound her arms around his neck and feasted back.

Cameron raised his head. "If I asked it of you tonight, Ainsley Douglas, would come to my bed?"

The words of Phyllida Chase came back to her. *Lord Cameron doesn't take his women in a bed . . . Quite known for it, is our Lord Cameron.*

"I thought you didn't like beds."

She felt him jerk, saw his eyes flicker. "True." His voice changed, from soft cajoling to hard edged.

Ainsley's own voice shook. "I should think a bed would be more comfortable."

"Comfort is the last consideration, Mrs. Douglas."

The tingling became hot waves of excitement. He was right: a bed was sedate, a place for a well-acquainted husband and wife who pulled on nightcaps afterward and rolled to either side to sleep. Lovers would use a chair, say, or a thick carpet in front of the fire. Or perhaps Cameron wished to learn what could be done on the top of a desk.

Words stuck in her throat. Ainsley, who could talk her way into or out of anything, suddenly couldn't form a sentence.

She raised on tiptoe and kissed him instead.

Ainsley felt the change in him, from a man wondering what would happen in this room tonight to a man knowing what would. As he kissed her again, his competent fingers unclasped her bodice, his broad hand spreading the fabric.

Wild heat seared her body. She'd never forgotten the fire of the first time Cameron had kissed her, six years ago, and the fire had only grown hotter since. Ainsley molded hungrily to him, seeking his mouth. He kissed her back, lips taking, teeth scraping where he'd already bruised her. His hand on her back was an imprint of fire, and her bodice was falling. She wanted his touch on her breast, ached for it. She would give him anything she wanted, and propriety could go hang. She wanted this. She *needed* this. She arched to him, seeking.

Cameron's whole body suddenly stilled. His kiss died on her mouth, and his hand froze on her back.

Ainsley, still swimming in dark madness, couldn't decide what had happened. Then she felt a cool draft on her back, heard the click of paws on bare floor, and realized that someone had opened the door.

"Daniel," Cameron said, voice hard. "Turn around and go out."

"Fat chance." Daniel Mackenzie blazed into the room, followed by McNab and the hound called Ruby. Both dogs circled Daniel, scattering the papers Ainsley had so carefully sorted. "I've come to save Mrs. Douglas's virtue," Daniel said. "Aunt Isabella's looking for her, and I thought I'd better come up before she did."

The frank expression of the boy who looked at Ainsley with his father's eyes returned her to reality with a rush.

She'd been about to succumb to Cameron's seductions—again. But Ainsley Douglas couldn't afford to indulge in that joy. She wasn't a sophisticated lady, lover to aristocrats, one who gadded off to the Continent to host salons in Paris and be wooed by wild gentlemen like Lord Cameron. Ainsley was a glorified errand-runner, trusted by the queen to solve domestic dilemmas, asked by her highborn friends to help with their social events. Dependent on others for her living. Exotic men like Lord Cameron Mackenzie were not for Ainsley. That dream was dust.

Cameron removed his hand from Ainsley's back, straightened to his full height, and stepped a little in front of her.

"Daniel." His voice held frustration, but at the same time, Ainsley knew Cameron was keeping a rock-hard rein on his patience. "Wait for Mrs. Douglas in the hall."

Daniel grabbed a newspaper from the top of the stack and

plopped himself into a chair. His kilt fluttered around his bony knees. "She's a lady, Dad, I told ya. I'm not taking the chance that you'll ravish her as soon as my back is turned."

The absurdity of it all brought Ainsley back to herself. She stepped out from behind Cameron and rescued her lace shawl from Ruby's questing mouth.

"Not to worry, Daniel, I wouldn't dream of letting him ravish me." Ainsley pulled the shawl, now a bit damp with drool, around her bare back. "Tell Isabella I'll be with her directly."

Daniel threw down the newspaper and sprang to his feet. "I'll walk with ye."

Ainsley looked back as she left the room behind Daniel. Cameron remained by the fireplace, stance rigid, his shirt open to reveal his brown throat. For the first time, Ainsley saw something naked in his eyes, not anger or frustration or old pain, but a longing so intense it stabbed at her from across the room.

Then Daniel slammed the door, and Ainsley's view of him was lost.

"I'd better do up your back."

"Pardon?" Ainsley stopped at the top of the stairs as Daniel jumped two steps past her. The dogs slithered by and ran all the way down the staircase, then hurried up again to see what was keeping the human beings.

"If someone sees ye like that, they'll talk," Daniel said. "Especially when ye disappeared so sudden."

She'd forgotten about the undone clasps under her shawl, but Daniel had a point. Running about with a bodice undone would make even the dullest person realize what she'd been up to.

Smothering a sigh, Ainsley lowered her shawl and turned her back. Daniel, at her head height when he stood two stairs down, quickly hooked the clasps together. His skill told her that he, at sixteen, already had experience doing up women's dresses. The apple didn't fall far from the tree, she supposed.

"How did you know I was in your father's study?" Ainsley asked Daniel when he finished.

"I saw you go inside the house with him. I always keep an eye on my Dad. Don't worry, I made sure no one else noticed."

When she turned around, Daniel was studying her with his Mackenzie eyes, darker than his father's, his face sharp and fine boned rather than hard. Daniel could look at a person with remarkable percipience, seeing through every layer they tried to put in his way. While Ian Mackenzie didn't like to meet a person's gaze directly, Daniel Mackenzie bored into their eyes to the point of rudeness.

"Do you like my dad?" Daniel asked it without rancor. He simply wanted to know.

"I barely know your dad."

"You were about to let him have his way with ye. I hope you like him a little."

Ainsley flushed. "Well, if you put it like that."

"I do put it like that. I like you, ye see, and I know Dad does too. But I don't want him toying with you and then turning his back on ye a month later, with a pretty gift for compensation. I told him tonight that I was interested in you meself, and you should have seen him come over growling, telling me to stay away." Daniel grinned. "I only told him that to see if he fancied you enough. I guess he does."

"You shouldn't have said it at all, Danny," she said. "He probably believed you."

"Naw, Dad don't take much heed of what I say." Daniel folded his arms. "But I don't want him leading you down the garden path, so to speak."

Ainsley adjusted her shawl. "Well, you have nothing to worry about on that account, my boy. I'm not naïve, nor am I the sort of woman your father prefers."

"No, but I'm thinking you're the sort of woman he needs."

Ainsley slowly let out her breath. Her body still sang from Cameron's touch, and she found it difficult to focus on his son's practical words.

"Put *that* out of your head," she said. "At the end of the house party, it's back to Balmoral and the queen for me. I'll not likely cross paths with your father for a long time."

And won't that be a shame?

Daniel didn't hide the disappointment in his eyes. "Mrs. Douglas, ye have to *try*."

"No, I don't. I need to get into my ball gown and go play hostess with your aunts." But wouldn't it be grand to be a glittering lady in bright silks, with diamonds on her bosom, dancing waltz after waltz in a sumptuous ballroom? Her partner would be Cameron, a big man who moved with grace.

Daniel stopped arguing, but his glower spoke volumes. He finally turned and led the way down the stairs, dogs scampering with him. He moved so fast that by the time Ainsley caught up to him at the bottom of the staircase, she was running.

Whiskey didn't calm him. Cameron tried to make himself feel better by using his foot to scatter the stacks of papers Ainsley had made, and then kicking them. Neither helped much.

He stormed back into his bedroom, did up his shirt, and pulled on another coat, not bothering with the cravat. He could never tie the bloody things decently. That's what women and valets were for.

He drank as he dressed, but half the decanter of whiskey couldn't erase the taste of Ainsley from his mouth. If Daniel hadn't come charging in, Cameron would be inside her by now, finally learning what she'd feel like around him.

He wasn't sure what to make of Daniel's interruption.

His look at his father had been one of annoyance, not jealous rage. Daniel's story about wanting Ainsley for a mistress seemed to have faded to smoke, the boy using it as a ploy of some sort.

Hell, Cameron never knew what Daniel really thought or wanted. They never talked—they bantered. Or argued. Daniel wasn't a bad lad, but his idea of obedience was doing what Cameron wanted only if Daniel had already decided on the same course. If Daniel disagreed with Cameron, he did what he damn well pleased.

Cameron gave up and let him. Cameron's own father had been the devil himself, controlling his sons so tightly that Cameron was surprised that any of the Mackenzies could still breathe.

The old duke had gone easiest on Cameron, because Cameron had been interested in horses and erotic pictures—*As a man should be,* their father had said.

The old duke had regularly beaten Ian, saying that Ian was being sullen when he wouldn't look at anyone. He'd beaten Mac for his love of art, *like a bloody unnatural*; and Hart every day regardless, *to make a man of him. When he's duke and beset by fools, he'll be strong.*

Cameron had stood by, troubled and angry, unable to stop any of it. Until the day he'd returned from Harrow at the close of a term and realized he'd grown bigger and stronger than his father. He'd entered the house to hear eleven-year-old Mac's terrified screams and found his father about to break Mac's fingers. Cameron had wrested his father from Mac and thrown the man against the wall.

After their father had taken himself out of the room, roaring, Mac had looked up from the beautiful pictures he'd drawn, bravely trying to blink back tears. "Damn good toss, Cam," he'd said, wiping his eyes. "Would ye teach me?"

Cameron had vowed that Daniel would never know fear like that. Daniel might run a bit wild, but that was a small price for Cameron to pay for Daniel's happiness. Cameron would be damned if he'd become the kind of monster who would think nothing of breaking his own son's fingers.

He got himself downstairs and to the main wing of the house in time to hear strains of music coming from the ballroom. Scottish music, a reel. Hart Mackenzie always made sure that, along with the popular German waltzes and polkas, his hired musicians played plenty of Scottish dances. No one was allowed to forget that the Mackenzies were Scottish first, the entire branch of their clan nearly wiped out in '45, except for young Malcolm Mackenzie who survived to marry and rebuild the family. He'd kept the title of duke bestowed on the family in the 1300s but lived in a hovel on the grounds that had once housed Malcolm and his four brothers, all but Malcolm gone under English guns. Hart Mackenzie enjoyed stuffing the Mackenzies' current prosperity down English throats.

As Cameron strode toward the ballroom, Phyllida Chase glided down the hall from the guest wing, fashionably late as usual. Intent on adjusting her gloves, she didn't see Cameron until she nearly ran into him.

"Do get out of the way, Cam," she said in a cool voice.

Cameron didn't move. "Give Mrs. Douglas back her letters," he said. "She's done you no harm."

Phyllida gave her glove one last tug. "Gracious, are you her champion now?"

"I find all blackmailers disgusting." Yes, Ainsley had asked Cameron not to interfere, but he refused to stand by while Phyllida plied her extortion. "Give her the damn letters and leave her alone, and I'll think about not having Hart throw you out."

"Hart won't throw me out. He's trying to cultivate my husband's support. If you hadn't been so thickheaded as to give Mrs. Douglas back that page, she'd have been able to come up with the price."

"Give her the letters, or I will make your life hell."

Phyllida's eyes flickered, but damned if she didn't return

a stubborn look. "I doubt you could make it any more hell than it already is, my lord Cam. I'm selling Mrs. Douglas the letters because I need the money. As simple as that."

"For what, your gambling debts? Your husband is rich. Go to him."

"It has nothing to do with gambling, and it is my own business."

Damn the woman. "If I give you the money you need, will you cease troubling Mrs. Douglas?"

Phyllida's worried look dissolved into a smile. "My, my, you *are* smitten, aren't you?"

"How much do you want?"

Phyllida wet her lips. "Fifteen hundred wouldn't go amiss."

"Fifteen hundred, and you return the letters and let it go."

Phyllida made a show of considering, but Cameron could see her salivating at the prospect of fifteen hundred guineas in her hands. "Fair enough."

"Good. Fetch the letters."

"My dear Cameron, I don't have them with me. I'm not that foolish. I'll have to send for them."

"No money until I see them."

Phyllida pouted. "Now, that's not fair."

"I'm not interested in fair. I'm interested in you leaving Mrs. Douglas the hell alone."

"Goodness, what do you see in that little termagant? Very well, but have Mrs. Douglas give the money to me."

"Why?" Cameron narrowed his eyes in suspicion.

"Because I don't trust you. Mrs. Douglas is a paid toady, but at least she's an honest toady. She will make a fair exchange without doing anything underhanded."

"*You* had better not be underhanded," Cameron said. "If you try anything, I'll throttle those letters out of you. Understand?"

Phyllida smiled. "That's what I've always loved about you, Cam. You're not afraid to be forceful."

"Just give her the letters," Cameron growled and walked away from her, not missing her delighted laughter behind him.

The fiddles and drums were loud inside the ballroom. Some English guests grimaced or openly mocked the music, but the Scottish guests had formed circles to dance in Highland delight.

In the center of the ballroom Isabella and Mac led a circle. Although Isabella was English born and bred, she had taken to all things Scottish with a vengeance.

In Mackenzie plaid, her red hair twined with roses, Isabella swayed in the circle. Next to her was Mac, who was a damn good dancer. He led the wide circle in and out, feet moving in quick rhythm, but his eyes were for Isabella.

The look Mac gave Isabella when he looped his arm around her waist to turn her was so damn loving. Mac and Isabella had struggled a long time for their happy ending, and Cameron was glad to see them have it.

Hart didn't dance, but Hart never did. He liked to put people together and then stand back and watch them, like a general surveying his troops. Hart spied Cameron entering and moved to him, dressed in cool finery and a kilt, Mackenzie malt in his hand.

"Where did you disappear to tonight?" Hart asked.

Cameron shrugged. "Bored." No reason to mention Ainsley to Hart.

"Isabella is complaining about having to shoulder much of the burden of this thing." Hart gestured with his whiskey at the crowd. "And when Isabella complains, Mac is the very devil."

As distracted as he was, Cameron took time to laugh at the exasperation in Hart's voice. Hart lived to orchestrate things, and Isabella and Beth were happy to help him. But Hart had discovered quickly that his brothers' wives weren't docile creatures he could bend to his will. And when Beth and Isabella weren't happy, Ian and Mac became walls of angry protection.

A quick scan of the room told Cameron that Ian and Beth were missing. "Beth's not helping tonight?"

"The crowd at the fireworks unnerved Ian. He retired with Beth."

Cameron met Hart's golden gaze, which held the same skeptical amusement Cam felt. "Of course he did," Cam said. "Ian Mackenzie is a bloody genius."

"I can't force him to stay downstairs," Hart said.

No, when Ian wanted to do a thing, neither God nor all his angels could prevent it. Only Beth could, and Beth generally took Ian's side.

Ainsley and Daniel rushed in, hand in hand, to join the dancing. Ainsley had changed into a gown of subdued Douglas plaid, more black than anything else, and wore a big plaid bow in her hair. Mac opened the circle to welcome them. Mac liked Ainsley, telling Cameron that it was refreshing to talk to a lady who used to rob the school pantry of cake and divide the spoils among her friends.

Daniel threw himself into the dance with enthusiasm if not grace. He dragged Ainsley around the circle until she laughed, and he twirled her hard when the circle broke off into couples. Ainsley's silvery laughter drifted over the music, her smile lighting the room.

Cameron watched her supple waist bending as she danced, imagined his own arm around it. Cam would turn Ainsley in the dance and keep his arm around her, pulling her up for a slow, burning kiss.

He felt Hart's eagle gaze on him, and he scowled. "Mind your own damn business."

Hart took a sip of whiskey. "You might be interested to know that I saw Mrs. Douglas pick open the lock of the Chases' suite the other night and sashay right in when she thought no one was looking. Chase and I are in agreement about the German question, but I don't want things discussed too soon, especially not with the queen."

Hart worried about Germany's steady advances in industry, viewing them as a potential threat to Britain, while many of his fellow politicians assumed that Germany was their strongest ally. Cameron, his attention buried in racing, paid little attention to those details, but Hart was no fool, and Cam trusted Hart's instincts.

"It has nothing to do with the German question," Cameron said.

Hart's gaze sharpened. "Then you know what she was looking for. Interesting. Enlighten me."

Cameron looked back at Ainsley—dancing, happy, smiling—and knew in that instant that he would never betray her to Hart. Cam would be as growling and protective of her as Mac and Ian were of Isabella and Beth.

"I can't tell you," Cameron said. "But I can assure you it has nothing to do with politics. Just female silliness."

Hart's gaze could have cut glass. "Female silliness can hide a wagonload of secrets."

Cameron met the famous Hart Mackenzie stare with a stubborn stare of his own. "This doesn't. You're going to have to trust me, because I'm not saying a bloody word."

"Cam . . ."

"Not a bloody word. It has nothing to do with your politics."

Hart's mouth tightened, but Hart knew exactly how far he could push his brothers. He pushed Cameron least of all, remembering exactly who'd won all those fistfights and scraps they'd had as youths.

But Cameron always forgave Hart for his high-handedness. Hart had saved Cameron's life after Elizabeth's death but had never demanded anything in return; they'd never even spoken about it. Hart would do anything to keep the family safe and together. That was why they all lived so well, although Hart would never go into the details of their father's sudden wish to bestow generous trusts on his younger sons instead of having Hart inherit the entire fortune.

"Fine, I'll take your word," Hart said, as the music wound to an end. "Just keep her under control."

The dancers dispersed to applause. Music began again, and guests moved to the floor to take up the waltz. Cameron looked for Ainsley and Daniel in the milling crowd, but both had vanished.

"That's her. My father's prized possession. Although she's *not* his possession, which is why he's all bothered about it."

The prized possession that Daniel had dragged Ainsley from the ballroom to view was a horse. A three-year-old filly to be precise, and a most beautiful creature.

The horse had slender, delicate-looking legs, but there was power in her body and fire in her eye. She was brown, her coat rich and dark, her mane and tail as dark. The pink lining of her nostrils spoke of fine breeding, and the way she watched Ainsley and Daniel approach told Ainsley that she was perfectly aware of how beautiful she was.

"Night-Blooming Jasmine, I presume," Ainsley said. The mare had her head over the half door of her box, ears pricked, nostrils expanding as she inhaled Ainsley's scent. "No, I didn't bring you sugar, you greedy thing."

As Ainsley reached out to stroke her, a tall man with black hair materialized from the shadows. Angelo, the Romany who was ostensibly Cameron's valet, but in reality assisted with all aspects of Cameron's life, leaned casually on the door of the next stall. "Careful of her, ma'am," he said, his dark voice holding tones of lands far away. "She's got the devil in her."

Ainsley rubbed the end of Jasmine's nose, smiling at the warm, velvety feel of it and the prickle of her whiskers. "She just wants a bit of attention, don't you, love?" Ainsley said. "You want someone to tell you how beautiful you are, and how much they appreciate you." Ainsley rubbed under the horse's mane, and Jasmine half closed her eyes in enjoyment.

"She does that." The Romany smiled, the corners of his eyes crinkling, gaze softening in approval.

Ainsley hadn't spoken to Angelo before, but she knew that Cameron keeping a Romany as his most trusted companion shocked many people, who were unnerved by Angelo's appalling lack of manners. Seeing him up close, Ainsley realized that they meant the man's lack of deference. Angelo obviously didn't consider aristocrats and the genteel his "betters," and saw no reason to treat them as any different from himself. Ainsley had to admire Angelo's utter confidence in who he was and where he stood in the world.

Daniel snorted. "Jasmine's a runner all right, but she don't like the bit. Yesterday, she tossed off Dad's best jockey and ran for the hills. Took them hours to find her."

Ainsley imagined Lord Cameron's reaction to *that*. No wonder he'd been out of sorts when he'd brought Phyllida Chase to his bedroom last night. He'd been a man trying to take his mind off his troubles, and he'd found Ainsley hiding in his window seat instead.

Jasmine nuzzled Ainsley's plaid hair bow with interest, and then decided to grab it with her teeth. Ainsley stifled a shriek as the bow came off, pulling strands of Ainsley's hair with it.

Jasmine backed up and shook her head until the bow unraveled into a long ribbon. She snorted playfully and kept shaking her head, dancing away from the ribbon that snaked around her feet. The Mackenzie dogs that had followed Ainsley and Daniel started barking, wanting to play too.

"You're right, she is a little devil," Ainsley said. "I'd better get that away from her before she swallows it."

Angelo's dark eyes were full of laughter. "Let me."

But when Angelo opened the stall door, Jasmine lunged

at him, ears flat on her head, teeth bared, the ribbon still between them. Angelo said something softly in Romany, but Jasmine ignored him.

Ainsley grinned. "She doesn't want you taking away her toy. Danny, get me a bit of oats."

While Daniel trotted off, Ainsley ducked in around Angelo and lifted the end of the unraveled bow. She quietly began to roll up the ribbon, ending at the piece Jasmine still held. Daniel thrust a handful of oats over the stall door, and Ainsley caught them in her bare palm and offered them to Jasmine.

Jasmine's nostrils widened as she whuffed a warm breath over Ainsley's hand. Then came the velvet nose, the wet tongue, and touch of teeth as Jasmine dropped the ribbon for the unexpected treat. Ainsley folded the rest of the ribbon and thrust it into her pocket as Jasmine crunched oats.

Once the oats were gone, Ainsley made to leave the stall, but Jasmine suddenly swung her hindquarters around, blocking the way out.

Ainsley patted the mare's side, unafraid. "Move, you daft beastie."

Jasmine decided she didn't want to budge. She kept crunching the oats in her mouth, pinning Ainsley between her and the corner of the stall.

"I'd say she likes you, ma'am," Angelo said.

He slid into the stall and made soft clicking noises between his teeth. Jasmine paid absolutely no attention. She turned to nuzzle Ainsley, making Ainsley have to back up against the wall.

It was a fine thing to be liked and trusted by a horse, quite another to be held captive by her. Ainsley tried to step around her keeping her movements slow, but Jasmine turned again, pressing Ainsley back. The dogs barking outside and Daniel's worried voice weren't helping.

Then Jasmine shied, swinging her hindquarters toward

Ainsley as a heavy tread sounded in the stable yard. Ainsley dove aside in case the horse decided to kick, but Jasmine wasn't intent on kicking.

She bolted through the half-open door and ran for freedom, shoving aside Angelo, Daniel, the dogs, and the large form of Cameron Mackenzie, who was bearing down upon them.

Chapter 9

"What th' devil did ye think you were doing?" Cameron shouted at her in the dark of the stable yard.

Angelo, sliding bareback onto another of the horses, rode quietly out in pursuit of Jasmine. Daniel and the dogs followed Angelo on foot, while a stable boy hurriedly saddled a horse for Cameron.

Cameron's big hands clamped Ainsley's shoulders, but her annoyance at being manhandled was mitigated by the fact that Cameron had every right to be angry. Jasmine was a racer worth a lot of money and had been entrusted to Cameron's care. The Scottish wilderness was full of holes to break Jasmine's legs, icy streams to carry her away, bogs to swallow her.

"Don't blame Angelo," Ainsley said quickly. "Or Daniel. I left the door open."

"Oh, no worries there, lass, I blame all three of ye. Angelo had no business letting you in, and Danny had no business bringing you out here at all." His anger wiped away any English veneer he might have—he was an enraged Highlander ready to reach for his claymore.

"I believe the horse didn't spook until a large Scotsman came charging in to see what we were up to."

Cameron's eyes flashed. "I never thought you'd be daft enough to crawl around a stall with a half-crazy racehorse!"

"I had to get my ribbon back."

Cameron let go of her, but his rage didn't lessen. "Ribbon—what the devil are ye talking about?"

"She was eating my hair ribbon. I didn't think you wanted her to choke on it."

He stared at Ainsley's bare head. "What possessed you t' give it to her in the first place?"

"I didn't *give* it to her. She has a long neck and strong teeth."

Cameron's palm pressed where Jasmine had ripped a lock from Ainsley's hair. His voice softened a notch. "Are you all right, lass?"

"I'm fine. My brother Patrick had a horse who regularly took chunks out of anyone near her. I still have the teeth marks to prove it. If she couldn't reach your flesh, she'd happily chomp on your hat or coat, skirt or shirt. Jasmine only pulled out my hair ribbon."

Cameron didn't appear to be listening. He caressed Ainsley's hair with a gentle hand. "Jasmine's gotten away from Angelo before," he said. "No horse gets away from Angelo. The little sweetheart is giving us a lot of bother."

"Shouldn't you be running after her?"

"I wanted to make sure ye were all right, first."

Ainsley's heart sped at the gentleness in his voice. "Not to mention shout at me."

"And shout at you." His eyes sparkled again. "Do ye always walk into a horse's stall so fearlessly?"

"Since I was three and liked to stand under their bellies."

"Good Lord, lass, I pity your parents."

"Brothers. My parents died when I was very young. My

oldest brother was already twenty and looked after the lot of us. Pity poor dear Patrick. I drove him mad. Still do."

"I don't doubt." Cameron's voice had lost its anger, his hand continuing to caress.

Ainsley wanted to step to him, to absorb more of his heat against the chill wind that cut across the meadow. In her rather lonely existence the last six years, she'd never been so warm as this night.

"You'd better go find your horse," she said.

"She's not mine. She's only borrowed."

"All the more reason."

"Angelo's the best horseman and tracker in the world, and I'm not finished with ye yet."

Why did the words make her shiver with pleasure? "No?"

The stable boy was approaching, leading the horse he'd saddled. Cameron slid his big hand behind Ainsley's neck and scooped her up to him for a fiery kiss.

It was a kiss filled with promise, one that told her he hadn't forgotten what he'd started in his study, nor his intention to finish it.

Cameron released her, turned as the stable lad reached them, and swung up on the horse with easy grace.

Ainsley folded her arms against the sudden cold as Cameron rode off into the night, the stable lad waving him away.

It took the rest of the night to catch the bloody horse. By the time Cameron led Jasmine in, lathered, scratched by bramble—and if he didn't know better, smug—the sun was up, and his two trainers were already out with horses on lounge lines. Cameron rubbed down Jasmine himself, and Angelo watered her as Cameron quit the stables for the house.

He bathed, dressed in fresh clothes, and went to the sunny room in Mac's wing where a private breakfast was served for the family. It was only eight, but during a house party, Isabella and Beth rose early to coordinate the activities for the day.

These breakfasts involved whatever family members were awake and hungry—brothers, sisters-in-law, Daniel, valets, dogs. When Cameron entered, Isabella and Beth were already chattering about the day's schedule. Mac sat close to Isabella, reading a paper and stealing his hand to his wife's whenever he could. Ian ate slowly and steadily, listening to Beth and no one else. Ian's valet, Curry, ate with gusto, the former pickpocket still reveling in the fact that he now lived the high life. Angelo was absent, the man deciding to remain in the stables with Jasmine, as were Daniel, Hart, and Mac's pugilist valet, Bellamy.

Curry jumped up to serve Cameron, but Cameron waved the little man back to his chair and helped himself to eggs and sausages, bannocks and coffee. He plunked the plate and cup to his usual place across from Isabella and snatched part of the racing newspaper from Mac.

Without looking at it, he said to Isabella, "Tell me everything you know about Mrs. Douglas."

Isabella's brows rose in surprise, then she smiled. "And why are you so interested in Ainsley Douglas?"

"Because she's busy corrupting my son, my valet, and my horses. I want to know what I am up against."

Cameron didn't miss Beth's sudden smile and Mac's knowing grin.

"I wondered when you'd confess," Mac said. "I noticed the way you looked at her when you saw her in Isabella's front parlor last year."

"Was she in Isabella's parlor last year?" Cameron asked.

Cameron knew damn well she had been, though he'd seen her for only a moment. He'd walked into Isabella's London parlor, bent on helping Isabella and Mac through a crisis, and seen Ainsley there looking sweet as you please. She'd flushed as she'd moved fluidly past him and out the door, skirts pressed to the side as though fearing they'd touch him.

Mac only chuckled. "Cam, old man, you're going to be snared as thoroughly as the rest of us."

A pot of honey for the bannocks reposed near Cameron's plate, and he lifted the dripper, letting the honey trickle back into the bowl. "Talk," he said to Isabella.

Isabella rested her elbows on the table and planted her chin on her hands. "Let me see, Ainsley's father was a McBride, her mother the only daughter of Viscount Aberdere. Ainsley's mother and father both died of typhoid in India when Ainsley and her youngest brother were just babies."

"She told me that her oldest brother raised her," Cameron said.

"He did. Patrick McBride was already twenty. He got Ainsley and her three other brothers out of India and all the way back to the family home in Scotland. Patrick married soon after that, and he and his wife, Rona, brought up the others. They sent Ainsley to Miss Pringle's Select Academy, wanting to make a lady of her. That's where I met her, and we became fast friends."

"Partners in crime," Mac added. "Mrs. Douglas taught my dear wife how to pick locks and climb into and out of windows."

"Ooh," Curry said. "Sounds interestin'."

"I never mastered the art," Isabella said. "Not like Ainsley. She was our ringleader for midnight feasts and practical jokes. We were quite awful."

"I can imagine," Cameron said. "What did she do after she finished at the academy?"

"Ainsley never finished," Isabella said, sounding surprised he didn't know. "In the summer before her final year, Patrick and his wife took her on a trip to the Continent. They decided to stay there for a year, in Rome, I think. When I next saw Ainsley, in London, she was already married to

John Douglas. Mr. Douglas was a very kind man, but at least thirty years her senior. Ainsley seemed content enough, but I always wondered why she married him. I've speculated, but she's never told me, and I don't like to pry."

"Yes, you do," Beth said. "When you first met me, you made me come home with you the moment I mentioned Ian."

"That was different, darling," Isabella said. "That was family."

Cameron lifted the honey dripper again. The amber folds cascading down made him imagine swirling the honey over Ainsley's naked body. Slowly, slowly licking it from her skin, savoring each sticky drop.

He looked up to find Ian watching him, no doubt guessing Cameron's exact thoughts. Ian so rarely looked at anyone straight in the eye that when he did, it could be unnerving.

Cameron put down the dripper. "And since her husband's death, Mrs. Douglas has worked for the queen?"

"Indeed, she has. Ainsley's mother and Lady Eleanor Ramsay's mother were good friends, and the queen adored Ainsley's mother. So one year when the queen was at Balmoral, Ainsley and Eleanor Ramsay were staying with a mutual friend nearby. The queen visited with them, and when the queen discovered who Ainsley was, there was nothing for it but that Ainsley should come and work for her. The queen finagled Ainsley into her household somehow and made her a lady of the bedchamber."

Mrs. Yardley had told him much the same thing. "So, she and the queen are chummy."

"Not really. Ainsley is grateful for the position and the salary, but she finds it trying at times. The queen doesn't like to let her leave very often. I'm surprised Ainsley was allowed to spend two weeks with me here, but I'm happy for it."

Isabella picked up her coffee and sipped, clearly finished with her story.

"Is that all?" Cameron asked.

"Isn't that enough? I've chattered on about my friend's private life long enough, and I told you that much only because Daniel told me he caught you kissing her."

Mac started laughing, damn him, and Curry was getting an earful to spread below stairs.

"Stop all the confounded smirking," Cameron growled. "I'm not looking to marry her. She's disrupting my life."

Isabella lost her smile. "She's a dear friend, Cameron. Do not hurt her."

"I have no intention of hurting her. I want her to cease pulling me into her affairs and to quit meddling in mine."

"Stop kissing her then."

Cameron saw by the faces turned toward him that they were going to line up against him. None of them understood the damage a woman like Ainsley could do to his sanity. The thrumming in his body wouldn't go away when he was around her, and he'd already lost two nights of sleep because of her.

What Cam should do was pack his bags, load up the horses, and retreat to his house in Berkshire where he had his main racing stables. He could join his other trainers and continue with Jasmine in his big, open paddocks.

But Cameron had already promised Hart to stay at Kilmorgan until the races at Doncaster, and he didn't like to break promises to his brothers. Aside from that, Jasmine was too jittery for a long journey south. If she were Cameron's horse, he'd back her off to light training, build her up slowly, get to know her, teach her to trust. As it was, he had to work her carefully. A long trip now would ruin her.

No, he had to stay at Kilmorgan and finish this. Once he'd had Ainsley, as he'd vowed to, he could forget her and return to sanity.

Ian slid the pot of honey toward his plate. "We should go back upstairs," he said to Beth.

"What?" Beth looked up from a list she was writing. "Why?"

Ian rose and pulled back Beth's chair without answering. Ian had difficulty lying, so when he knew he shouldn't say what was on his mind, he'd learned to keep his mouth firmly closed.

Beth knew him well, though. Without arguing, she let him take her arm and steer her from the table. Before he walked away, Ian reached back and snatched the honey pot from the table, balancing the pot in his hand as he led Beth from the room.

Two days later Ainsley sat among a sea of costly fabrics at a dressmaker's in Edinburgh. Rain fell outside, the sort that obscured everything in mist, but inside with Beth and Isabella, all was dry and snug.

Ainsley had telegraphed Phyllida's new demand to the queen, and while waiting for the reply, she'd restlessly searched the house again, just in case. She'd recruited Daniel to help her look, and Angelo too, although she didn't tell either exactly what she searched for and why. But both knew the house better than she did, surprisingly well, in fact. The Romany and the youth found hidey holes that she wagered even Hart didn't know about. But Phyllida hadn't made use of them, because they found no letters.

Phyllida herself refused to speak to Ainsley at all. She'd walk away when she saw Ainsley approach, deliberately surround herself with people, or confine herself to her chamber, claiming a headache.

A rather exasperated reply came from the queen that she could not send Ainsley any more money. Ainsley would simply have to be resourceful, and the queen would reimburse her later.

Blast and botheration. Ainsley didn't have anywhere near enough to make up the difference, and her brother Patrick would never lend her five hundred guineas without demanding a full explanation of why she needed it. Patrick couldn't know the truth, and Ainsley didn't want to lie to him either. Her barrister brother Sinclair would have the same curiosity, Steven could never keep money in his pockets anyway, and Elliot, who had the most resources, was away in India.

The only thing to do was borrow the money from Cameron. He already knew about Phyllida's demands and had offered the cash. Ainsley could give him her mother's jewelry as collateral and pay him back once Ainsley received the money from the queen.

This sort of situation was exactly why the queen employed her, Ainsley thought darkly, because Her Majesty knew that Ainsley would finish the job no matter what it took.

Hence, Ainsley hadn't fussed when Isabella suggested that she, Ainsley, and Beth take an afternoon's holiday from the house party for shopping in Edinburgh. She could take the opportunity to get her mother's jewelry valued, so that she could offer Cameron a fair exchange for the loan. Despite what Phyllida claimed Cameron would demand for helping, Ainsley was determined to keep the transaction businesslike. She had to.

Ainsley admitted to a pleasant warmth sitting at Isabella's dressmaker's surrounded by costly and beautiful fabrics. Isabella instructed the dressmaker's assistants to bring out bolt after bolt of moiré, taffeta, fine broadcloth, crushed velvet, and cashmere, and yard upon yard of laces, ribbons, and trims.

Ainsley fingered a china silk so fine it felt like mist in her hand. "This is heavenly. Pity she doesn't have it in lavender. You could wear this, Beth." Its dark sapphire tones would exactly match Beth's eyes.

"Beth?" Isabella repeated. "My dear Ainsley, everything Madame Claire is bringing out is for *you*. You are going to have an ensemble of dark blue, with this cream stripe for the underskirt, and the china silk for the lining." Isabella pulled out swaths of blue velvet and laid it over a cream and white striped satin. "With light blue silk for the ruffles and finish."

Ainsley looked at her in alarm. "Isabella, I can't. I'm still in mourning. Or half mourning, at least."

"And it's high time you left it off. I know the queen swoons when you wear anything lighter than dark gray, but you'll need smarter frocks for when you visit me in London—for the opera, and balls, and my soirees. I intend to show you off, my dear, and I have excellent taste in clothes."

"Her ladyship does have an eye," the dressmaker, Madame Claire, said.

Isabella waved away the compliment. "Living with an artist has taught me things. I will concede mauve or violet for you, Ainsley, but never lavender." She shuddered and reached for a swath of burgundy moiré. "Trim this with black piping and you'll have a lovely tea gown. But for your new ball dress, you will have this glorious sky blue. With your eyes and coloring, you can make this fabric sing. What do you think, Beth?"

Beth, who'd grown up poorer than poor and hadn't had a pretty dress in her life until she'd turned twenty-eight, nodded but with caution. "It is beautiful, Isabella."

"Then we shall take it. Now, where did the book get to?" Isabella dug around for the fashion book that she'd buried under fabric. "I know I saw some silver tissue, Madame Claire. I want that for Ainsley's ball dress as well."

While Isabella and Madame Claire searched for the book and the tissue, Ainsley whispered to Beth, "Does she know that I can't afford this? One gown, maybe, but certainly not a new ball gown. I bought the gray only last week."

"You've been seen in it once," Beth whispered back, her lips twitching. "That's what Isabella will say."

"But I can't pay for all this." Isabella, the indulged daughter of an earl and now the wife of wealthy Mac Mackenzie, might not understand that most people couldn't buy a new wardrobe on a whim.

"Darlings, are you being sordid and discussing money?" Isabella sat back down and spread the fashion book across her lap. "This is my gift to you, Ainsley. I've been dying to get you out of those dull gowns for ages. Don't spoil it for me."

"Isabella, I can't let you . . ."

"Yes, you can. Now, stop protesting so we can get down to business." She smoothed out a page. "I like this design—we'll have the tissue gathered over the underskirt in the front, with a big rosette off center on the hip. Then the blue and silver stripe for the overskirt over the bustle, which will also make up the back of the bodice, with a slice of the blue silk in front."

Madame Claire and her assistants bustled off to bring more fabrics, while Ainsley undressed for her fitting. Morag, one of Isabella's maids, followed Ainsley behind a curtain and helped pull off her gray gown. The fabric now seemed drab and dull compared to the brilliant colors on the floor.

"And the electric blue taffeta for a morning dress," Isabella went on. "That will be splendid."

Ainsley put her head out between the curtains. "Why so much blue?"

"Because you're fair-haired, and it looks well on you. Besides, Cameron is particularly fond of blue."

Ainsley froze, hands clutching the drapes. Behind her Morag made a noise of impatience as she tried to reach buttons. "What has Lord Cameron's preference for blue to do with me?"

Isabella gave her a pitying look. "Really, Ainsley, do you think *anything* can go on in the Mackenzie household without Beth or me knowing? Cameron was seen kissing you in the stable yard *and* in his private study, all dutifully reported to me by Daniel."

"Your brother-in-law hasn't spoken to me in two days," Ainsley said. "He is very angry at me because I almost lost him a horse."

"He hasn't spoken to anyone, because he's been too busy working with said horse," Isabella returned. "All the more reason we finish you well. He'll come 'round, and when

Cam sees you shining like a butterfly, he won't be able to resist you."

"Butterflies don't shine," Ainsley said. "And please do not tell me that, when you parade me past Cameron in my brand-new blue clothing, he will fall to his knees and propose."

Isabella shrugged. "Anything is possible."

Ainsley jerked the curtain closed. "Isabella, I love you like a sister, but I refuse to continue with this absurd conversation."

Isabella laughed, but Ainsley thought her optimistic. Cameron had made it very clear that marriage was not a state he'd willingly enter again. Besides, a man like Cameron would not drop to one knee and propose in a conventional way. John Douglas had done that, so sweet of him, because his knees had been quite rheumatic. No, Cameron Mackenzie, on the small chance that he should propose to a woman, would take said lady rowing on a lake, or riding in the hills. He'd swing her down off her horse, cup her face in his hands, and kiss her—a long, thorough, burning kiss—and then he'd say in his gravelly voice, "Marry me, Ainsley."

Ainsley would have to nod her answer, unable to speak. Then he'd kiss her more deeply while the horses wandered away. They'd consummate the engagement there in the grass—which would be miraculously neither muddy nor boggy.

"If it is so absurd," Isabella said as Ainsley stepped out from behind the curtains in her combinations, ready to be measured, "why did Cameron follow you to Edinburgh, today?"

Ainsley suddenly found it hard to breathe. "Of course he didn't. Isabella, don't invent things."

"I wouldn't." Isabella stood up and held the beautiful blue velvet to Ainsley's face. "I saw him plain as day, boarding our train and looking furtive as the devil. He certainly didn't want to be seen. Yes, this blue I think. Madame Claire, *where* is that silver?"

Not many streets away, Cameron scowled at Lord Pierson, Night-Blooming Jasmine's owner. Pierson's elegant drawing room was filled with cigar smoke and Scottish memorabilia. Claymores hung on the walls on top of swaths of plaid, a collection of sporrans lay in a glass-fronted cabinet, and knives Pierson swore had been collected from Culloden field rested inside a glass-topped table.

Pierson was Cameron's least favorite kind of Englishman—one who pretended to have a passion for all things Scottish but in reality despised the Scottish people. The junk in this room had been sold to him by crafty dealers who capitalized on Pierson's need to embrace the romance that he thought embodied the Highlands. Pierson always spoke to Cameron with a sneer in his voice, his absolute belief in his superiority obvious.

"I expect you to turn out a winner, not put me off with excuses," Pierson said. He poured Scots whiskey—from a cheap distillery, not the Mackenzies'—into glasses and handed one to Cameron. "I need her to fetch me top price at auction."

At auction. *Give me strength.* "I haven't had enough time with her," Cameron said. "She's too nervous to run well. Leave her with me another year, and she'll take the four-year-old races by storm. She'll finish Ascot like a queen."

"No, damnation, I need her to win at Doncaster so I can sell her when the season ends. I thought you were supposed to be the best trainer in Britain, Mackenzie."

"And when the best trainer tells ye *not* to run the horse, ye ought to listen to him."

Pierson's lips pinched. "I can always pull her from your stables."

"Good luck finding another trainer this late. You won't and you know it."

Damn the man. If not for Jasmine's sake, Cameron

would walk away from the idiot, have nothing to do with him. But Pierson would ruin Jasmine, and Cameron didn't have the heart to let him.

Jasmine had been fine after her wild run. Though Angelo had said nothing, Cameron knew the man felt a world of shame for letting Jasmine out like that. The only explanation for Angelo's lapse was that Ainsley had bewitched him. Why not? She'd bewitched everyone else in the household.

"Let me buy Jasmine from you, as I proposed before," Cameron said. "I'll give her whatever you'd fetch at auction for her if she were a winner. She's a fine bit of horseflesh. Make a nice addition to my stock."

Pierson looked shocked. "Indeed no. She's an English mare of purest blood. She doesn't belong on a Scottish farm."

"My main training stables are in Berkshire. I could do magnificent things with her there."

"Then why aren't you there with her now?" Pierson demanded.

Cameron tilted his whiskey glass. The whiskey was awful, and he'd taken only the smallest of sips. "An obligation to my brother."

"What about your obligation to me and my horse? She races at Doncaster, or I pull her from you and spread the word of your incompetence. Is that clear? Now, I have other appointments. Good day to you, Mackenzie."

Cameron resisted punching the man in the mouth, set down his glass, and turned to take his greatcoat from the servant who brought it. If he struck Pierson and relieved his temper, Jasmine would suffer, and Cameron couldn't let that happen.

The servant—who was English, Cameron noted—led Cameron to the door and opened it for him. Cameron clapped on his hat and stepped out into the rain.

He strode down the street, misty rain obscuring sky, buildings, and people, relieving his anger by walking fast and hard.

Bloody arrogant bastard. In usual circumstances, such a man wouldn't get under his skin, but Cam liked Jasmine and wanted her. He thought about enticing Pierson into playing cards with him and winning Jasmine, but Pierson wasn't a gambler. He didn't even bet on the horses.

Cameron could calm Jasmine down to run her at Doncaster, but not to win. If he pushed her too hard, he risked her health. Jasmine might win but drop dead at the finish line—or, if Pierson had his way, the moment the buyer walked off with her. That was the way Pierson did things.

Damned bloody English Philistine.

Cam's thoughts cut off abruptly when he saw the woman dressed in gray, with hair the color of sunshine, dart out from a jeweler's shop. Ainsley slipped a little pouch into her pocket, glanced surreptitiously about, opened her umbrella, and hurried away down the misty street.

Chapter 10

Ainsley felt the presence of Cameron even before his large gloved hand closed around her umbrella handle.

Did he tip his hat, give her a polite hello, offer to escort her down the street? No, he regarded her with angry eyes from a granite face and wouldn't let go of the blasted umbrella.

"I told you I'd give you the money for the letters," he said.

Ainsley gave him a cool nod. "Good afternoon to you too, Lord Cameron. I know you did."

"So why were you in a damned jeweler's? You don't have the money to shop. You were trying to sell jewelry to pay Phyllida, weren't you?"

And didn't he look enraged about it? *High-handed, arrogant Scotsman.* "I wasn't trying to sell the jewels, I was having them valued. For collateral."

"Collateral? What collateral?"

Ainsley again tried to take back the umbrella and was surprised when he let it go. "For the loan you offered me. I give you collateral, and then when my friend sends me the money, you return the jewels to me."

Cameron's eyes became topaz-colored slits. "I never said it was a loan. I'll pay Phyllida, and that's the end of it. Your 'collateral,' if you insist on it, is to have a conversation with me that's not about the damned letters. I'm sick to death of them."

"I can't take a gift of money from you and remain a lady," Ainsley said. "Unless it's a loan, a business transaction, and then only because I'm a friend of the family. Of Isabella."

"You make it too complicated. No one has to know that I gave you the money."

"Mrs. Chase will know, or she'll guess. And you can be certain she would tell everybody."

Ainsley turned away and resumed walking.

Cameron had to stride quickly to catch up. Hell, if anyone had told him that one day he'd be racing through the streets of Edinburgh, chasing a lady determined to shut him out with her umbrella, he'd have laughed uproariously. Cameron Mackenzie didn't chase women, those with umbrellas or otherwise.

"The jeweler said my mother's earrings and brooch were enough to cover the five hundred," Ainsley said. "Which is lucky."

Cameron decided not to tell her that Phyllida now wanted fifteen hundred. He didn't need Ainsley sending home for the family silver.

"They were your mother's?"

"Yes. The only thing I have from her, really. I've always regretted that I never knew her."

The sadness in her voice tugged at him. Cameron's own mother had been a terrified creature admonished to stay away from her own sons. She'd died right after Cam had turned eighteen, while he was away at university, from a fall, he'd been told.

Hart had related the truth to Cameron later, that their father had killed her, shaking her so hard when he fought with her that he broke her neck. Hart had deduced this over time—the only witness had been Ian, and their father had locked ten-year-old Ian into an asylum even before the funeral, in case the very truthful Ian blurted out what really had happened.

Cameron had nothing of his mother's, his father having rid the house of everything belonging to her after her death. The way Ainsley mentioned her regret in not meeting her mother did something to his heart.

Ainsley cut off the discussion by opening the door of another establishment, where a well-dressed shop assistant smiled up at them. Ainsley looked at Cameron in surprise when he followed her in.

"This is a dressmaker's," she said.

"I know what it is. I take it you're here for a wardrobe, not baked bread. And put down that umbrella before you spear someone with it."

Ainsley let the assistant take the umbrella, but she quailed as Cameron followed her straight into the back room. Madame Claire gave him a welcoming smile. "Now then, your lordship."

Isabella waved at him from her comfortable chair. "Oh, Cameron, excellent. Just who we need."

Cool as he pleased, Cameron rid himself of his great-coat, seated himself in an armchair, and accepted the glass of port the assistant brought for him.

"You look very comfortable," Ainsley said.

"I'm a good customer."

Which meant Cameron sent his mistresses here. Ainsley slapped open one of the fashion books and busied herself looking at the colorful dresses inside, not seeing a line of them.

"We're fitting out Ainsley," Isabella said. "I want her to be radiant."

Ainsley sat still, her throat dry, while Isabella showed Cameron the fabrics that she'd chosen and told him what each were for. Cameron voiced his approval at her choices and seemed to know all about gussets and half sleeves and fichus. Ainsley might not even be in the room.

"I'd like to see her in red," Cameron said.

"Not with her coloring," Isabella answered. "Bright red will wash out her skin instead of enhancing it, and her eyes will be lost."

"Not bright red. Dark. Very dark. And velvet. A cozy winter dress."

Madame Claire brightened. "His lordship has exquisite taste. I have just the thing."

Ainsley should shout, protest, tell them to stop. She could only watch, half dazed, as Madame Claire returned with a swath of red velvet so dark its shimmer was black.

Cameron rose, took the velvet from Madame Claire, and approached Ainsley with it. Ainsley jumped to her feet, half afraid he would simply throw the cloth over her head if she remained seated on the stool.

Cameron cradled her face with the folds, the velvet soft as down against Ainsley's skin. "You see?" Cameron said to Isabella.

"Yes, that's excellent." Isabella clasped her hands. "You have a wonderful eye, Cam. She'll be beautiful in that."

Ainsley couldn't speak. Cameron's hands were firm through the velvet, all his strength from working his horses now softened to caress Ainsley.

She caught sight of Beth watching beyond Cameron. The look in Beth's blue eyes was knowing, understanding. Beth had been ensnared by a handsome, irresistible Mackenzie, and she knew full well that Ainsley had been ensnared by one too.

More rain the next afternoon meant indoor entertainment at Kilmorgan, so Isabella arranged a scavenger hunt. She and Beth and Ainsley drew up the lists of items to obtain and handed them out to the guests. Those who had no interest in the game retired to the card room in the main wing and proceeded to win and lose fortunes.

Daniel scoffed at the rather tame scavenger hunt and enticed Ainsley into the billiards room for a game. Isabella, relieved to have Daniel out from underfoot, released them both.

"Isabella says your brothers taught you to play," Daniel said to Ainsley. "I don't quite believe a girl can do it."

"No? Then prepare to be amazed, my boy."

Ainsley let Daniel bring out the cues and red and white balls, while she fingered the note in her pocket that Phyllida Chase's maid had brought her that morning.

Phyllida wanted the money tomorrow night, she said. *Rowlindson, Hart's nearest neighbor, will host a fancy-dress ball on the morrow, Friday evening. Meet me in the conservatory of his home at one o'clock in the morning, and we will make the exchange there. Only you, Mrs. Douglas, not Lord Cameron.*

Ainsley had read the note in exasperation. Really, why did the woman have to be so clandestine? All Phyllida had to do was visit Ainsley in her bedchamber, and they'd finish the matter.

But, very well, Ainsley would meet Phyllida at the fancy dress ball. Ainsley hadn't even been invited to the dratted ball, and Isabella hadn't mentioned it. But later that morning, Morag had given her a hand-delivered note from Lord Rowlindson's secretary that included an invitation. Phyllida was certainly thorough. Morag was even now putting together a costume for Ainsley.

As Daniel set up the balls, Ian Mackenzie walked into the room and shut the door behind him. Ian never spoke much to Ainsley, but he'd become comfortable with her during her visits to Isabella, which meant he didn't avoid her. But he didn't seek her out either; he simply accepted her presence as he did his family's.

Ainsley noticed the change in Ian from her visits in previous years. He moved more confidently now, his quick agitation replaced with a calm watchfulness. Whenever he held his tiny son, his stillness became even more pronounced. Quietude, that's what it was, the sort of peace that came from deep, unshakable happiness.

"Not on the scavenger hunt?" Ainsley asked Ian as she lined up her cue to the white ball.

Ian poured himself whiskey and leaned against the billiards table. "No."

"He means he'd win it too quickly," Daniel said. "Same reason he don't like to play cards."

"I remember every card on the table," Ian said.

Ainsley imagined the other players wouldn't much like this. "Sporting of you to stay away then."

Ian looked uninterested in being sporting, and Ainsley understood in a flash that he stayed away from card games because they weren't a challenge to him. He had a mind so quick that it solved problems before others were aware there was a problem.

Cameron was a bit like that with his horses, Ainsley mused, knowing when one would founder before it happened, and exactly why. She'd watched him stop a training session and lead a horse away, with his grooms protesting that nothing was wrong, only to have the horse doctor confirm that Cameron had been correct.

As Ainsley lined up her cue, Ian tapped the table two inches to his right. "Aim here. The red ball will fall into that pocket and the white will return there." He pointed.

"Aw, Uncle Ian, no fair helping."

Ian sent Daniel the barest hint of smile. "You should always help the ladies, Danny."

Ainsley knew enough about the mathematics of billiards to know that Ian had given her good advice. She shot. Her white ball struck the red, sending it exactly where Ian pointed.

It caromed off the wall and into the pocket, the white ball gently rolling back toward Ainsley's cue.

Daniel grinned. "You're good for a lady, I'll give you that."

"I'll have you know that I've rousted my brothers on many occasions," Ainsley said. "They regretted teaching me all these games after they started losing money to me."

Daniel chuckled. "Good for you. What else do you know how to do?"

Ainsley lined up another shot. "Shoot a pistol—and hit the target, mind you. Play cards, and not womanly games like whist. I mean poker."

"Aye, I'd love to see that. There are some games going in the drawing room even now."

Ainsley shook her head. Ian, more interested in the billiards than the conversation, again tapped the table where Ainsley should aim.

"I don't wish to embarrass Isabella by draining her guests dry," Ainsley said with good humor.

She'd thought of joining a card game to try to win the money to pay off Phyllida, but while her brothers Elliot and Steven had taught Ainsley to be a good player, there was still the risk that other players might be better. Many of Hart's guests were hardened gamblers, and one needed a large amount of money to even enter the games. Thousands of pounds moved around those tables in the drawing of a breath. She couldn't risk it.

Ainsley tapped her ball. That ball struck the second, which bounced against the cushion where Ian's hand had rested and rolled into a pocket with a definite thud.

Daniel whistled. "I wish you *would* play for money, Mrs. Douglas. The two of us, we could win a great deal together."

"Certainly, Daniel. We'll get a wagon and travel about, waving a banner that says 'Champion Exhibition Billiards by a Lady and a Lad. Be Amazed! Test Their Skill and Try Your Luck.' "

"A gypsy wagon," Daniel said. "We'll have Angelo do acrobatics and Dad show off his trained horses. And you can shoot at targets. People will come from miles to see us."

Ainsley laughed, and Ian completely ignored them. When Ainsley finally missed her shot, Daniel took the balls from the pockets and lined them up for himself. Ian abandoned the table and came to stand in front of Ainsley.

The golden gaze that roved her face before settling on her left cheekbone was as intense as any of the Mackenzies', even if Ian didn't look directly into her eyes.

Ian had spent his childhood in a madhouse, and while Ainsley knew that Ian never had been truly insane, he wasn't an ordinary man either. He had intelligence that came out of him in amazing bursts, and Ainsley always had the feeling that his enigmatic exterior hid a man who understood everyone's secrets, perhaps better than they did themselves.

"Cameron's wife hated him," Ian said without preliminary. "She did everything she could to hurt him. It made him a hard and unhappy man."

Ainsley caught her breath. "How very awful of her."

"Aye," Daniel said cheerfully from the billiards table. "Me mum was a right bitch. And a whore."

Ainsley's correct response would be to admonish Daniel for speaking so harshly of his mother, especially when she was deceased. *Good heavens, Daniel, that cannot be true.* But from what Ainsley had heard about Lady Elizabeth, Daniel likely spoke the unvarnished truth.

"I never knew her," Daniel said. "But people tell me about her. I used to punch the fellows at school for saying that my mother had bedded every aristocrat in Europe, but it was mostly true, so I stopped."

The matter-of-fact tone in Daniel's voice made Ainsley's heart ache. Lady Elizabeth's reputation had been bad, but to hear the facts of it so baldly from her son's lips was heartbreaking.

"Daniel, I'm sorry."

Daniel shrugged. "Mum hated Dad for not wanting her to go tarting about after they were married. She thought she could carry on as before, you see, but with all Dad's money behind her. Plus she had the prospect that she might become a duchess if Hart pegged it. In retaliation for Dad not letting her run wild, she tried to convince him that I wasn't his son, but as ye can see, I'm very much a Mackenzie." Daniel was, with that sharp Mackenzie stare. No denying it.

"How could she?" Ainsley asked indignantly. That a mother could use her child as a pawn in a game with her husband made Ainsley sick. Stupid Elizabeth—she'd had Cam's wicked smile, the warmth in his dark gold eyes, his kisses of fire all to herself, and she hadn't treasured them.

"Like I say, she was a right bitch."

Ainsley didn't question how Daniel knew this about his mother. He'd have been told—by the servants, his schoolmates, well-meaning friends, not-so-well-meaning acquaintances. She imagined the anguish of the little boy learning that the mother he didn't remember hadn't been the angelic being a mother was suppose to be. Ainsley had very few memories of her own mother, and she could imagine how she'd feel if she were told repeatedly what a horrible person she'd been.

"I'd like to give Lady Elizabeth a good talking-to," Ainsley said. A good tongue-lashing was more like it.

Daniel laughed. "So would Aunt Isabella and Aunt Beth. And my uncles. But Dad never let anyone go up against her. Well, no one but him."

Ian broke in. "I never knew her. I was in the asylum when she was married to Cameron. But I heard what she did to him."

Ian, not a man who showed emotion except in his love for Beth, held a spark of rage in his eyes for his brother.

"Daniel." Cameron's voice rumbled from the other side of the room. "Out."

Daniel looked up at his father without surprise. "I was just telling Mrs. Douglas things she needed to know."

Cameron gestured at the door he'd just opened. "Out."

Daniel heaved an aggrieved sigh, shoved the cues back into the rack, and shuffled out of the room. Ian followed him without a word, closing the door and leaving Ainsley and Cameron alone.

Chapter 11

Cameron looked at Ainsley, her color high, her eyes sparkling with righteous anger, and he wanted her. He'd take her on the billiards table, on the chair near it, or the settee, he didn't much care. He wanted to kiss the lips parted in indignation, run kisses down the chest that rose with agitated breath. Cam wanted to bury himself inside the woman who's said with such outrage, *I'd like to give her a good talking-to.*

He could imagine Ainsley, with her frank eyes and bold stare, telling Lady Elizabeth Cavendish exactly what she thought of her. Elizabeth, the rich, spoiled daughter of an aristocrat, as wild and bright as a tropical bird, wouldn't have stood a chance against Ainsley. Ainsley was more like a sparrow—a matter-of-fact woman, more interested in the practical matter at hand than displaying her plumage.

No, not a sparrow. That was too plain for someone like Ainsley. Ainsley was deeply beautiful, with beauty that shone from the depths of her. Cameron wanted to learn that loveliness, every single inch of it.

"I know such things are none of my business," Ainsley was saying, her voice like fine wine to his senses. "I should have stopped Daniel when he began, but I admit to a morbid curiosity about your late wife. If any of what Daniel said is true, I am sorry."

She *was* sorry, that was the thing. Other women might pretend that Daniel must be making things up, or be disgusted—at Elizabeth, at Cameron, at Daniel for telling the tale. But not Ainsley. She saw the truth for what it was.

There were reasons Cameron hadn't divorced Elizabeth, all of which had to do with Daniel. He'd realized early on that Elizabeth couldn't be trusted not to try to rid herself of her baby, and so Cameron kept her close, much to her fury. Elizabeth had claimed repeatedly that the child wasn't Cameron's, and Cameron knew there was a risk that she told the truth. Elizabeth had had a string of lovers, some regular, some brief encounters. But Cam had been willing to risk it. Elizabeth had been wrong—Daniel was a Mackenzie all right.

Cameron knew now that he should have sent Elizabeth away as soon as she'd given birth to Daniel, but he'd been young and sentimental. He'd truly believed that once Elizabeth had a son to care for, she would change. But she hadn't; she'd only sunk into a strange melancholy, her rages growing worse, and she'd started trying to hurt Daniel.

Cameron had the strangest feeling that Ainsley, if he explained all this to her, would understand.

"I'm not here to talk about my wife," he said.

Ainsley's eyes were filled with anger for him. "Very well, what did you come here to talk about?"

Cameron touched the top button of her dull gray afternoon dress and forced his voice to soften. "I came to ask how many buttons you'll undo for me today."

Ainsley's sharp intake of breath pressed her bosom

against the very buttons Cameron wanted to undo. Her cheeks were flushed, eyes starry, Ainsley at her most beautiful.

"I thought you'd forgotten about that game," she said.

"I never forget games. Or what's owed me."

He stepped closer still, inhaling her sweet scent. Current fashion dictated that women's skirts were worn tight against thighs and legs, and Cameron took full advantage, standing right against her. When she opened her bodice, he'd be able to peer into her soft cleavage.

He again touched the top button, which was a little bar of onyx. "How many buttons, Mrs. Douglas?"

"It was ten last time. This time, I think, I should only go a half dozen."

Cameron frowned. "Why?"

"Because we're indoors with people barging about the house looking for odds and ends. Billiard balls were on a few lists for the scavenger hunt."

"Twenty," Cameron said firmly.

Ainsley choked. "Twenty?"

"Twenty buttons will put me here." He ran his finger down her bodice almost to her waist.

Cameron felt her heart pounding behind the stiffness of her corset. "Not fair," she said. "These buttons are more widely spaced than the last set."

"I'm not interested in what your dressmaker designed. I'm interested in how many I can open."

"Very well, twelve. My final offer."

"Not final at all."

The billiards table stopped Ainsley from stepping back. All Cameron had to do was lift her, and he'd have her lying flat upon it. They'd tear the cloth and exasperate Hart's housekeeper, but replacing the damn thing would be worth having Ainsley.

"I will concede fourteen," she said.

"Twenty."

"Lord Cameron, if someone bursts in here, I will never have time to do up twenty buttons."

"Then we'll lock the door."

Ainsley's eyes widened. "Good lord, no. I'd have a devil of a time explaining why I was behind a locked door with the notorious Lord Cameron Mackenzie. Leave the door unlocked, and they'll think we were scavenging."

Cameron smiled, putting as much sin into it as he knew how. "I'm getting impatient, Mrs. Douglas. Twenty buttons."

"Fifteen."

Cameron let his smile turn triumphant. "Done."

She flushed. "Oh, very well. Fifteen. But let us be quick."

"Turn around."

She looked at him with startled gray eyes. Did she know how sensual she was? She could make a man long to see those eyes regarding him sleepily across a pillow, and Cameron did not like women in his bed. Bed was for sleeping. Alone. Safer that way for all concerned.

Ainsley faced the billiards table, her breathing still rapid. Her stupid bustle was in his way now, loops of wire that kept her skirt stuck out behind her. An idiotic fashion. Whatever fool had designed bustles had obviously had no interest in women.

Cameron made do by standing half at her side, his thigh against her hip. The next time he stood thus with Ainsley, he vowed that the bustle would be gone.

Cameron pressed a kiss to her cheek as he undid the first button. Ainsley stayed true to the game, no maidenly flutters or begging off. She'd finished the bidding and would stick to the bargain. Brave, beautiful woman.

Her eyes drifted closed as Cameron undid the second button and then the third, her body relaxing against his. He kissed the corner of her mouth, and her faint noise of longing made his cockstand ache.

By button eight, Cameron was kissing her neck, tasting

her—salty tang over the faint bite of lemons. One day soon, Cameron would peel away her clothes and lick her entire body. Then he'd kneel before her and drink and drink, while her toes curled into the carpet, her hands tangled his hair, and she made those precious sighs of pleasure.

Ten, eleven, twelve. Cameron touched her bosom, heady heat inside her corset. He'd have the corset off her next time too.

"Thirteen," he whispered. "Fourteen." He dipped one hand into his pocket and opened button number fifteen one-handed. "Don't move."

Ainsley stood very still, eyes closed. Cameron breathed her scent, kissed her skin one more time, and then slid the necklace he'd taken from his pocket around her throat, closing the tiny clasp in back.

Ainsley's eyes popped open. She stared in amazement at the strand of diamonds that now lay across her chest and then up at him. Her bodice gaped enticingly, breasts lifting above a corset with small, decorative bows on the front.

"What is this?" she asked.

Cameron made his tone careless. "I bought it at that jeweler's in Edinburgh after you and Isabella and Beth left. I thought it would go well with your new finery."

Ainsley looked at him in pure astonishment. No squealing excitement that most of Cam's women succumbed to when he bought them jewels, no sly looks of promised payment later. Ainsley Douglas was dumbfounded.

"Why?" she asked.

"What do you mean why? I saw the damned necklace, and thought you'd like it."

"I do like it." Ainsley fingered the diamonds. "It's beautiful. But . . ." Her expression held longing, loneliness, and a sudden hurt that surprised him. "I can't accept it."

"Why the devil not?"

Cameron looked so angry—at her. He who'd interfered with Ainsley's business with Phyllida and had taken over her session at the dressmaker's, the man who wanted to give Ainsley money without collateral and bought her jewelry as he would for his doxy, now looked angry at *her.*

"Because, my dear Cameron, you know how people like tittle-tattle. There would be much speculation on why you gave me this necklace."

"Why does anyone have to know I gave it to you?"

Ainsley wanted to laugh. "Because you're not exactly discreet."

"Bugger discretion. It's a waste of time."

"You see? You can say that because you are so very rich, not to mention male. You can get away with much, while I must be a good little woman and follow all the rules." And didn't those rules chafe?

"The queen should give you a damned sight more than she does for drudging for her. You are worth more than she understands."

Ainsley shivered at his dark voice. "You are flattering, and believe me, I adore you flattering me, but I have to be so careful." She touched the necklace again. "Anyone discovering that you bought this for me will assume me your mistress. Phyllida already believes it."

Cameron leaned to her, moving his hands to either side of her on the billiards table. His body hemmed her in, his arms a cage.

"Then be my mistress in truth, Ainsley."

His breath touched her lips as she gasped in surprise, his mouth following. The swift kiss burned like a brand.

"I could give you so much," he said. "I want to give you so much. Is that so bad a thing?"

So bad a thing? Ainsley clutched the lip of the billiards table and tried to stay upright. No, it wouldn't be a bad thing to be this man's lover. She'd lounge in his bed—or wherever he preferred—while he unbuttoned her frock and tasted her skin. Surrender to Cameron would be breathless, a wild, heady freedom.

He was a man who took everything he wanted, whose women were meltingly grateful to him and didn't mind the strings attached. But then, Cameron's usual ladies were courtesans, merry widows, and women whose reputations had been soiled long before they took up with him. They had nothing to lose, and Ainsley had everything. *And wouldn't the downfall be heavenly?*

But once upon a time, Ainsley had succumbed to a seducer's skilled touch. She'd hovered on the brink of complete ruin, terrified to confess her sins to the brother who'd been everything to her. She remembered the shock in Patrick's eyes when she'd at last told him, the gasp of dismay from his upright wife, Rona.

And then Patrick, instead of chucking Ainsley into the street as he could have, had worked quickly and compassionately to save her. Only his and Rona's intervention, and John Douglas's kindness, had kept the world from discovering her shame. Patrick, Rona, and John had covered up what Ainsley had done, and Ainsley owed them everything.

"My lord . . ."

"My *name* is Cameron."

"Cameron." Ainsley closed her eyes and drew a breath for strength. "I want to. I very much want to be your lover. But I can't." The words dragged out of her, holding all the regret in the world.

"Why the devil not? You live like a servant and dress like a dowd. We'll go to Paris if you're worried about what people will say in London. You'll dress like a queen instead of fetching and carrying for one, and I'll drape you in jewels that will make this little bauble nothing."

A vivid image arose, Ainsley in satin gowns the colors Isabella and Cameron had picked out for her, ropes of diamonds around her neck, rubies glittering in her ears. "Would there be sapphires?" she asked wistfully. "They'd go nicely with all those blue frocks."

Cameron's smile made her limbs weak. "There can be

anything you want. A new gown every day, jewelry to go with it. A fine carriage for you to ride in, pulled by the best horses. I know a man in France who breeds the most amazing carriage horses. You could pick out the ones you liked."

Of course, he'd give Ainsley the best horses. Horses were to him what diamonds were to most women. Precious, beautiful, worth seeking the best.

"You have fire in you, Ainsley Douglas. Let it out with me."

She wanted to. She could have *this*, Cameron's strong arms around her, the man in him awakening the woman in her. She'd never experienced anyone like him—a virile male who could arouse her simply by whispering her name.

"Please, don't tempt me like this," she said.

"I want to tempt you. I want you with every ounce of strength I have, and damn the scandal. Isabella is right—it's past time you threw off your widow's weeds and enjoyed your life."

"It's not the scandal I'm afraid of." Ainsley drew a breath, her chest aching. "Believe me, were I alone in the world, I'd tell scandal to go hang and do as I pleased." She'd realized a long time ago, however, that it wasn't the scandal that was important, but the people she hurt with the scandal.

Raw pain flickered in Cameron's eyes, an old hurt that had never gone away. "At least tell me you'll think about it. Spend the winter with me in Paris. Promise me you will, Ainsley."

Ainsley bit her lip so she wouldn't blurt out the word, *Yes!* She could take what he offered and wring every bit of enjoyment from it before it was over. He'd move on, but she'd have that brief time to remember.

Cameron stilled, reading refusal in her silence, and what she saw in his gaze nearly undid her. Loneliness, years upon years of it, locked away behind the façade of a libertine. Cameron's rakehell reputation hid a man broken and numbed long ago, a man seeking physical pleasure because he knew he'd obtain nothing else from life.

An offer like this from any other man might have angered and insulted Ainsley, but her eyes welled with sudden tears as Cameron lifted himself away from her.

"Do up your frock," he said curtly. "The scavengers will be along."

Ainsley reached for the buttons. "Cameron, I'm sorry."

"Don't be sorry. If you don't want to, you don't."

To her surprise, she realized she'd hurt him. For her, the decision was whether or not to break her brother's heart all over again, but Cameron must see only a woman not wanting to be with him.

She touched his sleeve. "My hesitation has nothing to do with you, Cam. Of not liking you, I mean. I like you very well, and I'm sorry that I constantly make you angry. Regardless of all this, I hope that we can continue as friends."

"Friends?" With breathless suddenness, Ainsley found herself caged against the billiards table again. "I don't want to be *friends* with you, Ainsley Douglas. I want to be your lover. I want to bury myself inside you, I want to find out whether you taste as good all the way down, I want to feel you squeezing me, and I want to hear your cries as you take me inside you."

Oh, yes, that would be . . . yes, quite wonderful. *I want to be your lover too, Cameron. I want it with everything I have.*

"Being friends with you will never, ever satisfy me," Cameron finished.

"Me either, quite frankly."

"Then why the hell did you offer it?"

Ainsley gave a little shrug. "Better than nothing?"

Cameron growled. He hauled her into strong arms that would never let anything bad happen to her and crushed a brief, hard kiss to her lips.

"Ainsley, what am I going to do with you?"

"Let me borrow five hundred guineas?"

"The devil." Cameron let her go. "I'll give you the money, but if you go on insisting on drawing up a loan document, understand that I'll have nothing more to do with it. Has Phyllida fetched the letters?"

"She'll have them tomorrow, she says."

Cameron only nodded. "Good. Then you take them from her and be done. If she tries to cheat you or asks for more money, tell me, and then Phyllida will deal with me." His smile was vicious. "She doesn't want to have to deal with me."

The finality in his voice told Ainsley that Phyllida wouldn't win that fight. "Thank you for your help, Cameron. I mean that."

"And I mean it when I say I want you. I intend to finish what is between us. Whether you wish to make it a longer affair is up to you. Now, do up your frock."

Ainsley started buttoning. The blasted man had been in such a hurry to *un*button her, but when it came time to tidy up, he turned away, finished. So like a male.

Her fingers brushed the diamonds as she buttoned. "What about the necklace?"

"Keep it. Sell it. Hell, I don't care what you do with it. Just don't give it to Mrs. Chase for those damnable letters."

Cameron spoke carelessly, but Ainsley saw him preparing for the hurt of having Ainsley give him back the diamonds. Would he return them to the jeweler, or throw them into a drawer and wait to give them to the next lady on his list?

Fat chance. *These diamonds are* mine. *Hard luck on those other ladies.*

"I wouldn't dream of letting Mrs. Chase get her bony hands on my necklace." Ainsley threaded her fingers through the strand and lifted the diamonds to her lips. "Thank you, Cameron. I will treasure this."

The next night, Ainsley, wearing a large white wig of an eighteenth-century lady, face hidden by a gold paper mask, squashed uncomfortably in a carriage between the cushioned wall and Phyllida Chase, who must be wearing half a bottle of perfume.

Ainsley had enjoyed fancy-dress balls in her youth, inventing costumes that won her praise from her amused family and friends. She'd been everything from a china doll to a dragon—for the dragon she'd worn a papier-mâché dragon's head she'd made herself, and let her little brother Steven chase her around the house with a sword.

For this fancy dress party, Ainsley wanted anonymity. If anyone happened to witness the exchange of money for letters, Ainsley wanted no one to recognize her. Neither Isabella nor Beth would be attending, which made her task a bit easier. Lord Cameron wouldn't be there either, as far as she knew, for which she breathed a sigh of relief.

She hadn't seen anything of Cameron today, but that afternoon, Angelo had approached her in a deserted hall and quietly pressed money into her palm. Funny that most people didn't trust the Roma, yet Cameron was perfectly sanguine to let one carry fifteen hundred guineas to Ainsley.

Fifteen hundred. Apparently, Phyllida had persuaded Cameron to give her that much. The annoying woman had been playing both sides up the middle.

However, the sum might keep Phyllida from reneging on the bargain, so Ainsley didn't argue. She'd tried to explain to Angelo that the queen was providing the first five hundred, and so Cameron had to relinquish only a thousand, but Angelo had walked away, uninterested.

Morag, sworn to secrecy, had helped with Ainsley's costume. They'd made panniers out of cushions that Morag strapped to Ainsley's waist, which spread the flowing skirt Morag had found in the attics. The skirts were bright red—yards and yards of red velvet that swished as Ainsley walked. She felt a frisson of enjoyment wearing the costume, even if the brocade bodice was very tight and wig itched a bit.

Phyllida had insisted Ainsley ride to the party in her sumptuous carriage with a few English ladies and gentlemen Ainsley had seen at Hart's house party but didn't know. They'd blithely ignored Ainsley all week and didn't seem to recognize her now.

Six of them crammed into the carriage, the woman with Phyllida dressed as a shepherdess, complete with long crook, and the three gentlemen opposite dressed as a cardinal, a sheik, and a Spanish matador. Phyllida had chosen the costume of an Egyptian princess—or what she must imagine an Egyptian princess to be—all shimmering silks and thick gold jewelry and a black wig. She radiated sensuality, and from what Ainsley could feel from being stuck against Phyllida's side, Phyllida had left off her corset.

Phyllida and the shepherdess laughed and flirted with the gentlemen without compunction as they rolled along the country road. Innuendos about *staffs* and *goads* were tossed thickly about. One gentleman decided that he was a naughty sheep that needed to be chastised, and he and the other two gentlemen baa-ed the rest of the way to Rowlindson's mansion. Ainsley was never happier to climb down from a carriage in her life.

When Phyllida descended, Ainsley pulled her aside. "Can we not make the exchange now?" The banknotes were heavy inside Ainsley's corset, and the sooner she retrieved the letters, the better. Then she could go home, pull off the absurd wig, and turn her mind to other matters, like Lord Cameron's most wicked offer.

"No, indeed, darling." Phyllida laughed in real pleasure, more animated than Ainsley had ever seen her. "I'm here to enjoy myself. And you look divine. Come and meet our host."

Phyllida's fingers curled into Ainsley's arm as she marched Ainsley up the long staircase in the open hall. Lord Rowlindson, an Englishman who, according to Isabella, had purchased his estate from an impoverished Highlander and remodeled it, waited at the top. He was tall and dark haired with brown eyes, an ordinary face, and a friendly smile. The guests seemed to like him, and even the shepherdess and her new flock behaved decorously when they greeted him.

"Mrs. Chase, how delightful." Rowlindson pressed Phyllida's hand and smiled with genuine warmth. "Thank you for gracing my humble establishment. And for bringing this lovely young lady with you." He gave Ainsley a wide smile.

"Yes, she and I are great chums," Phyllida said. "This is Mrs. . . . um . . ."

"Gisele," Ainsley broke in and held out her hand. "Tonight, I am Gisele." She tried to make her voice throaty, her accent French, but it came out scratchy and wrong.

"*Bienvenue*, Gisele." Rowlindson took her hand, bowed, and pressed a light kiss to the back of it.

"*Merci*, monsieur." Ainsley gave him a little curtsey. He was courteous at least, and his smile wasn't lascivious. Just friendly with a twinkle of amusement.

Rowlindson turned to greet the next set of guests, and Ainsley followed Phyllida into the cathedral-like drawing room, complete with gothic arches and packed with people. Phyllida sashayed in, waving at female friends, cooing at male.

The guests talked in shrill voices, the noise grating on Ainsley's ears. Perfume and body heat were dense. Phyllida slid through the crowd like an eel through water, leaving Ainsley with her wide panniers straggling behind.

Phyllida had said she wanted to make the exchange in the conservatory. That would be a peaceful room filled with potted plants and places to sit. Cool solitude. There Ainsley could wait quietly, far from innuendo about sheep. Heaven.

Ainsley turned to leave the drawing room, but more guests surged in from the hall, carrying Ainsley with them like the tide. She was buffeted about, and felt more than one hand on her bosom, before she erupted into a relatively empty corner by a window. The window was open, mercifully, and Ainsley dragged in breath after breath of damp but refreshing Scottish air.

Movement in a nearby embrasure caught her eye, and she saw a man and a woman entwined there. The woman's costume plunged in a V almost to her navel, and the gentleman had his face in her bosom. The lady in turn firmly rubbed the man's crotch.

Ainsley swung away, only to find the sheik from the carriage on a circular divan around a pillar, a lady on either side of him. The ladies' hands roved under his bed sheet, and all three were giggling.

Oh, dear.

Ainsley understood now why Beth and Isabella hadn't mentioned the party. Ainsley had thought them simply too busy with Hart's do, but in truth, they were too respectable to be added to Lord Rowlindson's guest list.

Some of the people here had come over from Hart's house party, but most Ainsley didn't recognize. Many ladies wore costumes like Phyllida's: loose, uncorseted, scandalously low cut. Another lady had come in eighteenth-century dress, but her décolletage dove so far downward that the pink brown of her nipples showed.

Drat Phyllida. It was just like her to decide to make the exchange at an orgiastic gathering. If Ainsley made a fuss, perhaps refusing to pay her or trying to steal the letters, Phyllida could expose Ainsley to all and sundry. What a scandal. Mrs. Douglas, the prim little widow, one of the queen's favorites, at an orgy.

"*Cherie*." A man and a woman stopped in front of Ainsley, *both* of them looking her up and down. "Perhaps you'd like to walk with us?"

Ainsley's face flamed. "No. That is, no, thank you. Excuse me."

She lifted her too-long skirts and scurried past them. The conservatory. Now.

Ainsley wormed her way through the crowd, ignoring the evil looks of those she shoved with her panniers. She finally popped out of the drawing room to the relative calm of the upper hall, and tried to catch her breath as she made for the stairs.

Lord Rowlindson, shaking hands with new arrivals, saw her and sent her a smile. Was the smile now sinister? Ainsley couldn't decide. Rowlindson still looked like a benevolent host, concerned only that his guests have a good time.

She thought it prudent not to ask Lord Rowlindson for directions to the conservatory, and started on the journey to find it herself. Conservatories, modern additions to older houses, would be on the ground floor, probably at the end of a wing. Ainsley clutched the cool iron balustrade and started pattering down the stairs.

A strong hand jerked her to a halt. She stifled a shriek as she was pulled around and found herself looking into the unmasked, enraged face of Lord Cameron Mackenzie.

Chapter 12

"Bloody hell, Phyllida told ye to meet her *here*?"

When Angelo had reported that Phyllida had taken Ainsley to *Rowlindson's*, Cameron's rage could have burned down the house. Rowlindson, a fellow collector of erotica, had perversions that would fill volumes. The man enjoyed gathering the most scandalous people in the country to his house, mixing them with courtesans both male and female, and standing back to watch what happened.

Watch was the key word, because Rowlindson lived to observe the act, especially when it involved three or more people. He also liked to take photographs. It was quite a hobby for him, and he had a large collection of photos, which he was always offering to show Cameron.

The fact that Phyllida Chase had dared bring Ainsley here made him sick. She'd done it to take revenge on Cameron—not for Cameron breaking off his affair with Phyllida, but for Cam siding with Ainsley about the letters.

Phyllida might have promised Rowlindson access to Ainsley in return for letting Phyllida bring her.

If Rowlindson touched Ainsley, or more likely, let her be touched by others while he photographed the event, Cameron would kill him. Cameron might kill Rowlindson for even contemplating the matter.

Ainsley looked more or less intact as she gaped up at him, delectable in her frowzy wig and mask. She'd disguised herself well, but Cameron would have known those gray eyes anywhere.

Cameron pulled her the rest of the way down the stairs, along a hallway, and into an anteroom. Thankfully the little jewel box of a chamber was empty. Cam closed the door and locked it behind him.

"What are you doing?" Ainsley jabbered. "I need to meet Phyllida in the conservatory."

"Dear God, Ainsley, what the devil possessed ye to meet her *here*?"

He was so angry, his eyes so fierce. In the billiards room at Kilmorgan, Cameron had looked at her with such longing, and now his rage was strong, all sensuality forgotten.

"I didn't know it would be this sort of fancy-dress party, did I?" Ainsley said. "I never knew people truly did this sort of thing."

"They do. Rowlindson's masquerades are famous."

"Well, they're not famous in my corner of the world. I wondered why Phyllida wanted to meet here, but I assumed she worried that I wouldn't pay her if she didn't take me somewhere by ourselves. She is a treacherous snake."

"Which is why you're going back home."

"Not until I get those letters. Besides, it's not my home. It's yours. I don't have a home."

The last words came out more pathetically than Ainsley had intended. She heard the ring of sorrow and tried to mask it, but too late.

She turned from Cameron, wide skirts nearly knocking over a delicate little table with a gilt clock on top. Rowlindson had some fine pieces and good taste, incongruous with his friends and entertainment.

Cameron's arms slid around her before she'd gone two steps. No bustle kept him at a distance tonight; his warm kilt pressed her backside through her skirts.

"You're always welcome in my home, Ainsley."

He'd melt her. She couldn't meet Phyllida and get the letters if she were a puddle on the floor.

Cameron pulled back a curl of the wig and kissed her neck. "I have a house in Berkshire where I train the horses in the spring. I want to show it to you."

"Sounds lovely."

"Muddy and cold. Flat. Full of sheep."

"Gracious, I've had enough of sheep tonight."

"What?"

"Never mind," Ainsley said. "I'm sure your horses love it."

"They do."

Cameron continued kissing her skin, seducing her into compliance, the wretch. She turned, her panniers pressing him away. "I'd love to see it."

Ainsley had no idea when she'd ever have the chance, but she wanted to learn about every part of Cameron's life. He spent winters on the Continent, Isabella had told her—Paris, Rome, Monaco—before rejoining his trainers in Berkshire as soon as the coldest part of winter had finished. In Berkshire Cameron spent all his waking hours with his horses, readying them for the start of the flat racing season in Newmarket.

It sounded fine to Ainsley, a routine of his own making, a life with a purpose. So why, when she looked at him, did she see longing, an emptiness unfulfilled?

Cameron's eyes darkened as he cupped her face. "I want you," he whispered. "Ainsley, damn you, I want you so much."

"I want you too, truth to tell."

The look in his eyes was one of desperation, and Ainsley hurt with longing. But the little clock on the table was marching on to the appointed hour.

"There is no time," she whispered. Would there ever be?

Cameron sat down on one of the tiny chairs and lifted Ainsley to his lap. The stupid wig got in his way, but he pushed it aside and kissed her.

She tasted so damned good. She arched up to him willingly, her need as hot as his own. Her bodice was nicely low, allowing Cameron to cup the bosom that overflowed her corset.

He wanted her unfettered. He wanted to close his mouth over her breast, to taste and suckle her. Cameron had wanted that, he realized, for more than six years, and not only because she'd confounded him that long-ago night. He wanted *her*, Ainsley, the beautiful, brave woman.

He'd have this damned costume open before the night was over and finally learn the taste of her. Cameron slid a hand to her hip, finding whatever padding she'd used to plump out the skirt.

"I want this off."

"It will be a great relief to me too," Ainsley said as she kissed him.

"It will come off. All of it. I want you bare for me, Ainsley."

She gave him a little smile. "And I want to see what you wear under your kilt." Ainsley wriggled her hips, which stroked his cock.

"Little devil."

"I'm not an innocent debutante. I've heard much about Mackenzies and their kilts."

"I like you not being an innocent debutante." He kissed her lips again. "I'm going to thoroughly debauch you."

"Oh, heavens." She smiled and tapped her fist to his chest. "Oh no, you wicked thing, you mustn't."

Cameron nipped her mouth. "Vixen." *A man could fall in love with you.*

That troubling thought was broken by the chime of the little gilt clock next to them. Cameron wanted to throw it across the room.

Ainsley struggled up, her smile gone. "I have to go."

Cameron deserted the chair and pressed her back into it. "You will stay in this room. I'll make the exchange."

Ainsley popped off the chair. "Don't be daft. It has to be me. Phyllida's instructions were very clear. 'Only you, Mrs. Douglas, not Lord Cameron,' she said."

Cameron sat her back down again. "I'll get those damned letters, every single page of them. You're right that Phyllida Chase is a viper. She'll try to cheat you. She doesn't trust me, but she knows she can't cheat me."

He saw thoughts dancing through her gray eyes, Ainsley calculating the risks. "We should go together," she said.

"I'm not letting you out of this room, not at one of Rowlindson's blasted soirees. He's a bad man, Ainsley."

Ainsley slanted him a smile that made his blood hot. "But that's what everyone says about you, Lord Cameron."

Cameron smiled right back at her. "I *am* a bad man, very bad, but in a different way. I want to ravish you until we're both senseless with it, and then I want to do it all over again."

She flushed at his candor, but she didn't flutter and faint. Not Ainsley.

"I know you're right about Phyllida, but the letters . . ." She looked unhappy. "You must promise me you won't look at them but bring them straight back to me."

"I have no interest in the letters." Cameron leaned over her, stroking his gaze to the shadow between her breasts. "Is that where you're hiding the money?"

Ainsley reached deep into the corset and dragged out the wad of banknotes. "That's all of it."

Cameron took the notes, warm from her body, lucky things. "I didn't expect they would get lost down there." He pressed a brief kiss to her mouth and straightened up. "Stay *here*. I'll return with the letters, and we'll go home in my carriage."

Ainsley nodded again. She looked delectable, edible even, in that oversized wig, her gray eyes sultry through the mask. She looked like the best of harlots, half innocent, half seductive, the sort of woman in high demand in upper-class brothels.

The sort of woman Rowlindson best liked to photograph being pawed over by one or two brutes of males. Ainsley might declare she wasn't an innocent, but she had no idea about the things Rowlindson and his friends could get up to.

The beast in Cameron awoke, the violent, dangerous thing Cameron tried with alcohol, women, and horseracing to keep at bay. But tonight the beast found a place to direct its anger, and Cameron smiled. He'd had seen the look in Rowlindson's eyes when the man had watched Ainsley descend the stairs. Cameron could enjoy himself breaking Rowlindson's neck, and maybe Phyllida's. *After* Cameron retrieved the blasted letters.

"Wait." Ainsley bounced out of the chair. She jerked Cameron's handkerchief from his pocket and started dabbing at his lips. "You have lip color on your face."

Cameron gave her a hot smile. "I want to see it all over my body."

Ainsley blushed. Beautiful, beautiful Ainsley.

Cameron kissed her again then took the handkerchief and wiped the rest of the scarlet paint from his mouth as he made himself turn from her and leave the room.

When the door clicked shut, Ainsley blew out her breath and collapsed back into the fragile chair.

Any other woman watching a gentleman who interested her going off to meet his former lover might be apprehensive, but Ainsley felt only relief. If anyone could make certain Phyllida handed over the letters, it would be Cameron Mackenzie. He wasn't a subtle man—he'd get the letters whether Phyllida wanted to give them up or not.

Ainsley was warm all over, warmer than she'd been in a long while. And excited and worried and just a little bit scared about what she intended to do.

Even before Cameron had started kissing her in this little room, Ainsley had decided she'd allow herself one night with him before she returned to Balmoral. One glorious night of being Lord Cameron Mackenzie's lover, and then she'd retreat and become plain Ainsley Douglas again, dutiful sister and reliable confidante of the queen.

She was older and wiser and far more knowledgeable than when she'd been fresh out of finishing school, she reasoned. She'd go into the liaison, as Phyllida had said she had, with eyes wide open. Ainsley would be cautious but, for one night, she'd be happy in Cameron's arms, and treasure the romance of it for the rest of her life.

First, she had to wait for Cameron to return the with letters. Ainsley sweated as the clock wound to one fifteen—marked with a little chime—then on to one twenty. At one thirty, she gave up and jumped from the chair, but before she could start for the door, it opened to admit Lord Rowlindson.

He's a bad man, Ainsley, Cameron had said with quiet certainty. What did it say about a gentleman when someone like Cameron, black sheep of the notorious Mackenzie family, derided him?

Lord Rowlindson didn't look very dangerous at the moment. He stood with his hand on the door handle and sent Ainsley a look of concern. "Gisele, is it? Is everything all right?"

Ainsley plopped down in the chair again, fanning her face with her hand. "The crowd was rather overwhelming. I decided it a good idea to sit quietly."

"I thought I saw Lord Cameron leaving this room."

"You did." Ainsley looked him straight in the eye. "He was showing me where I could sit quietly."

Lord Rowlindson's expression turned worried. He came all the way into the room and closed the door.

"Gisele, I must give you this advice for your own good. Beware of Cameron Mackenzie. He might be charm itself when he needs to be, but he's not to be trusted. In truth, he's a hard and ruthless man. He uses his ladies until they are desperate for what he gives them, and then he discards them. I would hate to see that happen to you."

A little chill went through her. "I appreciate your concern, my lord. I truly do. But I will be well." *Now, do, please, go away.*

He didn't. "Forgive my prying. It's simply that I don't wish to see someone as young as yourself hurt. Please, stay and enjoy my soiree. Or, if you do not like crowds, we can adjourn to my private study. I have a friend, he's quite a gentleman, and very discreet, who might join us—or not, as you wish. Do you enjoy photography?"

What had that to do with anything? "I really don't know much about it, except to have my portrait done. But that was a long time ago." After her wedding, in hastily sewn wedding attire, standing next to John Douglas. Ainsley had not worn the wedding finery to the brief ceremony; there hadn't been time.

"It's rather a hobby of mine," Rowlindson said. "I'd enjoy teaching you about it."

Ainsley still wasn't certain Rowlindson was dangerous, but he was decidedly odd. "Perhaps another time."

"I always show new guests my pictures—rather a treat for me. And then I could take a photograph of you."

Definitely odd. "No, thank you, my lord. I will be returning home directly."

Rowlindson let out a breath. "If you must. My carriage is at your disposal. Shall I fetch it?"

"No, no." Ainsley fanned herself again. "I've made other arrangements. I'll sit until the servant fetches me."

Rowlindson watched her for a moment, then, to her vast relief, gave her a nod. "A wise idea. But if you need help, or my carriage to get you home, you must send for me immediately. Promise?"

"Oh, yes, my lord. I will. You are so kind." *For heaven's sake, go!*

"And heed my advice about Lord Cameron. No matter how he might tempt you."

Rather too late for that. "Yes, indeed. I thank you for your warning."

Rowlindson's mouth softened into a smile. "Perhaps you and I can speak on a later occasion. May I send you word, through Mrs. Chase?"

"I'm not sure that would be proper," Ainsley said, trying to sound prim.

Her worry about propriety seemed to delight him. "I will be most discreet. Good evening, Gisele."

Rowlindson gave her a final nod, opened the door, and at long last, left her alone.

Ainsley made herself wait an excruciating ten minutes, giving Rowlindson time to get himself back upstairs, before she slipped out of her costume's clunky shoes and crept out of the room in her stocking feet.

Phyllida was late, as usual. Cameron waited in the shadows, and sure enough, not until half past one did Phyllida casually stroll into the conservatory. She was dressed as her idea of an Egyptian queen: long, straight sheath that showed off every curve of her body, eyes painted black, gold jewelry dripping from her arms, neck, ankles, and ears.

She paused on the walkway, looking around for Ainsley. Cameron stepped from behind the screen of vines. "Phyllida."

She gasped in a satisfying way, then she flushed. "Devil

take it, Cam, what do *you* want? I told you I'd only make the exchange with Mrs. Douglas."

Cameron slid the roll of money from his pocket, and Phyllida's gaze turned sharp with greed.

"Is it fifteen hundred?" she asked. "As promised?"

"As promised. You give me the letters and never bother Ainsley again."

Her painted eyes went wide with delight. "You call her by her Christian name now, do you? How quickly things progress."

"Do you have the damned letters or don't you?"

"This is delicious. Mousy Ainsley Douglas and the decadent Lord Cameron Mackenzie. How the *ton* will delight."

Cameron felt rage building inside him. "Say one word about her, and I'll throttle you."

"You were always so violent. Did I ever tell you how exciting that was?"

"The letters, Phyllida."

Phyllida's gaze flicked beyond Cameron, and her face lit with genuine pleasure, an expression Cameron had never seen on her before.

"There you are, darling. Please, come and protect me from Lord Cameron's threats. You know what I told you about the Mackenzies."

Cameron turned to see the last person he expected: a tall, black-haired young man with the dusky skin and dark eyes of a southern Italian. Cameron thought he vaguely recognized him from the stage. Opera, perhaps.

"Apologize to the lady," the Italian said. His accent was very slight, his English good. "I know she was your lover, but that is finished now."

"I agree," Cameron said. "It is finished. Phyllida, who the devil is this?"

"None of your business," Phyllida said crisply. "He is here to see that I don't get cheated." She turned back to the Italian. "Darling, did you bring the letters?"

Cameron closed his fist around the money, not about to let Phyllida take it until she gave over the precious documents. The Italian reached into his pocket and brought out a stack of folded papers.

"Is that all of them?" Cameron eyed them. "Ainsley said there were six."

"It is all." The man held them out at arm's length. "You can trust the signora to deal fairly."

Fairly? Phyllida? Either the man was a good liar, or Phyllida had well and truly beguiled him.

Cameron reached for the letters. The Italian held them back. "You give her the payment, first."

Like hell. "Let's do this at the same time, shall we?"

The man gave a cool nod. He held out the letters again, and Cameron let the wad of money dangle from his fingers. Phyllida snatched the cash, and Cameron took the letters from the Italian man's grasp.

Phyllida ran her thumb over the corner of the banknotes. "Thank you, Cameron. I hope I never see you again."

Cameron unfolded the first letter. "Wait," he said sternly. "Neither of you are leaving until I know that I have them all."

"I've told you . . ."

The Italian held up his hand. "No. Let him look. The treacherous always must believe that others play treachery against them."

Definitely opera. The man's speeches came straight from them. Cameron seated himself on a scrolled iron bench and scanned the first page.

"You're not going to read *all* of them, are you?" Phyllida said in exasperation.

Cameron didn't answer. He would damn well read every word of them to make sure he had the letters in their entirety, no pages missing with which Phyllida could blackmail Ainsley later. Cam hadn't lied to Ainsley when he'd said he had no interest in the letters, but he'd never promised he wouldn't actually read them. He needed to, for her own good.

They were love letters without doubt. The lady addressed them to "My most beloved Friend," and then the paper flowed with overblown adjectives and flowery phrases that sang of this friend's manly physique, his prowess, his stamina.

In spite of this, Cameron could see that the writer had an excellent grasp of vocabulary and poetry, if in an overly sentimental style. The first letter eased from this poesy into a breezy, newsy epistle and then back out again to the flowery phrases. She'd signed it, "Ever your loving, Mrs. Brown."

Mrs. Brown.

Oh, bloody hell.

Cameron opened the second letter and found it to be much like the first, noting the writer's references in the middle of the letter to "trying children" and other such domestic issues. But these were the domestic issues of a palace, the trying children princes and princesses of this realm and rulers of others.

He finally understood Ainsley's secretiveness and furtive concern. The nameless friend she'd been trying so desperately to protect was the Queen of England.

"It's scandalous, isn't it?" Phyllida said when he folded the last one. "She ought to be ashamed of herself."

"Did you make any copies of these?" Cameron asked her. What a weapon Phyllida could have made of them, and yet she'd demanded, in retrospect, so little. Something was off.

"Why should I?" Phyllida shrugged. "I'm not interested in the queen's rather pathetic fantasies."

Cameron rose and stuffed the letters into his pocket. "These letters could utterly humiliate the queen, and you're ransoming them to me for fifteen hundred guineas?"

"Very generous of you too. Enough for a start, I think."

"A start of what?"

Phyllida laughed, and for the first time since he'd met her, Cameron saw the hardness depart from her. "To leave my husband, of course." She slid her hand through the crook of the Italian's arm. "Thank you, Giorgio. Shall we?"

Giorgio. Now Cameron recognized him. He was Giorgio Prario, a tenor who had recently taken London by storm. Isabella had hosted a soiree to help launch his career, one of those little gatherings that Isabella loved and Cameron avoided like the plague.

Prario regarded Cameron with deep brown eyes and a proud tilt to his head before he drew Phyllida away. Phyllida had her claws into him all right, poor sod.

Cameron watched them walk away, Phyllida swaying into the body of the large man. Phyllida Chase, who loved her comfort and social position above everything else, was ready to throw it all away to run off with a young opera singer. The world was becoming a strange place.

Still more bizarrely, Cameron was becoming more and more entangled with the young lady in red who crashed through the palm fronds next to him, breathless and pink-faced.

"Did you get them?" she asked.

Chapter 13

Cameron's eyes betrayed his anger, but he didn't growl at Ainsley for not waiting in the anteroom. He must have known that she would never be that patient.

Ainsley held out her hand for the letters, but Cameron didn't give them to her. "I'll keep them for now. I don't trust Phyllida not to waylay you and try to steal them back."

Ainsley kept her hand out for a moment, her fingers itching to feel the letters in them. "My friend will be most grateful for what you're done."

"Your friend, Mrs. Brown? Dear God, Ainsley."

Ainsley lowered her arm, eyes wide. "I asked you not to read them. I remember distinctly."

"I did it to make certain Phyllida wasn't holding anything back. I've got them all, even the one with the missing page."

He was so tall and solid. And angry. "Cameron, for heaven's sake, please don't tell your brother. Hart Mackenzie is notorious for opposing the queen's policies. I can't think what he'd do with letters like these."

"Probably toss them onto the fire."

Ainsley blinked. "What? But he could embarrass her, sway people's opinion of her, turn those on the fence to his side."

"If you think that, you have a wrong view of Hart." Cameron closed his warm hand over her cold one. "Hart wants to win by proving he's right—about everything—not with tittle-tattle and bedroom gossip. Hart wants to be God Almighty. No, he already thinks he's God Almighty. Now he wants to prove it to everyone else."

Ainsley ran her thumb over Cameron's fingers, which were calloused and rough from his days working with horses. These weren't the well-kept hands of a gentleman who lifted nothing heavier than cards or a glass of brandy. Cameron worked alongside the other men in the stables, doing whatever jobs had to be done.

She kissed one broad, blunt finger. "Please," she said. "Don't tell him. Just in case."

"I don't intend to. This is none of Hart's bloody business."

His eyes sparkled with heat, and Ainsley lifted herself on tiptoe and kissed the corner of his mouth. "Thank you."

Cameron scooped her up to him and caught her mouth with his in a full kiss. As she kissed him back, Ainsley wormed her hand inside Cameron's coat and touched the letters in his pocket.

Strong fingers clamped her wrist. "Devil."

Ainsley reluctantly let go. "When do I get them back?"

"When you leave Kilmorgan. I'll hand them to you when you get into your carriage." Cameron closed his arms around her. "Now, stop playing. I'm kissing you."

He was in a playful mood himself, she thought. He nipped and kissed her lips, and she nipped and kissed back, but when she looked into his eyes, she saw stark need. No playfulness at all.

She drew a breath, steeling herself for what she'd decided. "I want to spend tonight with you," she said.

Heat flared in his eyes. "I hope so.

How could he sound so casual? "But not, I think, *here*."

"Good God, no. We'll go somewhere far more comfortable and far less sickening."

She tried to match his light tone. "I thought you said comfort was the last consideration."

"Minx. I meant I want *you* to be comfortable."

"While you thoroughly debauch me?"

"Damn you, don't look at me like that. Or I won't be able to stop myself, no matter where we are."

Ainsley's heart beat faster. Why did such declarations excite her?

Cameron brushed another kiss to her lips. "Walk out with me, and I'll hunt down my carriage. I don't want you out of my sight."

Ainsley didn't much want to move from his sight either. Not in this house. "My shoes are in the anteroom." She wondered whether they could rush back and fetch them without encountering Rowlindson or anyone else, but her thoughts cut off when Cameron swept her up into his arms.

Cameron's strength took her breath away. He didn't waver under her weight and the drag of her skirts, cushions and all, as he strode for the door at the end of the conservatory and out into darkness. The night was cold, but Ainsley would never be cold tucked up against Cameron.

"You've done so much for me," she said, touching his face. "I'm not sure how I can—"

"If you start talking about repayment, I will drop you in the bushes." His breath fogged in the chill. "I don't want the money back, or your gratitude, or payment with your body."

"If you won't even accept gratitude, then what *do* you want?"

His voice lost all humor. "What I can't have."

Ainsley started to quip that surely a Mackenzie could have anything he wanted, but something in his face made her stop. Ainsley had lived in the queen's houses long enough to know that money and position were no guarantee of happiness. They made life more comfortable and less desperate, but there could still be grief, anger, emptiness.

"I want to do *something*," Ainsley said. "I am obliged to you—" She broke off and squealed as Cameron pivoted and strode straight for a line of rhododendrons. "Very well, very well. I will do nothing."

Cameron lowered her to her feet on a patch of grass. "The business with the letters is concluded. I don't want it between us."

"No, I see that." Ainsley didn't want it between them either. "But you can't stop me from being grateful. Thank you for your help, Cam."

She half feared he would make good his threat and drag her to the nearest clump of bushes, but Cameron only cupped her face with a gentle hand.

He hadn't had to help her. He could have demanded the price Phyllida had said he would before he'd even lend Ainsley the money. But he'd fought this battle for her, and now he'd turned back to what was between them.

Cameron's coachman must have been alert, because a carriage circled the drive not far away, its coach lights bright. Cameron picked up Ainsley again and made for it.

Stars were out in profusion, the night dry and cold. "I miss this sky when I'm in London," Ainsley said. "It's breathtaking."

"It's bloody freezing."

"I notice most Scotsmen complain about the weather while we're surrounded by beauty."

"Right now, I'd rather be surrounded by warmth."

They reached the carriage. A footman materialized out of the dark as the carriage rolled to a halt and opened its door.

"In you go." Cameron lifted Ainsley inside, where she sank onto comfortable cushions.

Cameron dropped a tip into the footman's hand, glanced up at his coachman, and made a circling motion with his finger. "Right ye are, sir," the coachman said cheerfully.

Cameron folded the steps and pulled himself into the carriage as it jerked forward. He slammed the door and dropped onto the seat next to Ainsley, smelling of the night and the good scents of the outdoors.

Without a word Cameron pulled off her wig and mask and tossed both to the opposite seat. Cool air touched Ainsley's face, and her head felt suddenly light.

"That's better," Cameron said. "My little mouse is back."

"Hardly flattering to call a woman a mouse, you know." She knew she was babbling, nervous, but she couldn't still her tongue.

"You hide behind my curtains and scuttle around my rooms. What else should I call you?"

"You said *ferret*, once. But you wouldn't give a diamond necklace to a mouse or a ferret. Well, not unless you were very silly. They'd try to eat it or use it to line their nests."

"I don't give a damn what you use the diamonds for." Cameron slid his arm around her shoulders and kissed the top of her head. "As long as you like them."

"I do. They're lovely."

"No more talk about giving them back or not accepting them?"

"I wouldn't accept them from any other gentleman, no," she said in a decided voice. "But for you, I will make an exception."

"You'd damn well better not accept them from any other gentleman. Any other man tries to give you jewelry, and I'll pummel him. Right after I pummel Rowlindson for letting you come here tonight."

She shivered. "He *is* rather strange."

"He's disgusting. He understands only crudity. Not beauty."

Ainsley touched the velvet wall of the coach. "This is a very comfortable carriage. Quite large and warm."

"I travel a lot during the horse season. I like a big traveling coach, especially if I have to sleep in it."

"You could take trains, surely. Even with the horses."

"The horses don't like the train, and the coal smoke is bad for their lungs."

He sounded like a worried father. "You are very kind to your horses."

Cameron shrugged. "They're expensive animals, and they give me all they have. Idiots ruin them by not taking care of them."

"You take good care of Jasmine, even though she's not yours."

"Because she's a damn fine horse."

His voice held longing. "You truly want her, don't you?" Ainsley asked.

"Yes." Cameron's fingers under her chin tilted her head back. "And I truly want you."

"I hope not for the same reason. I don't gallop very fast."

"You have a lot of the devil in you, Ainsley."

"So I'm told—"

Cameron silenced her words with a kiss.

Soft lips, trembling and nervous, but determined at the same time. Cameron tasted her need to be held and touched, her laughter. He'd never, ever met a woman like her.

His heart beat faster, his body beginning to perspire in the coach's heat. Whenever he seduced a woman, Cameron was calm and cool, knowing the steps it took to reach the brief part of coupling that brought him alive. The spark lasted only a short while, but it was heady when he got there.

He always made sure the ladies enjoyed great pleasure, his gift to them for releasing him from numbness. He reflected that the women often had a much better time with the whole thing than he did.

Tonight he was impatient, clumsy with need. He tugged at the waistband of Ainsley's skirt. "I want this off."

Pins that held skirt to bodice tinkled to the carpet. When Ainsley reached forward to catch them, Cameron unfastened the clasps on the skirt's back. The velvet folds came away, so many yards of them.

Cameron knelt on the floor in front of her as he pulled away the last of the skirt. Underneath the skirt's smothering fabric he found—sofa pillows. He burst out laughing.

"We didn't have panniers," Ainsley said. She pulled a cushion out from the sash that tied them around her waist. "It was Morag's idea."

Cameron pulled the pillows away and plumped them behind her. "There, now there's your comfort."

He laughed again, the sound of it grating, because Cameron had never had the velvet tones of his brothers. Working in the cold outdoors had broken his baritone long ago.

Ainsley lolled against the old sofa pillows in her white stockings and plain cotton pantalets. Cameron's laughter died away as he put his hand to her bodice. "How many buttons, Mrs. Douglas?"

"They're clasps." Her breath was warm on his face. "I suppose that doesn't sound as enticing."

"I didn't ask you what it sounded like, I asked you how many."

Ainsley's mischievous smile flashed. "All of them, I think."

Cameron was already undoing the clasps until the old-fashioned bodice and stomacher came loose in his hands. Ainsley, being her modest self, wore a small corset under it, and under that, her combinations, its lacy straps on her shoulders.

Cameron ran his hand down the corset. "I want this off too."

"It would be a relief, yes."

Ainsley shivered as Cameron spread the corset's laces, as he had that long-ago day in his bedchamber, his big hand like fire on her back. He lifted the corset away, and there

Ainsley sat, in nothing but her combinations, undressed in front of a man for the first time in years.

And what a man. Cameron knelt in front of her, his big body filling so much space. His coat followed her corset and bodice to the seat behind him, then his waistcoat and cravat. He unbuttoned his shirt, and she beheld him as she had the night she'd crept into his room looking for the letters—the brown of well-muscled chest, kilt hugging narrow hips, Cameron folding back his loose cuffs to bare his arms.

The scars on his thick wrist came into view, those burns that someone had given him long ago, pain deliberately inflicted. Ainsley hated whoever had done that. From her brothers, she knew that young men at school sometimes tortured each other, she supposed to prove how masculine they were. But Cameron didn't seem the type to let bullies shove him down and press lighted cigars to his skin.

Ainsley caught his hand, lifted his wrist, and kissed the burn marks. His skin was smooth, the scars puckered.

He pulled away. "Don't."

"I dislike to see you hurt," she said softly.

Cameron rested his hands on either side of her. "Stop being kind, Ainsley. Not while I'm ravishing you."

Ainsley smiled. "If you'd like me to be *un*kind, I certainly can be."

"I doubt that. What I'd like is for you to wrap your legs around my waist."

"But I'm still wearing my combinations."

"I know, devil woman."

Cameron slid his hands under her thighs, lifted her legs, and eased them around his hips. Ainsley felt him through the fabric of her pantalets, warm wool of the kilt and the hardness beneath it.

"That's my girl." His hands were hot on her legs, moving around to her buttocks while he rocked against her.

Ainsley felt shivery and hot at the same time, nervous

and happy. This was going to happen. She was a wanton courtesan tonight, like her imaginary lady who held salons in Paris and had the most handsome men in France after her. But she didn't want handsome Parisians, she wanted Cameron, her hard, powerful Scotsman.

"Stop laughing," he said against her mouth.

Ainsley cupped his cheek. "Not laughing. Wondering how you plan to ravish me in the close confines of this carriage."

The answering heat in his eyes fired her blood. "I don't know yet. I've never had a lady in this carriage."

"Never?" Ainsley's heart beat faster.

"Never until you, vixen."

"Good."

Cameron slid one hand through her hair, dislodging pins, letting tendrils tumble to her shoulders.

"I love your hair," Cameron said. "I've always wanted to see it down."

"A bit difficult to tame, I've always found."

"I don't want it tame." Cameron fisted a lock of hair, kissed it. "I want it wild. I want *you* wild, Ainsley. I know it's in you." He put his hand between her breasts, right over her heart.

"Wild? Me?" She contrived to look innocent.

"I work with horses all day, every day. I know which ones are happy to plod along and which ones are bursting to throw off their fetters and run free."

"Like Jasmine."

"Exactly like Jasmine. I look at you and see fire, love. You hide it behind drab clothes, and you pretend to be so dutiful, but that fire wants to burst out of you. You're a woman of passion, wanting to run." Cameron's voice softened but was still rough, still deep. "Why not let yourself run?"

"No one wants me to," she said. "No one but you."

Cameron closed both hands over hers. "Reconsider my

offer, Ainsley. Come to Paris with me. I'll take you to Nice, to Monte Carlo, to Rome if you want. I'll dress you in beautiful clothes and put you in a carriage behind the finest horses, and you'll eclipse everyone we see."

Ainsley couldn't stop her happy sigh. "Wouldn't that be grand? Me a sophisticated and glittering lady."

"Say you'll come with me." His smile was sudden and wicked. "Say you will or I'll have my coachman stop, and I'll put you out into a Scottish meadow in your combinations."

"As though such a thing would frighten me, my lord. I'd fly home through woods and dance lightly across bogs, unhampered by my confounded corset and false panniers."

Cameron's laughter filled the carriage. "Ainsley, you have to come with me. Say you will. Promise me."

She touched his face. "Cameron."

"Damn you, don't say no."

Ainsley started to speak, but Cameron put his hand to her lips. "Not now. Don't refuse me now. Think about it. Be on the train from Doncaster to London after the last St. Leger race—I leave from there for the Continent. If you want to go with me, tell me then. Now, stop talking, woman, and let me ravish you."

Chapter 14

He was going to have her, touch her, taste her. Everything he could of her.

Tonight if no other time. He'd do everything he could to persuade her to come away with him, but right now, he was going to enjoy this.

He undid the pretty bow that tied the top of her combinations and slid the lacy fabric from her shoulders. Her breasts came into view, round globes, firm and tight. Not the small breasts of a virgin, but the wonderfully full ones of a woman who'd grown into her body.

Ainsley was as beautiful as Cameron had dreamed. He cupped one breast reverently before he leaned forward and licked it.

He tasted fire, felt her heart beating swiftly. Cameron nuzzled her skin, flicked his tongue to the taut peak of her nipple. She gasped. Cameron touched his tongue to her again, and again, the gasp. Delightful.

"Has no man ever tasted you, Ainsley?"

"No." The word was breathless. "Not like that."

"Fools. You taste good." Cameron licked a circle around the areola. "You're like the best wine, Ainsley, lass."

He suckled her gently, then drew one nipple between his teeth. She reclined on the cushioned seat, eyes half closed, breasts bare in the lamplight, legs spread for him. He hadn't seen so beautiful a sight in a very long time.

Cameron kissed between her breasts, moving his way downward. Her belly was a little soft, a little round, despite the constant cinch of her corset. There were scars here, pink lines on her skin, signs that her abdomen had once been much fuller than this.

He flicked his gaze to her face, and Ainsley stilled. She knew he'd seen and that he understood what he'd seen.

Isabella had never mentioned that Ainsley had borne a child. Where was that child now?

The sorrow in Ainsley's eyes told him. The baby had not survived.

It was a common thing, even in this day and age, for a child to die at birth or shortly thereafter. But that didn't mean every death wasn't mourned, every grief felt. John Douglas had been elderly; perhaps his seed hadn't been strong.

Cameron remembered his conversation at breakfast with Isabella, her story that Ainsley had gone to the Continent and returned a year later, married, to Isabella's surprise. There had been no announcement, not even a letter, simply Ainsley McBride returning as Ainsley Douglas. Interesting.

Not that he'd question her about her secrets right now. They all had them, dark secrets of the soul. The only way to deal with them was to live, and forget.

Cameron feathered kisses along the lines, tracing them with his tongue. He enjoyed himself, tasting her skin, inhaling the salt sweet scent of her. He dipped his tongue into her navel, and she let out a laugh.

She pushed at the open placket of his shirt. "Not fair that I'm the only one undressed. I want to see you."

"No need." Cameron could feast his eyes on Ainsley all night. When it came time to finish, he didn't need to bare his scarred body. He rarely undressed all the way for his ladies.

"There is need. *My* need." Ainsley lolled against the cushions, bare, delectable, erotic. "I have hidden nothing from you, my Cam."

My Cam. Damn her.

My Ainsley.

He could give her some but not all, and the carriage was dark enough. Pressing another kiss to her belly, Cameron knelt back and slid off his shirt.

Ainsley held her breath, her heart beating fast and hard. Her Mackenzie male was large, strong, delectable.

She'd only glimpsed his chest before, and now she saw Cameron in full, a huge man, sculpted with muscle, skin glistening with perspiration. Perfect, except for a thin scar that marred where his collarbone joined his right shoulder. Ainsley traced the scar with her fingers, then leaned forward to kiss it, to lick it.

"Ainsley, you do have fire," he whispered. "I want to feel that fire all around me."

Ainsley kissed his scar one more time, lifted her face, and lightly kissed the scar on his cheek.

Cameron's ensuing kiss was hard, hot, taking. Strong fingers undid the buttons that held her pantalets closed, and the cotton moved down her legs.

Ainsley thought he'd lift her around him there and then, but Cameron pressed her again to the cushions. He parted her legs and bowed over her lap.

And then his mouth. Ainsley jerked as Cameron closed lips and tongue over her most intimate place. Her legs came up, knees bending as her feet rested on the seat. She was open all the way to him, but she felt no shame, only heat and a burning need.

The carriage listed, but Cameron didn't stop. Ainsley furrowed his hair as he went on, his strokes and pulls harder. She hurt for him, she wanted him, and the friction of his tongue was glorious, glorious. His mouth was hot, tongue skilled and swift, the burn of his whiskers on her thighs wicked.

She was coming apart, the noises she made muffled by the cushioned walls. Cameron went on and on, and Ainsley couldn't see or hear or breathe. The only thing in the world was Cameron's mouth on her, the bulk of his warmth so close to her, the dark fire spreading through her.

"Cam, *please*!"

Ainsley didn't know what she begged for, she only knew she wanted him against her, with her, inside her. Always.

Cameron raised his head and dabbed his lips with his fingers. "Sweet Ainsley. Has no one ever done that either?"

She shook her head, beyond speech.

"All men are fools," he said. "To pass you by when they could have *this*." Cameron stroked his fingers through the curls between her legs. "You're sweet and wet for me, my Ainsley. Wet and ready."

He pulled aside the folds of his kilt, and no, he wore nothing beneath it. Only him, his shaft long and dark.

The drapes of the plaid got in Ainsley's way, but she easily found him. She smiled as she closed her hand around him, not hiding her pleasure at how hot and hard and so very big he was. Cameron was a large man, large all the way down.

Cameron groaned as Ainsley squeezed, her tightly controlled man coming undone for her. He studied her with half-closed eyes, his cheekbones flushed. Enjoying what she did to him, and letting himself enjoy it.

"You are quite . . . long," she said. "Have you ever measured it?"

A glint flashed in Cameron's eyes. "No."

"I must fetch a tape measure then."

Cameron seized her wrist in an impossibly strong grip. "You are not going anywhere or fetching anything. Not now."

He removed her hand from him and drew her up off the seat.

The wool of his kilt prickled her as Cameron moved between her thighs. His tip touched her opening, and Ainsley ached with need. Her body wanted to squeeze, wanted to pull him in, to have him all the way.

"Not too fast, love," Cameron said. "I don't want to hurt you."

Ainsley shook her head. She was past caring, past remembering what pain was. "I'm ready." She'd been ready for six years.

"Stop me if I hurt you. Promise me."

His eyes held anguish mixed with need, and Ainsley realized that her answer was very, very important to him.

She nodded. "I promise."

Cameron relaxed, as though Ainsley had said the right thing. He cradled her in his strong arms her, held her gaze with his, and slid inside.

I belong here.

I belong inside this beautiful woman who tastes like dreams.

Cameron's thoughts scattered, and all he could feel was Ainsley, her heat and her scent. Deeper, deeper into her. *Ainsley, I need you.*

His breath came fast, the noises in his throat hoarse, Cameron who never lost control.

Cameron couldn't afford to lose control, never, ever. But Ainsley was stealing him. She was tight, so damn tight, and he was sliding into her so deep he never wanted to come out.

He kissed her throat, feeling her groans with his lips. He kissed her face, up under her hair. Ainsley was making beautiful noises, and Cameron kissed her throat again. He felt the slight scrape of her fingernails on his back, Ainsley not even knowing she scratched him.

"Ainsley." Saying her name was joy.

Cameron couldn't move inside her much in this position, but their bodies were tight against each other's, the feeling raw. Later, he'd take her on cushions on the floor of her chamber, and then he'd be able to move. Stroking into and out of beautiful Ainsley. The thought excited him beyond measure.

But right now was good too. Ainsley touched his face, looking straight into his eyes with her beautiful gray ones. She was around him, part of him, and he was part of her.

Ainsley couldn't believe what she was feeling. Cameron was thick and firm inside her, spreading her, yet there was no pain, only *rightness*. He held her so gently, but his body had such power that it undid her.

If she'd known there would be this joy, six years ago, Ainsley would not have waited so long. "I'd have found you," she heard herself saying. "Chased you through London like a fool, and begged you to do *this*."

Cameron's smile was hot. "Wicked, wicked lady. I'll give you everything you want, do anything to you. All you have to do is ask."

He moved inside her, and Ainsley gave in to the bright, hard feeling. "Would you do this for me?" She moaned as he sent forth another burning thrust. "Any time I wanted? If I went to Paris with you?"

"Hell, yes." His voice was dark. "Again, and again, every damned night. I know pleasure, Ainsley, and I'll show you every bit you ever dreamed of."

She sucked in a breath as he pressed even tighter into her, spreading her so wide. "This seems adequate."

"There's so, so much more, Ainsley, love." He cupped her head in his large hand, his breath tangling with hers. "So much more. But—*God*—now. You're beautiful. My Ainsley. Always *mine*."

Cameron felt the finish coming—too soon, too damned, damned soon. But Ainsley was squeezing him hard, sending little pulses of pleasure up and down his cock. Nature, damnably controlling, wanted him to bury his seed deep inside her. *Now.*

"No." He fought it. *No, no, no, I don't want to stop. I never want to stop.*

"Cameron." It was a whispered groan. "Cam, I feel so *good.* What do I . . ." Words vanished as Ainsley's climax took her, her sweet feminine sounds undoing him.

Cameron let out a savage growl. He lowered Ainsley quickly to the seat and slid out of her, his cock protesting all the way. He yanked a handkerchief from the coat behind him, wrapped it around his hardness, and spilled his seed into the innocent cloth.

Ainsley couldn't catch her breath. She lay limply against the cushions, clutching the lip of the seat so she wouldn't slide off.

Cameron remained unmoving on the carpeted floor, head bowed, handkerchief pressed to himself, his chest swiftly rising and falling.

"Cameron, are you all right?"

He raised his head and gave her a wide, hot smile. Cameron rose over her, fists on either side of her, caging her on the seat.

"Am I all right?" His Highland accent rang through. "Of course I'm all right, lass. I'm better than I've ever been."

"But you—"

"Pulled out of ye? Aye, so I won't give ye a babe."

"Oh. Yes." Ainsley wasn't certain whether she felt grateful or disappointed. "It was—"

"Far too soon." His smile broadened. "I know. I want more. I want ye all night, love."

"Cameron, stop interrupting me." She sat up to him, met the dark golden eyes that held so much warmth. "I wanted to say that it was beautiful."

"But far too quick. I want ye the rest of the night."

"Yes." Ainsley dissolved into a smile. "I think that would be quite an excellent thing."

Cameron looked her up and down, his eyes taking in everything, a man liking what he saw. "You're beautiful, lass."

His look was like a touch, his words burning. She laughed nervously. "A bit long in the tooth."

"Ye stop that, now. When I saw ye tonight, Ainsley, when you looked up at me through that mask and ran your tongue over your red-painted mouth, I wanted you so hard. I'd have taken you right there on the stairs if I could have. I showed bloody good restraint not even kissing you until I got you into the anteroom."

Ainsley stretched, her body pliant. "So I had to hide my face with a mask to gain your attention?"

"Careful with me, woman. I'm barely stopping myself ravishing you all over again."

Cameron growled and swept a kiss across her mouth. Ainsley splayed her hands against his chest, feeling his heart pounding as swiftly as hers. She loved how large he was, how powerful. How safe she felt with the cushions at her back, and Cameron's body between her and the world.

"Damn you, Ainsley," he said. "You are the most enticing, beddable, *sensual* woman I have ever seen. I want to lie with you all night and all the next day. I want to do things to you and have you do them to me. There are cruder words for what I want, but I'm trying to keep in mind that you're a lady."

Ainsley's heart tripped, but she smiled. "Now you have me curious. Tell me, Cameron. I'm not a fainting flower."

Cameron put his mouth to her ear. The blunt syllables tapped through her—*fuck . . . suck . . . cunny . . . cock.* Ainsley felt a lightness in her limbs, a floating sensation that was warm and freeing.

Cameron raised his head, his smile so hot she thought she'd slide from the seat. "Is that what ye wanted to hear?" he asked.

"I don't regret the question," Ainsley said breathlessly.

"Good." Cameron licked between her breasts. He tugged her legs around him again, but instead of pushing inside her, he held her close, the two of them entwined, face to face.

Ainsley kissed him as he kissed her, both of them tasting, licking, nipping, exploring. So many different sensations under her tongue—the sandpaper roughness of his whiskers; the smoothness that was his scar; the hot, wet point of his mouth; firm, masterful lips.

She kissed his cheek, smoothed his eyes closed with kisses, nibbled her way down his throat. Cameron murmured in pleasure and did it all back to her.

The carriage hit a hole in the road. Cameron held her so protectively that she never felt the bump, but the carriage abruptly slowed.

"Damn," Cameron growled.

Ainsley didn't want to let go of him. "What is the matter?"

Cameron gently unwound himself from her and hauled himself into the seat beside her. "We're almost home."

"Oh." Ainsley fought back a wave of disappointment.

Cameron swept up her combinations and dropped them onto her bare skin, then knocked on the coach's roof. The coachman, thank heavens, didn't look down at them through the little peephole to see Ainsley in her naked glory. He merely halted the coach.

"Why are we stopping?" She felt cold without him around her, and she hugged the cotton combinations to her chest. "We haven't turned into the drive yet, have we?" She hadn't felt the turn, anyway.

"I'm getting out here." Cameron slid on his shirt then shrugged on the waistcoat. He paused to kiss her, lingered, kissed her again. "I don't want to risk us arriving together. I'll walk across the fields, and you take the coach all the way home. Go upstairs and straight to your bedchamber. I'll come to you there."

Ainsley warmed. Again, she saw the gentle caring of this rough, brutish man. Cameron was leaving now to protect her and her reputation, not disappearing into the night, finished, having taken his pleasure.

"In my chamber?" she asked. "Wouldn't it be better to be in yours?" His wing of the house was almost deserted, while Ainsley was housed in a corner of the very busy guest wing.

Cameron draped his cravat around his neck but didn't tie it. "Easier for me to explain why I'm in the guest wing if anyone happens along."

Ainsley opened her mouth to protest, but Cameron growled. "Can you do *nothing* without arguing, woman?"

"Not really. I'm not used to following orders without question."

"The Queen of England must put up with much, then. Turn around."

Ainsley decided to do that without asking him why, and Cameron laced up her corset. He did it with quick competence, as skilled as any lady's maid.

Cameron turned her around and kissed her again, this kiss lingering and slow. "You're a beautiful, beautiful woman, Ainsley Douglas. And I want to drink you down."

And wouldn't Ainsley love that? She touched his face. "Soon."

"Very soon." Another kiss, and Cameron snatched up his coat and opened the door.

A rush of cold air filled the coach, blocked a little by Cameron's body as he descended. "Damned soon," he said.

He flickered his tongue, promising and sensual, and then he slammed the door, and was gone.

Before Ainsley could draw a ragged breath, the coach lurched forward, and she scrambled for her bodice and skirts. Outside she heard Cameron go, his cheerful whistle cutting the night.

Cameron paced his bedchamber, poured himself whiskey, paced some more, and drank, his eye on the clock. McNab lay sprawled on Cameron's bed, the dog fully at home. McNab thumped his tail the first few times Cameron passed; then his eyes drooped and he began to snore. It was like a rusty saw, that snore.

Cameron drank and walked, his focus nowhere. He had to give Ainsley enough time get herself upstairs, give her maid a chance to fuss as she undressed Ainsley and put her to bed. Another quarter of an hour perhaps. His blood burned with impatience.

Again and again he felt the warmth of Ainsley around him, heard her laughter. Her astonishment when she'd reached climax told him she'd never had an orgasm before. Cameron couldn't help but smile in triumph to know he'd been the first to make her feel it.

He knew he should be finished with her, having at last obtained what he'd wanted since that night six years ago in this very bedchamber. Challenge completed, the game won. He should at least be finished for the night, sated and sleepy, ready to make plans for the morning's training. But he paced and wanted Ainsley again. Not just tonight but night after night.

He'd convince her to come to Paris with him. She had nothing to look forward to—more drudgery to the queen and duty to her brother and sister-in-law, hidden away until she became faded and forgotten.

Ainsley was too vibrant to be forgotten. Cameron would take her to Paris then Monaco. He'd dress her in the most costly gowns, give her jewels that would make every other woman on the Continent ill with envy. He'd take her to the finest restaurants and best theatres and let her enjoy herself. Then they'd retreat to the townhouse he leased in the best district and watch the city lights.

Ainsley was a delight to be with—she threw herself wholeheartedly into whatever she did, whether it was helping Isabella organize guests for Hart or fetching compromising letters for the Queen of England.

Cameron would watch her take Paris by storm. She'd grace his side at glittering Parisian soirees, stand at his elbow at the gaming tables in Monte Carlo. She was a beautiful, enticing woman, and Cameron wanted to be with her as much as he could.

"Devil take it all. She makes me insane. And damn it to hell, I can't stop wanting her."

McNab opened one eye, saw that nothing very interesting was happening, and closed it again.

The dog came alert a moment later at the same time Cameron heard hurried footsteps in the corridor. McNab gave one hopeful woof, then someone pounded on the door.

Damn it, I told her to stay put.

"Sir," Angelo called through the door. "It's Jasmine. I think you'd better come."

Chapter 15

Night-Blooming Jasmine stood in the middle of her stall, her head bent to forelegs, sides heaving. Cameron slipped inside her stall, the heat in his body evaporating into fear.

It wasn't colic or gas, because Jasmine would be circling the stall in agony or trying to roll. Instead she stood dejectedly, not raising her head as Cameron ran expert hands along her body. "What is it, girl? What's wrong with my lass, eh?"

He tapped a fetlock, and Jasmine readily turned up her hoof. Cameron held it, Jasmine taking the opportunity to lean her entire body weight on him. The hoof wasn't hot or the frog mushy or pus-filled. The hoof wall felt solid and sound as well. He checked her other feet, but all four hooves seemed fine.

Cameron set down the last hoof, Jasmine sighing disappointment that he wouldn't hold her up any longer. When she raised her head, mucus ran from her nose and mouth to dribble down Cameron's white shirt. She whuffed softly, a picture of misery.

Cam stroked her nose and turned to the stable hands who were hanging over the stall. "Not thrush or colic and nothing's broken."

Angelo flicked a dark Romany gaze over the horse. He'd have examined her already as soon as he noticed a problem, but he wasn't offended that Cameron had checked her again.

"Could be poison," one of the stable hands said.

Cameron's heart constricted. "Let's hope to God it's not. Anyone been around here tonight?"

"No, sir," Angelo said. "We keep a good watch."

The other stable hands nodded. The men here worked for Cameron or Hart, had for years, and Cam doubted any of them could be bribed—both Hart and Cam paid high salaries and the men prided themselves on their loyalty. They loved the horses as much as Cameron did.

"Nothing to do but wait it out," he said. "What did she eat?"

Angelo shook his head. "Nothing tonight. I tried to give her a few oats, and she didn't want it, or good hay."

Always a bad sign when a horse wouldn't eat. They loved to eat, their raison d'être. Humans might think they'd tamed horses, Cameron reflected, but horses knew they'd trained humans to feed them.

"Could be pneumonia," Angelo said, eyes unhappy. "Or the cough. What with her legging it through the countryside, there's no telling what she might have picked up out there."

Angelo's explanation was the most likely one. The Scottish hills were cold, far colder than Jasmine's home near Bath, and if she'd taken chill on her adventures, it could develop into something worse.

"What about the other horses?" The cough—a malady that made horses cough and sneeze, similar to the human cold—could spread quickly, and while it might not be deadly, horses couldn't run until the disease played itself out. Pneumonia was a different matter. Jasmine could die tonight if she'd contracted it.

"Nothing wrong with the others," Angelo said.

"Get warm water inside her," Cameron said. "I'll rub her down."

"Warm water's coming." Of course, Angelo would have already sent someone running for some.

Cameron stripped off his coat, rolled up his sleeves, and fetched curry comb and dandy brush. Brushing horses was good for their circulation and kept them warm. They could send for the horse doctor, but no doubt he'd tell them the same things that Angelo and Cameron had concluded. Large bottles of tonic stood waiting in the tack room, but Cameron didn't want to shove medicine down Jasmine until they knew what they were dealing with. Keeping her warm was the first consideration.

Jasmine didn't react much while Cameron brushed her, except to lean her head on his shoulder. Angelo came with blankets, which they buckled around her. They had to put the water inside her with a tube, because she refused to drink.

The night was crisp and cold now, and Cameron thought regretfully of Ainsley's bedchamber warmed with fire and her body against his. But he also knew that when he told Ainsley tomorrow why he hadn't come to her, she'd understand. Not only understand, but demand to be kept informed of Jasmine's progress. He couldn't think of any other woman who'd not be angry that she'd been eclipsed by a horse, but he knew Ainsley would think him right to stay with Jasmine.

Cameron finished and left the stall. Jasmine draped her head over the door, seeking Cameron, and he stroked her neck.

"It's all right, girl. I'll not leave you."

Angelo had already run for a blanket, a fresh shirt, and a new coat for Cameron. Cam wondered often what he'd do without Angelo, the Romany he'd rescued from certain death one night near Cameron's Berkshire estate. A group of men from Hungerford had run eighteen-year-old Angelo to ground after they'd caught him stealing enough food to get his family, waiting on a canal boat, through another day. They'd trashed the food and started beating Angelo, knives coming out to assure that the Romany thief wouldn't live to see the morning.

This had happened not long after Elizabeth's death, when Cameron had first purchased the estate. Cameron had been riding in the dawn light, drunk and unable to sleep. He'd welcomed the chance to join the fight, ran off the locals, took Angelo home, and gave him food for his family from his own kitchen. He'd walked with Angelo to the boat waiting on the Kennet and Avon Canal, which had been overflowing with people—Angelo's parents, grandparents, bothers, and sisters, and about a dozen children.

Cameron had left him there, assuming he'd seen the last of the man, but Angelo had turned up again at Cameron's stables not many weeks later. There was no better race fixer in the country than himself, Angelo had claimed, so he'd know how to watch out for all the tricks. He'd protect Cameron's horses in exchange for a place to sleep and the occasional money to give to his family.

That's how it started, but Angelo proved to be more competent and loyal than anyone Cameron had ever met. Now Angelo looked after Cameron with the same intensity. Angelo knew Cameron's moods and what plagued him, knew of his nightmares and dark memories, and was always there with a drink or a sleeping draught or just an ear to listen. Without Angelo, Cameron knew he'd have gone mad long ago.

Now Angelo arranged the blanket and flask of brandy for Cameron and folded himself into another corner to watch.

In spite of his worry for the horse, Cameron felt loose, warm, still filled with the sensation of Ainsley. He was half drunk with the whiskey he'd downed while pacing, and as he slid into waking dreams, he reached for the scent and joy of Ainsley.

What he got was a recurring nightmare about Elizabeth. After Daniel's birth, Elizabeth had fallen into severe melancholia. Whenever she roused herself from it, the first thing she tried to do was hurt Daniel. The nurse and maids at Kilmorgan protected him fiercely, but Elizabeth could be cunning.

Cameron's dream turned to the fateful day when he'd rushed to his bedchamber after hearing Daniel's screams, to have her come at him, knife in hand. Elizabeth had stolen the knife earlier that day from Cameron's father's collection, which meant she'd thought this through. She'd lain in wait in Cameron's chamber with Daniel as her hostage, intending to kill them both.

The dream turned from the streak of pain when Elizabeth had slashed the knife across Cameron's cheek to her turning that knife toward the innocent Daniel on the bed. Cameron relived his watery panic as he dove for Daniel and rolled across the bed with him. He'd had to fight Elizabeth when he gained his feet, trying to keep the already bloody blade from Daniel.

He couldn't remember what he'd roared at her, or what he'd done, but Elizabeth had stumbled backward, screeching obscenities at the top of her voice. Cameron had whirled Daniel away to the other side of the room.

Elizabeth had turned the knife on herself. Cameron heard again the horrible gurgle as the knife slid into her throat, saw the scarlet blood that rained down her neck to her dress. She'd stared at it in shock, then up at Cameron with a mixture of fury and hurt betrayal, before she'd crumpled to the ground.

Then the shouting as the household tried to get into the room, Daniel's infant screams, then Hart's gruff voice bellowing at Cameron to open the damned door. Hart had broken it down to find Cameron cradling Daniel in his arms, desperately trying to quiet him, and Elizabeth on the floor in a pool of her own blood.

Cameron's dream jumped forward to the funeral—Cameron in soot black, wind stirring the crepe trickling from his tall hat. He stood rigidly next to his father and Hart as the Scottish vicar droned on about the wickedness of this transitory world and how Elizabeth was welcomed as a sister with joy into the next.

He remembered how their father had growled as soon as the vicar finished that Cameron had made bad job of it, losing himself a wife before she could push out more babies. If Cameron had only brought Elizabeth to heel, the old duke said, she would have been more obedient and not such a damned whore.

Hart had turned and crashed his fist into their father's face, while the vicar watched in horror. Hart's voice had held terrible anger as he'd said to their father, "You are dead to me."

Cameron had stood by numbly, not really giving a damn. Afterward, he'd gone upstairs, told Daniel's nurse to pack his things, and had taken Daniel, nurse and all, to London that very afternoon.

Cam's dreams were cut by feminine laughter and a scent he already loved. He opened his eyes to see Ainsley, dressed once more in sensible gray—buttoned to the chin again—give Jasmine a bannock. The horse sniffed it, lipped it, then took it from Ainsley's hand and crunched it down.

"Daniel, another," she said.

Daniel took a second oat cake from a hamper and handed it to Ainsley. Ainsley fed it to Jasmine, who ate it with enthusiasm and reached for more. Angelo sat cross-legged in his corner, arms on his knees, watching with interest.

The images and dreams floated away in the cold dawn light, birds coming awake outside in the yard. Cameron's eyes were sandy, but he felt strangely alert and rested.

"Was that meant to be my breakfast?" he asked.

Ainsley turned beautiful gray eyes to him. "That's what I told your cook. My brother Patrick's horse always loved bannocks when she grew ill. It seems far more effective than any draught in a black bottle."

"She does seem to be perking up, Dad." Daniel stuffed another bannock into Jasmine's mouth, and Jasmine ate it greedily. Her nose still dripped mucus, but her miserable look had gone.

Horses were maddening. They could be right as rain in the morning and drop dead that night, or be as near death's door as a horse could get and then make a full recovery a few hours later.

Jasmine couldn't not feel better with Ainsley hand-feeding her. The horse crunched the next oatcake as Cameron got to his feet.

"You're awake then," Ainsley said. "You were twitching a bit when we came in. Bad dreams?"

"Nothing important." Cameron heaved himself to his feet and went to stand next to her, absorbing her warmth. He couldn't very well tell her, *I'm sorry I didn't come to your room and finish our debauch,* in front of his son, Angelo, and the other men, but the look she gave him told him he didn't need to say a word.

"Are the letters safe?" she whispered to him.

He nipped her earlobe as he answered. "Locked in my room, and no one, but no one is allowed in there but Angelo, and he's incorruptible." He gave her a pointed look. "Remember that."

Ainsley sent him a cheeky grin. "I'll consider it."

Jasmine ran her horsy nose across Ainsley's placket and closed her teeth over one of Ainsley's buttons. Ainsley squeaked as Jasmine jerked off the button. Cameron swiftly took it out of Jasmine's mouth before she could swallow it and pulled Ainsley back as Jasmine reached for more.

"You see?" Cameron said, lacing his arms around Ainsley from behind. "She knows exactly what should be done with all those buttons."

Ainsley and Daniel went inside for breakfast soon after that, but Cameron remained. Training needed to begin, sick horses or no. The routine never stopped, and Cameron had the other racers to consider.

But he felt good. His crazed dreams had dissolved like mist in the sunlight, and he was back to remembering being inside Ainsley. Jasmine seemed to have passed her crisis, and if she were truly better, Cameron would arrange to spend that night with Ainsley. And the next night, and the next. All winter, in fact. He'd send telegrams to his man of business in Paris to begin the lease of his usual house and to hire a lady's maid for Ainsley.

He hoped that Ainsley would return to the stables while he worked, but she didn't. Cameron rode with Angelo and the others and didn't see her among the guests that turned up to watch the training. She'd likely been pressed into service by Isabella again.

When Cameron returned to the house hours later to wash and change, he nearly ran into Beth coming in through the front door in bonnet and gloves. The house was quiet, the guests nowhere in sight.

"Is Ainsley with Isabella?" Cameron asked Beth.

Beth blinked at him in surprise. "With Isabella? No, Ainsley's gone. I've just come back from putting her on the train."

Chapter 16

Cameron stared at Beth while the color drained from his world. "Gone? What do you mean *gone*?"

"Back to Balmoral. She had a telegram from the queen this morning." Her voice softened. "I'm sorry, Cam. You didn't know?"

"No, I bloody well didn't know." No good-bye, no bothering to send him a message.

"She didn't even have time to pack," Beth said, tugging off her gloves. "She took a few things with her and asked me to send everything else on."

"And you let her go?" Cameron's voice thundered.

Beth's dark blue gaze burrowed past his anger. "It was a summons from the queen. She couldn't refuse." She hesitated. "Do you remember when you taught me how to ride a horse?"

"What the devil does that have to do with anything?" The world had dropped from under Cameron's feet, and he was falling, falling.

"You were so patient with me, even though I was completely ignorant about horses. You found me a horse that would be gentle and easy to ride, and you went slowly. I learned to trust that you wouldn't let me fall. And not only because Ian would throttle you if you did."

"I remember."

"Then trust me when I say that you will see Ainsley again. And everything will be as it should be."

Beth looked wise, but this was wrong, all wrong. "Did she leave any message for me?"

"No." Beth looked apologetic. "She barely had time to say good-bye to Isabella and ask me to kiss the babies for her."

No good-bye for Cameron, no answer to his pathetic plea. *Ainsley, you have to come with me. Say you will. Promise me.*

"Damnation."

Beth touched his arm. "Cameron, I am so sorry."

Cameron looked down at Beth, the kind but resilient sister-in-law who'd made Ian so happy. He started to answer but just then his jumbled thoughts clarified into a single one.

The letters.

The exasperating Ainsley would never have rushed off to Balmoral without the letters. If Angelo had given them to her . . . Cameron should have remembered that she'd already swayed Angelo to her side.

Without another word, Cameron strode to his wing of the house, took the stairs two at a time, and stormed into his bedchamber. Everything looked as Cam had left it the night before, including the dog-haired impression McNab had left on the bed. The dog in question now padded back into the room.

Cameron slammed across the room to his bedside table. A painting of a cheerful tart hung above it, she sitting on the edge of her bed in her chemise, grinning while she pulled on her stockings. Mac had painted the picture for him a long time ago. Though Cameron had never met the model Mac had used, he liked the way the woman's cheeky smile beamed at him every morning.

She laughed at him now as Cameron yanked open the drawer. Cameron had locked the drawer, but the little lock was no match for Ainsley's skill.

The stack of letters had gone.

"Damn it," Cameron said. McNab sat down next to him. "Bloody rotten guard dog you are."

McNab thumped his tail.

Cameron drew out a scrap of paper from the drawer that hadn't been there the night before. Unfolding it, he found Ainsley's clear handwriting.

On the train, after the St. Leger. I will give you my answer.

She hadn't signed it.

"Dad!" The outraged cry had McNab's tail going faster. Cameron slid the note into his pocket.

"Dad!"

"I heard you the first time." Cameron shoved the drawer closed and faced his son, who'd been running, his kilt dirty as usual.

"Dad, Mrs. Douglas is gone."

"I know that."

"Well, go after her. Bring her back!"

Cameron glared, and Daniel took a worried step back. Cameron checked his rage, not liking the frustrated violence boiling up inside him.

"She went to the queen," he said as calmly as he could. "She had to go."

"Why? What does the bloody queen need with her anyway? She's got enough people to look after her without Ainsley."

Cameron agreed. The beast inside him wanted to rush to Balmoral and damn anyone who got in his way. "I know."

"This is your fault," Daniel snarled. "She's gone, we'll never see her again, and it's all your fault."

"Daniel—"

Daniel whirled and fled the room, McNab trotting worriedly after him.

Hell and damnation. Cameron sank to the bed, the strength going out of him. He hadn't slept all night, and his head pounded with whiskey, exertion, and memories of Ainsley.

On the train, after the St. Leger. I will give you my answer.

Cameron could barely breathe.

He wouldn't let her go. Mackenzie men were good at getting exactly what they wanted, and Cameron would have Ainsley. He'd not let her go again, not for the Queen of England or any other reason on God's earth.

The declaration didn't return color to his world, but he clung to it as he stripped off his soiled clothes and bellowed to the footmen to fetch Angelo.

Queen Victoria opened the keepsake box Ainsley had brought to her and slid the bundle of letters inside it. She locked the box with a little key on a ribbon and tucked the key back into her pocket.

"You have done well, my dear," the queen said, her quiet smile satisfied.

"Begging your pardon, ma'am, but shouldn't you burn them?" The lock on the keepsake box was flimsy, and Phyllida's toady had found no difficulty stealing the letters from it the first time.

"Nonsense. It scarcely matters now. Mrs. Chase is long gone."

Yes, but there might be others just as intent on embarrassing you, Ainsley argued silently.

However, the queen was right that Phyllida Chase would no longer be a threat. As soon as Ainsley had alighted from the train that evening, the maid who'd come to fetch her had told Ainsley the delightful rumor that Mrs. Chase had fled to the Continent with a young Italian tenor.

The rumor was confirmed at Balmoral by a colleague of Mr. Chase. Phyllida had written a letter to her husband, baldly stating that she'd left him and outlining why. Mr. Chase was outraged, ready to sue her, and he fully blamed the Duke of Kilmorgan for hosting licentious house parties. Ainsley wondered how Hart Mackenzie had reacted to that.

Victoria went on. "I heard that you returned my five hundred guineas to my secretary."

"Yes, I was able to retrieve the letters and not spend your money, ma'am."

"Very clever of you." The queen patted her cheek. "So frugal, so very Scots. You've always been resourceful, my dear, as was your mother, God rest her soul."

"Thank you, ma'am."

It alarmed Ainsley how easily she slid back into the role of the queen's trusted servant. Ainsley wore mourning black again, but she couldn't help but touch the onyx buttons of her bodice and imagine the wicked smile Cam would give her as he asked how many she'd let him undo.

Ainsley thought of the note she'd left him, poor recompense for all his help. But when Ainsley had telegraphed the queen that she'd successfully retrieved the letters, she'd received an almost instant reply that she should return to Balmoral at once.

Cameron had been on a horse in the fields with Angelo and his trainers, and Ainsley knew she wouldn't have time to wait for him to finish so that she could say good-bye. When the queen said *at once*, she meant it.

Besides, Cameron might have demanded an answer then and there, and Ainsley's mind whirled with the question. He wanted her to flee to the Continent with him, as Phyllida had done with her tenor, and Ainsley hadn't the faintest idea what to tell him.

If she did go with Cameron, how on earth would she

explain it to Patrick and Rona? As she'd tried to tell Cameron, she didn't so much worry about scandal but who she would hurt by it. *If I were alone in the world, I'd tell scandal to go hang and do as I pleased.*

But Cameron was tempting Ainsley. It wasn't simply lust for the bedchamber that made her long for him—there was his smile, the warmth in his eyes, the way he worried over Jasmine, the way he'd helped lame Mrs. Yardley so very gently across the croquet green. Ainsley wanted all of Cameron, the whole man.

"I'm thinking of going to Paris, ma'am," Ainsley said.

The queen blinked. "Next summer, with your family? Of course, you must. Paris is lovely in the summer."

"No, I mean in a few weeks."

"Nonsense, my dear, you can't possibly. We have the ghillies ball at the end of the month and so much to do after that, and then Christmas."

Ainsley bit the inside of her mouth. "Yes, ma'am."

To the queen, nothing was more interesting or important than royal entertainments, and Ainsley knew that Victoria would not want Ainsley to leave her side. Victoria smiled at Ainsley now.

"Play for me, dear," the queen said. "You soothe me."

She had her hands around her box, the queen's plump face serene now that she's regained the evidence of her secret love. Ainsley hid a sigh, went to the piano, and started to play.

Two days later, Ainsley walked into a long drawing room and found Lord Cameron Mackenzie standing in it, his back to her while he warmed his hands at the fireplace.

Before she could choose between running away and facing him squarely, Cameron turned around. His sharp gaze moved up and down her, and he didn't disguise the fact that he was angry. Very angry.

"I left you a note," Ainsley said faintly.

"Damn your note. Shut the door."

Ainsley walked across the room to him without obeying about the door. "What are you doing here?"

And why did he look so wonderful in his worn riding kilt and muddy boots?

"I came to visit my mistress."

Ainsley stopped. "Oh."

"I meant you, Ainsley."

Ainsley's breath came pouring back. "I'm not your mistress."

"My lover, then." Cameron sat on a sofa without inviting her to sit first, removed a flask from his coat pocket, and took a long sip.

Ainsley seated herself on a nearby chair. "You make us sound like characters in a farce. I'll wager you didn't tell her majesty that you were here to visit your mistress."

Cameron shrugged and took another sip. "She asked for my advice on a horse, and I decided to give it to her in person."

"Very clever."

"The queen likes to talk about horses."

Ainsley nodded. "She does. I told you I'd give you my decision after the St. Leger. I need time to think."

Cameron crossed his booted feet. "I've changed my mind. I want my answer now."

"Does that mean you've come here to carry me off? They do have guards and things."

"No, damn you. I came here to persuade you."

"You are an arrogant man, Cameron Mackenzie."

Cameron thrust the flask back into his pocket. "I'm a damned impatient man. I don't understand why the devil you insisted on rushing back here to be the queen's best servant."

Ainsley spread her hands. "I need the money. I'm not a rich woman, and my brother can't be expected to keep me forever."

"I told you, I'll give you all the money you need." Cameron flicked his gaze up and down her frock. "I hate you in black. Why do you keep wearing it?"

"It is what I wear when I'm working for the queen," Ainsley said. "And I wear it because John Douglas was a kind, caring man, and he deserves not to be forgotten."

"Kind and caring. The opposite of Cameron Mackenzie."

Something in his eyes stemmed her anger. "You can be kind and caring. I've seen you."

"Why did you marry John Douglas in the first place? No one seems to understand why, not your closest friends, not even Isabella."

Ainsley did not want to talk about John with Cameron. "You were enticing her to gossip and speculation, were you?"

"I have to, mouse, because you won't answer a straight question. But tell me this." Cameron held her gaze with his. "Were you carrying his child?"

Chapter 17

Ainsley's breath went away again. "What?"

"I saw the marks on your abdomen, Ainsley. I understand what they mean. You had a baby."

No one knew. Only Patrick and Rona, and John. Even Ainsley's three other brothers, nowhere near Rome at the time of Ainsley's hasty marriage, hadn't known the full story.

Ainsley rose from her chair, walked across the room, and closed and locked the door. Cameron watched her, not moving, as she returned to her seat.

"The child lived for a day," she said in a quiet voice. "But she wasn't John's."

Cameron sat perfectly still. "Whose, then?"

"I met a young man in Rome. I fell in love with him and allowed him to seduce me. I thought he'd rejoice that I was having his child and marry me." She wondered that she'd ever been so naïve. "That's when he told me he was already married, and even had two children of his own."

Cameron stared at her while red fury rose inside him.

Ainsley—beautiful, fiery, innocent Ainsley—used and discarded by a gigolo. "Who was he?" he asked.

Ainsley glanced up at him, cheeks red. "It was a long time ago, and I'm certain he gave me a false name. I was so very young and stupid, and I believed every word he told me."

"Damn it, Ainsley . . ."

Cameron wanted to rage. He wanted to race to the Continent, find the blackguard and throttle him. The selfish fool had ruined Ainsley's life before she'd even tasted the world.

"This is why you married an old man and buried yourself," he said.

Her smile was sad, full of regret. "Patrick and Rona had taken me to Rome to expand my mind with art and music. Training me to be the wife of a cultured man. And then . . ."

The look on Patrick's face when Ainsley had told him . . . she cringed from the memory even now. But Patrick, her good brother, had put aside his disappointment and taken care of her.

Ainsley remembered her nights of weeping, from shame, over betrayal of her young, fragile love, plus the knowledge that her brother was pairing her with a man nearly three times her age to save her reputation.

Patrick was kind, but he was firm, and he knew, very realistically, what the world was like. Rona, though sympathetic, had stood solidly with Patrick. Ainsley must marry John Douglas, and marry him quickly. And she must show the world that she was happy with her choice.

John Douglas had come to the house Patrick had rented in Rome, a tall man whose fair hair had gone to gray, his blue eyes warm but worried. Ainsley had met him before but not paid much attention to him, as he'd been, to her, merely an acquaintance of Patrick's. Now he was there to be her husband.

John had been patience itself, and when Patrick and Rona had left them alone, John Douglas had taken her hand and gone down on one knee. His grasp had been warm, steady, even comforting.

I know I'm not what you want, he'd said. *A young lady wants a dashing young husband, doesn't she? And I know what this is all about. But I promise you, Ainsley, I will look after you. I'll do my utmost. I can't promise to make you happy, because no one can promise that, can they? But I'll try. Will you let me?*

He'd been so kind, so aware that barely eighteen-year-old Ainsley would rather be dragged behind a cart than marry an old man, that Ainsley had burst into tears. She'd ended up sitting on the sofa with him, being held and soothed. She'd clung to him and realized that, as bizarre a match as this was, he was a man, a good man, not a villain.

She did feel safe from the world with John Douglas—Patrick had made a wise choice. Ainsley had told John that of course she'd be happy to marry him, and vowed then to be as good to him as she could. Poor man, not his fault.

John had wiped away Ainsley's tears, pulled a silver necklace from his pocket—his mother's, he'd said—and clasped it around her neck. It rested there even now, under her high-collared black frock.

John had taken Ainsley's hand and led her to Patrick and Rona, who were trying not to hover in the next room. Thus, Ainsley McBride had been engaged and, the next week, married.

"John Douglas must have been a hell of a man," Cameron said softly.

Ainsley looked up at him, eyes blurred with tears. "He was." John had accepted a pregnant young woman as his wife, agreed to treat another man's child as his, and not say a word. "He knew he'd not likely have the chance to marry and be a father on his own, so Patrick's favor was welcome. He told me."

Cameron's face was so still that Ainsley couldn't read it. What was he thinking? Contempt at her weakness? At

John's? Understanding for what she'd done? He sat forward on the sofa, his hands clasped loosely in front of him, his dark gold eyes fixed on her.

"This is why you put me off that night, six years ago," he said. "You didn't want to betray him."

Ainsley shook her head. "John didn't deserve it. As much as I wanted to stay with you, he didn't deserve the betrayal."

"I admired you for that, you know. Until I learned that you were a picklock, and a thief." He gave her a hint of smile.

"I admitted to stealing the necklace, for a misguided reason. I thought *you* a blackmailer."

"So we were at cross-purposes."

"It was difficult to push you away. Believe me, Cameron, when I tell you how difficult it was."

Cameron's voice hardened. "I hope he appreciated it. What I sacrificed that night."

"He never knew, of course. He must have wondered, though, whether I ever betrayed him. I didn't."

"No, you were most devoted and grateful."

"Don't sound so patronizing. I *was* grateful. John took me on out of kindness."

Cameron gave her a withering look. "Ainsley, trust me, it wasn't only kindness."

"He was especially kind when my daughter . . ." Tears rushed at her. So long ago, and still the loss cut her deeply.

"I'm sorry, Ainsley." Cameron's voice gentled. "I truly am sorry."

"I named her Gavina." She raised her head, but she couldn't see him through her tears. "Do you know what it was like when I was grieving, and all those around me told me her death was for the best? They thought they were making me feel better—I'd never have to answer awkward questions about why my daughter had black curls while John and I were both so very fair . . ." Her voice broke.

Cameron was standing above her, lifting her, holding

her close. Ainsley leaned into his broad chest and let the tears come.

Gavina had been so beautiful, so perfectly formed. Had fit in Ainsley's arms with the knowledge that she belonged there. She'd lived one day, one wonderful day, and then she'd weakened and gone. Her small body now lay in the Scottish churchyard near Ainsley's mother and father.

His hands were warm, comforting, Cameron so tall and strong. The man who could make Ainsley's body sing in passion now knew how to hold and comfort her, to let her know that he understood her grief.

She could remain here for the rest of her life, in this room, in his arms, and be perfectly happy.

The door handle rattled, then came a knock, followed by the hollow voice of a footmen. "My lord? Her Majesty is ready for you now."

"Damn and blast," Cameron whispered.

Ainsley wanted to say the same. She peeled herself away from Cameron, wiping her eyes.

"Meet me here in the morning," Cameron said rapidly. "At nine o'clock. Can you do that? Without a bloody argument?"

Where he'd want to continue prying into her life, demanding to know why she'd not simply fly off with him. But he deserved to know. Ainsley nodded.

Cameron leaned down, gave her one hard kiss, and headed for the door where the footman was still knocking. "Yes, yes, I'm coming."

He opened the door, shielding Ainsley from the footman's view, then closed it, and was gone, leaving Ainsley alone with her tears.

At five minutes before nine the next morning, Ainsley was back in the drawing room, alone. She was still alone at five minutes past, still alone at half past. The clock on the mantel ticked ponderously, heavy chimes marking the quarter hours.

Cameron didn't come.

When the clock reached five minutes before the next hour, a maid entered. She approached Ainsley, curtseyed, held out a folded piece of paper, and said, "For you, ma'am."

Without betraying any interest in the note, the clock, or Ainsley, the maid curtseyed again and glided out of the room.

Ainsley unfolded the thick paper to find a few words written in a bold hand.

Daniel never stays where I tell him to stay. I'm off to Glasgow to extract him from a scrape. You win, mouse. On the train from Doncaster, after the last St. Leger race. The conductor will know how to find me. À bientôt.

Ainsley folded the creamy paper, pressed her lips to it, and tucked it into her bosom.

When she retreated to her room that night, once the queen had dismissed her for the evening, Ainsley sat down and wrote a long letter. She posted it off to Lady Eleanor Ramsay in the morning, directing it to Eleanor's father's tumbledown house near Aberdeen. Ainsley enclosed enough money for a railway ticket from Aberdeen to Edinburgh and told Eleanor quite sternly that she was to use it.

Ainsley Douglas and Lady Eleanor Ramsay faced each other over a corner table in the tea shop at the main station in Edinburgh a few days later, the shop a bit empty this early. A train stood ready outside, its steam hissing, the black bulk of its engine like a mighty ship.

Ainsley had not seen Eleanor in a while, though the two wrote regularly. Their mothers had been close friends, both at one time waiting on the queen. The queen had wanted Eleanor, higher born than Ainsley, to enter her household as well, but Lord Ramsay had tearfully begged for his daughter to stay home, and Eleanor couldn't refuse him. Eleanor's father was by no means feeble, but Ainsley agreed that the man would be entirely lost without Eleanor. That fact might explain why Eleanor had entertained no more offers of marriage after she'd famously jilted Hart Mackenzie, Duke of Kilmorgan, years before.

Eleanor had never revealed the reason she'd broken her engagement with Hart, though Ainsley, knowing Hart Mackenzie even the little she did, had some inkling. Hart had been enraged at the jilting and had a little while later married an English marquis's daughter. The wispy Sarah Graham had died trying to bringing Hart's son into the world, the child dying as well. Hart never spoke of Sarah, nor had he ever made any indication he would pursue marriage again. Eleanor had remained quietly at home and that had been that.

"Thank you for making the journey, El," Ainsley said warmly.

Eleanor heaped sugar into her tea, stirred, then put her spoon backward into her mouth and licked it clean.

"Not at all, my dearest Ainsley. A summons to Edinburgh to stuff myself with cakes is quite the most exciting thing that's happened in a twelvemonth. The entire household walked me to the station—cook, maid, the gardener. Even dear father left his books to escort us, though he had to stop along the way and collect every botanical specimen he saw. They put me on the train and waved me off, all cheering like mad and fluttering handkerchiefs. I felt like a princess."

Eleanor paused to sip her tea, and Ainsley laughed, feeling better already.

In the last ten years, Eleanor's father, Earl Ramsay, whose finances had always been shaky, had slowly slipped into poverty. Lord Ramsay wrote books on science and philosophy, and Eleanor assisted him. But though the books were highly praised by scholars, they brought in no money.

None of this had changed Eleanor's frank disposition or her sense of humor. Her hair was gold with a touch of red, elegant under her out-of-date hat, and her eyes were delphinium blue. She regarded Ainsley with keen intelligence while she piled cake on her plate with a long-fingered hand.

"Now, then," Eleanor said. "Your letter said that you wanted my advice about one of the maddening Mackenzie males. But Ainsley, dearest, you neglected to tell me *which* Mackenzie. Never say it's Daniel." She spoke lightly, but her eyes tightened.

Ainsley felt sudden remorse. "Oh, Eleanor, I'm so sorry. I assumed you'd naturally conclude who I meant. I'd never be so callous as to ask you for advice about *Hart*."

Eleanor let out her breath. "Well, that is a relief. I was preparing myself to be generous and tell you that I wished you every happiness, but truly, Ainsley, I think I'd rather have clawed your eyes out."

"I am sorry, El," Ainsley said. "I should have made myself clear. I didn't realize you still cared for him."

"You never forget the love of your life, Ainsley Douglas, no matter what he did to anger you, and no matter how much time has passed." Eleanor took another sip of tea, making her voice light. "Especially not when he's paraded through every newspaper and magazine you set eyes on. But we are not here to talk about me; you invited me all this way to talk about you. The remaining unmatched Mackenzie male is Cameron, so I conclude that it is he. Now, tell me everything."

Ainsley did, leaning forward and relating the entire tale in a low voice. Eleanor listened while she ate seedcake, avidly interested. Ainsley ended with Cameron's sudden visit to Balmoral, and her promise to give him her answer after the races at Doncaster.

She finished, and Eleanor sipped tea in thoughtful silence. Ainsley picked up her now-cold tea and drank, not noticing its chill.

Finally, Eleanor set down her cup and fixed Ainsley with a sharp look. "The fact that we are discussing Cameron's proposition at all means that you didn't simply slap him in high dudgeon and storm away. So, my dear, the question is, have you asked me here to persuade you into it or out of it?"

"I don't know." Ainsley pressed her hands to her face. "Eleanor, I can't possibly go off with him, but oh, if I don't . . . He'll move on to the next woman in the wings, won't he? I'm under no illusion that he wants to marry me. He said once that he even hated the sound of the word *marriage.* I understand, I suppose. I didn't know his wife, but she sounds ghastly."

"She was more than ghastly, my dear," Eleanor said around her next sip of tea. "Lady Elizabeth used to beat him."

Chapter 18

Ainsley's mouth dropped open. "She *beat* him?"

"With a poker mostly." Eleanor's voice was quiet but held vast rage. "Cameron is a large and strong man, of course, so he'd stop her, but usually he'd take the brunt on himself because he was keeping her away from Daniel. Or, Elizabeth would wait until Cameron was drunk and asleep, and then she'd go at him. She slipped him laudanum once or twice, Hart told me. Cameron had to begin ensuring he didn't fall asleep anywhere near her."

Which explained why Phyllida Chase had said that Cameron never took a woman to his bed. He had her everywhere else, yes, but not in a bed. That must have been a habit he'd cultivated, to avoid the chance that the woman he fell asleep with would wake him with a poker across his back. The scars on his thighs suddenly took on new and horrible meaning.

Ainsley realized she was clenching the handle of her

teacup too tightly for fragile porcelain. She set it down. "Dear heavens."

Eleanor shook her head. "Elizabeth was a cruel and crazed woman, and she resented Cameron for trapping her in marriage. She was a few years older than Cameron, and according to Hart, Cam fell wildly in love with her. I imagine that Cameron being the son of one of the richest men in England, standing to inherit the title if anything happened to Hart, was too tempting for Elizabeth to resist. Her parents did nothing to warn Cameron about her, being happy to be rid of the girl. Elizabeth had thought she'd simply do what she pleased, you see, after she married, with whatever man she pleased, and she did at first. When Cameron insisted that Elizabeth be faithful to him, she grew uncontrollable. It was an unfortunate match from the beginning."

Ainsley thought about the Cameron she knew—single-minded, stubborn, knowing what he wanted and letting nothing stand in his way. He could laugh, but there was always a bitter tinge to his laughter. Cameron had a reputation for taking up with women here, there, and everywhere, and he'd never fixed on one woman after his wife's death.

Ainsley had assumed he played the rakehell from boredom, but Eleanor's explanation told her a different tale. After a wife so awful to him, who'd destroyed whatever trust he had, Cameron would not have rushed eagerly back to the altar. This was Cameron's view of women then: Grasping and selfish like Phyllida Chase, or cruel and tormenting like Lady Elizabeth Cavendish.

"Poor Cameron," Ainsley said.

Eleanor smiled as she lifted her teacup. "Do be careful, Ainsley. They entice you, these Mackenzies, first with their wickedness and then with all that is heartbreaking."

"Why did Cameron not divorce her?" Ainsley asked. "He surely had grounds. Or at least tuck her into a remote house somewhere, away from him and Daniel?"

"Precisely because of Daniel." Eleanor refilled their cups then dropped five lumps of sugar into her freshened tea. "Elizabeth became with child very soon after they married, which infuriated her. She never wanted to be a mother. She would fly into rages, threaten to harm herself or to try to rid herself of the baby. Cameron didn't want to let her out of his sight—he was protecting Daniel from her even then. Elizabeth tried to tell Cameron—repeatedly—that Daniel wasn't his son, claiming any number of men to be his father. The trouble was, you see, any one of them could have been. Elizabeth was most generous with her body."

Ainsley remembered the look on Cameron's face when he'd found the letter from his wife's lover in the hidden drawer. The anger, the disgust, the old pain that hadn't quite dispersed. He'd kissed Ainsley right after that with a desperation, a need to forget.

"I think I rather hate her," Ainsley said.

"I'm not much fond of her myself," Eleanor said decidedly. "Cameron has a big heart, and it didn't deserve to be broken by someone like Elizabeth." She looked thoughtful. "Though I've come to believe that her need to rush about with other men was a kind of illness. Father read a piece from a scientific journal to me that explained that some people become obsessed with coupling just as others have a mania for gambling or alcohol. They can't stop themselves. They must lie with someone and experience that . . . ecstasy, let's call it, or they go a little mad. Father and I decided that perhaps Elizabeth must have been one of those people."

Ainsley blinked. "Good heavens, Eleanor, your *father* talked of this with you?"

"Of course. Dear Father has no idea that such things shouldn't be mentioned in the presence of a young lady. He's keen on all branches of science and has a wide-open mind, which means he'll discuss the mating habits of frogs or human beings and not have an inkling that there's a difference between them. Proprietarily, I mean. Frogs reproduce rather differently from human beings, of course."

Ainsley couldn't stop her laugh. Certainly anyone bringing up the mating habits of frogs, let alone human beings, at Patrick's dinner table would face the horrified silence of Patrick and Rona. Her brother and sister-in-law weren't unkind people, but they had very stringent ideas about manners and proper topics of conversation.

The laugh ended in a sigh, and Ainsley sat limply in her chair. "What do I do, Eleanor? Cameron goes on about diamonds and hotels in Monte Carlo as though I'll clap my hands and rush with him to the train."

Eleanor gave her a sympathetic smile. "Because Cameron is used to women who cross their eyes and fall over when he dangles diamond necklaces in front of them. They don't want him, they want his money, and he knows it."

He did know it. Cameron was a generous man, but not a stupid one. He knew exactly why the ladies flocked to him.

"I don't care about his money," Ainsley said.

"*I* understand that, but I wager Cameron hasn't the faintest idea how to woo a lady without bribing her. None of the Mackenzies do."

Eleanor spoke with conviction. Hart must have lavished gifts on Eleanor until she couldn't see, and still, Eleanor had told him to go.

Ainsley let out her breath. "If I refuse Cameron, I know that I will regret it for the rest of my life. But if I go, I'll ruin myself and disgrace my family." *Again*, she did not say. "My brothers would never forgive me."

"Well, you do not have to advertise that you are running off with him, you know. If you will forgive me for saying so, you are not the most socially prominent young lady in Britain. Go incognito."

Ainsley laughed, thinking of her costume at Rowlindson's party. "In a wig and mask?"

"Nothing so theatrical. Simply leave for a jaunt to the

Continent on your own. Ladies do such things nowadays all the time. They take walking tours of far-off countries by themselves and write books about their adventures. You're not an unmarried miss, but a respectable widow. If you meet Cameron on your travels, what of it?"

Ainsley stared across the table at Eleanor, and Eleanor looked unflappably back at her. "El, you are telling me to run away with a man to become his mistress."

"I am telling you to be happy. Even if it lasts only a little while. We must snatch what we can when we have the chance. Life is so very lonely when we don't."

Ainsley sat back, realizing that Eleanor probably hadn't been the wisest choice for advice on this matter. Ainsley had hoped for a clear-eyed, uncolored view of the Mackenzie family—and Eleanor had that—but Eleanor still loved them as hard as did Beth or Isabella. Ainsley hadn't wanted to go Isabella or Beth, because she knew Cameron's offer would become a family discussion, and Ainsley had not wanted that, and she knew that neither would Cameron.

But Eleanor, she saw, though she'd shown Hart the door, wasn't exactly an outsider. Eleanor obviously regretted her decision to jilt Hart, though she'd likely had good reason for it. Ten years ago, Hart Mackenzie hadn't had a pristine reputation. Ainsley had heard from Beth about the house he'd bought for his mistress, a woman called Mrs. Palmer. He'd visited Mrs. Palmer in this house for many years, and the things he'd done there hadn't been exactly conventional. Not until after his wife and child had died had Hart become much quieter and more discreet. He'd stayed with Mrs. Palmer, though, until that lady's death.

Eleanor lifted her teacup. "You're not an ingénue, Ainsley. You know exactly what you are getting yourself into. You know about men and what they want. You know the Mackenzies. You will be walking in with no illusions."

Ainsley poked at the seedcake on her plate. She loved cake but at the moment had lost her appetite. "Tell me, El.

If it were you—if Hart popped in and asked you to go away with him and be his lover—would you do it?"

Eleanor's eyes flickered. "He never would."

"But let us enter the realm of make-believe and suppose he did. Would you go with him?"

Eleanor flashed a smile. "Let Hart Mackenzie drape ropes of jewels about my neck and beg to share my bed at night? I would be sorely tempted. But my circumstance is a bit different than yours."

Ainsley drew an impatient breath. "But in a castle in the air, where all else is unimportant, *would you do it*?"

Eleanor studied her teacup for a moment, and when she looked up, her eyes were quiet. "Of course I would," she said. "I would in an instant."

Eleanor's train to take her back to Aberdeen pulled into the station not long later, and she and Ainsley left the teashop for the platform.

Eleanor wasn't certain what Ainsley would do, but she saw in Ainsley a lonely young woman who badly needed a moment of happiness. Whether Ainsley would be brave enough to snatch that moment remained to be seen.

Ainsley pressed the seedcake she'd asked the waitress to wrap for her into Eleanor's hand and thanked her as they exchanged a kiss good-bye. It was like Ainsley to disguise generosity as gratitude, Eleanor thought. Eleanor wasn't too proud to accept the cake, though. She'd take it home to Father, and they'd have such a treat.

Ainsley hurried from the station after their good-byes, likely having stolen this time from whatever errands she was supposed to be doing for the queen. Poor Ainsley had less freedom than Eleanor did. Eleanor still managed to maintain a circle of friends—at least, those friends who didn't give a toss about money. Only the very rich or the very poor could be so cavalier, so Eleanor's friends came in an odd range.

Eleanor turned from waving Ainsley off to step from platform to train compartment. She slipped, failed to steady herself, and was caught by a large, strong hand.

All the breath went out of her when she looked back and down at the face of Hart Mackenzie.

The golden gaze that studied her had grown, if anything, harder and harsher with experience. Hart's body was still broad and strong, shoulders stretching his finely tailored greatcoat, under which he wore his Mackenzie plaid kilt. Unshaved whiskers dusted Hart's jaw, a sign that he'd been working around the clock as usual, but no exhaustion tinged his intense gaze.

Eleanor sensed something new in him, however, a focus that hadn't existed before. She knew that Hart's ambition was as honed as ever—she read the newspapers—but the hope and humor that had once lightened his eyes was gone. This was a man who had experienced loss, first of his wife and only child, then of his longtime mistress. He seemed to exist on ambition alone, now.

"I heard about Mrs. Palmer," Eleanor said softly. "Hart, I am so very sorry."

His eyes flickered in surprise, and in that moment, Eleanor looked at the true Hart Mackenzie, the man who'd sacrificed so much that his family would not suffer. It had been Hart who'd forced the old duke to make generous trusts for his three younger brothers, so that they could live independently. Their father would have been happy to let Ian, Mac, and Cam starve to keep all the money in the dukedom.

How Hart had persuaded his father to do this, Eleanor never did discover. Eleanor was one of the few who even knew he'd done it. And now Hart, a man with so much power, so much wealth, and so much might, grieved for a simple courtesan.

His look told her that he wasn't certain of her motives, but he nodded. "Thank you."

Eleanor gave his hand a squeeze, her heart fluttering at the strength she felt through his gloves.

Hart smiled suddenly, a smile that held the challenge of a predator about to make a kill. A lion might look like that right before he leapt upon a gazelle that couldn't run away quite fast enough.

Eleanor tried to snatch her hand from his, but Hart closed his fingers on hers in an unshakable grip. The signal man on the platform blew a whistle, indicating that the train was about to leave. Hart transferred his grip to Eleanor's elbow and half shoved her up into the compartment, following her inside.

"This is your train?" Eleanor asked nervously. *Oh, mother mine, he can't mean to ride with me all the way to Aberdeen!*

"No." Hart stood in the open door frame until she fell into the seat, the package with the precious seedcake landing beside her.

The engine's whistle shrilled, and a waft of black smoke rolled back along the train. The car jerked.

"We're leaving," Eleanor said, frantic.

"I see that." Hart reached into his pocket, pulled out a folded note, and thrust it into her hand.

Not a note, a banknote, for one hundred pounds sterling. Eleanor opened her hand and the money fluttered to the floor.

"Hart, no."

Hart retrieved the note and tucked it under the string that bound the seedcake. "For your father, for research on his next book."

Without bothering to hurry, he took out a small gold case, extracted a pristine card, and held it out to her. When Eleanor wouldn't reach for it, Hart tucked it into the décolletage of her high-collared dress.

The heat of his fingers tore through her, and Eleanor realized at that moment that she would burn for this man for the rest of her life.

"If you need to see me for any reason, give that card to my majordomo," Hart was saying. "He'll know what to do."

Eleanor fought herself for control. "How very, very, *very* kind of you, Your Grace."

The cool duke's façade cracked and fled. "Eleanor." Hart cupped her face in gloved hands, and Eleanor's heart sped faster than this train would ever go. "Whatever am I going to do with you?"

She couldn't breathe. His mouth was so close to hers, his breath warm on her skin. He'd kiss her, and Eleanor would crumple, and he'd know the truth.

Hart touched the corner of her mouth, the movement so gentle she wanted to die.

The train jerked. Hart gave Eleanor a smile, stepped away from her, and dropped to the platform as the train started to glide forward.

He slammed the compartment door and gave Eleanor a lazy salute through the window as the train pulled out. Eleanor couldn't look away from him. Hart kept his gaze locked on Eleanor's until the train moved out of the station, and he was finally lost to sight.

One week later, Cameron Mackenzie lifted the shade of the train carriage window then let it fall again. He'd seen no woman hurrying across the dark platform, no form of Ainsley rushing for the last train from Doncaster.

"Bloody perfect ending to a damn rotten day."

Jasmine had come in sixth in her race, and Lord Pierson had been furious. He'd accused Cameron of deliberately throwing the race and had made a huge scene, threatening to get Cameron barred from the Jockey Club. An empty threat, because Cam had a better reputation in the club than Pierson.

Even so, one of Cam's trainers had to stop Cameron from punching Pierson in the jaw. Cameron had made the offer again, through clenched teeth, to simply buy Jasmine, but Pierson had refused. He'd had his grooms load Jasmine to take her away, and walked off.

Jasmine had looked back at Cameron like a child wondering why it couldn't stay where it wanted to. Cameron's heart had burned—*Damn it, I've fallen in love with a horse.*

Daniel, too, had been distraught, but he'd meekly agreed to remain behind with Angelo while Cameron wrapped up racing business in London, knowing that Cameron was still angry about Daniel's Glasgow adventure.

Daniel had decided, when his father had charged off to Balmoral, to go down to Glasgow for reasons Daniel hadn't yet made clear. While there, a gang of street youths had tried to rob him. Daniel had fought five of them manfully, but when the police came to arrest them, Daniel allowed himself to be arrested too instead of letting on that he'd been the victim. Apparently he'd gained the street youths' admiration, and they'd cheerfully shared a cigar and smuggled whiskey in the cells, until Cameron had arrived to wrest Daniel away.

Instead of being remorseful that he had pulled Cameron from his argument with Ainsley, Daniel had been angry that Cameron hadn't simply put Ainsley over his shoulder and run off with her.

Cameron was beginning to agree with Daniel, because Ainsley wasn't coming. The queen was notorious for keeping her clutches into ladies she liked, not wanting them to leave her for any reason. The bloody woman had about seven hundred children and grandchildren, but she kept her favorite ladies pasted to her side, angry when they wanted to leave her to marry or to return to husbands and families. They all slowly froze to death together in the monstrosity that was Balmoral, the queen's recently built "castle" that was about as Scottish as strudel.

The train engine huffed, the whistle blew, doors slammed up and down the train. Cameron took one more look at the platform, then let the shade fall again. His first-class carriage was comfortable, so he'd sleep well on the overnight journey. Alone.

The train jerked once and then began to creep out of the station. Six years had dragged by between Cameron's first encounter with Ainsley and this one, and . . . *Damn it all to hell, I can't wait another six years.*

Cameron got to his feet, ready to haul open the door and leap down. He'd go back to Balmoral, fetch Ainsley, and to hell with it.

The door to the corridor swung open, and the conductor stepped out of the way to let someone pass. "Is this it, ma'am?"

"Yes, thank you." Ainsley spoke in a breathless voice, dropped a tip into the man's hand, and breezed into the carriage. "You'll see to my luggage, won't you? I'm afraid there is rather a lot of it."

The conductor, looking smitten, touched his hat, and said, "Right away, ma'am."

He backed out and slammed the door. Ainsley drew the shades down over the corridor-facing windows, plucked off her gloves, and dropped into a seat.

Cameron remained standing as the train glided into the night. Ainsley looked fresh and bright, despite her hurry, different somehow. He realized after a moment that she wore vibrant blue instead of her usual gray or black, one of the ensembles Isabella had purchased for her in Edinburgh. Though her bodice was still buttoned to her chin, the fabric hugged her like a second skin, and her matching hat and veil turned her gray eyes almost silver.

"I'm sorry I nearly missed the train," she said. "I had to rush from Edinburgh, because the clothes Isabella ordered for me were ready, and they take up three trunks, which all had to be packed at the last minute. Isabella and Mac kindly gave me use of the townhouse they lease there, so

I'm afraid they know I've run off with you. Mac was rather pleased about it."

"He would be." Mac's method of persuading a woman to stay with him was to abduct her and make her think it was her own idea.

"I assume we'll make a stop in London?" Ainsley asked. "I can't imagine you'd run straight through to Paris tonight, would you? If I could find a room at a respectable hotel, I can sort through my things and decide what I truly need to take. Isabella thought the lot, but I think she is optimistic."

Cameron unstuck his tongue from the roof of his mouth. "We'll stop in London," he said, his voice gruff. "Not at a hotel. In Hart's house; he keeps it ready. In the morning, we'll marry."

Chapter 19

"Marry?" Ainsley felt suddenly light, floating, unreal. But no, Cameron was standing solidly above her, announcing that tomorrow he would marry her.

"Vows exchanged, a license," he said. "You'll have heard of it."

His eyes held anger and also something Ainsley didn't understand. "But I'm running away with you."

Cameron hauled her off the seat and sat down again with her firmly on his lap. "Are you mad, woman? You were right to turn me down. I'll not let you destroy your life for the likes of me."

Ainsley looked into his hard face and realized that what she saw in his eyes was fear. Not the nerves of a man contemplating matrimony, but stark panic.

"I won't promise to be a model husband," Cameron said. "Home at six for tea and the like. I work the horses all day during racing season and stay out all night in the off season. I drink, I play cards, and my friends are not respectable. I'd treat you like a mistress, a lover, because I sure as hell don't know how to treat a woman like a wife. If that's not what you want, tell me now and go back to your queen."

His voice grated, a man saying things he didn't know how to say.

Ainsley made herself laugh. "Do you know, I once thought that if you proposed to a woman it would be wildly romantic, perhaps in a boat on a crystal blue lake. You'd sweep the lady off her feet—or maybe off her oar—and have her swooning with delight."

"I'm not romantic, Ainsley. I just want you with me."

His words rippled fire through her, warm against the September cold. "Are you saying that you want us to behave as lovers but marry to save the scandal?"

"This way, if you tire of me, you won't have to risk your brother refusing to house you. You'll always have money and a place to live as my wife. I'll provide for you no matter what you think of me."

She blinked. "Goodness, you're ending the marriage before it's begun."

"I was a rotten husband before, and I can't promise I won't be a rotten one this time. If you don't want this, you can leave the train at the next stop."

They were picking up speed, racing through the darkness.

"All my trunks are on the train," Ainsley said. "So I have to marry you or risk you chucking out my new wardrobe."

Again she saw the flare of panic, which he masked with anger. "The minute you don't want to live with me, you tell me. Understand? No divorce, no separation, no bloody rows. You tell me, and I give you a house to live in and money to do whatever you want."

"I will bear it in mind."

Cameron growled. He slid his strong hand behind her neck and pressed an openmouthed kiss to her lips.

Warmth, delight, strength. Ainsley wrapped her arms around him and gave in. Deciding to go through with running off with him had been the most difficult choice she'd ever made. But she'd known in the end that if she didn't go, she'd regret it forever. Fate had given her a chance, and she'd realized that she couldn't turn her back on that chance. Or on Cameron.

Changing the decision into one of marrying him was ridiculously easy. She belonged to this man—she was eloping with him. She could do anything she wanted with him.

Ainsley leaned back, encouraging him down with her, and he ended up on top of her on the seat. His weight on hers made her heart hammer with excitement. Ainsley dared stroke his back down to his hips to cup his tight backside under the plaid.

The door slammed open. Ainsley tried to scramble up, but Cameron pushed her protectively behind him while he prepared to lambaste the intruder.

Daniel banged the door shut and more or less fell onto the opposite seat. He grinned at Ainsley, ignoring his father. "So you're here at last, are ye? Excellent. Now we'll have some larks."

The next morning, Ainsley Douglas stood in the parlor of Hart Mackenzie's London townhouse and married Lord Cameron Mackenzie by the special license he'd obtained before he'd even gone to Doncaster. The witnesses were Hart's housekeeper and butler and the vicar's wife. Daniel stood at his father's side, smiling like mad.

Ainsley was sandy-eyed as she repeated her vows, because the train had run through the night, arriving in London early that morning.

Before Ainsley could recover from the shock of the vicar pronouncing her and Cameron man and wife, Ainsley was in a train again with Cameron and Daniel, a heavy gold band on her finger, heading for Dover. Cameron wanted to start the Paris trip right away.

Ainsley was happy to leave England, because, though she and Cameron had legally married, their elopement stood to be the scandal of the decade. An affair Ainsley might discreetly conceal, as Eleanor had suggested, but the sudden marriage of the black sheep of the Mackenzie family to a nobody would be all over the newspapers.

Cameron was not only the brother of a duke, he was heir to the title while Hart remained childless. Despite Ainsley's mother having been a viscount's daughter, the McBride family was neither prominent nor powerful, nor particularly wealthy. The marriage would be decried as a misalliance and talked about up and down the country. Particular consideration would be given as to by what means Ainsley had duped Lord Cameron, the notorious womanizer who'd vowed never to take another wife, into the marriage. The queen would have apoplexy.

Therefore, Ainsley was happy to board the train and flee to the Continent. Patrick and Rona, when they received her telegram, would be as stunned and bewildered as the queen.

But Eleanor had been right: Ainsley was no longer a dewy-eyed debutante. She was a respectable widow with experience of the world, making choices with a clear head.

Well, an almost clear head, Ainsley thought as Cameron, having settled the tickets, sat down next to her in the compartment. His large body took up most of the seat, not allowing an inch of space between them. With Cameron, it was difficult for her to be sensible.

Daniel went right along with them, beaming at them from his side of the carriage. Cameron's usual practice was to leave Daniel with Angelo in Berkshire until Michaelmas term began, when Daniel would return to school. It was the arrangement they had every year, Angelo not wanting to leave England and his family behind, Cameron not trusting anyone else with his horses while he was away. Traveling abroad was risky for a Romany anyway.

But Daniel had begged to accompany them. Ainsley, seeing the lonely desperation in the lad's eyes, had taken his side. Cameron, already looking out of his depth, agreed.

They broke the journey in Le Havre, where Cameron booked three rooms in the most expensive hotel, one each for himself, Ainsley, and Daniel. When Ainsley pointed out that, now they were married, they could share a bedroom, Cameron gave her an unfathomable look and told her that the rooms were small and he'd take up too much space.

Ainsley thought she wouldn't mind Cameron filling the space in her bedchamber, but Cameron didn't give her a chance to argue. In the restaurant that night, Daniel ate with gusto, and Cameron consumed his meal steadily, like man determined. Ainsley found herself jumpy and without appetite.

Later, as Ainsley brushed her hair for bed, Cameron entered her room, closed the door, and locked it behind him.

Ainsley froze, hairbrush poised. She hadn't seen Cameron alone since Daniel had burst in on them in the train compartment at Doncaster. As though the young man played chaperone, he'd stuck to them until after supper tonight, when he'd bade them a cheerful good night outside the dining room.

Not to go to bed, Ainsley noted. Daniel had strolled off to the lounge, probably to smoke cigars and play cards. Cameron let him without a word, and Ainsley thought it wisest not to interfere on her first night as Lady Cameron Mackenzie.

Lady Cameron. That would take some getting used to.

"Have you settled in?" she asked in a bright voice.

Cameron came to her, plucked the brush from her hand, and laid it on the table. His mouth was hot on her neck as he began unbuttoning her nightdress.

Ainsley half closed her eyes and leaned back against him. "I think all the buttons tonight, don't you?"

Cameron bit her cheek. His fingers made swift work of the buttons, and he plunged his hands inside her warm nightgown. "I've been dying for you."

Dying. Yes. Ainsley had been burning for him for weeks. They'd sat upright together on the train to Dover, Daniel across from them, and on the ferry they'd watched England recede from the deck, standing side by side but without touching each other. Agony.

Cameron's blood went hot at the taste of her, so sweet and delectable. Look at her, with the little half smile, her eyes with that wicked gleam. *I'm hurting for you, my wife.*

My wife.

Her breasts were heavy in his hands. Ainsley breathed against his mouth while he played with her, then his hand went lower, cupping between her legs to find the curls there damp and hot. Ainsley's intake of breath excited him, as did the scent of her, warm and aroused.

Cameron reached up and turned down the gaslight. The room dimmed to near darkness, but Cameron wanted that. He had too many scars, too many old hurts, that he didn't want her to see.

He stood Ainsley up and pulled her nightdress all the way off. Ainsley leaned one hand on the dressing table, his cool, nude lover, waiting to watch her man undress.

Cameron divested himself of coat, cravat, waistcoat, stiff shirt, too many layers between himself and her. He pulled the undershirt from his flesh, jerked socks and shoes from his feet.

Then he hesitated, standing only in his kilt. He could keep the kilt on, because he'd gotten out of the underbreeches before he'd come in. He didn't mind so much if she saw the scars on the backs of his legs, but there were terrible ones on his buttocks that Cameron wasn't sure he wanted her to see.

Ainsley hooked her finger around his waistband and tugged. "Now then, laddie, don't be bashful."

Cameron dissolved into laughter. Cameron Mackenzie had never been called bashful in his life.

What the hell? He unpinned the kilt and let it drop, at the same time he sat down on the chair. It was a delicate chair, a lady's dressing room chair, and Cameron felt its slender legs wobble.

Ainsley gave him a sly smile as she ran her fingers up his long and already throbbing shaft. Cameron groaned at the fire that raced up his cock. *Dying for you* wasn't much of an exaggeration.

Cameron clasped her waist and pulled her down to him, fitting her to him and the chair. Ainsley half closed her eyes, her smile becoming a moue of passion as Cameron guided himself into her.

Ah, back where I belong. The position shoved him deep inside her, Ainsley closing around him like a fist. And like a fist, she squeezed.

Cameron eased his hands to her hips, kissing her neck, taking the flesh in his teeth. He suckled, and she made a soft noise in her throat. Cameron suckled harder, marking her. *Mine. Forsaking all others.* Damn, it had felt good to say those words.

Ainsley rocked on him, her body instinctively wanting to join with his as much as it could. Cameron guided her to the movement that would give them both the most satisfaction.

Her breasts flattened against his chest, nipples pressing him with pleasing friction. She kissed his mouth, the kisses clumsy with passion.

"That's the way," Cameron whispered. He nibbled her earlobe. "That's the way to love me, my Ainsley."

Her answer was a soft noise of pleasure.

"You're so tight and wet," he said. "Wicked Ainsley, so wet for her lover."

Her little, "Umm," made his heart beat wildly.

They rocked together, the chair creaking its protest, Ainsley's legs wrapped firmly around him. Cameron braced his bare toes in the carpet, stroked hands through Ainsley's silk swath of hair, and lost himself.

He was going to finish too soon. Cameron groaned with it, not ready, wanting to rock here with her far into the night. But his body was too excited, Ainsley too soft and beautiful. The scent of woman, and loving, undid him.

Ainsley's breath started to come faster as she reached her peak, her hips rocking in a rhythm that didn't have to be taught.

Cameron went with her willingly. His buttocks left the chair as he drove hard up into her, bracing her hips so the joining would be fast and strong.

The words that poured out of his mouth were blunt and filthy in praise of her body and what it did to him. Ainsley flushed, her eyes starry, her cries of delight growing louder as he spoke.

As her voice broke—*Yes, yes, Cameron, please!*—Cameron came. He was halfway off the chair, Ainsley screaming in pleasure. Cameron's shout joined hers.

He crashed down on the chair again, its legs definitely creaking, but they held.

"Did I hurt you?" He kissed her, tumbled her hair. "Love, did I hurt you? Are you all right?"

Ainsley stilled his word with her fingers. "Cam, I'm fine. It was beautiful. So beautiful."

"You're beautiful, Ainsley." Cameron cradled her close, breathing hard with the finish. She was soft and warm and tasted and smelled so good.

Not until he knew he was hardening again for the next round, did Cameron realize he'd spilled his seed inside her. It hadn't occurred to him to pull out, and not because he'd remembered she was his wife. The marriage ceremony and all it meant hadn't yet made an impression on his senses.

He'd wanted only to be inside Ainsley and stay there, where everything was safe and splendid, and her tenderness wrapped him and eased every hurt in his soul.

Cameron loved her twice more on the chair, then he carried her to the bed. Ainsley half woke when he pulled the covers over her naked body and caught his wrist as he made to turn away.

"Stay here with me," she whispered.

He looked down at her for a long time, not debating, Ainsley thought, but fighting something inside himself. He wasn't speaking because he couldn't.

Cameron clenched his fists, a muscle moving in his throat, a large man delectable in nothing but a kilt wrapped carelessly around his waist. She saw him deliberately calm his anger, second by second, while he fixed his gaze on her. He wasn't seeing her, but his eyes never left her.

"It's almost morning," he said in a careful voice. "Our train leaves early. Go to sleep."

He turned and strode out the door, banging it so hard that the curtains fluttered on the bed. Ainsley heard him move across the suite and slam the door to his own room. Then, ever so faintly came the click of the lock.

Ainsley lay down again, her breath hurting her. Her body hummed from the warm, sweet love they'd made on the chair. Cameron gave all to lovemaking, his entire body engaged in the act. He was such a big man, and yet he'd held her so that she didn't fall, had taken their combined weight all on himself.

How a man with such raw brutality could be so tender, Ainsley didn't know, but Cameron managed it.

But his fear when she'd asked him to stay had been real. Deep panic had flashed in his eyes, and he'd fought himself away from her.

That such a strong man should fear angered her. Ainsley determined then and there to delve to the bottom of it, to have Cameron explain how he felt, and erase what had been done to him the best she could. She would do it.

The dual emotions—elation at lovemaking and worry for Cameron mixed together and kept her eyes open. As tired as she was, she couldn't relax into sleep until she was on the swaying train to Paris in the bright sunshine of the morning.

~

Once they reached Paris, a lavish coach took them to the townhouse Cameron rented in a street off the Rue de Rivoli. The house rose six stories, with a wrought-iron railed staircase twisting through its grand foyer to a dome at the top.

Ainsley would have her own bedroom here as well, with windows that overlooked the garden behind the house. Cameron's room was in the front of the house, with Daniel's on the floor above theirs.

The townhouse was elegantly beautiful, modern, and quite unlike anything Ainsley had ever lived in. The queen's private spaces tended to be crowded, cluttered, and full of family photos, her public rooms vast and lavish. Cameron's house sported cool marble tiles and light-colored paneling, and was filled with paintings in the new styles of Degas, Manet, Monet, and the young Renoir. The furniture was clean-lined in the new handcrafted style that was a backlash against the ornately carved and mightily uncomfortable manufactured furniture of the day.

Money had gone into this house, and good taste—likely Mac had suggested the paintings and Isabella the décor—but it was still a bachelor's house. Cool and elegant, but a bit bare.

When Ainsley suggested she might stitch a few pillows for the parlor, Cameron looked at her as though she'd lost her mind. Then he took her shopping.

Ainsley had visited Paris once, on her fateful trip to the Continent with Patrick and Rona, but they'd taken rooms in a small hotel in an inexpensive district. Rona had been so nervous about the city that she hadn't wanted to venture very far from the hotel, so Ainsley had seen little of Paris.

Cameron showed her a new world. He took her to boutiques that sold everything a householder could want, to art dealers eager to sell Cameron the very best, and shops that dealt in expensive objets d'art. Ainsley could buy pillows ready-made or order some made to her taste. She did so, but then she went to a shop that specialized in luxurious embroidery skeins and outfitted herself with a new embroidery basket filled with everything she needed. Heaven.

They lunched in a café, and Ainsley discovered something else Paris did well—cake. Ainsley loved cake, and the confections of many thin layers separated with chocolate or jam or sugar syrup satisfied her soul. She ate an extra-large piece during their fourth shopping expedition and licked her fork, looking up to see Cameron watching her with amused eyes.

Ainsley shrugged. "I like cake."

"Paris has the best cakes," Daniel said, diving into his second slice. "Every café on this boulevard has their own specialty. You could go up and down and try a different one every day."

Ainsley grinned. "Yes, let's."

Cameron only laughed at them, the sound warm. It was the first time he'd laughed since Ainsley had joined him in Doncaster. Ainsley savored the laugh as she savored the last morsel of chocolate cream on her plate.

That night, Cameron took her to another new world, one Ainsley had glimpsed only in newspapers depicting the high life. Cameron himself picked out what she'd wear—a dark red and silver satin confection Isabella had dreamed up that went well with the diamonds Cameron had given her at Kilmorgan.

"It's hardly matronly," she said as Cameron laid the diamonds across her bosom and snapped the catch.

Cameron's gaze met hers in the mirror of her dressing

table. "Nothing matronly for you any longer, Ainsley Mackenzie. You are a beautiful woman. I want all to see how beautiful you are, and envy me."

"I was joking."

He kissed her neck. "I wasn't."

Ainsley found it heady to look so unlike herself as Cameron took her out into the Paris night, plunging her into the whirl of the avant-garde. More so having Cameron beside her in his black coat and Mackenzie plaid kilt. He was a powerful man of raw handsomeness, and now he belonged to her. Ladies looked at her in envy and curiosity, wondering who was the fair-haired nothing who'd snared the very eligible Lord Cameron.

"We must have cake after," Ainsley said as she sipped champagne at the restaurant Drouant. "That chocolate one with the cream in the middle. I think it's my favorite, though I'm not certain. I have many more to try."

Cake was a safe topic. Despite her determination, whenever Ainsley tried to bring up the question of the two of them sharing a bed, Cameron's eyes would harden, and he'd change the subject. Usually in a bad-tempered way. He'd started doing so if he so much as thought Ainsley would mention the word *bed*. Their conversations had been reduced to inanities, their lovemaking intense but without words.

"Most women want to rush up and down the boulevards buying jewels and hats," Cameron said now. "You head straight for the *boulangerie*."

Ainsley matched his careless tone. "Perhaps that is because we were allowed only very stingy slices of cake at Miss Pringle's Academy. I learned that if I wanted cake, I had to steal it."

"So that is the explanation for your life of crime."

"The cake was worth stealing, you can be certain. The cook was French, and she knew how to make tortes with the layers and layers of caramel and cream between them.

I realize now that she only gave us the barest taste of the joys of France."

"I'll take you all over the country so you can try the cake of every region," Cameron said.

"Truly? That would indeed be splendid—"

Ainsley's words cut off in a surprised squeak as a woman sat down in the chair next to her and helped herself to Ainsley's champagne.

"Lady Cameron Mackenzie, I do believe," Phyllida Chase said, and laughed. "Really, darling, it's too bad of you."

Chapter 20

"Oh, don't look so alarmed." Phyllida set down the glass, then took an oyster from Cameron's plate and tipped it down her throat. "I think it wonderful that you've gone and eloped with the elusive Lord Cameron. I'm happy for you, even if he did throw me over for a younger woman."

Her eyes glittered in mirth, the brittleness gone from her laughter. Phyllida Chase's ice had melted.

"Would you like to join us, Phyllida?" Ainsley asked her coolly. "They'll bring you your own plate and glass if you ask them."

Phyllida sent her a sunny smile. "That would be lovely." She turned and waved through the crowd. "Giorgio, I'm here. I've found friends."

A broad-shouldered, dark-haired man moved past the tables toward them, and Cameron rose to meet him.

Phyllida caught the man's hand when he reached them. "Look, darling, it's Lord Cameron and his new wife. Ainsley, this is Giorgio Prario, the famous tenor. Giorgio, love, they've invited us to dine with them."

The Italian man was alarmingly tall, and he stood toe-to-toe with Cameron. But Signor Prario held out his hand in a friendly manner and took Cameron's in a firm grip. "Yes, the Scottish lord who provided us with the means to remove to a happier place. I thank you." He bowed to Ainsley. "My lady. I also thank you."

Ainsley blinked. "*Cameron* provided you the means?"

The two men sat down and the ready waiters appeared with extra plates and cutlery, glasses and napkins. More champagne was poured, and the maître d'hôtel personally offered them the best from the kitchen. Cameron was a very rich man, and every restaurateur in Paris knew it.

"Money for the letters, darling," Phyllida said when the waiters finally departed. "You didn't think I truly cared for what the queen gets up to with her horseman, did you? I only cared that she'd pay dearly to save herself embarrassment." She beamed at Cameron. "Cam's generosity gave me the last bit I needed so that Giorgio and I could set up a house here. My husband is busily divorcing me in London, and when that's all done, Giorgio and I will be married."

Phyllida radiated happiness. Her smile was wide, her eyes soft, and she looked far younger than the cold, remorseless woman Ainsley had faced in the gardens at Kilmorgan.

"Giorgio is now the most sought-after tenor on the Continent," Phyllida went on, voice filled with pride. "The crowned heads are all demanding him. He's giving a concert tomorrow night at the opera house. Darlings, you must come. You'll understand my infatuation with him when you hear him sing."

"But, Phyllida," Ainsley burst out as soon as Phyllida paused for breath. "Why all the scheming with the letters? Why not just tell me what you wanted the money for? I might have been a bit more sympathetic, or even tried to help you get it."

Phyllida's eyes widened. "Confess to the prim-and-proper confidante of the queen that I wanted to run away from my lawfully wedded husband? You, who were so famously devoted to an elderly man who bored you senseless?" Phyllida lifted her glass of champagne. "I am *delighted* to see you've let Cameron corrupt you."

Giorgio had turned to Cameron to ask him a question about horses, and the two men were already deep in conversation about that. Ainsley watched Cameron become interested in their discussion about differences in various race courses.

I was already corrupted, dear Phyllida. Cameron simply made me acknowledge it.

"Surely you could have raised the money without resorting to blackmail," Ainsley said.

"Not at all. My so-called friends were as upright and closed-minded as you. They'd rather obey the rules and live in misery than boldly snatch a few moments of happiness. Besides, I wanted to punish Her Little Majesty for forcing me into marriage with an ice-cold man. To Mr. Chase, a wife is little more than an automaton to stand beside him and say the right things at the right time—to benefit *him*. I'm surprised he didn't store me in a closet every night and wind me up again every morning."

"Was Signor Prario the happiness the queen had taken from you?" Ainsley asked, remembering their conversation in the garden. "The reason she made you marry Mr. Chase?"

"No, no, I didn't meet Giorgio until about a year ago. But it was a similar thing—ten years ago, the most delightful man in the world asked me to marry him, but the queen refused to let me. He wasn't rich enough or well-born enough to be able to override the queen's objections, and she persuaded my family to her side. I was too young and too afraid to simply run away with him. He's long gone, in America, probably married to someone else by now. Mr. Chase was looking for a society wife about the same time, and the queen influenced my family to marry me off to him instead. Our Victoria buried me in misery for ten long years. I decided that she needed to suffer a little for it, though she'll never quite understand what she did to me."

Ainsley thought she understood a little. Phyllida was a woman of strong emotions, and being locked to a man who had no interest in her must have been very, very hard. Ainsley's marriage hadn't been her choice either, but at least John Douglas had been a warm man. Friendly and kind, he'd done his best to make his young bride happy. The fact that he hadn't entirely succeeded hadn't been his fault.

One thing Ainsley *didn't* understand, however. "If you were so in love with Signor Prario, Phyllida, why did you take up with Cameron?"

Phyllida waved this away. "Because Cameron has a reputation for lavishing very expensive gifts on his ladies." Phyllida glanced pointedly at Ainsley's diamonds, and Ainsley stopped herself touching the strand on her bosom. "Giorgio and I wanted to elope, but neither of us had a bean. He raised money by singing, and I by the only way I knew how—out of other men. Cameron is very generous, you must admit."

"And Signor Prario didn't mind this?"

Giorgio was now engrossed in his discussion with Cameron, which had moved to sport in general. He didn't look in the least worried that Cameron had once been his mistress's lover.

"Giorgio understands that I love him to distraction," Phyllida said. "He knows that people like us need patrons—singers no different than ladies. Now he's attracted a patron of his own, a very rich, elderly Frenchman who dotes on young tenors. So we have no more worries about money." Phyllida gave Ainsley an open look. "You don't know, darling, what it's like to fall asleep at night with a man who adores you. To open your eyes in the morning and look upon him, knowing that your day will be filled with delight. It's absolute bliss."

No, Ainsley didn't know what it was like. She had to glance away, to pretend interest in the last drop of champagne in her glass.

Phyllida rattled on, not knowing that she'd said anything awkward. "I can already tell that you're good for Cameron—heavens, he *married* you, the man who put it about, loudly, that he'd never go to the altar again. The Mackenzies are hard, hard men, but you seemed to have softened this one a little." She squeezed Ainsley's hand. "Do come to the concert, you and Cameron both. You won't regret it."

Too damn many people here. Cameron shifted on his seat in the crowded box high above the stage while below them, Prario burst into song.

The fact that Phyllida has stuffed Prario's box with as many people as she could meant that Ainsley sat slap against Cameron on his right. This was fine, but the presence of so many others meant that he couldn't take advantage of the closeness as he'd like. He had to sit, hard and aching, with Ainsley's scent under his nose, and not be able to do anything about it.

Phyllida sat on the other side of Ainsley, with Phyllida's Parisian friends taking up the other chairs. The box was tiny in the eighteenth-century jewel box of a theatre, and Phyllida sat forward to watch Giorgio Prario, her face glowing with love.

Cameron had to admit that Prario was good. His voice filled the theatre with solid sound, his notes unwavering. Cameron tried to lose himself in the beauty of the music, while his trousers stretched too tight. He should have overridden his Parisian valet's horror and worn his kilt.

Ainsley leaned to him, her warmth heady, and her sweet voice drifted into his ear. "How many buttons, Lord Cameron?"

Cameron's breath stopped. He felt a hand on his waistband,

but their corner of the box was too dark for him to see his own lap. Ainsley's hair and eyes glowed in the light from the stage, and her smile was sultry.

"Devil," he murmured back.

"I say four." Her breath tingled down every nerve.

"Eight." That would open him all the way. "The whole bloody lot."

"You're daring, my lord."

"I don't believe you'll do it," he whispered back.

Ainsley popped open the first button, bold as brass. She kept her eyes on the stage, sitting modestly in her chair while her fingers opened buttons too damn slowly for his taste. Cameron's heart hammered as each one came undone, and then he was sitting in the opera house with his trousers open.

Cameron wore thick underwear against the cold of October, but damned if Ainsley didn't find a way inside. She'd removed her gloves, he noted as her bare fingers closed around him.

On the stage, Prario launched into an aria. The crowd hung on every note. Ainsley's hand slid down Cameron's immense and burning hardness and squeezed.

He hid a groan. The music swelled, and the noise released from Cameron's throat was drowned in Giorgio's notes.

Cameron leaned his forehead in his hand as Ainsley worked him. Ainsley, the minx, kept her gaze on the stage, even plied her fan languidly, all the while her left hand squeezed, pulled, stroked, twisted.

When her fingers touched his tight balls, Cameron almost left the chair. He made himself still, his hand clenched on his thigh while her hand tightened on *him*.

What she did drove him wild. He wanted to pull Ainsley onto the chair with him and burrow under her skirts until he was satisfied. He wanted to drag her to him for a long kiss; he wanted to rip the buttons from her bodice and feast on the package inside.

"Damn you," he whispered.

Ainsley smiled. She glided her hand up and down him in fine, hot strokes. God, he was coming apart. He clenched his jaw to stifle his groans, but he wanted to shout to the world what his sweet little lover was doing to him in the dark of the box.

Below them, Prario wound to the top of the aria, his voice clear and true as he scaled the notes. He reached the top one and held it, and Cameron broke.

Cam snatched a handkerchief from his pocket and pressed it over himself, Ainsley moving her hand away just in time. Cameron's seed spilled in an ecstasy of feeling and music, joy in the heat of Ainsley pressed against him.

"I want to be doing this inside you," he said savagely into her ear. "I want to feel you taking me, knowing that you're mine."

"I'd like that too," she whispered.

Cameron rode out his climax as Prario's voice slid downward in glissando. At the end, Prario threw out his arms and bellowed his last, loud note.

The crowd roared its appreciation, and Phyllida leaned to Ainsley, eyes shining. "Didn't I say he was wonderful?"

"Indeed," Ainsley said calmly as Phyllida sprang to her feet. Ainsley pulled on her gloves and rose to join the ovation, leaving Cameron to hastily refasten his trousers in the dark.

As soon as the door closed behind them in the townhouse, Cameron said to the footman, "Leave us."

Well trained, the footman turned down the last gaslight and discreetly faded away. Ainsley's heart fluttered in excitement. Cameron had refused Phyllida's invitation to a grand soiree after the performance and had nearly shoved Ainsley into his town coach, telling the coachman to get them quickly home.

Now Cameron pressed Ainsley into the paneled wall in the dark, pinning her wrists above her head. He kissed her without a word, not letting her speak or ask questions. He was taking, lifting Ainsley up the wall until their faces were level.

His kisses were brutal, burning. Cameron might have kept his wanting dammed after she'd played with him in the theatre, but now he let the dam burst.

"Vixen," he whispered. "Unmanning me in public."

Ainsley licked across his mouth. "I enjoyed it. I believe you did as well."

His voice went soft but savage as he used words that should offend her but instead excited her beyond measure. He told her what he wanted to do to her, and what pet names he'd call her. No lady should listen to such things, but, as Cameron had pointed out weeks ago, Ainsley wasn't quite a lady.

He kissed her bosom, diamonds catching in his teeth. His hands went to the clasps on the back of her bodice, and he made a grunt of frustration as he tugged.

"Tear it open," she whispered. "I don't care."

She didn't. Why stop this sensation when a simple needle and thread would repair the damage?

Cameron smiled a feral smile, and he ceased being gentle. He yanked wide her bodice, kissing and licking her flesh as the fabric came away. The cool of the panel pressed into her back, the hot hardness of Cameron into her front. Ainsley felt dizzy, decadent, wicked.

He disrobed her, a layer at a time, right there in hall beneath the curve of the spiral stairs. So many layers a lady had to wear, and Cameron kissed her and touched her as each one came off.

Ainsley didn't protest until he tugged open his trousers, not even bothering to remove his coat.

"We're in the front hall," she said.

"We were in a box in the theatre. You didn't worry about propriety then."

"It was dark."

"It's dark here, and my servants know damn well better than to disturb me."

While Cameron spoke, he lifted Ainsley against the wall, cushioning its hard surface with his arms. He supported her hips, and by now she knew how to wrap her legs around him as Cameron entered her in one smooth stroke.

The erotic feeling of him awakened her, excited her. His words died to whispered breaths, and his strength kept Ainsley from falling.

Nothing existed at that moment but herself and him. The raw sensuality of Cameron, the smooth lip of the paneling, the sounds in his throat as he loved her.

Hot, hard, sensation. Ainsley arched against her lover, the feel of his coat exciting against her bare skin. Cameron caught the sounds of her aching need in his mouth.

They rocked into the paneling, and then his eyes went dark, his pupils spreading, and she felt him release inside her. Cameron kept thrusting, his kisses hotter but more relaxed, the frenzy dying into warmth.

Cameron carried Ainsley upstairs, where the coal fire heated her bedchamber, and laid her on the chaise while he quickly got out of his clothes. Ainsley's clothes they'd left all over the hall. She started to protest that they should retrieve them, but he silenced her with a kiss. That's what he'd hired the damn servants for, he growled.

Cameron wanted loving, not talking. The armless chaise was perfect for having Ainsley on top of him, and soon, Cameron was buried inside her again, Ainsley sighing in pleasure.

Damn, but she was beautiful. Ainsley's breasts moved while she rode him, nipples dusky pink against her Scots-pale skin. Her hair was still piled on top of her head, some of the little curls dripping down her neck.

When Ainsley gave him a little smile, her eyes half closed, Cameron knew that no woman would ever be more beautiful than Ainsley. The softness of her body, even the fading, snaking scars on her belly, made her so, so lovely. She belonged to him, always, forever.

He'd loved her squeezing him with her hand, but being inside her was ten times better. She was tight, damned tight. He loved it. He loved *her.*

The last thought made Cameron lose all control. He rocked against her, hands on her thighs, her hands splayed on his chest as she swayed. She made sweet noises in her climax, but Cameron's coming was raw. He held on to her, tight, tight, and his *Oh, fuck!* rang through the room.

Never go, never. I need this. I need you.

He pulled Ainsley down to him and they drowsed in afterglow, warm by the fire. He pressed his cheek to Ainsley's hair as she skimmed her fingers across his chest, both of them exhausted by passion.

He didn't let himself think much as they cuddled together. This moment was too important for stray thoughts. There was only Ainsley, and himself, and now.

Cameron rested with her until the window lightened to gray. Ainsley slept against his chest as he held her, her breath on his skin.

Finally, he rose and carried her to the bed, Ainsley still sleeping. He laid her down and covered her as tenderly as he'd used to with Daniel, when the lad had been a boy in a cot.

Ainsley's eyes fluttered open. "Stay with me," she whispered. "Please, Cam."

Chapter 21

She hadn't asked him that in a while. Cameron was already hard and hot for her again, but something dark twisted inside him, tendrils wrapping him so tightly he couldn't breathe.

Ainsley's eyes held longing, but Cameron was already moving from the bed, shaking his head.

"Eleanor Ramsay explained to me what your wife did to you," Ainsley said behind him. "I understand why you don't let yourself sleep in the same room with a woman."

Cameron turned around. Ainsley was sitting up, the sheet pulled to her chin, watching him.

"With anyone," Cameron said. "And Eleanor didn't tell you all of it."

No one knew but Cam. Cameron hadn't been able to confess every truth, even to Hart, and he didn't want to tell beautiful, unmarred Ainsley that his wife had not only beaten him with that poker, but on two occasions had tried to rape him with it.

He remembered the incidents with clarity, even though so much time had passed. The wash of pain that had jerked him out of deep slumber, Elizabeth's laughter, more pain, blood, his own screams. He'd flung Elizabeth away, and still she'd laughed.

He'd started allowing himself to sleep only when he was alone, behind a locked door. But damned if Elizabeth hadn't tricked a servant into letting her into Cameron's chamber late one night so she could go at Cameron again. The only thing that had worked after that was posting a guard, both on his own door and Elizabeth's. She'd railed about that too.

The darkness cleared a little to let him see Ainsley's gray eyes, shining in the equally gray dawn.

"It's not just what she did to me," Cameron said with difficulty. "It's what I might do to you. If you woke me suddenly, I might strike out and hurt you."

He could tell she didn't understand. Cameron went back to the bed and leaned down to her, resting his fists on the mattress.

"Daniel woke me up once, when he was about ten years old," he said. "I threw him across the room. My own son. I could have killed him."

The horror of that moment had never gone away. Daniel had lain still on the floor, unconscious, while Cameron had rushed to him, lifted his limp body in his arms. Resilient, Daniel hadn't been badly hurt, thank God. Daniel had later said, cheerfully, that it had been his own fault. He'd forgotten that his dad was a little crazy.

Daniel taking the blame for the incident had kicked Cameron in the gut. Then Angelo had tried to blame himself for not realizing that Daniel had crept upstairs to his father's bedroom. Cameron had wanted to shout at both of them, and ended up moving to a hotel, no longer trusting himself around those he cared about.

"Was Daniel all right?" Ainsley asked.

"Aye, but that's not the point, is it?" Cameron's fists tightened. "He was only a little boy. I could have hurt him. Do ye think I want to wake up and see I've done the same to you?"

Ainsley stared up at him, eyes unreadable. Cameron would never understand her. Just when he thought he knew Ainsley, the lively young woman who picked locks and ran about Paris in pursuit of cake, she decided to bring him off him in public, then tried to pry out the secrets of his soul.

"Perhaps if you grew used to it," she began.

"Damn it, have ye heard nothing? There's something wrong with me, understand? I can't even think about settling down to sleep with you without the world going black. That's why I wake up tossing people about. The blackness doesn't let me go until it's too late."

Ainsley listened in silence. She was supposed to be afraid of him, of the terrifying, raging thing inside him. Some women enjoyed being afraid of Cameron, liking the danger, but they didn't truly understand what Cameron was capable of. Cameron had never let them know.

He swung away and snatched up his clothes.

"I positively hate this woman," Ainsley said behind him. "Your wife, I mean."

Cameron gave a bitter laugh as he pulled on his trousers. "I'm glad you do. She wrecked me. She wanted her revenge, and now she has it."

"Cam . . ."

Cameron shook his head. "No more talking. Go to sleep."

He turned his back on the beautiful woman he'd do anything in the world for, shrugged on his shirt, and banged out.

Behind him, Ainsley hugged her knees, wiping tears on the sheet. "I do hope it is hot where you are, Lady Elizabeth Cavendish," she whispered. "Very, very hot."

Ainsley walked into Cameron's bedroom the next evening while his Parisian valet readied him for another night of restaurants and cabarets. Cam glanced at the afternoon dress Ainsley still wore and frowned.

"Aren't you coming out with me?"

"I'll get dressed in a moment. Felipe, will you leave us?"

The valet didn't even look to Cameron for confirmation. The servants, both Scottish and French, now obeyed Ainsley without question. Felipe simply left the room.

Cameron finished closing the collar stud Felipe had been setting in place. "I told you, I don't want to talk about it."

"How do you even know what I intend to say?"

He gave her an impatient look before he turned back to the mirror to slide his cravat around his neck. "Because you're a ferret and can't leave well enough alone."

Ainsley went to him, took the cravat ends from his hands, and started to tie the knot for him.

"I came to tell you about my brother."

Cameron tilted his head back so she could work. "Which brother? There are as many confounded McBrides as there are Mackenzies."

"There are only four. Patrick, Sinclair, Elliot, and Steven. I want to tell you more about Elliot."

"Which one is he, the barrister?"

Cameron knew full well which of her brothers was which, because Ainsley had talked quite a lot about each of them. Her brothers were a safe topic of conversation, plus she was proud of their accomplishments. Ainsley was willing to wager that Hart too had told Cameron about her brothers, likely with dossiers on each one. Cameron was trying to be difficult.

"Elliot went to India with the army," she said. "When he left the army, he stayed in India to start a business helping other colonials settle. Once when he was traveling in the northern region in the course of this business, he was captured. He was kept imprisoned for so long there that we were certain he was dead. But at last he managed to escape and make his way home."

Cameron's voice softened. "I remember. I'm sorry. What about him?"

"Elliot stayed with Patrick a while to convalesce, and he seemed to mend, but I could tell that there was something very wrong. Elliot made too light of his broken bones and the torture he'd suffered, almost joking about the whole thing."

"I understand why," Cameron said. "He didn't want to think too much about it. Or talk about it."

Ainsley gave Cameron's knot one last tug. "I realize that. What he went through must have been horrible. One night, when I looked in on him, I found him huddled on the bed, shaking and unable to speak. When I went to see what was the matter, Elliot wouldn't respond to me, wouldn't even look at me. I was about to run for Rona and Patrick when he came to himself. He told me he was all right and begged me to say nothing."

"It had happened to him before, then."

Ainsley nodded. "He told me that sometimes, out of nowhere, even when he sat quietly in Rona's front parlor, the world would . . . go away. He'd feel himself floating, and then he'd be back in the tiny hole where his captors had kept him. They sometimes didn't feed him or even look in on him for weeks. Logically, Elliot knew that he was safe and whole and in Patrick's house in Scotland, but his mind made him relive the entire horror of what had happened. He said he worried that the visions made him a coward, but that can't be true—Elliot is one of the bravest men I know. He even went back to India—he's still there—because he feared he'd be cowering in Patrick's guest room for the rest of his life if he didn't."

Cameron looked down at her with an unreadable expression. He was delectable in kilt, shirt, and waistcoat, in undress only his valet or wife was allowed to see. "You are telling me this story because you think I feel about Elizabeth the same way your brother felt about being imprisoned and tortured."

"Well, not quite, but it must be a similar thing."

Cameron turned away from her. "Which I asked not to talk about, I remember."

"I think we should talk about it. It's our marriage, Cam. It's our life."

Still he wouldn't look at her. "I told you, I don't want rows with you. We rub along, or we don't."

"Then we ignore the fact that my own husband refuses to sleep in a bed with me?"

Cam dragged a hand through his hair. "Plenty of married people don't share a bed. God knows my mother and father never did. They had separate rooms, separate spaces. It's not unusual."

"It is in my family. Patrick and Rona sleep together every night, and my parents did too."

"I'm glad you had such an idyllic upbringing."

"I even shared a bed with John."

Cameron's eyes flashed as he swung around again. "And I don't want to hear you talk about you and John Douglas."

"But we must talk about you."

"Why?" His big hands clenched. "Why must we, Ainsley? Have you come into my life to fix every little problem? I don't want a be-damned nanny, I want a lover."

"So do I."

"For God's sake, Ainsley, what do you want me to say? That Elizabeth was insane? You've heard the stories. Eleanor must have given you an earful—Hart spilled all the family secrets to her. Eleanor ran far away from us, wise woman."

"She told me that Lady Elizabeth hurt you."

"Aye, she did." Cameron ripped the button from his cuff and yanked the sleeve up his arm. "You were interested in these? All right, then, I'll tell you. Elizabeth was in my bedroom, smoking a cheroot. Her lovers liked her to smoke them, so she did it to remind me that she didn't belong entirely to me. Daniel was there, and she thought it would be interesting to see what kind of scars the ends left on a baby's flesh."

Ainsley's mouth dropped open. Eleanor hadn't mentioned *that.* She thought of the precious body she'd cradled to her bosom for one day, and rage that knew no end filled her. "How *could* she?"

"I grabbed for Danny, and while I was wrestling my own son away from her, she jabbed me with the damn cigar. She said she'd leave Daniel alone if I allowed her make a pattern on my arm, so I let her. She enjoyed it. Then I carried Daniel back to his nursery and stayed with him, in case she decided to come up there and try something more awful. Elizabeth hated Daniel, because she knew he was mine. I started making arrangements that very day to send her away, but before I had the chance . . ." He made an empty gesture as he wound down.

Ainsley pressed her arms to her chest, trying to stem her shivers. "Cam, I am so sorry."

"It hurts, Ainsley. I loathed her, and still it hurts." He dragged his sleeve back down and flipped the ruined cuff closed. "That's why I don't want to talk about it."

Ainsley picked up the button he'd ripped off and rummaged silently through the dressing table for a needle and thread. Miraculously, he held still while she put the button back into place and started sewing, though she had difficulty seeing the needle through her tears. The cuff closed, hiding the round scars again.

"Cam," she said softly. A tear fell to his wrist.

Cameron's broad fingers tilted her face up. There was fire in his eyes, and anger, and pain. "Let me be, Ainsley. Don't try to remake me in one night. I told you, I'm a wreck of a man."

A man I'm in love with. Ainsley kissed his palm.

Cameron stared down at her a moment, thumb stroking the curls at the nape of her neck. Then he cupped her head in his hand and swiftly kissed her.

The kiss held passion, hunger, need. He dragged her up to him, the kiss turning deep. They'd not be going out that night.

Cameron didn't speak of the matter again, but Ainsley refused to forget it. Cameron had said he didn't like rows, and Ainsley didn't either, but she also didn't wish to pretend away the problem.

Meanwhile, during the whirl of life in Paris, Daniel was packed off to Cambridge to begin the Michaelmas term. Daniel wasn't happy about leaving, but he kissed Ainsley good-bye, shook his father's hand, and grudgingly boarded the train.

Ainsley's heart ached to see him go, and she noticed that Cameron was more gruff and scowling as well. He missed his son, the son he'd endured torture to protect.

But a mere two weeks later, Daniel was back.

Chapter 22

Daniel walked in out of the rain, soaked and without the valise with which he'd left. Or the servant either. He'd left both, he said, in Cambridge.

Cameron was suffused with fury, his Highland Scots coming through with his rage. "Damnation, lad, can ye nae stay put?"

"At a bloody boring English university?" Daniel plopped himself on a sofa, his wet coat smearing one of the cushions Ainsley had finished embroidering. "While you're here in Paris with Ainsley? Not likely. I don't need to go to university, Dad, especially not with the same blokes I knew at Harrow telling me what they'll do when they start running the country. God save us. I'm going to help train the ponies with you, anyway."

Cameron swung to the window and glared out of it, breathing hard. Controlling himself, Ainsley realized. He didn't want to burst out at his son.

Ainsley sat down next to Daniel and rescued her cushion.

"Danny, the acquaintances you cultivate at university might be the very men who send you horses to train later."

Daniel rolled his eyes. "I don't want to cultivate acquaintances, I want to learn something. The professors at Corpus Christi are wheezy and talk a lot of philosophy and rot. It's ridiculous. I want to learn good Scottish engineering."

"Perhaps, but I imagine your father paid rather a lot of money to send you to Cambridge."

Daniel looked marginally ashamed. "I'll pay it back."

Cameron turned to him, still tightly controlled. "That's not th' point, son. The point is I send ye off, and ye run away, again and again."

"I don't want to be sent off! I want to stay with you. What's wrong w' that?"

"Because my life here is not one a boy should live, damn you." Cameron stopped short of shouting. "My friends are hard, and I don't want you anywhere near them."

"I know," Daniel said. "I've met them. So why do ye want *Ainsley* around them?"

"I don't."

Observing Cameron's anger, Ainsley realized he truly didn't. Cameron's Paris acquaintance were people who lived the idle life as hard as they could—staying out all night, sleeping all day, and spending money without noticing.

Ainsley had found it exciting at first, but she soon realized that there was no stillness in this life, no contemplation, no absorbing beauty for the sake of it, and no love. What Cameron's friends called love was infatuation and obsession, which began with ferocity and ended in rows and drama, sometimes violence.

These were hot-blooded people, and Cameron was as hot-blooded as they were. He thought nothing of kissing Ainsley in public or holding her to his side, and his friends looked on with amusement rather than shock. Every night was another play or opera, or a party that lasted well into morning. Each night Ainsley wore a new gown, and Cameron draped her with more and more costly jewels.

But there was no quiet happiness among these people. No reaching for a friend and finding one, warm and comforting, at the end of your hand.

"We should leave then," Ainsley said.

"Why?" Cameron demanded. "Are ye tired of it already?"

"No, but you are."

Cameron scowled at Ainsley's all-knowing gray eyes. Did she have to understand *everything* about him? "Who the hell told you that?"

"No one had to tell me," Ainsley said. "You're not comfortable with this life, and you know it. When you're out riding horses or even watching them, as we did at the horse fair the other day, you're far more sweet-tempered and companionable. Too many nights under the gas lamps and you start growling."

Cameron made a rumbling noise in response, and Ainsley smiled. "Exactly like that. Don't stay here for me, Cam. Go where your heart is, and I'll follow."

Cameron looked out the window again, studying the Parisian rooftops. Daniel waited on the sofa, as tense as his father.

It had been bad of Daniel to run away from school, but Cameron secretly agreed with his reasons why. Cameron had sent Daniel to Cambridge because all the Mackenzies had gone there, and he'd had a place secured there when he was born.

Truth to tell, Cameron hadn't minded Daniel underfoot on this trip. He'd enjoyed watching him and Ainsley laugh uproariously over whatever they found funny that day, the two of them trying every pasty in Paris or dragging Cameron to obscure parts of the city just to see what was there. Cameron knew he should be more strict about Daniel and Cambridge. A lad needed to go to university, and Cameron should be a parent in control of his son's life. But he didn't have the heart. If Daniel were truly unhappy, they'd think of something else.

Cameron looked back at the two of them waiting side by side on the sofa for his answer, his wife and his son watching him with the same intensity.

"Monte Carlo," he said.

Ainsley blinked. "Your heart is in Monte Carlo?"

Cameron didn't smile. "I'm tired of self-satisfied Parisians and artists full of their own genius. I put up with that enough with Mac. At Monte Carlo, you'll meet a much more interesting mix of people."

"I will?"

Cameron turned to them, fixing them both with his topaz gaze. "You'll like it, Ainsley. Not one person there has pure motives in mind. A picklock might find such corruption entertaining."

"That does sound more interesting than self-satisfied artists full of their own genius."

"And the sunrise over the sea from the top of the city is beautiful." That was true. Cameron wanted to show the view to Ainsley, to see her delight when she beheld it. He remembered Ian watching Beth watch the fireworks, finding more joy in her than the show of light. Cameron understood now.

Ainsley winked at Daniel and stretched her feet in her new patent-leather boots. "I have only one question about this oh-so-exciting Monte Carlo," she said.

Cameron's gaze fixed on her ankle boots, primly buttoned against silk stockings. He imagined himself unfastening each button, licking the ankle that came into view, running his tongue all the way up to the back of her knee. Ainsley and her buttons.

"What question is that?" He managed to say.

She gave him a smile and Daniel a wink. "In Monte Carlo, do they have cake?"

They did have cake, and also the casino of which her moral majesty, Queen Victoria, vastly disapproved. When they reached their hotel in Monaco, Cameron asked Ainsley to wear the dark red velvet he'd picked out for her in Edinburgh, and he took her straight to the casino.

Ainsley found herself in a long, elegant, cupolaed building filled with glittering people. The foyer rose to a gigantic rectangular stained-glass window with classical-looking paintings and statues all around it. The game rooms opened from this rotunda, and Cameron strolled into them with ease.

He was greeted by name by the croupiers and smiled at by the butterflies—beautiful women hired by the casino to entice gamers to tables. More than one interested gaze of that crowd fixed on Ainsley, society there also having learned of Cameron Mackenzie's astonishingly sudden marriage.

But Ainsley realized quickly that Cameron didn't like Monte Carlo any more than he had Paris. He could talk and laugh with his friends, drink whiskey and smoke cheroots as he played cards, but his heart wasn't in it.

Ainsley grew to know the true Cameron better as the days slipped by—the mildest winter Ainsley, used to Scottish cold, had ever spent. She found that she could talk easily with Cameron about many things—news of the world, sports, games, their opinions on Scotland's history and relations with England, books, music, drama, art. Cameron was well read and well traveled, joking that he'd absorbed *some* knowledge at Cambridge, though it must have been in his sleep. He'd spent his waking hours drinking, gaming, racing horses, and chasing women.

He was quite open about his debauched life, rumbling that Ainsley deserved to know everything, and besides, he despised hypocrites. But even with this openness, Cameron hid some part of himself from her, never letting Ainsley so much as glimpse it. The feeling of being shut out was a lonely one, even if Cameron would make crazed love to her every night.

Most evenings the three of them dined out or went to the theatre or opera together, and there was no more talk of packing Daniel off again to Cambridge. Cameron, Ainsley saw, though he didn't much know what to do with the lad, liked having him around. During the day, they visited museums and the gardens, or simply traversed the steep streets of Monaco. They walked from the harbor to the top of the hills so often that Ainsley declared it must be the healthiest winter she'd ever passed.

But Cameron would never, ever lie down with Ainsley in her bed.

Only one incident marred their glittering season in Monte Carlo. Daniel returned to the hotel one afternoon after New Year's with a black eye and half his face bloodied. Ainsley fussed over him as she patched him up, but Cameron watched with a scowl.

"Did you finish it?" Cameron asked him. "Or are the police going to come to my door and arrest you?"

"I didn't get into a fight, Dad. A chap had his toughs beat me up."

Ainsley looked at Daniel in alarm. "Then we are the ones who should go to the police."

Daniel shrugged. "I'm fine. I got away from them."

"What chap?" Cameron demanded. "What happened?"

Daniel looked evasive. "You'll go spare when I tell you. Maybe I shouldn't with Ainsley here."

"I'm made of stern stuff, Daniel," Ainsley said. "I want to know about this chap, and I still think we should have his toughs arrested. What kind of man sets other men to punch up a lad?"

"Count Durand."

Ainsley had no idea who that was, but Cameron came alert. "Durand is still alive? I thought he'd be dead of the clap by now."

Daniel snorted, relaxing. "No, he's here, but he don't look good. Haggard, I'd say. Maybe he does have the clap."

"He set his men on you?" Cameron's words were quiet, but Ainsley sensed the fury in him rising like a geyser.

"I did hit Durand first, I admit. But that's because he started trying to claim again that he was my pa. I told Durand that it was impossible, because his wick's been limp for decades. *Then* he said that if I claimed to be a Mackenzie whelp, it meant I was as mad as my mother, so I laid him out. He screamed, and his toughs pulled me off him, and he told them to give me a good beating. Durand said he'd let them stop if I admitted I was his son, but damned if I would. I got away from them and lit out."

Ainsley listened in shock, the rag she'd been using to wipe Daniel's face dripping bloody water to the carpet. "Cameron . . ."

"I'll deal with Durand. Danny, you stay the hell away from him. No thoughts of vengeance. Understand? I don't want him to have ten toughs next time."

Daniel looked annoyed, but he nodded.

"Who is this Count Durand?" Ainsley asked.

Daniel shot a look at his father. "I told you we should have sent her out of the room."

"If Ainsley chooses to live with us, she deserves to know the worst. Count Durand was my wife's lover," Cameron said to Ainsley. "One of her most persistent."

"Oh." Cameron's explanation was all the more heartbreaking for the calmness with which he gave it.

"She was with Durand right before she married Dad," Daniel said. "She kept going back to him even after she married, and she gave him a lot of Dad's money. Durand's one of those old French aristos from an émigré family. Doesn't have a home, and pretty much lives off his friends and his women. Probably his male lovers too."

"Daniel," Cameron said.

"Well, ye wanted her to know. Somehow, the man got it into his head that he sired me."

From the look in Cameron's eyes, the uncertainty of that had once haunted him. Daniel, tall and broad-shouldered, his stance a mirror of Cameron's own, was certainly a Mackenzie, but Cameron must have lived with the agony of not knowing for certain before Daniel's birth.

That was another reason Cameron hadn't sent Elizabeth away, Ainsley realized. Cameron needed to find out whether the child Elizabeth carried was indeed his.

"But Count Durand *didn't* sire you," Ainsley said. "That's obvious."

"Yes, but he can't get the idea out of his thick head. Threatens to go to the police about it, or tries to blackmail Dad for keeping me away from him." Daniel laughed, his bruised eye swelling almost shut. "Durand doesn't really want a son hanging on him, he just likes to make trouble and get money out of Dad. Durand couldn't stand the expense of me."

Cameron made Daniel drop the subject, but he was tight-lipped for the rest of the day.

That night, at the casino, Cameron abruptly abandoned a winning hand of baccarat to stride out of the card room to a slender black-haired man whose satin-lined opera cloak hung in limp folds on his bony frame. Patrons of the casino scurried out of Cameron's way, opening a path between him and the dark-haired man.

Cameron grabbed the man by the neck and marched him into the rotunda and out the front doors. No one stopped him—the discreet guards and even the butterflies pretended to pay attention to something else.

Cameron pushed Durand down the drive in front of the pseudoclassical building, Ainsley pattering after them in her tight evening frock and high-heeled slippers. Cameron propelled the man along until they reached a place where one of the winding streets dropped to a street below it.

Ainsley followed, heart in her throat. She didn't blame Cameron for his anger, but who knew what Cameron would do to Durand? Or how many toughs Durand had waiting in the shadows to beat Cameron to a pulp?

She rounded the corner just as Cameron threw Durand into a wall. The man tried to guard himself, but Cameron hoisted Durand up by his cloak.

"You touch my son again," Cameron said clearly, "and I'll kill you."

"*Your* son?" Durand spoke French to Cameron's English, but Ainsley understood well enough. "My Elizabeth said you couldn't make your cock dance enough to give her a son. She said she'd fooled you well and good with my seed. The boy is mine."

"She was a fucking liar, Durand."

Durand took a swing at him, and Cameron easily caught his fist.

"She told me what you did to her, you filth," Durand cried. "She should have had me there to hold you down when she took her revenge the only way she knew how. Elizabeth gave you what you deserved, but if I'd been there, I'd have driven that poker up your ass until I ripped your heart out of your backside."

Cameron slammed the man into the wall again, and Durand's head knocked against the bricks.

"I don't give a damn what you say to me, but if you touch Daniel again, if you so much as look at him, I'll break your bloody neck. Do you understand?"

Durand tried to spit at him, but Cameron smacked his head into the wall again. "I said, *do you understand?*"

Durand finally nodded, gasping. Cameron hauled the struggling man by his collar across the narrow street and dropped him over a low wall side to the street below. The count screamed as he went, then the scream abruptly cut off.

Chapter 23

Ainsley rushed to Cameron. "Good heavens, you didn't kill him, did you?"

Cameron glanced over the wall. "No, he's landed in a wagon. Full of shit."

Ainsley pressed her hand over her mouth, stemming a hysterical laugh.

Cameron focused on her as though just seeing her. "Ainsley, what the devil are you doing out here?"

"Following you. I was afraid his thugs would waylay you."

"And if they had, what would you have done? Beaten them off with your fan?"

"I was going to shout for the police. I can scream very loudly."

Cameron took Ainsley's arm and steered her back toward the casino, where a crowd pretending not to be interested had gathered. "We're leaving."

"That's likely a good idea."

Cameron was already signaling for his servant to run for his carriage. Another hurried back inside for Ainsley's wraps, emerging with them as the carriage rolled up.

Ainsley and Cameron rode in silence as the coach bumped its way back to the hotel, Cameron staring out of the window.

She sensed his restlessness and knew that but for her presence, he'd have been striding up and down the streets of Monte Carlo to burn off his rage. Cameron was escorting Ainsley home for *her* protection, not because he wanted to go himself.

"I thought you were going to kill him," she said into the darkness.

Cameron looked down at her. "Hmm?"

"Durand. You couldn't have known that wagon would be there."

His eyes glinted. "The drop wasn't that high. I wanted to scare him off. I am many things, my wife, but not a murderer."

"Not when there's a cartload of dung handy, certainly."

"I hope it ruined his opera cloak. I hate the damn things."

Ainsley wormed her fingers under the crook of his arm, felt his rigidity, his knowledge that she'd heard every word Durand had said. "I dislike to ask an obvious question," she said. "but why did you marry Lady Elizabeth in the first place?"

Cameron grunted. "She dazzled me, I suppose. I was still at university, saw a glamorous woman, and I snatched her up. I found out too late what she was like, and by then, she was carrying Daniel."

And Cameron had wanted to keep her close to protect the unborn Daniel. "I know you don't wish me to say this, but I'm sorry," Ainsley said. "I'm sorry about all that's happened to you. It shouldn't have."

Cameron rested his big hand over hers. "But it did. And I live with the ghosts." He looked down at her, his eyes holding more warmth. "The ghosts haven't plagued me as much lately."

Now she did dare to snuggle into him, and he kept hold of her hand.

"I had some other news today," Cameron said after a time. "From Pierson. I meant to tell you, but then Daniel . . ."

Ainsley felt a chill. "About Jasmine? Is she all right?"

"She's fine, or at least, I think she is. I wrote to Pierson, and I got his answer today. Bloody man won't see reason. I want that horse, Ainsley."

"And he won't sell?"

"No, but I've at least browbeaten him into letting me train her again. He now informs me I will do it for no training fee, in return for the money he lost because I couldn't make her win at Doncaster." Cameron made a noise of disgust. "I wager all other trainers turned him away, and he's desperate. He wants to pretend he's not desperate, that he still has the upper hand. Ingrate."

"You'll turn him down, then?"

Cameron looked at her, eyes still burning with anger. "Hell, no. I don't need the money. I need Jasmine."

Ainsley rubbed his shoulder. "You want to go back to England, don't you, Cam? Right now, I mean."

He didn't look at her. "I want to train her, Ainsley. I'll make her into a damn good racer. She has so much potential, all wasted by Pierson."

"What I mean is, you hate it here. It doesn't matter how many sunrises we watch from the top of the hill, or how many times you win at cards. Your heart's not in it. You're made to be standing in a paddock holding a lounge line, not sitting at a baccarat table."

Cameron reached down to smooth a lock of her hair. "And what the devil will you do while I'm standing in a paddock holding a lounge line?"

"Watch. Ride. Be the lady of the manor. Trust me, I'll have plenty to do."

Cameron ran his thumb along the thin gold bracelet he'd given her for New Year's. "My estate in Berkshire is far from any city. There's nothing to do there *but* horses. And my brothers will drift down to the estate when I start training. They use it as an excuse to escape whatever it is they're supposed to be doing."

"It sounds perfect." Ainsley grew animated. "We can invite them all, Beth and Isabella and the children if they can manage it. They're both due in late spring. Or afterward if they can't come in spring. I'm certain we can have a lovely summer party with everyone there."

Ainsley broke off when she saw Cameron's look, a man contemplating his bachelor home overrun with women, babies, and nannies.

"It's just a thought," she said quickly. "Are you telling me, Cam, that we've stayed here all this time because you thought I liked it here?"

"You do like it here."

"Well, yes, it's exciting, but not what I want to do forever."

Cameron watched her with a pensive look. "You're a woman, Ainsley."

"Yes, I know that. I have been for many years."

"You're supposed to want a constant flow of gowns and jewelry and to be seen in them every night."

"The endless parade of fashion can become a bit dull."

"You're bored?" His frown deepened. "You should have told me. I can take you anywhere. Rome, Venice, even Egypt if you want."

Ainsley put her fingers to his lips. "Why should we flutter around the world? I don't wish to if it means I watch you be unhappy and impatient."

Cameron gave a restless sigh. "I don't understand what you want, Ainsley."

"I want to be with you."

"While I'm knee deep in mud? My estate is miles from any restaurant."

"Good. I'd love a bit of old-fashioned Scottish cooking. Your Berkshire cook knows how to make bannocks and porridge, doesn't she?"

"She's Scottish."

"Well, then that's settled."

"Ainsley, stop. Stop being so damned cheerful about everything."

"I can be grumpy if you want." She gave him a mock scowl.

Cameron didn't laugh. "I can't give you what you want if you don't tell me what it is."

Ainsley lifted the fist he'd rested on his thigh and kissed his large fingers. "I'm trying to tell you. You're a generous man, and I can't lie and say I don't want the beautiful frocks and jewels you give me. But really, I ran away from my respectable life to be with *you*. You, Cameron Mackenzie. I don't care if we're in the most expensive hotel in Monte Carlo or in a hovel with nothing but oat cakes for dinner."

The look he gave her bordered on the anguished. "Why the hell would you want that?"

"I like oat cakes. Especially with a little honey."

"Damn it, I mean why would you want me? Look at you. I've introduced you to the most corrupt of the demimonde, and you sit there all pristine and innocent, smiling at me, for God's sake."

"What should I be doing? Demanding more jewels? Breaking plates and screeching if I don't get them? Threatening to leave you for a man who will buy me more?"

"It's what they all do." His voice was hollow.

"You see, you do despise women. I told you that before, remember?"

"I despise women like what you describe, yes."

"Then have nothing more to do with them. Let's go to Berkshire and say to hell with the lot of them." When Cam eyed her skeptically, Ainsley wrapped her arms around him and ruffled the hair on the back of his neck. "It's what I truly want, Cameron. The horses, the mud, and you." She kissed him.

And so, they went to Berkshire.

Cameron had never brought a woman to his Berkshire estate, Waterbury Grange, which lay south of Hungerford. He'd bought the place after Elizabeth's death, needing a retreat far from Kilmorgan and his father and Elizabeth's grave.

He'd hired a houseful of servants, let Daniel run wild, and concentrated on horseracing. Newmarket, Epsom, Ascot, the St. Leger—these were the events around which his world revolved.

Needy mistresses didn't fit into that world. Ainsley, on the other hand, slid into it without breaking stride. She took over the running of the house from the moment she arrived, soon discovering and curtailing the servants' long-running practice of keeping the best foodstuffs for themselves while serving the offhand Cameron what was left over.

Cameron found her indignation about the way they took advantage of him amusing. "These people kept me alive when I first moved here, and they looked after Danny for me. I don't begrudge them."

"There is a world of difference between begrudging them and dining on gristly salt pork while they feast on tender beefsteak."

Cameron shrugged. "Do what you like. I'm not good with domestic arrangements."

"Obviously not," Ainsley had said with a frown.

Cameron couldn't deny that Ainsley had been right to bring them back here. January winds were brisk and raw, but the worst of winter's grip soon departed and he and Angelo, with Daniel in tow, began training in earnest. Cameron found that he looked forward to rising before dawn every morning and leading out the horses with Daniel as the sun rose.

Pierson had not yet rolled up from Bath with Jasmine, and Cam wondered whether the man would bring her at all. Other than that, training commenced in a satisfactory way.

Cameron's stables were true working stables, with multiple trainers, people coming and going, and a well-run routine. Angelo was second-in-command, and any trainer, stable hand, or jockey who had trouble with this was asked to leave. Angelo knew the horses as well as Cameron did and could glide onto them bareback to run them to the clock. The trainers who'd been with Cam the longest had come to respect Angelo, saying, "He knows what he's doing, that Romany."

As for Cameron, once he had the Berkshire wind in his hair, and felt the young horses' excitement coming to him through the lounge line, his ennui fled. Once again, he was awake and alive. When he and Daniel went back to the house each afternoon, Cameron had another bright spot in his life—Ainsley.

She fit smoothly into the household as though she'd lived there her entire life. The housekeeper, who'd never spoken much to Cameron except when absolutely necessary, kept a constant conversation running with Ainsley as Ainsley questioned her on all aspects of the housekeeping. Ainsley now had her own set of keys, and the housekeeper began saying, "Let me ask her ladyship," when any question came up.

The staff here were quiet, undemonstrative, well-trained domestics, apart from their now-ended habit of skimming off the foodstuffs. If they didn't actually burst into song and dance about Ainsley, they at least respected her.

Even the one point of contention between Cameron and Ainsley—the fact that Cameron left her every night to sleep in his own bed—seemed to ease a little as spring commenced.

Or so Cameron thought. He should have remembered that Ainsley was very good at stealth.

The locks in Cameron's old manor house were easy to pick. The doors and locks were leftover from a hundred years ago, when the house had been built, and several of them even opened with the same key. Ainsley had practiced picking the locks from the day she arrived, which was how she'd discovered the cache of foodstuffs the servants had kept for themselves.

On a moonless night, she crept down the hall the short distance from her bedroom to Cameron's, hairpin at the ready. She knelt softly on the carpet, listening to his snores from within for a time before she quietly moved the old-fashioned keyhole cover on its tiny hinge.

And found herself faced with a shiny new lock. He'd changed it.

Botheration.

Ainsley let out her breath, but she refused to give up. She had to work a little harder on this lock, and in the end it took two hairpins, but finally Ainsley had it open. She stood up, her heart beating swiftly, and very quietly opened the door.

The room was dark, save for the glow of coals on the hearth. She'd made certain to visit Cameron's bedchamber often, so she'd studied the lay of the land. Unless he'd decided to rearrange the furniture at eleven o'clock last night, his bed would be *that* direction. The continuing snore told her she was right.

Ainsley softly closed the door behind her and started across the room.

"Ainsley."

The word was hard, clear, and told her that Cameron was fully awake.

"Drat you," she said. "You only pretended to be asleep."

A match spurted and a kerosene lamp glowed to life. It showed Cameron sitting up in his bed, his lap covered with a sheet, the rest of him delectably bare.

"I *was* asleep. Then I heard the unmistakable scratch of a thief trying to pick my lock."

"Your hearing must be very good then."

"It is."

Ainsley took another step. "Did I frighten you?" He'd told her he'd wake up in violence when he was startled.

She'd planned to wake him as gently as she could, to show him that nothing terrible would happen.

Cameron's smile was hot. "When I hear someone picking a lock, I immediately think of you. Not to mention the little mutters of frustration you make when the lock proves challenging. What are you doing in here?"

Ainsley closed the distance between the door and his bed. "I came to sleep with my husband."

"Ainsley."

She put her knee on the mattress. "You refuse to talk about it, but I refuse to let matters stand as they are. Beds are for sharing. Especially beds as large as this one."

Cameron lunged for her. Before she could scramble away, Ainsley found herself dragged onto the bed and pinned to the mattress, much as he had the night she'd broken into his room to search for the queen's letters. The difference was that last time, he'd been more or less fully dressed. This time, nothing rested between Cameron's bare body and Ainsley but a sheet.

She felt every inch of his hard body—*every* inch—the strength of his hands, the heat of his breath.

"Do you need reminding how dangerous I am?" he growled.

"You're not dangerous."

Cameron pinned her wrists to the mattress with his weight and gave her his hot, wicked smile. "No? Perhaps I should demonstrate."

Did she want him to or didn't she? A wise woman should be frightened of a giant rising over her in the dark, looking ready to ravish her, but Ainsley was not wise. Or maybe she was. She'd married him.

"Not necessary," she said.

Cameron licked across her mouth. "Necessary. I don't want things becoming *too* domestic."

So he'd told her on the train when he'd proposed. He wanted a lover, not a wife.

"Well," she said. "Perhaps a small demonstration."

Cameron rose abruptly from the bed, lifting her up with him, and the sheet fell away. He was naked in the dim light, his cock long and hard, his wanting unashamed. From Ainsley's position on the edge of the bed, it was easy to grasp him in her hand, draw him a little to her.

Cameron tensed all over as he felt Ainsley's sweet lips and tongue brush the tip of his cock. *God help me.* He'd been about to lay her on the floor and make deep, hard love to her, in retaliation for her sneaking into his room, but she'd turned the tables on him. *Again.*

She'd not done this before, but she'd seen his erotic drawings and heard the naughty things Cameron whispered into her ears. Ainsley wasn't naïve, and she obviously wanted to play.

He almost came as he watched her open her lips and then his hardness slide between them. Cameron clenched his fists, his entire body rigid as he held himself back. If he came now, he'd miss this feeling of being inside Ainsley, the feeling of her licking him, nipping him, the wonderful pull when she began to suck.

"Ainsley." The word was ragged, his breathing hoarse. He put his hand on her head, rocked his hips. "Ainsley. Love. What are you doing to me?"

Happily, she didn't answer. Ainsley kept her mouth busy with him, her hands steadying herself on his thighs.

"Devil woman," he whispered. "I am supposed to be making *you* pay."

For answer, Ainsley worked him harder. Cameron heard the words spill out of his mouth, naughty syllables that had led to this situation in the first place.

Beautiful, beautiful Ainsley . . . damn it.

He shouted out loud as his seed spilled from his body, and he didn't want to stop when she demurely pulled away and wiped her lips with her fingertips.

Cameron growled, a bestial sound. When Ainsley merely smiled at him, he swept her up into his arms and carried her across the room, where he proceeded to make deep love to her on the thick rugs before the fire. He loved her so thoroughly that she was fast asleep by the time he carried her back to her own bedroom and left her there.

Lord Pierson delivered Jasmine in the first week of February. Cameron watched him driving up the road at a snail's pace, following the low-slung cart that contained Jasmine.

Cameron dismounted the horse he'd been riding and tossed his reins to the jockey, who sprang lightly into the saddle. Cam walked out of the paddock to meet the cart and carriage at the stable, but he stopped in surprise when another low-slung cart turned in.

Pierson stepped out of his carriage, making sure his pristine boots didn't land anywhere muddy or damp. His neatly tailored clothes were a sharp contrast to Cameron's rough coat and riding breeches.

"Well, Mackenzie," Pierson said. "I've brought her back. You won't make a pig's breakfast of it this time, will you?"

Cameron watched the second cart approach and halt. "And what's in that, then?"

"A stallion. He's called Raphael's Angel, and he's giving me problems. I'd like you to sort him out for me."

"And why should I do that?"

"For losing me the St. Leger. No one wants Raph's Angel, but everyone says if anyone can turn him around and make him sellable it's you. I thought that you'd do it for me as a favor."

Jasmine's cart had been taken all the way into the stables. Daniel and Ainsley appeared as if by magic as Angelo started to unload her.

"And I don't want that Romany anywhere near my horses," Pierson said loudly. "I wouldn't be surprised if *he's* why she did so poorly."

Ainsley turning, heard, and opened her mouth. Cameron held up his hand to forestall her.

"There's nothing wrong with Angelo, and there's nothing wrong with Jasmine," Cameron said.

He would rather bash Pierson in the mouth, dump him back in the carriage, and send him home, but Cameron controlled himself. He wanted to train Jasmine—wanted to save her from this bastard—and if he angered Pierson, the man would simply take Jasmine away again.

Cameron turned to gesture Angelo away, but Angelo had already moved from Jasmine, leaving her to one of Pierson's grooms. Angelo would comply without rancor, which was why Cameron trusted the man.

"Fine," Cameron said. "Leave them both. I'll see you at Newmarket."

Pierson didn't even gloat. He simply looked down his long nose and turned back to his carriage, ready to rush back to his overly ornate house in Bath.

Ainsley pressed her lips together. She knew what a struggle it was for Cameron not to shout what he thought at Pierson. He'd chosen to hold in his temper for Jasmine's sake.

Poor Jasmine looked a bit rattled from traveling. Her coat was flecked with lather, and her eyes were wide. A good rubdown and a turnout in a paddock so she could run off her nerves, that's what she needed.

Pierson's groom, however, started leading Jasmine straight to a stall in the U-shaped stable yard. Jasmine obviously didn't want to go. She'd bolt the moment she had the chance, if Ainsley were any judge.

"Let her have a run," Ainsley said. "Angelo."

Angelo said nothing, leaning against another stall door to watch.

The groom shook his head. "His lordship's order, m'lady. He'll not let us go home until she's safely locked away."

"Horses don't like being locked away."

Ainsley had learned that as a child, and she'd seen it watching Cameron every day. If you had a nervous horse, you let them wander about the paddock and investigate the scary new landmarks, preferably with a horse who was calm and sedate. The new horse needed to feel safe, needed time to get used to things.

The groom sighed. "Well, Lord Pierson likes it, and I like me job, so in she goes, begging your pardon, m'lady."

Ainsley folded her arms and let him go. What happened after Lord Pierson left would be different.

Jasmine didn't fight the groom, though she danced nervously. All would have been well, except for the stallion.

He didn't want to be shut up for the night. As soon as Raphael's Angel was backed out of his cart, he snorted and danced and threw off the two grooms trying to keep him quiet. Cameron started for him, and Angelo clenched his fists as he watched, not daring to interfere.

Jasmine heard the stallion and looked back to see what was happening. Not in fear, but with the calculating eye of a mischievous child.

"Watch her," Ainsley warned.

The groom gave her an irritated scowl. *She*, a mere lady of the manor, was presuming to tell an experienced groom how to handle horses.

The stallion danced out of reach, spied Jasmine, and headed toward her. Jasmine swung her hindquarters around and flicked up her tail—the horse equivalent of a lady sashaying her hips at a randy gentleman.

The stallion let out a low, rumbling neigh and ran for her, two thousand pounds of black horse barreling into the narrow yard. Stable hands scrambled out of the way, and Ainsley danced aside as Jasmine, at the last minute, got the jitters.

Jasmine threw up her head, breaking the halter rope, and whirled around, frantically looking for a way out. The stallion charged to pen her in, and both horses swung straight toward Ainsley.

Chapter 24

Ainsley's world slowed. She saw Angelo's eyes widen, the groom lunge for the stallion. Jasmine's sweaty brown hide coming too close, the mare's back undulating as she bucked. The stallion, a huge wall of horseflesh, ducked Jasmine's flailing hooves, and swerved directly at Ainsley.

Ainsley heard her own shout, felt herself raise her arms, her attempt at scaring them off. Then the acrid odor of excited horse, the forequarters and flying hooves of the stallion, his huge chest, his hot breath, wide red nostrils, white-rimmed eyes.

Dimly she heard the stable hands and Daniel shouting, the whinnies of the other horses, and over it all, Cameron's voice, terrible and harsh.

The instant before the combined might of Jasmine and the stallion came to crush Ainsley alive, she felt herself rising into the air. A tight band squeezed her chest, choking out her breath, but she slid rapidly upward and over the top of the stall behind her.

Both horses crashed into the wall where Ainsley had been standing, smashing through the boards. Ainsley landed in the soft hay in the back of the stall, rolling over Angelo, who seemed to be tangled up with her.

Jasmine and the stallion whirled from the corner stall and out the way they'd come. They charged from the yard and lit out for the fields, two streaks of horse on the green.

Angelo scrambled to his feet. "Are you all right, my lady?" He held out his hand to Ainsley, who took the bronzed lifeline.

I think so. Ainsley opened her mouth to speak, and nothing came out.

Cameron threw open the broken door and snatched Ainsley to her feet. Ainsley found herself crushed against him, Cameron's strong arms like iron.

"Ainsley." His voice was broken. "Dear God . . ."

I'm all right. Again, the words wouldn't come. She couldn't breathe, couldn't swallow, couldn't feel. She tried to put her hands on his shoulders, but they slid limply off. *Shock,* she thought. *I'll be fine once my heart starts beating again.*

Cameron lifted a flask to Ainsley's lips, the metal cool, and the burn of whiskey trickled inside her mouth. Ainsley coughed, swallowed, and coughed some more.

"Cam," she whispered. Tears filled her eyes and spilled over.

Cameron held her. Ainsley sank into him, closing her eyes as chill terror rushed through her. That had been too close.

"Make sure Jasmine is all right," she said worriedly.

"Angelo's gone after her."

"Angelo." The word choked in Ainsley's throat. "He pulled me out of the way."

"Aye, and I'm having a medal cast for him. Damn it, Ainsley." Cameron cupped her face in his hands. "I thought . . ." His throat worked, and moisture formed on his lashes. "I thought I'd lost you."

"Angelo is a quick thinker." Her whisper was still too faint, and the words were lost.

Cameron's lips shook as he kissed her. Ainsley held on to him, Cameron the anchor in her spinning world. He was the only thing that kept her from tumbling down, and she clung to him, loving him hard.

"Mackenzie!" Lord Pierson's voice rang through the yard. "I told you to keep that Romany away from my horses."

Cameron set Ainsley aside, gentleness itself, and then he ripped open the stall door and went for Lord Pierson. The volley of broad Scots and filthy swearing that followed flooded the yard and drowned out Pierson's bleated protests.

By the time Ainsley picked her way out of the stable yard, her knees wobbling, Cameron was throwing Pierson into his carriage.

A ring of men stood about, Pierson's coachman and grooms doing nothing to help their master. Cameron's grooms and jockeys glowered their anger and disgust. The unruly stallion had been caught by Angelo, the Romany speaking gently to it while it lowered its great head to Angelo's hands.

Jasmine, still elusive, cantered around the paddock, a string of grooms and Daniel trying to corner her.

"Ye take your bloody stallion and get out," Cameron bellowed. His voice was hoarse, the beast inside him no longer contained.

Pierson, incredibly, still defied him. "If the stallion goes, you don't get Jasmine."

"Take her off, then. Get your fucking horses out of my sight!"

"Cam." Ainsley tried to hurry to him, but her feet were too slow, her voice too soft. "No, don't lose Jasmine."

The grooms moved to let her through, the men furious, but not at her. "You all right, my lady?" more than one asked.

"Yes, thank you." Her voice was breathless. "Cam."

"Ye haven't even bothered to ask if my wife is all right."

"She shouldn't be out here at all," Pierson said. "Women belong in bed, not the stable yard."

Cameron's fist flashed out, and Pierson fell backward into the coach, his face bloody. Cameron slammed the carriage door, and the coachman leapt up to the box, quickly turning the vehicle.

The carriage's hurrying wheels sprayed mud over Cameron, but he turned back to Ainsley, not noticing. As Pierson's carriage moved toward the drive, Angelo managed to maneuver the stallion into his cart. A groom shut him in, and Angelo climbed out to head for the field to round up Jasmine.

"Cameron," Ainsley said as Cameron's arms came around her again. "You can't lose Jasmine. You love that horse."

"I almost lost *you*. Pierson can go to hell."

"But Jasmine. She doesn't want to go with him." Ainsley felt reaction setting in, her mind seeing again the black horse's body and hooves swerving to crush the life out of her.

Cameron caught her as her legs gave way. He swept her up into her arms and carried her swiftly to the house, past the servants who'd rushed out to watch, and up the stairs to Ainsley's bedchamber.

He set Ainsley down on her chaise near the fire, and she waved a weak hand in front of her face. "When did my life become so dramatic?"

"When you agreed to marry me. It's confounded cold in here." Ainsley's large bedroom had a fireplace, not a stove, and Cameron further ruined his shirt by shoveling more coal onto the hearth.

The fire built, and the room warmed until Ainsley was sweating. Or maybe it was the heat of delayed shock.

"Don't go," she whispered.

"I'm not going anywhere, love."

"But Jasmine." Ainsley's teeth chattered. "She didn't mean to. They were just being horses. I was standing in the wrong place."

"Ainsley, shut it."

Cameron trickled water from a large pitcher to its basin and wet a towel. He tugged Ainsley's torn gloves from her and began wiping her dirt-streaked hands. The water stung where her palms had been sliced by her fall.

"Your hands are just as filthy," Ainsley said. She caught sight of herself in the mirror and started to laugh. "And so is my face. I look awful."

"Hush now."

Ainsley heard voices outside the door. Two maids and a footman came in with a tub and ewers of steaming water, though Ainsley didn't remember Cameron sending for them. Just as well he did. The mud in the stable yard, plus her scrambling journey over the door into the empty stall, had left her coated with dirt and horse leavings.

She'd have to speak to Cameron about installing taps in his house—the maids had to haul water up the back stairs. It was too far for them, really. She tried to break away from Cameron to help them, but he held her back.

"Hurry before it gets cold," was all he said to them.

The splashing of water sounded heavenly. The maids quickly filled the tub, and then all the servants filed out, including the lady's maid who'd tried to stay to undress Ainsley. Cameron closed and locked the door behind them.

Ainsley tugged at the buttons of her riding habit, but she couldn't manage to open one. Cameron turned her around to face the roaring fire and undid all the buttons himself.

"You're growing quite skilled at that," she said.

Cameron peeled the broadcloth bodice from her back and rubbed her bare wrists. "You're too cold. Are you sure you aren't hurt?"

"A few bruises, I think."

"More than a few." Cameron loosened her corset and pulled it off, hand going to the tender spots on her back. "But these are from your rescue. Nothing broken, thank God."

"Thank God and Angelo. Very clever of him to climb through to that stall from the one beyond."

She'd seen the pulled-away partition between the stalls, the board walls made to be moved in case Cameron needed one large stall instead of two smaller ones. Ainsley had noted this absently while Angelo had helped her to her feet, the significance not really dawning on her.

"I'd kiss him," Cameron said. "If it wouldn't make both of us sick. But he will get a huge rise in wages."

"He's told me about the canal boats his family lives on," Ainsley said. "I'd love to see them. I've never been on a Romany canal boat. Or any canal boat for that matter. Not something for a lady to do, I've been told."

"I will take you to his canal boat, and we'll have his family glide us from the Thames to the Avon and back again, but *after* I get you warm."

Cameron was kneeling before her, tugging off her stockings, the rest of her body bare. Ainsley wondered when that had happened, and then Cameron lifted her in his arms and deposited her into the hot water.

The water burned, stung, and felt so good. Ainsley sank back, letting the heat dull her senses.

She wasn't afraid of horses—she wasn't, she told herself. They were beasts that did what beasts did—but never had she come so close to dying because of one. If Angelo had been one moment too slow . . .

"Bloody Pierson," Cameron was growling. "I didn't ask him to bring that damned stallion. I was ready to kill him. If you'd been hurt, I *would* have killed him. I couldn't have stopped myself."

Ainsley put a dripping hand on her husband's arm. Cameron's shirt was already wet, and he impatiently pulled it off.

Ainsley rubbed her head on Cameron's bare shoulder, liking how warm and solid it was. This strong, beautiful man belonged to her. The vicar in London had made her say so. *With my body, I thee worship.*

Cameron let her go but only to take up the cake of soap and begin washing her all over. Soap got on him as he scrubbed her back and arms, slid soapy hands to her belly.

"Get in with me," Ainsley suggested.

Cameron grunted a laugh. "I'm too big."

"We should have a large bathtub built then. One big enough for two. In our new bath*room.* You really should hire some builders to start modernizing."

"Hush." Cameron nipped her ear. "Let me tend to you, love."

Ainsley liked being tended to. Cameron slid his hands around her waist again, gliding soap up under her breasts, and Ainsley leaned back in happiness.

"I love you," she murmured.

She probably shouldn't have said that—would he want such sentiments? But there was nothing she could do about it. She did love him, and that was that.

Cameron ended her speculations by kissing her.

She tasted fierceness in him, the rage and fear he'd been holding back. He let it go in the kiss, mouth shaking. Cameron half lifted Ainsley out of the tub, and water sloshed over the sides and over him.

"My Ainsley," he whispered between kisses. "Mine."

Yes, Ainsley tried to say. *Yours.*

Cameron's breath heated her flesh better than the hot water. Hard, blunt fingers slid across her body, which was still slick with soap. Cameron opened her mouth with his, kisses hard and biting.

He scooped her all the way out of the water. Cradling her against him, Cameron carried Ainsley to the bed, where he started to rub her dry with towels the maid had left warming by the fire. Ainsley's skin warmed, the friction of the towels good.

She especially liked the towel against her nipples, which began to tighten. Cameron leaned down and took a dusky point into his mouth, and Ainsley groaned. She leaned back onto the bed as Cameron teased the nipple with the tip of his tongue and suckled her again.

Ainsley pulled on the towel that he'd wrapped between her legs. She closed her eyes and let out another sigh, more friction in a wickedly sensual place.

Cameron's eyes darkened. He took the ends of the towel from her and pulled it himself, little tugs that stroked across her female places. A noise of pleasure escaped her. Cameron kept up the pressure, and Ainsley gave in to it, her fears dissolving.

Cameron wielded the towel masterfully. The mattress was soft on her back, Cameron's warm body over hers. He was heavy on her, his solid chest pressing hers, the towel between them. Cameron tugged the towel again, and the hot fire sent her over the top.

Ainsley wrapped her legs around him, wet feet against his boots. She couldn't stop the noises that came from her mouth, her groans and cries loud in the gloom of the dying afternoon.

When Cameron lifted away from her, taking the towel with him, Ainsley whimpered. Cameron's mouth was pressed into a firm line, his brows drawn down. He stripped off the rest of his clothes and stepped into the still-full tub. Standing up, he scooped water and soap over himself, washing away the dirt from the stables.

Ainsley lifted herself on her elbows and enjoyed the sight. Cameron's body gleamed with water, and soap clung to his chest, shoulders, and long, dark erection.

He rinsed himself, casually lifting his balls to wash away the soap there. Soap suds chased themselves down his legs, then Cameron bent down to rinse his hands and scrub water over his face.

He stepped out, snatching up another towel to rub himself

dry. Ainsley watched him come for her, her tall god of a husband, water darkening his hair and dripping to his broad shoulders. His hands, forearms, neck, and face were deeply tanned, as were his lower legs, the skin that the kilt covered more pale.

Ainsley assumed Cameron would lift her out of the bed to make love to her on a chair or the long sofa, or on the floor in front of the built-up fire. But Cameron tossed the towel away and pressed Ainsley back into the mattress.

Cameron licked her mouth, his damp, warm body so wonderfully heavy on hers. "I almost lost you," he said, voice harsh. "I never want to lose you. Never."

Ainsley's heart beat thick and fast. *He'll tire of her in a sixmonth,* she'd heard people say in Paris and again in Monte Carlo.

Cameron didn't look tired of her now. He feathered kisses to her chin and neck before he moved down to her breasts. He suckled her, his mouth hot and wet, then parted her legs and slid himself into her.

The towel had rubbed her hot, but when Cameron thrust into her, all was wet and slick.

He stopped, their faces together, and Cameron looked into her eyes. She saw so much need there, and pain, so much loneliness. Fear. The powerful, dangerous Lord Cameron Mackenzie was afraid.

Ainsley couldn't speak, the sensation of him stiff inside her robbing her of words. She responded to his stark fear the only way she could, by loving him.

Cameron moved slowly, the first thrust followed by another equally as slow. He was so big, but she loved the feeling of him inside her. The wide bed was at her back, and Cameron's warm, solid body was on top of hers. As always, he held himself back, muscles bunching as he took his weight on his fists.

Nothing existed but the heat of Cameron's skin against hers, his arousal spreading her wonderfully, his damp hair trickling water to her cheek. They rocked together, back and forth, Cameron moving faster now and then faster.

Finally he was driving into her in desperation, their bodies slick together, the joining fierce. Wild waves of climax rolled over Ainsley and lifted her into him. Cameron grunted with it, and Ainsley's pleasure rang through the room.

"My Ainsley," Cameron whispered brokenly. "I can't lose you. Never. Never, never. . ." His words moved with his body, Cameron losing control. "My sweet, tight, beautiful *wife*."

Ainsley cried his name, loving the sound of it. Cameron kept on, their bodies coming together, Cameron's words drifting into groans.

Then they were falling together, body to body, into the wide, comforting embrace of the marriage bed.

Cameron caressed Ainsley's skin, wondering again at how incredibly soft she was. Ainsley was a strong woman, but there was nothing coarse about her. Her skin was like satin, sleek now with perspiration and water from the bath.

He'd almost lost her today. When Cameron had watched the stallion swing his huge body right for Ainsley, and Ainsley stranded in that corner, his entire world had died.

He'd known he'd never reach her in time. He'd have to stand and watch the woman he loved be trampled to death, all because Cameron Mackenzie had coveted a horse. Only Angelo's quickness had saved her, a deed Cameron could never repay.

Cameron had screamed at Lord Pierson, but he knew blame lay at his own feet. If he hadn't bullied Pierson into bringing back Jasmine, Ainsley would never have been standing there, crooning over Jasmine, while a ton of dangerous horseflesh did its best to kill her.

Cameron's hand shook as he tucked the covers around

her, and Ainsley smiled sleepily. The smile he might never have seen again, because of his selfishness.

When Pierson had shouted that he'd remove Jasmine as well as the stallion, the decision to let them go had been easy. Ainsley was worth far more than a damned horse, and she always would be.

Ainsley's smile remained, though her eyes drifted closed. Cameron felt his own body relax, the crash of exhaustion after panic, coupled with intense loving. His eyelids grew heavy, everything in him willing him to let go, descend into oblivion, sleep . . .

Panic touched him. Cameron started to slide from the bed, but Ainsley's eyes snapped open. She caught his hand.

"No, not yet," she said in alarm.

Cameron kissed her forehead. "I have to go, sweet. I don't want to hurt you." He wasn't certain he could trust his own reflexes tonight, even with Ainsley.

Ainsley's grip tightened. "Please, not yet. I'm still shaky. Just until I fall asleep. Please."

Cameron saw the stark fear in her face. Ainsley might protest that she was fine, that all was well, that Angelo had been in time, but Cameron saw that the incident had scared the hell out of her.

She was asking for his comfort. Even while a cold finger of dread stole down Cameron's spine, he knew he couldn't walk away from her, not now. At this moment, when he had to choose between her peace of mind and his, he chose Ainsley's.

Without a word, Cameron nodded.

Ainsley visibly relaxed. Cameron pulled the covers over them both, curling into the warmth of her and drawing her back against him. Ainsley closed her eyes, sweetly trusting.

Cameron waited while the fire crackled and the window darkened with coming night. Ainsley slid into sleep while he held her, her body moving gently with her even, slow breaths.

He could leave now. Cameron could slide out of bed and pad to the door, slipping to his own room to crawl into bed and welcome exhausted sleep.

He didn't move. The silence of the room was soothing, as was the hiss of the burning coals and the rising wind that flowed under the house's eaves. He and Ainsley were safe together in this nest, warm and comforting each other. Stillness, that was what Cameron needed. Stillness to be with Ainsley.

His body relaxed as the room grew darker. Soon Cameron knew nothing but Ainsley's warmth, her presence, her scent. Then, oblivion.

Ainsley opened her eyes to sunlight and found herself nose-to-nose with her husband. Cameron lay on his side, cheek on the pillow, the covers kicked off in the stuffy room. His eyes were closed, his hair a mess. A faint snore issued from his slightly open mouth.

Lord Cameron Mackenzie was sleeping with her.

Chapter 25

Ainsley rose on her elbow to study him. Cameron lay like a recumbent beast, arms curled under his pillow, bare legs splayed. Morning sunlight pooled on the backs of his thighs, curls of wiry hair dusting his skin between the scars.

She'd not seen his body laid out for her like this before, showing plainly where his skin had been broken and gouged. Scars snaked from his thighs up and over his buttocks, dipping between the tight mounds of his backside. At the cleave, the skin had been scraped away entirely.

Cameron must have lain very much like this that horrible day about which Count Durand had taunted him—facedown, sprawled in sleep. Ainsley wondered how long it had taken for Cameron to feel safe sleeping in this position again, even behind the bedroom door he locked every night. A long time, she thought.

Now he slept hard, body limp, even the lines that marked the corners of his eyes smoothing to nothing.

Ainsley didn't touch him. She lay down again, watching

her husband until the sunshine soothed her back into warm sleep.

Something brushed Cameron's thigh, and he jerked his eyes open. The room was bright with sunlight, close from the overly stoked fire. Cameron lay in a warm tangle of sheets and blankets with Ainsley snuggled up to him. The thing that had bumped him was Ainsley's knee.

Her softly scented form nestled against his, her warmth like an embrace. Sunlight touched her spill of yellow gold hair and the lashes that lay against her skin. One plump arm cradled her head, the other rested across her body, hand on the mattress.

She was profoundly beautiful.

The realization worked into Cameron's brain that although Ainsley had startled him awake, he hadn't reacted. He hadn't swung fists or tried to shove her away from him. He'd awakened to peace, to this moment in the warmth and brightness of her bedroom.

Ainsley slept on, unaware, and a strange stillness crept over Cameron. One by one, his fears untwined and released him.

Here in bed with Ainsley, he was safe from the beast that lingered within him, safe from the cruelty of others. He must have instinctively gentled his reaction to her, knowing that, even in his sleep, he needed to protect her. Something about Ainsley's touch, her scent, had soothed him and kept him still.

Cameron let out his breath, his relief so vast that the world seemed too small to contain it. Ainsley was doing it again, awakening him, banishing the gray, letting him live.

He reached out and smoothed her hair, fingers shaking.

Ainsley made a little noise in her throat, and her eyes fluttered open.

She regarded him a moment in sleepy confusion, then her warm smile blossomed.

"Cam," she whispered. "You stayed."

Cameron skimmed his hand down her bare side, cupping the breast that was warm from the covers. "I decided that there is an advantage to waking up with you."

Her smile turned sly. "Oh, yes?"

Cameron stroked her lips apart with his tongue. Ainsley nibbled his lower lip, and Cameron's hardness throbbed.

"A decided advantage," she said.

Cameron rolled on top of her. "I'm taking *full* advantage."

Ainsley's smile widened as Cameron easily slid inside her. "I see that," she said.

Cameron silenced her by starting to love her with renewed vigor, in the safety and heat of her bed.

"Angelo."

Angelo finished unfastening the girth of the horse he'd been riding and pulled off the saddle. He carried the saddle to a hook in the wall, folding up the stirrups, leaving it to be cleaned once the horse was taken care of.

Cameron watched Angelo pick up a curry comb and start on the haltered horse's sweaty hide. The prize racer half closed his eyes in enjoyment.

Angelo said nothing, waiting as usual to see what Cameron had on his mind. He went on rubbing the stiff metal brush in a circular motion, loosening dirt and hair and sweat from the horse's back.

"I want to give you all the money in the world, Angelo," Cam said. "I want to make you King of England. Hell, a Romany would make a damn sight better king than the Saxe-Coburgs."

Angelo flashed him a grin. "Please don't. I wouldn't like staying indoors all day."

"All the money in the world, though. You deserve it."

"Money is good to keep the belly full and the fire warm," Angelo conceded. "But it's more fun to steal it."

"Don't make light of this. You saved Ainsley's life, yesterday. That's worth everything I have."

Angelo kept the curry comb moving. "I was close enough to do something, is all. I know how you think, so I know you're blaming yourself, but I saw how volatile that stallion was. I should have ignored Pierson and handled him anyway."

"And Pierson would have you sitting in a magistrate's court today for horse thieving. We're well rid of the man. But Ainsley shouldn't have had to suffer for it."

"Aye, that's true enough." Angelo gave him a quiet look. "Don't give me your kingdom. I don't want it, and I know that if it had been my sister or mother or lover in danger, and you'd been close enough, you'd have done the same."

"Yes."

Angelo finished currying, tapped the dirt from the comb, and started on the horse's coat with the softer dandy brush. This one he swept in the direction the horse's hair grew, and the champion racer, who'd finished first in his year at Newmarket, Epsom, and Doncaster, rocked his weight onto one hip and grunted with pleasure.

"Ainsley wants to see your canal boat," Cameron said.

Angelo's grin lit his eyes. "Let me send word to Mother first so she can have a good cleanup. She'd tan my hide if I brought her ladyship on board without warning."

Cameron, having met Angelo's mother, understood. Angelo's mother stood about four and a half feet tall, if that, and ruled Angelo's vast family with an iron fist.

They left it at that. Angelo understood Cameron's gratitude, and Cameron knew the man would take it in stride.

Cameron left the stable, still too agitated to ride—horses didn't need a jerky, anxious rider—and watched from the edge of the paddock as the jockeys did training runs.

He felt rather than heard Daniel stop beside him. Daniel

was, if anything, even taller than he'd been when they'd left Kilmorgan, and had filled out still more.

Cameron couldn't help remembering the child who'd followed him about on spindly legs, demanding to know everything about "the ponies." Even though Cameron had been offhand with Daniel, he'd always been acutely aware of where his son had been and what he'd been doing at all times, going after him when he went astray, as he'd done in Glasgow. He and his brothers between them had somehow raised him without making too much of a mess of it.

"Well, I'm off," Daniel said.

"Off? Where this time?"

Daniel stuck his hands in the pockets and gave Cameron a bland look. "University. Isn't that where you've been trying to shove me these last months?"

"I thought you hated Cambridge."

"I do. So, I'm not going to Cambridge. I'm going to Edinburgh. I thought maybe Glasgow, which is why I legged it down there that day."

Cameron's exasperation rose. "Is that what that was all about? Damnation, Danny, why didn't ye tell me?"

He shrugged. "I wanted to see the place before I begged ye to send me there. Didn't expect to get in a scrape. I dressed decently so the warden wouldn't toss me out on my ear, but it was too tempting for those lads. They wanted the clothes off my back, would you believe it? If they needed money, they only had to ask. I told them."

"So you went to jail with them? Noble of ye, son."

"They didn't think I'd fight back. I was fighting as hard as they were, so I didn't see I should get off. Their leader, ye know, he's not so bad. For a street tough."

God help us. "Ye chose Edinburgh, though. Why? Fewer street toughs?"

"Amusing, Dad. I like a professor there who's going to teach me engineering. And there's one who'll teach me architecture. No more philosophy, thank ye very much."

"If you didn't want to study philosophy, Danny, you only had to say."

Again the careless shrug. "I didn't much know, Dad, truth to tell. I had to wander about, find out for myself. But I'm fixed now. Hilary term's part done, but they say they'll give me private instruction to bring me up to scratch. I'll get the lay of the land, meet the chaps, see how it goes. I'll come back here between terms and then seriously start at Trinity. I'll catch the train today, send you a telegram when I arrive. Uncle Mac says I can stay in his house there."

The tight pain in Cameron's heart startled him. Cam had grown used to having Daniel with him all the time. He'd purchased the Berkshire estate partly because he'd be close to Daniel when he was at Harrow.

Now their paths were diverging. The son Cameron had fought so hard to protect was ready to start protecting himself.

"Why the sudden wish to rush off?" Cameron asked in a light voice. "I can always use more help with the horses. The Newmarket races will be here soon enough, and you can start at Trinity term."

Daniel looked his father straight in the eye. "Because I know you'll be all right without me. You don't need me anymore, Dad. You've got Ainsley looking after you, now."

"I thought I was looking after her."

Daniel snorted. "She might let ye think so. But you spent the whole night with her last night, didn't you? Sleeping and all?"

Cameron's face heated. "That's your business now, is it?"

"The whole house knows it, Dad. They're pleased that you have a chance for a good marriage, and so am I."

"Good God, doesn't anyone have anything better to talk about?"

"Not really. They all like Ainsley and want to make sure you treat her well. I like her too, and want the same. But ye proved yourself."

Cameron's eyes narrowed. "Is that why you've been staying with us all winter? So you could keep an eye on me with Ainsley?"

"Partly. That's why I know that it's all right for me to go now."

Cameron wanted to laugh. He wanted to hug Daniel, tell the lad he was a damn fool, and then tell him that he loved him.

Neither had ever been comfortable with that kind of sentimentality, so both turned to watch the horses. The filly called Chance's Daughter, a pretty bay Cameron had bought about the time Ian married Beth, ran with grace and enthusiasm. She'd do well this year in the three-year-olds' races.

"Daniel," Cameron said after a time. "I know I've been the worst father a lad can be stuck with."

"Not your fault, Dad. You're a Mackenzie."

"So are you. Don't forget that." Horses thundered toward them, Chance's Daughter smoothly pulling into the lead. "Don't make the mistakes I did."

"I'll make plenty of my own, I warrant. But I have an advantage, ye know. All you got was a dad who beat his sons and was jealous of them too. I have a dad who tries to do the right thing, even if he mucks it up most of the time. And then there's my sweet aunties and my stepmother to show me that some women ain't so bad. They don't all just want our money. Some of the lasses even like us."

Cameron let out a laugh. "Yes, some of them do. Now, I'm going to do something to embarrass you."

He grabbed Daniel and jerked him to him in a big bear hug. Instead of stiffening, Daniel laughed and hugged his father back. The embrace grew tighter and tighter until Cameron couldn't breathe. Daniel had certainly grown strong.

The two broke. "Come back to us soon, all right?" Cameron said.

"Of course. You're going to teach me everything you know about working with the ponies, so once I'm done with university I can become a partner in your stables. We're going to be world famous, Dad."

"You have that all planned out? What about your engineering and your architecture?"

"I can do that too. Might even invent a better transport for horses or build a better stable. Plus I'll work on the chaps at university and have them and their dads to send the horses to us." He clapped his father on the shoulders. "I already said good-bye to Ainsley. She cried and kissed me on the cheek, and then gave me a packet of cakes. Marrying her was the smartest thing you ever did, Dad. There's hope for you, yet."

With that pronouncement, Daniel hugged his father again. Cameron returned the embrace, then reluctantly released him.

Daniel waved at Angelo, who was coming to join Cam, and then strode back toward the house and the carriage waiting to take him to the station. Daniel walked as tall and strong as Ian or Mac, even Hart.

"They grow up so fast," Angelo said when he reached Cam. Cameron glanced at him, thinking the man joking, but Angelo's dark eyes were serious. "Childhood is gone in the wink of an eye, and then they have to be men. You Anglos are strange, sending your sons out into the world as soon as they get tall enough. My family has been together forever."

"I notice you don't live with them, Angelo, so don't become sentimental. Besides, my family is together. Just a bit spread out."

"Rich Anglos need too much space."

"That is true, but it keeps us from killing each other."

Angelo grinned. Daniel climbed into the coach, and Cameron watched it roll down the drive with a pang in his heart.

He'd miss Daniel with everything he had, but he took Angelo's words in the way the man meant them. Daniel would be welcome to stay with Cameron any time and for as long as he wanted. He'd done everything in his power to make damn certain that Daniel never had to fear coming home.

At that endeavor, Cameron knew he'd already far surpassed his own father.

Ainsley found the house emptier without Daniel, but Cameron now stayed all night every night with her, which meant that Ainsley got very little sleep. He'd wake her in the morning with loving, and they'd separate, sandy-eyed to their morning activities.

Cameron was unhappy about the loss of Jasmine, Ainsley could see, although he told her adamantly when she brought it up that it didn't matter. He had plenty of other horses that would do well, and Chance's Daughter would probably win the five top races of the year.

Ainsley wished Cameron could make his peace with Lord Pierson—or rather, that Lord Pierson wouldn't be such a pompous fool. Jasmine was the suffering for their quarrel, and Ainsley's heart went out to her.

But Ainsley had ideas for solving the problem. Legally of course. She wrote to her brother Steven, hoping to recruit him, but Steven replied that he couldn't get leave from his regiment. Sinclair was too busy with his practice, Elliot was out of reach in India, of course, and Patrick . . .

Hmm, perhaps Patrick would do very nicely.

Before Ainsley could put any plans in motion, however, a telegram came to jolt her out of the new and pleasant hum of her life.

Chapter 26

Cameron walked in while Ainsley was packing. Her upstairs rooms were a mess of boxes and bags, the maids hurrying in and out with articles of clothing. Ainsley had known she'd have to confront Cameron sooner or later, but she'd rather hoped his training would keep him out of doors a little longer.

She took the telegram from her pocket and thrust it at him. "Before you ask, *this* is what it's all about."

Cameron's eyes flickered as he read the words. *Mr. Brown is gone. Come to me at once.*

"Brown?" Cameron rumbled. "He's dead?"

"Apparently." Ainsley stopped a maid. "No, not the blue. I need the gray and the black. The queen will expect me in mourning."

Cameron held the telegram between two fingers. "Why does she want you? She must have other ladies who can hold her hand."

"She confided deeply in me about John Brown, how

fond she was of him. He saved her life, really. I understand what she's feeling."

"What I mean, Ainsley, is *why* the devil are you going?"

"It won't be for long," Ainsley said. "A few weeks, maybe a month."

"No." The word burst out of Cameron, and Ainsley looked at him in surprise. "A month is far too long."

"It will give me a chance to finish a few things I left hanging. To make a clean end of them."

"What things?"

"Things from my old life. I packed and left rather abruptly, as you know, once I'd made up my mind to."

Cameron slapped his hand to her open trunk lid, and the thing clattered shut. The maid looked startled then discreetly faded out the door.

"The queen has a houseful of servants and ladies at her beck and call," Cameron said. "Why should you go?"

Ainsley had seen Victoria grieve before, how ill she made herself with it. The queen was a robust woman, but she did not handle loss very well. She loved hard and she grieved hard, rather like Cameron in that respect.

"I had another telegram, from one of her ladies," Ainsley said. "The queen can't walk, is unable even to rise from her chair. If I can ease some of that, if I can help her again, take my leave of her as friends, then I can return here and begin my life."

"*Begin* your life? What the devil have you been living these past five months?"

"Please, Cam, this is important. She needs me."

"Damn it all, *I* need you!"

Ainsley watched him in silence. Cameron held himself rigidly, fists clenched in dusty gloves.

"Cam," Ainsley said. "I'll come back."

"Will you?" The words were bitter.

"Of course. We're married."

"Is that all?"

"That's rather a lot, to me."

Cameron knew she didn't understand. Her gray eyes were still, hands halted in the act of folding a shawl. The shawl complemented her, silver and satiny, dripping down her arms the same way her hair slid over Cameron's body when they made love.

Ainsley was leaving—Cameron losing her. The very thought made him break into a cold sweat.

"By the time I return, Daniel will have come home for his short holiday," Ainsley said. "We'll be a family again."

A family. *Again.* She sounded so certain, as though everything were simple. Cameron and Daniel had only ever been tense satellites circling each other, and they had both known it. Until Ainsley. Daniel had tried at every turn to shove Ainsley into Cameron's life, had turned up to winter with them, to make sure his father and Ainsley stuck it out. Now Daniel had gone, believing that everything was well.

"You won't come back," Cameron said.

"Yes, I will. I've just said."

"You'll intend to. But the queen will get her clutches into you, drag you back into her world, where she is the sun and the moon. She doesn't like the Mackenzies, and she'll do whatever she can to get you away from us."

Ainsley looked puzzled. "The queen takes your advice on horses. You even turned up at Balmoral to speak to her about it."

"Because she wants her horses to win. That doesn't mean she likes or even respects me. Victoria knew my mother, thought her a fool for putting up with my father. She pitied my mother and despised her at the same time. She thinks Mackenzie sons are cut from the same cloth as the father, and she's not far from wrong."

"She *is* wrong. I know that. Isabella told me about your father. He sounds horrible."

"But he's here." Cameron pressed his chest. "He's in here. The bully who beat us, who killed my mother, who locked Ian away in an asylum—he's in here with me. He's in all of us. You might have noticed that my family is not exactly sane."

She gave him her little smile. "Eccentric, certainly."

"Stark, raving mad. I ease the madness with the horses, but between seasons, I barely keep it contained. Until this year, with you. Instead of drinking and sexing until I couldn't remember which day was which, I strolled in parks and went to museums and to gardens, for God's sake. I watched you and Daniel discuss the virtues of pastries and play draughts together on rainy evenings. My friends in Monte Carlo told me I'd gone domestic, and I laughed, because *I didn't care*."

Ainsley sent him another puzzled look. "You were miserable in Monte Carlo."

"Restless, yes. Miserable, no. Hell, no. There, and in Paris, I was seeing everything as though it were new. All the things I took for granted for years suddenly had color and substance. Why? Because I saw them anew, through your eyes."

Ainsley couldn't know how beautiful she was standing there listening to him, brow puckered in confusion. "But your heart is *here*," she said. "In Berkshire. With your horses at Waterbury Grange. I'm not wrong about that."

"My heart is where you are, Ainsley. So when you leave . . ." Cameron made an empty gesture.

"I'll come back," she said stubbornly.

"To this wreck of a man? Why should you?"

"Because I love you."

Cameron stopped. She'd said that before, though not often, as though worried how he'd respond.

But damn it, Ainsley could say it as often as she bloody well pleased. Plenty of women had told Cameron they'd loved him, even Elizabeth had. Usually they cooed it after he gave them some expensive present. Ainsley stood forlornly in the middle of a room and said it.

With Ainsley, something whispered to him, it just might be true.

"Then why go?" he asked.

"Because of the things I need to do. Important things. I would ask you to accompany me, but I know you can't leave the horses, and you being with me would complicate things."

"What things?"

"Cameron . . ."

Cameron unfolded his arms and moved to the window. Out in the paddock Angelo was letting the horse he rode slowly canter, winding down from a gallop.

He felt her come up behind him then her soothing touch on his shoulder. "That night six years ago in your bedchamber," she said in a soft voice. "When you tempted me so sorely, and I refused you . . ."

"I remember." The horse was going well, Angelo riding as though he were one with the beast. "What about it?"

"I refused you because I wouldn't betray John, my husband. And I won't betray you now. I'll come back, Cameron. I promise."

Cameron turned and pulled her to him. They stood together, swaying in the sunshine. He felt Ainsley relax, relieved that he'd stopped fighting her. But Cameron was far from yielding.

"I don't want you back because you feel obligated to me, love," he said. "That's the devil of wedding vows—they make you do things for a person you maybe should run away from. Come back to me because you want to, not because you think you ought to. Do you understand?"

Ainsley looked up at him, her eyes a mystery. "I think I do understand you, Cameron."

Cameron heard more in the sentence than the bare words, but he couldn't decide what. He kissed her, dissolving in her warmth, and then he let her go.

~

Angelo went with her. Cameron insisted. Cameron said that he trusted *Ainsley* but not whatever fools she might meet on her journey. A maid and a footman weren't enough to guard her. Angelo, he knew, wouldn't let a damn thing happen to her. So Angelo went, without argument.

Once they reached Windsor, Angelo left to join his family on their canal boat that wandered up and down the nearby Kennet and Avon Canal. Ainsley loaded Angelo with packages of food and clothing, toys for his nieces and nephews, and sent him off.

She found Windsor cold, damp, and sorrowful.

My dearest Cameron,

The queen is quite distraught and most days cannot walk on her own. She has expressed relief that I am here and relies on me most strongly.

I am happy I came, because the others of the household, while sad that the queen is grieving, did not have much love for Mr. Brown. They grow impatient with Her Majesty's eulogizing and her talk of mausoleums and monuments to him. Their line of thinking is that Mr. Brown was only a servant, and one who got above himself at that. He deserves a proper burial, yes, but nothing more.

But they forget what a true friend Mr. Brown was to the queen after her husband's death, when her heart broke, and she hid herself away from the world. It was Mr. Brown that got her to do her duty as queen again and gave her the will to continue. He should at least be remembered for that.

I doubt, despite vicious gossip, and despite those letters over which Mrs. Chase was delighted to blackmail her, that the queen and Mr. Brown were ever lovers. A couple can be quite intimate without sharing bodies—though you will likely not believe that, my Cam.

But it can be true. What I feel for you is highly intense, whether you are standing next to me or living a hundred miles away. I do not have to be touching you at all to experience what I feel.

The queen and I go out seldom, and I look longingly across the fields from my high window, wishing I were at Waterbury with you. Here lambs wander across green fields and crocuses sprout the colors of spring. I imagine that Waterbury must look much the same, all misty and soft.

Unhappily I do not see much of spring because I sit most of the time behind thickly draped windows with nothing to do but read to Her Majesty, or embroider, or perhaps play on the piano. At least I have time to work on the pillows I'm doing for our parlor, in very bright and cheerful colors. I enjoy picturing what they will look like in our house.

I will write as often as I can, but truth be told, I don't have many moments to myself. The queen is in a very bad way and needs everyone who can be at her side.

But whenever I undo my buttons to ready myself for bed, I think of you. I imagine your fingers unfastening my gown, opening me like a Christmas parcel for your pleasure. I tingle even now as I think of it, and so I will close before I quite combust and burn the paper.

Please greet our household for me, and your trainers, and the lads at the stables, and the horses, and McNab. I so miss you all!

With my deepest love, my dearest husband,

Your,
Ainsley

"Now, my dear, I will speak to you about your unfortunate marriage to the Mackenzies."

The queen must be feeling better, Ainsley thought, *if she's bringing up the topic of my elopement.*

Ainsley kept her gaze on her embroidery, blue violets on a cream background. She was redoing the parlor at Waterbury in shades of blue and yellow, brightening it from Cameron's decorating scheme of "whatever happened to be in the house when I bought it."

She makes it sound as though I married the whole lot of them. Although, maybe I did.

"Their father was a brute," Victoria said decidedly. "I knew the duke, and he was awful. The apple doesn't fall far from the tree, you know. Marriage to a Mackenzie is no marriage for a genteel young lady, especially one as well brought up as you were."

Isabella and Beth were genteel young ladies too, Ainsley reflected. The queen, however, made no mention of them.

"Lord Cameron and I are managing to rub along quite well," Ainsley said. "You'll see us at Ascot, of course, but I imagine he'll win the Thousand Guineas Stakes at Newmarket with his new filly. You ought to wager on her. Chance's Daughter is a brilliant runner."

The queen gave her a severe look. "Don't change the subject. You eloped. You disgraced yourself. For once, I am glad your poor dear mother is not alive. You'd have broken her heart."

While Ainsley hadn't known her mother, she refused to believe that Jeanette McBride would have minded seeing her only daughter marry happily, if a bit unconventionally.

"What's done is done," Ainsley said. "Water under the bridge. I must make the best of it." She winced as the clichés fell from her lips, but all clichés held a grain of truth.

"I heard of your goings-on on the Continent," the queen went on. "Cabarets and the casino at all hours of the night. Your brother and sister-in-law hid their faces in shame."

Ainsley rather doubted that. Patrick, for all his emphasis on hard, honest work, could understand a bit of pleasure for pleasure's sake now and again. Plus, Patrick was far more open-minded than his rather dour countenance suggested.

As she'd told Cameron, Patrick and Rona definitely did *not* have separate bedrooms.

"And it's not quite true that what's done is done," Victoria said. "The marriage can be put aside. I'm certain that Lord Cameron tricked you into believing you married him legally. He knew you wouldn't let him seduce you until you had a ring on your finger."

Ainsley decided to keep quiet about the fact that Cameron had seduced her long before the ring was on her finger. "Ma'am, Lord Cameron isn't a stage villain. We had a license. I saw it. And a vicar, and witnesses."

"Hired actors and a forgery. I have caused letters to be sent to Hart Mackenzie, instructing him to take the legal means to declare the marriage null."

Ainsley imagined Hart Mackenzie's reaction on receiving *those* instructions.

But the queen's presumption that she could so coolly interfere with Ainsley's life and that Ainsley would simply obey, made her at last lose her temper.

"How dare you?" she said in a low but fierce voice. Victoria's eyes widened, but Ainsley plunged on, bravely taking to task the Queen of England and Empress of Britain. "After all I did for you. I risked everything to get those letters back for you, because I respected you and didn't want to see you embarrassed. Lord Cameron helped—did you know that? He gave me the money for the letters so that you'd not have to pay one farthing."

"You told him?" The queen's whisper cut through the room, and ladies on the other side looked up. "Do mean to say, Ainsley Douglas, that *Cameron Mackenzie*, of all people, knows about my letters?"

"If not for him, you'd have had greatest difficulty getting them back."

Victoria stared at her in outrage. "You little fool. Lord Cameron will have told the duke, and copies will be circulating even now."

"Cameron has told no one. I asked him to keep the secret, and he complied."

"Do not be ridiculous. He is a *Mackenzie*. He cannot be trusted."

"He can be perfectly trusted," Ainsley said. "But if you succeed in breaking up our marriage, do you not think Lord Cameron might retaliate with what he knows?"

Ainsley didn't truly believe Cameron would take his revenge with petty gossip, but then again, who knew what Cameron might do? She remembered his look when he'd watched her leave Waterbury: raw, empty, angry.

Victoria, on the other hand, did believe it. "That is blackmail."

"Yes, it is. It seems to be the only thing that anyone understands."

Ainsley was suddenly tired of this life—the court, the gossip, dealing in secrets and tittle-tattle. She had always been an outsider looking in, the nobody daughter of a nobody gentleman, hired by the queen for the sake of Ainsley's mother. Ainsley had never been important enough to be bribed for favors or blackmailed into them; she'd only watched others do so to each other. No one had much noticed Ainsley at all.

Now, as wife of one of the notorious and powerful Mackenzies, heir to the dukedom, Ainsley could be used, or she could be dangerous. She preferred to be dangerous.

"Therefore, I believe that I will remain married to Lord Cameron," Ainsley finished.

The queen glared at her, but Ainsley saw Victoria looking at her in a new way: not as a sycophant who could be sent on delicate errands, but as a woman to be reckoned with.

"Your poor dear husband will roll in his grave," Victoria said. "Mr. Douglas was a respectable man."

"My poor dear husband was quite generous, and I believe he'd want to see me happy." John had been kind to the end, and Ainsley had always been very, very glad that she'd stood by him.

The queen continued to regard her with cold eyes. "I will pretend that I never heard this outburst. The conversation never took place." She lifted her needlework from her lap. "If you had not been so rude, Ainsley, I would have told you that your brother has arrived. I'd arranged for him to take you home to wait for your annulment, but now, of course, you may do whatever you wish. We are finished. But there is a saying, my dear, that you might well heed, that those who make their beds must lie in them."

My, they were full of old adages today. But as long as that bed held Cameron Mackenzie, Ainsley would happily lie there.

Ainsley thrust her embroidery into her work basket. "Patrick is here? May I go?"

"Please do. Send Beatrice to me. I do not believe we shall be seeing you again."

Ainsley rose and curtseyed, relieved rather than dismayed to be dismissed.

On impulse, she leaned down and kissed the queen's faded cheek. "I hope you'll learn to be proud of me, one day," she said. "And I assure you, your secrets are safe with me."

Victoria blinked in surprise. Ainsley felt the queen's gaze on her as she made her way across the room and out of it. The click of the door that a footman closed behind her seemed to signal the end of Ainsley's old life.

Patrick McBride waited in a corridor not far away, looking uncomfortable and a little drab amidst the splendors of Windsor. Ainsley tossed down her sewing basket and ran the length of the hall to him, arms outstretched. Patrick's smile as he swept her up was worth every one of the queen's disapproving words.

"I'm so pleased to see you," Ainsley said, smiling into his dear face. "I need a cohort in crime, Pat, and you, my so-respectable older brother, will be perfect."

Chapter 27

The Mackenzies started pouring into Waterbury Grange in April, at about the time Ainsley's letters stopped coming. Cameron would leave for the meets at Newmarket soon, the racing season once more reaching out to embrace him.

Mac and Isabella arrived first with their two children in tow, Mac taking over with his usual ebullience. Fortunately the house was big enough to absorb them all plus give Mac a place to set up his studio.

Mac had been painting with gusto this past year, in his usual getup of nothing but kilt and painting boots and a gypsy kerchief to protect his hair. He now spent his time fully dressed in the stable yard, doing preliminary sketches of Chance's Daughter, while his wife kept her robust children from going too close to the horses, an arduous task.

A few days later Ian and Beth and child turned up, accompanied by Daniel, who'd traveled down with them.

In years past when Ian had visited Waterbury, he'd develop a rigid routine, allowing himself only into certain rooms and along certain paths around the unfamiliar house and grounds. He'd be fine if allowed to follow that routine, but the moment anything disrupted it, Ian would fall into confusion and rages, what he called his "muddles." Only Curry, his valet, had been able to calm Ian back into the comforting routine.

This year, Curry seemed to have been recruited as makeshift nanny. He bounced the ten-month-old Jamie Mackenzie in his arms while Ian assisted Beth from the carriage.

Ian called out that they'd arrived and took his son back from Curry. He slowed his steps for Beth, who was plump with child, as they entered the house. Beth hadn't been to Waterbury before—last year she'd been pregnant with their first child, and Ian had not wanted her to travel. This year, Beth had insisted.

Cameron greeted them, then stood back with Mac as Isabella hugged Beth and chattered with her about the journey. The two dogs that had accompanied Ian and Beth now swarmed around McNab, the three of them probably also chattering about the journey.

As Ian took Beth's hand and started to lead her up the stairs, Cameron's housekeeper blocked their path.

"I'm afraid you've been put into a different room this year, my lord," the housekeeper said. "Her ladyship—Lord Cameron's ladyship, that is—thought you'd be more comfortable in a bigger chamber. It's a front one, my lord." She smiled tightly, familiar with Ian. "It has a very nice view."

Behind Ian, Curry stopped, looking worried. Beth smiled encouragingly at Ian and squeezed his arm.

Ian didn't look at the housekeeper but glanced at Cameron, briefly meeting his eyes. "The one at the top of the stairs? I was going to ask you for it, Cam. My usual one will be too small. Ainsley was right to change it. This way, my Beth."

He glided on up the stairs, baby on one arm and Beth on

the other. Curry followed, the look of relief on his Cockney face obvious. The housekeeper relaxed as well, and Mac raised his brows at Cameron.

"Our baby brother has grown up," Mac said.

He had. Beth had taken the wreck that was Ian and given him a life.

"Ainsley is very perceptive," Isabella said, leaning on Mac's shoulder. "I believe I have mentioned that she is excellent at organizing. She's certainly done wonders with this dusty old place. When is she returning?"

"I couldn't say." Cameron's voice was stiff.

"I'm certain the queen has her running about on some mad errand," Isabella said. "Ainsley will finish it and sail back here before you know it." She tapped Cameron's wrist. "But I will never forgive you for marrying her in that underhanded way, without telling me."

Cameron thoughts flashed back to Ainsley in Hart's London parlor, promising in her unwavering voice to honor her husband and worship him with her body. "It was necessary."

Mac laughed. "Because Ainsley wouldn't have agreed if Cam had given her time to think about it." He kissed his wife's cheek. "It's the only way to get a woman to marry a Mackenzie."

"Yes, but *one* bride in this family should have a sumptuous wedding," Isabella said. "We could do a second one, as Beth did with Ian."

Cameron didn't answer. For now, his bride was elusive, buried with the queen at Windsor while Cameron grew surlier by the day.

Daniel went out with Cameron to the paddocks in the morning to watch the horses run. Cameron liked Daniel there, enjoyed standing next to the solid wall of his son. The idea of Daniel coming to partner with him after university was a good one.

After they watched Chance's Daughter leave the other

horses in the dust yet again, Daniel said. "You'll have to trust her, Dad."

"Who, Chance's Daughter?"

"Very funny. Ye know I mean Ainsley." Daniel's voice was even deeper now, his stance more confident. "If Ainsley says she'll do a thing, she'll do it."

The next set of horses came running down the flat, hooves pounding, mud flying. The roar and rush was supposed to make Cameron's world come alive, but without Ainsley to watch it with him, that world was flat and dull.

"Women change their minds at the drop of a feather, son," he said. "You'll learn that."

Daniel gave him a patient look. "She's not *women*, Dad. She's Ainsley."

He pushed away from the fence and strolled toward the stables, waving at the trainers on the way, but his words lingered.

She's Ainsley.

The world took on a flush of color. Ainsley would come home. She'd said she would, and the truth of that struck Cameron with force.

He'd never trusted a woman before. Elizabeth had long ago stolen that trust from him, and Cameron had held women at arm's length ever since. He'd always ended his affairs long before the lady in question had a chance to betray and hurt him, having learned, painfully, that he had to control any liaison he entered.

Then Ainsley had bowled into Cameron's life and taken over. No, not taken over. She'd become part of him, bonded to his heart. Cameron felt that bond now stretching between them, across the miles to Windsor, or wherever she'd gone by now. That bond would pull him to her, and her to him, and he would never lose her.

A peace stole over him, one Cameron hadn't felt in . . . Hell, he'd never felt anything like this in his life. He'd come close to it holding his son for the first time, the tiny being he'd vowed to protect with everything he had, but never since.

Cameron raised his gaze to the young man who'd grown from that tiny being, and his heart swelled with pride. Not for anything Cameron had done himself, but for what Daniel had become on his own. A good lad, smart and brave, who loved without resentment, who was as carelessly generous as the rest of the Mackenzies.

She's Ainsley.

Cameron thought of Ainsley: of her beautiful hair spilling across her body while she slept, of her frank gray gaze that undid his heart, of her laughter that heated his blood. He missed her with brutal sharpness.

When Ainsley returned—and she would return—Cameron would show her how much he'd missed her, every detail of it.

And he'd never let her out of his sight again. Being without her was too damned hard.

When Ainsley told Patrick that part of her scheme involved him accompanying her to a canal boat full of the Roma, he was naturally perplexed.

"Ainsley. Stop."

Ainsley set down her valise on the towpath of the Kennet and Avon Canal. A long canal boat rested beside them, rocking ever so gently. Children watched them from the deck, as did the adults, one man smoking a long pipe. Angelo had gone below to tell his mother that they'd arrived.

Patrick puffed from the walk from the village a little west of Reading, where the hired coach had left them. Ainsley's forty-five-year-old brother, though he'd let himself go a bit paunchy, looked so utterly respectable in his dark suit, hat, and walking stick that Ainsley wanted to hug him again. She'd missed him.

Patrick pulled out a handkerchief that had been folded into a perfect square and wiped his brow. "We've never discussed what we are to do on this boat."

"Nothing. It will take us, discreetly, to Bath."

"A Romany canal boat is discreet?"

"Unexpected, certainly. I need to get to Bath without making a fanfare of it, without anyone knowing we're coming."

"Where I will be your cohort in crime?"

"I use the term *crime* loosely," Ainsley said. "I'll tell you all about it on the boat."

"Ainsley."

Patrick's tone turned serious, and Ainsley sucked in a breath. She'd rushed him from his Windsor inn to his hired coach, and then kept up a steady stream of chatter about her life in Waterbury, the horses, Daniel, about redecorating her house, as they rode. Anything to prevent the talk she knew she had to face now.

"Ainsley, you haven't allowed me to discuss your elopement," Patrick said.

"I know that. I'm avoiding the scolding that I'll know you'll give me."

"I merely wish you had consulted me about it first. What a shock we had when we received your telegram! My little sister married to a lord. And *such* a lord."

"I know. I'm sorry, Patrick, but I had to choose quickly. There wasn't time to consult you. I knew that eloping would disappoint you, and please believe me when I say that it hurt me to disappoint you. Very much. But Cameron was right when he told me I'd deliberately let myself become a drudge. Because, you see, I thought that, if you and Rona saw how sorry I was, how grateful I was that you stood by me when I was so foolish—and how good I'd be for the rest of my life—maybe you, my brother, would forgive me." She ran out of breath.

"Ainsley." Patrick's gray eyes went wide. "Of course I

forgave you. I forgave you years ago. And anyway, there wasn't anything to forgive. You have such a large heart, of course you'd trust that blackguard in Italy. Why shouldn't you? It was my fault for being so wrapped up in my own business that I didn't notice and warn you in time. *You* should forgive *me* for not looking after you."

"But I never blamed you, Patrick. It never ever occurred to me to blame you."

"Well, I have blamed myself. You were so young and so trusting, and I should have kept a better eye on you."

Ainsley stopped. She'd had no idea that Patrick had felt that way. Perhaps she'd been so busy with self-castigation that she'd failed to notice her brother doing the same himself.

"My dear Patrick, we can stand here on this towpath and exchange declarations of culpability for hours, but perhaps we should agree to put it behind us. I will simply say that I've always been very grateful to you. You stood by me when you didn't have to."

"You are my sister. I would never dream of deserting you, or throwing you to the wolves. And you're avoiding my questions again. This elopement with Lord Cameron Mackenzie—"

"I had to jump the way my heart led me," Ainsley said.

Patrick wiped his forehead again. "Let me finish, dear girl. At first I suspected that Mackenzie had abducted you, had tricked you into running away with him by pretending to marry you. Her majesty certainly thought so and had her secretary write me her suspicions. I was inclined to investigate. I asked friends in Paris what they thought of the match. They wrote me how happy you were, how positively radiant, how Lord Cameron treated you like a queen." Patrick chuckled. "Better than a queen treated you, actually."

Ainsley stifled surprise. Patrick rarely criticized anyone, even obliquely, and especially not the Queen of England.

Patrick shrugged. "Bless her, she's Hanoverian. Not even

a Stuart. I rather agree with Hart Mackenzie that Scotland should be independent, although I'm skeptical at his chances to put it that way."

Ainsley looked at her brother, her heart full. "Then you forgive me? Or at least understand?"

"I told you, there's nothing to forgive. You followed your heart, and this time, you were wise enough to make the choice with your head as well. I would like to meet Lord Cameron before I fully make up my mind, but I trust you." Patrick let out his breath. "Now, what the devil is this crime you want me to help you commit?"

"Not a crime. Merely a little deception."

Before Patrick could answer, Angelo came out on deck, followed by a diminutive woman dressed in soot black, her head covered with a scarf. She peered from the deck to Patrick and Ainsley with vibrant eyes.

"Well?" she said in a loud, heavily accented voice. "Why are they just standing there? Help them on you lazy louts!"

The man with the pipe sprang to his feet and vaulted over the side to pick up Ainsley's valise.

"My lady," Angelo said, teeth flashing in a grin. "And sir. My mother."

The woman reached for Ainsley as Ainsley stepped across to the deck. "Welcome, my dear. Goodness, your hair is very yellow. It ain't dyed, is it?"

Patrick gave her a shocked look. "It's pure Scottish gold, madam."

"Humph, I thought Scottish gold was whiskey." Her look softened for Ainsley. "You're quite beautiful, my dear. His lordship has come to his senses at last, I see. Now you come over here and sit down with me. I've made a nice space for you to settle while you watch the world float by."

Patrick stuffed his handkerchief into his pocket as he followed Ainsley and the woman across the deck. The Romany with the pipe carried Ainsley's and Patrick's valises below, and Angelo cast off the ropes.

"I hope it doesn't rock too much," Patrick said as he sat down, the children eyeing him with curiosity. "You know how deucedly sick I get on boats."

When Ainsley's coach stopped, a week later, at Waterbury Grange in Berkshire, the carriage door was wrenched open for her by none other than Hart Mackenzie.

"Your Grace," Ainsley said in surprise as Hart reached in and swung her to the ground. "What are you doing here?"

"Looking after the family." The duke nodded at Patrick, who remained in the coach clutching his hat. "Where's Angelo?"

"Following," Ainsley said. "Where's Cam?"

"Snarling at all and sundry." Hart fixed Ainsley with a sharp stare. "You haven't written him. Not lately."

Ainsley reached for her valise. "I couldn't. First, I've been living on a canal boat, and we never stopped near enough to a village where I could mail a letter. Second, I have a surprise for Cameron, and I knew I'd never contain myself if I wrote him. My pen would betray me."

Hart clearly didn't believe the last part, but he led her to the house without further admonishment. Patrick, assisted by a footman, climbed down and followed, and servants swarmed to the coach to unload their baggage.

Ainsley broke away from Hart when they reached the house and its wide front hall.

"Cam," she shouted, dropping her valise. "I'm home."

She heard a squeal as Isabella ran out of the parlor, arms outstretched. Isabella was nicely round with her pregnancy, so soft to hug. Mac came from the parlor after her, and Beth, also pleased and plump, hurried down the stairs with Ian and Daniel.

Daniel swept Ainsley into a strong hug. "I knew you'd come back. Didn't I say so? Dad!" he bellowed up the stairs as he set Ainsley on her feet. "It's Ainsley!"

"He knows, lad." Mac laughed. "I think the whole county knows."

Cameron clattered in through the back passage, the entrance he used when returning from the stables, and everyone went silent.

Cameron halted on the flagstones when he saw Ainsley, his boots and riding breeches splattered with mud. It was all Ainsley could do not to rush to him, her tall, strong horseman with the topaz eyes.

"Hello, Cam," she said.

Cameron's scarred cheek moved, but the rest of him remained still.

"I've brought my brother with me. Cam, this is Patrick McBride."

Patrick made a little bow. "How do you do, your lordship?"

Cameron dragged his gaze to Patrick, made a stiff, polite nod, then moved right back to Ainsley.

Hart laid his hand on Patrick's shoulder. "Mr. McBride, why don't we wet your throat with a little Mackenzie malt?"

Patrick brightened and followed Hart into the parlor, where Hart pointedly closed the doors. The others began to fade up the stairs or outside, Beth taking Ian's arm and walking him out the front.

Only Daniel remained, stubbornly, by the foot of the stairs. "Don't say anything stupid, Dad."

"Daniel," Cameron said.

"Stay all you like, Danny." Ainsley removed her hat and tossed it to a table, then fished inside her valise and removed some papers. "I do apologize, Cameron, for taking so long to come home. But Lord Pierson is a bloody stubborn man. He took some convincing. Patrick did remarkably well, I thought. He ought to have gone on the stage."

Cameron unfolded his arms, finding it difficult to focus on anything but Ainsley's smile. "Pierson?"

"Angelo floated Patrick and me down to Bath, where Patrick visited Lord Pierson and convinced him to sell

Jasmine. To sell her to Patrick, I mean. I stayed in the canal boat, so that Lord Pierson wouldn't see me and recognize me, and Patrick did everything. He was quite wonderful. Do you know that canal boats can glide as smoothly as silk? I found it very relaxing. Although, Angelo's nieces and nephews know how make the boat rock so it will slosh about in the water. They taught me."

"Ainsley." Cameron cut through the heady flow of her chatter. "Are you telling me that you . . . convinced Pierson . . . to sell you Jasmine?"

"Patrick did. I gave Patrick the money, and he pretended to be a rich businessman interested in horses. Patrick almost fainted when I told him how much to offer for Jasmine, but I was firm. Patrick told Lord Pierson that he was new to racing, which is true, and that he'd heard that Lord Pierson might have a horse for sale, also true. Lord Pierson almost licked Patrick's shoes, he told me. Lord Pierson showed him Jasmine, and Patrick took a shine to her. Again, true, because Patrick agrees that she is a wonderful horse. Jasmine perked right up when she saw me when Patrick brought her down to the canal. I think she knew that she was on her way home. To her real home, I mean. Here."

Ainsley looked so damned pleased with herself, and Cameron could only look at her and bathe in her smile.

Daniel laughed. "And Pierson fell for it?"

"Lord Pierson was happy to sell Jasmine to Patrick McBride, the rather naïve businessman." Ainsley approached Cameron, the bundle of papers in her hand. "The next morning, Patrick McBride sold Night-Blooming Jasmine to *me*—for one pound sterling. We had it legally drawn up and everything." She pressed the papers to Cameron's chest. "And, now, my Lord Cameron, I give her to *you*."

Cameron stared at the pale ivory sheets against his coat. "Why?"

"Because you want her so much," Ainsley said.

Cameron was so stunned he could barely breathe. He

wanted to reach for her and pull her to him, to crush her to his body and never let her go.

He couldn't move.

A crunch of wheels outside interrupted, and Cameron heard a familiar piercing whinny. Ainsley whirled from him in excitement. "She's here."

Cameron grabbed Ainsley's hand. She couldn't go. Not now. Not yet.

Daniel laughed and raced outside, calling to Angelo as he went.

Cameron tugged Ainsley back to him, relaxing as she came. She was home, with him, where she belonged. His world took on color again.

"You can't be angry at me for buying Jasmine." Ainsley's eyes gleamed with mischief. "I can always send her back, you know."

"I'm not angry with you, devil woman. I'm madly in love with you."

Ainsley looked startled, then her smile blossomed. "Are you? That's splendid, because I love you too, Cameron Mackenzie."

The words went straight to his heart.

The papers fell, unheeded, to the floor as Cameron kissed her. He needed the taste of her, needed it every day of his life. Ainsley's lips were hot, her mouth wonderful. She slid her hands down his back, working under his coat to cup him in his tight riding breeches.

"Vixen," Cameron said against her mouth.

"The others are giving us a moment alone. We may as well take advantage of it."

"No." Cameron's voice went savage. "I want you for far more than a moment. I want to take you slowly, for a long time, in a place where no one will interrupt us."

"We'd better try your bedroom, then. That door has a stout lock, and as far as I know, I'm the only one who knows how to pick it."

Before she finished, Cameron had her in his arms, carrying her up the stairs. He wanted to hurry, but he couldn't resist stopping on the landing to kiss her, nibble her neck, nip at her lips.

When the bedroom door slammed behind them, Cameron set Ainsley on her feet and began stripping off her clothes.

"Never go away again," he said. "Whenever you leave this house, I go with you. I can't stand to be away from you. Understand?"

He peeled away her layers—pelisse and bodice, skirt and petticoat, bustle and corset, combinations and stockings. Ainsley's beautiful body came into view, dusky nipples tight, the brush of gold hair between her thighs sweetly damp. She was so beautiful that Cameron ached with it.

"I shouldn't travel very far anyway," Ainsley said as Cameron wrenched off his own clothes, his nude wife looking so demure. "I shall grow quite stout soon, but I can look upon it as an excuse to eat as much cake as I please."

Cameron flung off his shirt and stripped out of his underwear. "What are you talking about?"

"I'm talking about Daniel's little brother or sister. I wasn't certain before I left, so I didn't want to mention it, but I became much more certain during my visit to the queen. Her doctor confirmed it."

Cameron stopped. Ainsley smiled that secret smile, her cheeks flushed, while she stood before him stark naked. Lovely, impossible Ainsley.

"Don't look so shocked, my husband. It was inevitable, the way we carry on. I am only surprised it didn't happen sooner, but there's no predicting these things."

"Our child." Cameron's voice became an awed whisper. His dark world whirled around him one last time then dissolved into sunshine. "*Our* child."

"Certainly." Ainsley's smile faded, but the love in her eyes did not. "I am ecstatically happy, and honored, to carry her—or him."

Cameron read worry in her face, fear that hadn't quite faded from the death of her first baby. He cupped her face in his hands.

"I'll take care of you," he said. "You can be certain of that. You'll not have to fear."

"Thank you," she whispered.

"Damn you, Ainsley, I love you so much I hurt with it. I fell in love with you the night I first caught you in my bedchamber, my little thief. I was so drunk, and you were so lovely, and I wanted you like I'd never wanted a woman before in my life. How the hell did I live so long without you?"

"About as well as I lived without you." Ainsley touched his face. "Let's never live without each other again, all right?"

"That's what I've been trying to say." Cameron straightened from her. "Bed. Now."

Her brows rose. "My, aren't you commanding?"

"I am about this. March." He slapped his hand to her backside and half shoved, half walked her to the bed, Ainsley laughing all the way.

While he laid her down, he growled those naughty things that she loved to hear. Ainsley kissed him, and Cameron slid into her, completing their joining, completing himself.

He loved her until they were panting, sweating, shouting their joy. Cameron held her hard through it all, and still held her as they wound down to exhaustion.

"I love you," he whispered.

"I love *you,* Cam." Ainsley's voice was soft, tender. He believed her.

Cameron snuggled down beside her, pulling the covers over their nakedness, knowing that he could drift to sleep in complete safety and solace. He knew that he'd wake again in the peace she'd taught him, no more blackness, no more grief.

"Thank you," he said. "Thank you for giving me back my life."

"There will be much more of that, my Cam." Ainsley touched his cheek, breathed her cinnamon-scented breath on him. "Years upon years of it."

He intended there to be.

Cameron started to whisper that tender thought when he jumped, feeling a very determined hand close around his still-hard cock.

"Devil," he growled.

Ainsley laughed, her mirth ringing to the ceiling as Cameron rolled her into the featherbed and loved her all over again.

Epilogue

Ascot, June 1883

Hooves pounded on the track, mud flying, jockeys bent over brown and black and gray backs.

Ainsley whooped and flung her fists in the air as Night-Blooming Jasmine pulled ahead in the last furlong and romped home well ahead of the pack.

The Mackenzie box went insane. Daniel stood on top of the rail and screamed; Beth, Isabella, and Mac cheered at the tops of their voices.

The well-bred crowd in other boxes looked at them askance, and Ainsley hoped that Lord Pierson was among them. His own fault. The man did *not* understand horses.

Hart added his voice to the cheer. "Eat that, Pierson."

Mac laughed at him. "You must not need his vote."

"Shut it, Mac," Hart said.

Ian didn't join in with the cheering, but he pressed his fists into the rail in front of him and watched as Jasmine pranced about, proud of her victory. Beth planted a happy kiss on Ian's cheek, and Ian smiled down at her, far more interested in Beth than the horses.

Only Cameron had not said a word or done a thing. He simply watched, unsurprised, as the horse he'd lavished attention on all spring performed exactly as he expected.

Daniel jumped down from the rail. "I've just won a bundle. That will teach the bookmakers to do odds against on Dad's horses."

"They knew about Jasmine's past," Ainsley said. "They must not have believed Cameron could turn her around. More fool they."

Cameron held out his arm to Ainsley. "Time to go down."

"Before you do," Hart said, "I have something to say."

Cameron paused, not really interested, but Mac seemed to catch something in Hart's tone. "What?" he asked sharply.

"Nothing disastrous," Hart said. "But now that I have you lot married off, I'm contemplating taking a wife."

The silence was instant, stunned, and heavy. Ian looked at Hart and kept looking at him, straight into Hart's eyes.

And then everyone started talking at once. "Do you mean Eleanor?" Ainsley asked over the clamor.

Hart broke his gaze from Ian's and flicked it to Ainsley. "I've not said I've chosen a possibility."

"Yes, he has," Daniel shouted. "He just don't want to say, in case she turns him down again."

"Cameron," Hart said. "Cuff your son."

"Why?" Cameron shrugged. "Danny's right. Sort it out yourself, Hart, my horse is waiting. Come on, Daniel. This is your victory too."

Daniel took Ainsley's arm on her the other side, and sandwiched between father and son, Ainsley exited the box.

"What do you think, Step-mama?" Daniel asked. "A tanner on Lady Eleanor? For or against? I say she gives him the boot."

"No, indeed, Danny, my boy," Ainsley said. "Twenty says she accepts."

"Done. Dad?"

Cameron shook his head. "I never bet on Mackenzies. Way too risky, and Hart can be underhanded."

"Still, I think Eleanor will win, no matter what," Ainsley said. "Now, let's go see Jasmine."

Daniel dropped Ainsley's arm and ran ahead, bounding down the stairs. Behind them, the remaining Mackenzies continued their noise, also flinging about wagers on Hart's intended. Ian's voice rose above them all. "Thirty on Eleanor," he said. "She'll say yes."

Ainsley laughed. "Poor Hart."

"His own fault. He dropped the news on purpose when everyone was excited about Jasmine. He meant for us to treat it in fun, not something deadly serious. But Hart's deadly serious."

Ainsley knew he was. "I'm tempted to warn Eleanor," she said. "But no, they need to work it out for themselves."

"As we have."

"Hmm." Ainsley looked at her broad-shouldered, handsome husband, in black coat and Mackenzie kilt, and craved him with a bright suddenness.

"Cam," she said. "They'll wait for us in the paddock, won't they?"

"Probably. Unless Danny grabs the trophy."

"Good." Ainsley side-stepped and tugged Cameron with her under the shadow of the grandstand.

"What is it, vixen?" Cameron asked as they ducked out of sight. "Do you want to tell me a secret?"

"Ask you a question, rather." Ainsley touched the top button of her placket. "How many buttons can you open, my lord, before we have to go and rescue the trophy?"

His eyes darkened. "Little devil."

Ainsley laughed as Cameron swept her against him, mouth hard on hers, while his agile fingers began to unbutton her dress.

Turn the page for a preview of the next historical romance by Jennifer Ashley

The Duke's Perfect Wife

Coming soon from Berkley Sensation!

Hart Mackenzie.

It was said that he knew every pleasure a woman desired and exactly how to give it to her. Hart wouldn't ask what the lady wanted, and she might not even know herself, but she would understand once he'd finished. And she'd want it again.

He had power, wealth, skill, intelligence, and the ability to play upon his fellow man to make them do what he wanted and believe it their own idea.

Eleanor Ramsay knew, firsthand, that all of this was true.

She lurked among a flock of journalists in St. James's Street who waited for the Scottish duke to emerge from his club. In her unfashionable gown and old hat, she looked like a lady scribbler as hungry for a story as the rest of them.

The men came to life when they spied the tall duke on the threshold, distinctive with his close-cropped, red-highlighted hair and ever-present Mackenzie kilt. Hart always wore a kilt while in London, to remind everyone who set eyes on him that he was Scottish first.

"Your Grace!" the men shouted. "Your Grace!"

They surged forward, a sea of black backs, male strength shutting out Eleanor. A lady was a lady, but not when it came to newspaper stories about the elusive Duke of Kilmorgan.

Eleanor used her folded parasol to push her way through, earning herself curses and glares. "Oh, I do beg your pardon," she said as her bustle shoved aside a man who'd tried to elbow her in the ribs.

Hart barely glanced at them with his sharp golden eyes as he waited for his carriage to approach. He'd cut his hair shorter, Eleanor noticed, which made his face appear squarer and harder than ever. She knew she was the only one among this crowd that had ever seen that face soften in sleep.

The duke looked neither left nor right as he pulled on his hat and prepared to walk the three steps between the club and the open door of his carriage.

"Your Grace," one journalist shouted above the rest. "If you love Scotland so much, why are you here in London?"

Hart didn't answer. He was a master of letting what he didn't want to acknowledge flow past him.

Eleanor cupped her hands around her mouth. "Your Grace!"

Her voice rose above the masculine cries, and Hart turned. His gaze met hers and locked.

When they'd been in love, years ago, Hart and Eleanor at times had been able to communicate without words. Eleanor never knew how they did it, but somehow they'd been able to exchange a glance and understand what the other wanted. At this moment, Hart wanted Eleanor in his carriage, and Eleanor wanted that too.

Hart made a curt signal to one of the pugilist-looking footmen that followed him everywhere these days. The footman shouldered his way into the sea of rumpled suits, parting the pack of journalists like Moses at the Red Sea.

"Your ladyship," the pugilist said, and he gestured for her to precede him back through the crowd.

A second pugilist footman stood like a rock at the carriage door, anchoring the way. Hart watched Eleanor come, eyes on her all the way. When she reached him, he stepped in front of his footman, caught Eleanor by the elbows, and boosted her up and into the open carriage.

Eleanor's breath went out of her at his touch. But it didn't last long, and she landed on the seat as Hart followed her in. He took the seat opposite, thank heavens, and the second footman slammed the door.

She grabbed at her hat as the carriage jerked forward, trying to keep her grip on her parasol and the seat at the same time. Hart sat across from her, neat and tidy, his hat firmly on his head. She resisted the urge to reach over and knock it off.

The gentlemen of the press shouted and swore as their prey got away, the carriage heading up St. James's Street toward Mayfair. Eleanor looked back at them over the carriage's open top.

"You've made Fleet Street very unhappy today," she said.

"Damn Fleet Street."

"What, all of it?" Eleanor turned around again to find Hart's eyes on her, sharp gold in his hard face.

"What the devil possessed you to hang about a street corner with a pack of journalists?" Hart demanded. "If you wanted to speak to me, you should have come to the house."

"I did go to your house," she said. "But you've changed your majordomo, and he didn't know me. Nor was he by any means impressed by the card you gave me on that train in Edinburgh. Apparently ladies make a habit of trying to gain entrance to your house by false pretenses, and your guard dog of a majordomo assumed me one of those. I can't really blame him. I could have stolen the card, for all he knew, and you seem to be quite popular."

"I'll speak to him," Hart said when her breath ran out.

"Oh, dear, don't swat the poor man *too* much. Not on my account. He wasn't to know."

Damn her, how did she manage to turn every chastisement around on him? All the while smiling that little smile, her eyes so blue under her out-of-date hat?

Watching Eleanor bludgeon her way through those journalists with her parasol and bustle had awakened something light in him, something he hadn't felt since . . .

One hell of a long time.

"I'll instruct my majordomo," Hart said. "You can set an appointment with him when we reach the house."

"No time like the present. I really do need to speak to you, Hart."

The thought of Eleanor following him into his small private study, breathing the same air as he did, made his chest constrict. "Eleanor . . ."

"Goodness, you can spare me a *few* minutes, can't you? Consider it my reward for distracting those rabid journalists from you. You're making yourself quite controversial, you know, what with declaring Scotland should be a separate country and that the Germans are dangerous."

"If you already know so much, write your story about that. I'll not deny any of it."

"Oh, very generous of you. But I am not writing a newspaper story. And if I were, I wouldn't write about anything so boring as politics. No, I'd write about the personal life of the Duke of Kilmorgan. The most delicious and private gossip I could dig up, confirmed or unconfirmed. I'm certain any newspaper would froth at the mouth to buy it."

Again the smile, accompanied by a little nod of her head. Again the constriction in Hart's chest. Hart had verbally fenced with Otto von Bismarck, one of the most brilliant political minds of the century. Eleanor Ramsay in her flat hat trimmed with faded flowers could run rings around him.

"What is the appointment about, then?" he asked.

"Do you know that your face looks like granite when

you scowl? No wonder everyone in the House of Lords is terrified of you. What I want to speak to you about is a business proposition."

"A business proposition." With Eleanor Ramsay. God help him.

"Yes." She sat back and smiled.

Soft flesh beneath his, her blue eyes half-closed in sultry pleasure, Scottish sunshine on her bare skin. The feeling of moving inside her, her smile as she said, "I love you, Hart."

Did she remember? Did she regret, hate, or was it all gone?

Her smile was still as sweet, but Hart had learned the difficult way that Eleanor Ramsay was not a naïve, biddable young woman. Eleanor had the Queen of England eating out of her hand. When Her Majesty had wanted to make Eleanor one of her ladies of the bedchamber, Eleanor had refused, citing the need to stay home and look after her father. The queen, a woman famous for getting her own way, had meekly let her go.

"What business?" Hart asked. If they could take care of it in the carriage, no need for Eleanor to even enter his house.

"Business better discussed in private." Eleanor glanced about as the carriage turned down Grosvenor Street, heading toward Grosvenor Square. "Isn't that Lady Mountgrove? Of course it is. Hello, Margaret!" Eleanor waved heartily to a plump woman who'd descended from a carriage and was preparing to enter a house.

Lady Mountgrove, one of the most gossipy women in the country, looked up in surprise. Her mouth fixed in a round O when she saw Lady Eleanor Ramsay in the Duke of Kilmorgan's carriage, before she lifted her hand in a return acknowledgment.

"Haven't seen her in donkey's years," Eleanor said as they rolled on. "Her daughters must be, oh, quite young ladies now. Have they made their come-outs yet?"

Her mouth was still so damned kissable, closing in a little pucker while she awaited his answer.

"I haven't the faintest bloody idea," Hart said.

"Really, Hart, you must at least *glance* at the society pages. You are the most eligible bachelor in all of Britain. Probably in the entire British Empire. Mamas in India are grooming their girls to sail back to you, telling them, 'You never know. He's not married yet.' "

"I'm a widower. Not a bachelor."

"You're a duke, unmarried, and poised to become the most powerful man in the country. In the world, really. Of course, such a man will need a wife."

Breathing was becoming difficult. "Does this business proposition have anything to do with matchmaking? If so, I'll ask you to go. I might even tell the coachman to slow down." Hart didn't want to discuss his matrimonial contemplations with Eleanor—not yet.

"Very amusing. No, it doesn't. You'll learn about it in good time. I *can* converse about more than one topic, you know. I had very good governesses, and they taught me well."

Her tongue, her lips, moved in such a sultry way as she talked. A man who walked away from that had to be insane. Hart remembered the day he'd done so, still felt the tiny *smack* of the ring on his chest when she threw it at him, and the rage and heartbreak in her eyes.

He should have refused to let her jilt him, should have run off with her that very afternoon and bound her to him and never let her go. But he'd been young, angry, proud, and . . . embarrassed. The lofty Lord Hart Mackenzie, so sure he could do whatever he damn well pleased with anyone he damn well pleased, had learned differently with Eleanor.

That had been a long time ago.

"How are you, Eleanor?" Hart asked quietly.

The smile faltered. "Oh, about the same. Father is still writing his books, which are brilliant, but he can't tell you how much a farthing is worth. I left him to amuse himself at the British Museum, where he is pouring over the Egyptian collection. I do hope he doesn't start pulling apart the mummies."

He might. Lord Ramsay had an inquisitive mind, and neither God nor museum authorities could stop him when he wanted to find the answer to something.

"Ah, here we are." Eleanor craned to look up at Hart's house as the carriage pulled to a halt. "As elegant as ever. I see your majordomo peering out the door with a look of dismay." She put her fingers lightly on the hand of the footman who'd hurried from Hart's front door to help her down. "It's Franklin, isn't it?" she said to the footman. "Gracious, you've become quite tall, haven't you? And married, I hear. With a son?"

Franklin, who prided himself on his forbidding countenance while guarding the door of the most famous duke in the land, melted into a smile. "Yes, my lady. He's three now, and the trouble he gets into." He shook his head.

"Means he's robust and healthy." Eleanor patted his arm. "Congratulations to you." She waltzed on into the house while Hart climbed down behind her. "Mrs. Mayhew, how delightful to see you," he heard her say. He entered his house to see her holding out her hands to Hart's housekeeper.

The two exchanged greetings and were talking about, of all things, recipes. Eleanor's housekeeper, now retired, apparently had instructed her to obtain Mrs. Mayhew's recipe for lemon cakes.

Eleanor started up the stairs, and Hart nearly threw his hat and coat at the footman before he followed. He was about to order her into the large front parlor instead of his more intimate study when a large Scotsman in a threadbare kilt, loose shirt, and socks wrinkled around his ankles came barreling down from the top floor.

"Hope you don't mind, Hart. I brought the hellions, and I fixed myself a place to paint in one of your spare bedrooms. Isabella's got the decorators in, and you wouldn't believe the racket—" Mac broke off, and a look of joy spread over his face. He raced down the wide staircase to the first landing and grabbed Eleanor in a bear hug.

"Eleanor Ramsay, by all that's holy! What are you doing here?"

Eleanor kissed Mac, Hart's second youngest brother, soundly on the cheek as Hart gained the landing. "Hello, Mac. I've come to irritate your older brother."

"Good. He needs a bit of irritating." Mac glanced at Hart, his eyes glinting with his smile. "Come up and see the babies when you're done, El. I'm not painting them, because they won't hold still; I'm putting finishing touches on a horse picture for Cam. Night-Blooming Jasmine, his new champion."

"Yes, I heard she'd done well." Eleanor rose on her tiptoes and gave Mac another kiss on the cheek. "That's for Isabella. And Aimee, Eileen, and Robert." Kiss, kiss, kiss. Mac absorbed it all with an idiotic smile, damn him.

Hart leaned on the landing's railing. "Are we going to come to this proposition sometime today?"

"Proposition?" Mac asked, eyes lighting. "Now, that sounds interesting."

"Shut it, Mac," Hart said.

Mac opened his mouth to ask more questions, but just then screaming erupted from on high—shrill, desperate, Armageddon-has-come screaming.

Mac grinned and jogged back up the stairs. "Papa's on his way, hellions. If you're good, you can have sweets and Auntie Eleanor for tea."

The shrieking continued, unabated, until Mac reached the top floor, dodged into the room from whence it issued, and slammed the door. The noise instantly died, though they could still hear Mac's rumble.

Eleanor sighed a pleased sigh. "I always knew Mac would make a good father. Shall we?"

She turned and headed up to the next floor and the study without waiting for Hart. At one time, she'd become well acquainted with the rooms in his house, and she apparently hadn't forgotten her way around.

The study hadn't changed at all, Eleanor noted when she entered. The same warm paneling covered the walls, books still filled bookcases that climbed to the high ceiling, and the huge desk that had belonged to Hart's father reposed in the middle.

The same carpet covered the floor, though a different hound dozed by the fire. This was Ben, if she remembered correctly, a son of Hart's old dog Beatrix, who'd passed on a few months after Eleanor had ended the engagement. The news of Beatrix's death had nearly broken her heart.

Ben didn't open his eyes as they entered, and his gentle snore blended with the crackle of the fire on the hearth.

Hart touched her elbow to guide her across the room. She wished he hadn't, because the steel strength of his fingers made her want to melt.

If all went well today, she'd not have to be close to him again, but she needed to make the first approach in private. A letter could too easily go astray or be dismissed by his secretary or be burned unread by Hart.

Hart dragged an armchair close to his desk, moving it as though it weighed nothing. Eleanor knew better, though, as she sat. The heavily carved chair was as solid as a boulder.

Hart took the desk chair, his kilt moving as he sat, showing sinewy strength above his woolen socks. Anyone believing a kilt unmanly had never seen Hart in one.

Eleanor touched the desk's smooth top. "You know, Hart, if you plan to be the first minister of the country, you might give a thought to at least changing the furniture. It's a bit out of date."

Hart didn't give a damn about the furniture, and Eleanor knew it. "Mrs. Mayhew will be arranging tea. Whatever you have to say to me, say it quickly."

"It's nothing I want to say, really; rather, a favor to ask." Eleanor drew a breath, looked Hart fully in the eyes, and said, "I'd like you to give me a job."

Not what he was expecting. Hart's eyes flickered in

surprise; then the eagle gaze fixed on her again. "A job? Why?"

"The usual sort of reason. I need the blunt. Father is dear to me, but a wee bit impractical, as you know. He believes we still pay the staff wages, but truth to tell they stay and look after us because they feel sorry for us. Our food comes from their families' gardens or out of charity from the villagers. They think I don't know."

Hart listened with his usual assessing look, the one that knew everything without being told. "Eleanor, if you need money, I'll give it to you." His voice was deep, rumbling, a man who was in the habit of fixing other people's problems. "I'll buy your house if you want, to save your pride."

"Father would never let go of the house. It's been in the family for centuries. Never mind that every bit of land that can be sold has."

"That wreck of a house is going to tumble down one of these days and bury you both under rubble."

"Yes, but it will be *our* rubble. Call me an assistant to a secretary or some such. I'm sure you have several of those."

"I do. But what do you think the world will say when they find out I employ you? My former fiancée, a lady of the Scottish nobility, now assistant to one of my secretaries?"

"You don't have to tell anyone. I don't believe you'll wish to when I explain the sort of job I have in mind."

"What sort of job do you have in mind?" he asked, the question slow and careful.

Eleanor dug into a pocket on the inside of her coat and withdrew a large envelope. "I don't believe there's a name for such a job. Well, there might be, but I don't know what it is. I want you to pay me to help you find out about *this*."

She pulled a folded card from the envelope, laid the card on the desk in front of him, and opened it.

Hart went still.

The object inside the card was a photograph. It was a full-length photo of a younger Hart, shot in profile. Hart's body was a little slimmer than it was now, but still well muscled. In the photograph, he rested his buttocks against the edge of a desk, bracing himself on it with a sinewy hand. He was studying something on the floor that lay out of the frame, his head bent.

The pose, though perhaps a bit unusual, was not the unique thing about the photograph. The most interesting aspect of this portrait was that, in it, Hart Mackenzie was quite, quite naked.